ೞ Sylvio: Revelations ೲ

R.E. Beebe

GLASS
SPIDER
PUBLISHING

Published by Glass Spider Publishing
www.glassspiderpublishing.com
ISBN 978-0-9990096-6-6
Library of Congress Control Number: 2018954708
Cover design by Jane Font
Edited by Vince Font

Praise for R.E. Beebe's *Sylvio* book series

"I couldn't put *Sylvio: The Preternatural* down until I finished it. The author puts a whole new spin on supernatural."
—Virginia Babcock, author

"Overall, I would rate *Sylvio: Past and Present* a 4 out of 4 stars. I enjoyed each moment of this novel. I loved learning more about what powers Rachel had as well as how a 'good' vampire like Sylvio came to be. I am definitely putting the first book in this series on my to-read list."
—Onlinebookclub.org

"*Sylvio: Past and Present* does not only suit the preternatural fans, but all readers of all genres. It will catch them to the end. We'll find out that we decide what we are, not destiny. A great job the author did to develop the story."
—A. Shawar

I want to thank all those who supported me and my family as we carried on with our lives this past year. Writing is a solace and an escape. No book is written alone. Even random comments lead to ideas, and that helps the characters become more real as the series progresses.

I want to particularly thank family and friends who read the rough drafts and are brave enough to say, "What?" And especially the many people who now stop and ask, "When's the next one coming out?" It keeps me motivated. I'm glad others get enjoyment out of what I write.

I look forward to tomorrow.

–R.E. Beebe

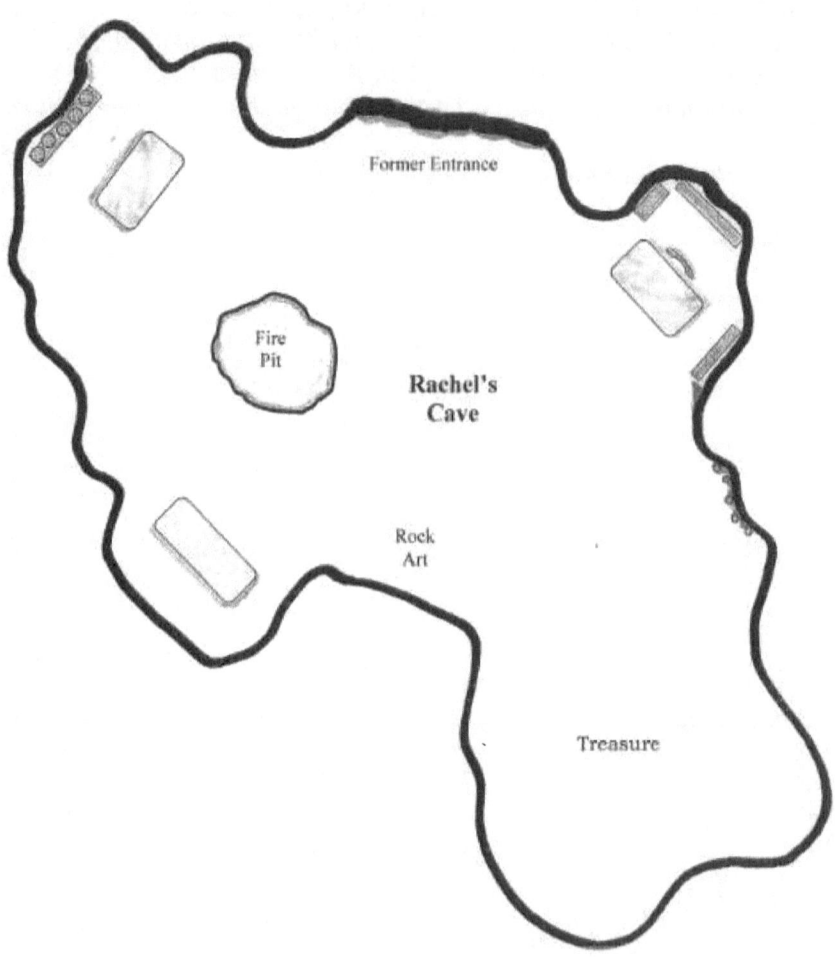

Former Entrance

Fire
Pit

**Rachel's
Cave**

Rock
Art

Treasure

ᔕᕼ Chapter 1 ᕙᔕ
Magic 101

We were on a mission. The activities of the nasty things out there were on the rise. Stories about black witch activities were being heard of in more places, and more often. Sylvio reported that the demon-possessed were approaching the level they'd been shortly after the Great Plague, and Carlisle informed us that malevolent poltergeists were cropping up everywhere. Sylvio was sure someone was pulling the strings, and if it was only one, then they were immensely powerful indeed.

However, life seemed to keep getting in the way of our pursuit of the culprit(s) behind it all. Like the time I went to meet a man who said he was interested in buying my condo. I'd bought the condo and rented out my house when I learned I had cancer and grew too ill to take care of the property. Then, I'd been given a second chance at life when Sylvio offered to save me in exchange for becoming one of the people he kept to feed him. He could save me because, to strengthen his tie to the human, he gave them a little of his blood. Vampire blood brings health and vitality with it.

To our mutual surprise, living with Sylvio, and the danger that went with it, brought out the power of witchcraft in me and made me impervious to vampire mojo. Sylvio could not make me his thrall. Still, I had decided to stay for the duration, which for Sylvio's people was ten to fifteen years.

My oldest son and his wife were making arrangements to buy my house in Clinton. With that worry out of the way, I had put the condo up for sale. So, when a man called to make an appointment for lunch claiming he wanted to discuss buying it, I accepted. And then . . .

ℰꙅ ᏣᏞ

I woke feeling groggy and unfocused, like what happens when you're waking from surgery. Someone had pumped me full of drugs. I tried to rub my hand over my face, but it was tied down. Panic seized me and stole my breath. The last time I'd been tied down had been a horrific experience. I still had regular nightmares about being trapped with no way out. They had become convoluted dreams now, intertwined with other events that were also terrifying—real events that had taken on a life of their own in my dreams.

"Rachel!"

Sylvio's voice in my head was like a balm. It soothed my nerves and helped me start breathing again. I took long, slow breaths. I didn't want to call him to me at that moment. I first needed to find out what was going on and where I was.

"I'm okay now, I was just scared," I replied with my thoughts.

I hoped Sylvio couldn't sense the lie. I turned my head and looked around. My mind was still somewhat fuzzy, but adrenaline had cleared it quite a bit. I could see an IV stuck in the back of my hand, and followed the tube up to the IV stand on my right, behind my head. I was lying on a gurney.

I was glad to find I still had clothes on. Whoever put me here had also covered me with a light blanket. I moved an ankle. It was tied down too. Panic started to crawl up my spine again, and I tried to squash the feeling.

"You're not okay," Sylvio responded.

Rage. That was what I felt through our bond. I could hear his growl, even though he had to be miles away. I felt a push as he tried to teleport to where I was, and I pushed back. I could sense his stunned silence that I could do that—I was as surprised as he was.

I took a couple more deep breaths and made myself sigh to relieve some of the tension. "True, but the spirits are not concerned. I'll see if they will help me out."

I knew we would be having an uncomfortable confrontation later about what I'd done. But first, I had to deal with the current situation.

I felt for the spirits. They surrounded me with comfort and were not worried. I looked around the room. It was singularly unattractive industrial. The walls were light green. The ceiling was old white tile, and the floor was cement painted gray. On the right was a large mirror which had to be one-way glass. I suddenly felt like I was in a movie or something.

"*Who took you?*" Sylvio sounded calmer that time.

"*He said he was CIA, and he wasn't lying.*"

"*I'm calling Shaw.*"

"*Perfect. I'll let you know what's happening here.*"

"*Promise you won't wait to call me to your side if you need me.*" Sylvio was not happy that I hadn't already done that.

"*I promise.*"

I could feel his frustration and worry. But if this was a trap aimed at him, which was more likely than any interest someone might have in me, I didn't want to be the one to spring it.

I focused on the spirits. I have decided they exist on a different dimension from that of normal humans, which is why so few of us can sense them and fewer still can enlist their aid. I really didn't like being trapped on that gurney. Keeping magic secret was important, but if my captors thought they could easily control me, they needed to learn a thing or two.

If they were CIA, their treatment of me meant this was a black op. Clearly, they had not done their research. Or, they didn't believe what they were told. Sylvio had carried out black operations centuries before there was a term for it, much less any of the agencies with their various acronyms. Holding one of his people captive could possibly cost them their lives. Sylvio did not tolerate harm to those he cared about. I needed to defuse this. I wanted my captors to learn that the rules of the game were different when they dealt with the preternatural.

I sent the thought out to the spirits that I wanted to be free. As always, they did much more than I intended. First, the air spirits formed a bubble around me. I felt a tickle as they pulled the tape away from my arm and the IV tube fell, taking the little plastic cannula they use these days instead of needles out of my hand. When it fell clear of me, the spirits ripped the Velcro straps away, tearing the metal buckles free also. The blanket covering me was stripped away when the straps across my chest fell to the floor. The metal buckles made a loud clink when they hit the cement.

Then it was the fire spirits' turn. Intense heat filled the space except for the protective bubble encircling me. The Velcro straps looked like weird flat snakes as they curled and twisted while they melted. The metal buckles scattered on the floor and the IV stand next to the bed began to glow. The plastic tubes were now mere globs.

I sat up and swung my legs over the side of the gurney so I was sitting in the middle of the pad. Even that was not spared. The ends of the gurney, which were suddenly not encased in my bubble or air, began to crackle and smolder. Then the blanket fell near my feet and burst into flames, sending curls of smoke up to the ceiling.

An alarm pierced the air, and the fire sprinklers in the ceiling sprayed a fine mist, which flashed into steam at first because the heat in the room was so intense. The fire spirits relented a bit to allow the water spirits to join in the show. Inside my bubble, the air was a little too warm, but I was otherwise comfortable and dry.

I glared at the mirror. I could feel the presence of people on the other side. It occurred to me that glass does not like heat or a sudden change in pressure. At that thought, the spirits did their thing, and the thick glass of the mirror shattered, blasting toward me and falling harmlessly into multiple shards that tinkled as they hit the cement. Tiny pieces of glass now covered the floor. I directed the water spirits to push them to the far wall and smiled at my captors. It was not a kind smile.

All of that happened too fast for the people in the room behind the broken mirror to do much more than stare. One of them grabbed a phone that hung on the wall. It was the old kind with a cord. He said, "Turn the sprinklers off! And the alarm! We don't need assistance. Something malfunctioned." Then he hung up.

Malfunctioned my ass, I thought. *I think things are working perfectly.*

I sat and watched their expressions turn from astonishment to fear, and then I felt their anger begin to rise. After mere seconds, the fire alarm and sprinklers stopped. I felt disappointment from the water spirits; they wanted to do more. I asked them to wash the floor clean, and the air and fire spirits helped, drying the cement and causing a miniature hurricane that swept the papers in the other room up into the air. The air spirits tossed them about while the normal humans in their little room grabbed at them. That's what they were, too—normal humans without any magic in them.

Finally satisfied with their show, the spirits settled down, and we all waited to see what my "captors" would do next. The people finished picking up the scattered papers. When they turned to look at me again, I recognized the man I'd met for lunch to discuss my condo. I scowled at him and said, "It was foolish in the extreme to take me against my will."

"What's happening?" Sylvio was still very angry. It sounded like he was gritting his teeth.

"*The spirits put on a show,*" I replied. "*There are four agents. They're trying to figure out what to do next.*" I made sure to sound smug, and I wasn't really faking it.

"*Keep them guessing and find out their names.*" Sylvio sounded slightly less miffed.

"*Will do.*"

I focused on the people on the other side of the hole in the wall again. They composed themselves on the outside, but inside, their emotions were a mix of fear, embarrassment, and anger. They were used to being the intimidating ones, not the other way around.

I sighed with relief and hoped I could persuade these people to cooperate. Being ignorant might not bring about their deaths after all. If Sylvio intended to kill them for what they'd done to me, he would not care what their names were. Except, perhaps, to get to whoever gave them their orders. The thought gave me a chill.

I needed to find out if they had good intentions, even if they were misguided, or if they were evil. I asked the spirits to show me their souls. A person's soul is not white or black; it is a balance. We all have done bad deeds, but it's the intent that matters. Is that person bent on evil, or did they do dark things in the pursuit of good—of justice? That was the question I posed for their individual spirits.

One man was truly evil. He hid behind the mask of the agency but carried out his own operations. The other three had done many dark things in their pursuit of justice. There was a weight on their souls, but their intent was pure.

They couldn't hear the silent exchange between Sylvio and me, of course, and they could not know that I was able to delve their souls. The man who I had met for lunch started to speak, but then we all jumped when the phone on the wall rang.

The man closest to the wall picked it up. In the sudden silence, the familiar voice at the other end was an angry growl that carried all the way to me. "This is Admiral Shaw. Put me on speaker. I want everyone there to hear this."

Now a feeling of uncertainty filled their room. The man nearest the phone said, "Yes, sir," and punched a button.

"Who is that?" Shaw snarled.

"Sir," the man said, "this is Karl Beckman."

I relayed that name to Sylvio and added, "*Shaw is on the phone with them. You work fast.*"

"*They won't argue with Shaw.*"

"*Good to know.*" Relief washed over me. Things might not go to hell for them after all.

"Let me speak with Rachel," Shaw demanded.

"Good to hear your voice, Admiral," I said. I couldn't help the smile that replaced my scowl. "There are four agents here, and they are badly misinformed." Werewolves have very good hearing. I did not need to be near the phone.

"Are you okay?" he asked.

"Getting better by the minute, but I don't think they truly believed in magic until a few moments ago."

Shaw's voice was deep and would easily carry through a vast auditorium. Confined to the two small rooms, it vibrated off the walls. "Now listen up. You should know already, but I'll state it anyway. I answer only to the director. Therefore, my orders override any others you might have been given. You picked the wrong target. Your mission is to find black witches. Rachel pursues black witches herself, as does her patron, who is someone I guarantee you do not want to offend any more than you already have. She is free to go. You will extend her every courtesy and give her any and all information she desires about your current operation."

There was silence for a moment, then the man I'd met for lunch said, "Admiral, sir, we have it on good authority that a white witch would not have the power to do what this woman has done."

"Who is speaking?" Shaw demanded.

"Agent Sean Donovan, sir," he said.

"Agent Donovan, your information would normally be accurate, but Rachel has access to magic that nearly all witches do not, no matter what kind of witch they are. I will not repeat my earlier demands."

I focused on Donovan's feelings and felt his frustration at having to follow orders he didn't agree with. The trouble was, he was not the evil one in their room. He needed to be an ally. I pushed the spirits to get him to lean the right way.

Shaw said, "Do I make myself clear?"

They all said, "Yes, sir."

"Rachel?"

"Yes."

"Call me as soon as you are safe." He didn't need to add what would happen if I didn't call right away. All of the agents understood heads would roll if I didn't.

"I'll be sure to do that." I relayed the conversation to Sylvio and told him I wanted to find out what I could first before he came to get me. He was not happy with leaving me in their hands any longer but understood the necessity.

It was dicey after that, but the agents did cooperate. In the end, they gave me a jump drive with their reports copied on it. I relayed each of their names to Sylvio, and by the time he came to get me, he was eager instead of angry. He loves hunting, whether on foot or with his new passion, the internet. It would take him no time at all to find out everything about the agents, from their individual shoe sizes to what grades they got in kindergarten.

ℰᏠ ᏣᎡ

I was back at home, sitting on a barstool in the kitchen looking over our shopping list. I was planning to take Eric and Shena shopping again. I thought we'd go to Ogden and wander the mall before going to Sam's Club. They'd love that.

Ray was cleaning up breakfast with Lucas, who was teasing him about something—I wasn't really paying attention. Ray took a swipe at Lucas with the wet dish towel in his hands, and Lucas made a grab for it. Ray flipped it up out of reach, and the end of it caught a vase that was sitting on top of the cabinets. It began to fall. The guys were watching each other, not the towel. Ray started after Lucas, who was dashing toward the long redwood kitchen table, so they did not see it happen. I was on the other side of the bar and knew I wouldn't be able to get there fast enough.

Sylvio did not own things simply to have them. Practically every knickknack in the house was either highly valuable or there was a story connected to it, or both. I didn't know the story behind that particular vase yet, but I wanted to save it. I sent that thought out as I despaired of anyone being able to do anything to prevent it from crashing to the tile floor.

"Oh, no!" I shouted and reached out with my hands, even though I was several feet away.

The vase stopped in midair, two feet from the floor. The spirits took my thought and wrapped it safely in a cocoon of air. Distracted by my shout, Lucas and Ray looked back. They halted mid-stride to stare at the vase. Slowly, I got up from the barstool and walked around the kitchen island to stand next to the vase. I reached out and took it in my hands. I could feel the blanket or air spirits dissipate when my fingers wrapped around it. I turned it in my hands and then glanced at Ray and Lucas, whose faces held a look of wonder. I'm sure my face reflected the same feeling.

Up to that point, my success with magic had been random. If I were in a serious situation, the spirits were more than willing to help out, and they did so with alarming strength and speed. But if I wanted to practice magic or do something simple, when nothing dire or important was happening, they seemed to enjoy making things difficult for me. When I tried practicing magic, things always went wrong. So far, I'd melted glasses and DVDs, burned two chairs and a big patch of lawn to a crisp, shattered mirrors, and exploded more than one hay bale.

I held the vase and wondered what I had done that was different. Why had it worked this time?

"Nice one," Ray said. He flipped Lucas on the hip with the wet towel and took off. Lucas chased him out the kitchen door.

I put the vase back where it belonged and stared at it. I hadn't really thought of magic when the vase fell. I'd only wished it could somehow be saved. My concentration had been on the shopping list and going to town. Then an incredible possibility occurred to me.

I looked around the room to locate things that would not be harmed by falling. A napkin holder was nearby. Lisa had brought it home; she liked the fawn and doe in the picture on it. It was made of plastic. I pushed it off the bar—and stopped it inches from the floor. Even the napkins that had begun to float out of the basket hung in the air.

There was a glass on the bar too. It was also plastic. I reached over and knocked if off. It stopped in the air beside a couple of the floating napkins. I was overwhelmed with joy and could not help a loud whoop escaping my lips, unable to contain myself anymore. Everything fell to the floor. I stared at them and wondered—*why?* I thought I had the answer, finally.

Could it really be that simple? Was emotional control the key? As I considered that possibility, it seemed so obvious. The shaman (or whatever name they go by in their various cultures) set great store on meditation, calming the mind, emptying it of random thoughts and unfocused feelings. Always before when magic did what I wanted, it was because I was in desperate need of it. I'd been terribly frightened, or angry, or worried and under stress, and focused on a particular goal— survival; our very lives. They did more than I could have imagined possible because of the *degree* of emotion.

I spent the next hour making things float in the air until I had a collection of objects surrounding me. Utensils, measuring spoons, magazines, and cups joined the napkin holder and napkins. I moved into the living room to try it out. Kita, Nero, and Cactus were standing on the couch, watching. Cactus and Nero kept trying to snag a napkin each time one passed them.

I had figured out how to move them so they were all spinning in a slow circle as though I were Saturn and they were the rings. Lisa and Lydia came in while I was figuring out how to move things, and they helped out by tossing stuff toward me to add to the ring. Each time something was caught in the spiral, the girls clapped and laughed.

I'd forgotten about going to town until Shena opened the kitchen door with Eric right behind her. It distracted me enough that everything fell to the floor with a crash and a clatter. All of us stared at the circle of stuff. Then Shena's green eyes met mine. At that moment, they were old eyes, wise eyes. Very much like Micah's. "Congratulations," she said.

"Did you know how to do that?" I asked.

Sylvio said Atshena was the only witch he'd known who could perform such feats of sorcery as I seemed to be able to.

Shena thought for a moment, her eyes turned inward to a distant past—in fact, an entirely different lifetime. "I was taught not to use my magic unless it was for a purpose. Was there a specific reason to move these things?"

"Other than learning a new use for my magic, no."

She bent down and picked up the napkin holder and turned it in her hands, looking at it instead of at me. "You must be careful, Rachel. Magical power is . . . seductive. Once it's been used, it's hard not to do more, and then even more, and then justify using it although your heart says you shouldn't."

Exasperated, I said, "How am I supposed to learn about magic if I don't practice it?" I understood, intellectually, what she was saying, but it was frustrating.

"Have you needed to practice previously, or has magic come to your aid without it?"

She knew the answer to that and was certain that I did, too. Since there was no need to answer her question, I said, "Well, I'll clean things up and take you to town as promised."

"Can you put the things back by using magic?" Lisa asked.

I looked at the odd collection strewn on the living room throw rug. At that moment, they seemed as immovable as a mountain. "Nope. Looks like putting them back will have to be done the normal way."

"Bummer," Lisa said.

It didn't take long to clear up. As we did, I thought about what Shena said and what Micah told me previously. There were a *lot* of rules the witches followed; endless restrictions on how and when to use magic. I was ignorant of most of them. But I couldn't help wondering if those rules were a help or a hindrance. Did they actually keep witches and others safe, or did they limit their options and prevent them from doing more with their own magic?

We all create barriers in our minds. Sylvio told me once that I was able to do what I did because no one told me it was impossible. What would be possible if the witches did not limit themselves to a few spells only used sparingly? And, even more to the point, would they listen to me if I tried to explain that to them?

ஒ Chapter 2 03
Fly on the Wall

Sylvio had been asked to attend a couple of meetings at the Pentagon, and he brought me along. I wasn't originally invited to the first meeting, but it worked out so we could be there at the same time for both. He told those we were meeting that he wouldn't participate without me. I was certain that caused some ruffled feathers.

When I asked him about protocol and clearances, he smiled and said in his case, those rules were set aside. I asked if the powers that be were okay with that. That got a chuckle out of him. He placed a cold hand on my face and brushed a thumb across my cheek. "They put up with me because of the results. Don't worry about what they think of you."

When we arrived, I was surprised at the size of the building. It is *huge*. I had seen its image in countless pictures and TV shows, but the reality was quite impressive.

We wrote our names on a chart as we entered the door. It was one of those charts you see at museums that lists a spot for your name and state. The Pentagon *is* a tourist destination, after all. I was curious what state Sylvio would pick. Today, it was Kentucky, which is the location of one of the three houses where he keeps his people. He signed it *S. Costa*.

Further in the entrance was one of those security scanners that you walk through. I was surprised when the scanner went off as Sylvio walked through. I knew he didn't have any metal on him, and all I had on was my silver necklace, which I'd taken off and put in the tray with our cell phones.

The three guards at the door all stopped what they were doing and stared at their monitors. Then they all looked at Sylvio. I scanned their feelings and found a mixed bag. Mostly, they were astonished and hiding it behind impassive faces. The guard manning the walkway, who happened to be a woman, said, "Please, sir, will you stand in the archway?" I could tell from her uniform that she was the sergeant in charge of their detail.

Sylvio obliged, and their monitors pinged again. It was not the usual buzz when metal is detected. The sergeant's eyebrows rose as she gazed at the screen. She cut a quick glance at Sylvio then looked away and said, "Please step over here for a moment." She indicated the space next to another guard. Sylvio walked to the spot she pointed at. He was feeling amused.

"Please, ma'am, step into the monitor," the sergeant said to me.

I stepped in, and it did not ping. All three watched their monitors for several seconds and exchanged glances. The sergeant asked Sylvio, "Please, sir, will you step into the monitor and stand next to your companion?"

They were being exceptionally polite, but they were all feeling more alarmed.

Sylvio stepped into the monitor, and the ping did not sound.

"Step out of the monitor, please, ma'am," the guard said. As soon as I was clear of the archway, the ping sounded. They exchanged incredulous glances again.

The sergeant cleared her throat and said, "Please, have a seat over here. It appears our monitor is not working properly, but procedures require that we have a supervisor come speak with you."

That statement was partly a lie—the part about their monitor. Sylvio and I sat in the chairs that were indicated. The other people who were waiting to enter were redirected to another door. One of the guards walked out onto the sidewalk and put up a sign to block anyone from using the door. The other guards, attempting to be inconspicuous about it, kept their hands near the holsters and kept Sylvio in their line of sight as they moved around.

Sylvio was still feeling amused, not worried, and that helped settle my nerves quite a bit. The three guards were very concerned and were doing a fair job of hiding it. When the guard who'd placed the sign came back in, Sylvio turned to the sergeant. "We need to let the people we were meeting know we've been detained," he said. "May I have my phone?"

The sergeant brought the tray over with our phones. With every step she took toward Sylvio, her fear mounted, but she steeled herself and held out the tray. We took our phones, and Sylvio sent a short text message. It said, *Your new door monitors are working. Rachel and I are stuck at the south door.*

The reply took only about a minute. I leaned over to read it. *I'll make sure they let you through. You were supposed to be escorted in to bypass the monitors.*

The guards spoke in whispers, but I was sure Sylvio could hear them. "What are they saying?" I asked.

"I'm certain these chairs are bugged," was his reply. "But in any case, it seems that detector checks for temperature and heartbeat, not only metal."

It was late afternoon, many hours since Sylvio last fed. I took his hand and felt how cold it was. "What's your guess at the temperature reading on that monitor?" I didn't think it mattered now what the bugs on the chairs would tell whoever was listening.

"Several degrees too low. Pretty clever, really. That's one of few ways there might be to detect preternatural beings."

The third officer on duty was checking the monitor systems for any problems while the other three watched over us. I was impressed with these guards; they kept their air of authority and professionalism while inside, they were feeling quite apprehensive.

A few minutes later, a colonel walked up and began speaking with the guards. The colonel's emotions went from annoyance to alarm as he looked at the screen. He glanced at us and then down at some papers in his hand. He flipped through them then stopped at one page and read it. We could see his profile as he took a deep breath and licked his lips, composing his expression before turning toward us.

"I'm sorry for the delay," he began. "I am Colonel Riggs. Please come with me." He didn't offer a hand to shake and didn't approach very closely. He turned to the three guards and said, "Thank you for alerting me. You can take the sign down. The monitor is in good working order."

Instead of feeling reassured, all three in the guard detail felt even more alarmed and couldn't help sneaking furtive glances at Sylvio.

Colonel Riggs waited for us to stand and then gestured to a door. He did not lead the way, but rather followed us and allowed Sylvio to open the door. It was clear he did not want Sylvio out of his sight, even for a moment.

The room we entered was not large. The centerpiece was an oval desk made of walnut, surrounded by five leather chairs. As we sat down, I was surprised to note that they were quite comfortable. I wondered absently what kind of monitoring equipment was in the room. The sylph decided my random thought was a request. Immediately, I saw flashes of tiny lights. They were little golden beacons indicating each item used for surveillance. The room was full of them.

"*What?*" Sylvio asked, noticing the change in my mood. I was trying to stifle a laugh.

"You're not kidding the place is bugged. The spirits have shown me what's in this room. It's like we're sitting in the middle of a sparkler."

Sylvio kept his humor to a wide smile that he directed at the colonel. The man seemed taken aback by the friendly expression. Apparently, he had assumed we would be irritated at the delay. Perhaps, if Sylvio viewed time in the same way as mortals, he might have been annoyed. Instead, Sylvio was enjoying keeping the man unsettled.

Colonel Riggs cleared his throat and said, "My duty is the safety of the people in this building. Given the readings from that monitor, I cannot guarantee anyone's safety with you in it." He kept his tone neutral, but the man was ready to fight if need be and felt certain he would die if it came to that. I decided I liked him. The world needs more people willing to protect what they believe in.

"I assure you, no one in this building is in danger from me," Sylvio said in the silky tone he used when he was amused. "My name is Sylvio Costa. This lady is Rachel Burns. Admiral Shaw invited us here to discuss a national security issue." He paused a moment to let the names sink in. As he had expected, the tension in the colonel went down a notch.

Colonel Riggs dared look down to scan the papers in his hand. Then he looked toward Sylvio, but I noticed he was careful to look to the side and not directly into Sylvio's eyes. There was uncertainty and a smidgen of hope in him when he said, "I've been told you are trustworthy."

"What did your monitor tell you?" Sylvio asked.

The spirits were telling me there were now two guards outside our door. I knew Sylvio would be able to sense them as well. The colonel decided to be frank with us, and my respect for the man grew. "Alright," he said. "The monitors were changed last year after an attack on the building. In addition to scanning for metal, they check temperature . . . and heartbeat."

Sylvio smiled. "The one who attacked this building is dead. Permanently so."

The colonel twitched, unable to hide his surprise, and fixed Sylvio with an astonished stare. "Do we have you to thank for that?"

"No, that would be Miss Rachel here."

I was as surprised as the colonel. He looked me up and down, not really believing Sylvio. I turned to Sylvio. "Jiang?"

He smiled wider. His amber pupils had a hint of red in them. "Yes." He turned that same smile on the colonel, and magic filled the space around us. Catching his intent, I added the power of the spirits to the mix. "So, colonel. Tell me, what happened during the attack?" Sylvio asked.

Colonel Riggs may have spoken freely without magic, but he had no choice at that point. "Two field agents came back from China with a report they composed on . . . what did you call it? Jiang?"

Sylvio nodded. The colonel went on. "The night after they arrived back in the States, the building was breached and their report was taken. It killed five agents and was shot more than once. It was on film from our security system, although the film has since become corrupted. The next night, the two agents disappeared. There has been no trace of them since."

Sylvio released the spell on the man. The colonel was confused momentarily, then wary, probably wondering why he'd said so much. Sylvio said, "I'm sorry you lost those agents. But I am not Jiang. What did your monitors reveal to you since they've been installed?"

The colonel hesitated, and I pushed the spirits for him to speak freely again. "We found we have thirteen werewolves working here. Their temperatures are high, and their heartbeats low. There is also a fae, who happens to rank rather high here. No one has had readings like yours, though."

"What readings are those?" Sylvio inquired.

"It shows your temperature is ninety-one. And there was no heartbeat."

"Disconcerting." Sylvio continued to smile benignly.

The colonel blinked at him. After nearly two years living with Sylvio, I was now amazed at how hard people tried *not* to believe. Everything was telling this man Sylvio was undead, but still he refused to accept it. He believed somewhat the things the papers in his hands told him about the preternatural. He was also discovering that believing in it abstractly was quite a bit different from having it walking and talking to you.

Colonel Riggs licked his lips, unable to hide his unease, and said, "I saw the video. The thing moved too fast for the cameras to catch a clear image, even before the film was corrupted. Bullets didn't even slow it down. Locks meant nothing to it, either. We got the idea for changing the monitors because the room that held the report was a meeting room like this one, and it was rigged for tracking heartbeats and temperature. The thing didn't even register on the system. But how did it know which room the documents were in?"

"He could smell the two agents, track where they went," Sylvio said. "Or he had them enthralled, and they gave him the information." Sylvio didn't seem to be bothered by the colonel calling Jiang an "it."

The colonel leaned forward, his palms flat on the table. "What *are* you?"

"I'm sure the werewolves have told you. I suggest you listen to their advice. I'm a vampire, Colonel Riggs, as was Jiang."

The colonel sat back and blinked, still doubting the reality sitting in front of him. He rubbed a hand over his face and was rapidly losing his battle at appearing composed. He turned to me. "How is it that five highly qualified agents were unable to harm that thing—Jiang—to any great degree, but you could? What are *you*? Your readings are normal."

I shrugged and said in a matter-of-fact tone, "I'm a witch, Colonel Riggs. Not many of us have power that would trump that of a vampire such as Jiang, but I do."

He sat back in his chair and shook his head.

We heard a loud exchange outside the door—a challenge. The voice that responded was a low, commanding growl. I knew that voice. Admiral Shaw opened the door. He was wearing his uniform, which I'd never seen him in, but it suited him more than anything I'd seen him wearing before. Colonel Riggs got to his feet and saluted.

"At ease, colonel," Shaw said. "I'll debrief you later. For now, these two are needed elsewhere. They are not a danger to anyone here unless their safety is threatened." He held the colonel's eyes to make sure he got the message. I felt Colonel Riggs' relief when we were taken out of his hands.

Many eyes followed us as Shaw escorted us down the long corridor. I couldn't help gawking around like the tourist I was, although I did listen attentively while we walked. A major had been dispatched to escort us to the meeting but was detained. Shaw was going to investigate why he was detained, but for now, we were meeting to discuss a terrorist they had located. The man was highly placed in ISIS and was a high-profile target for America's security interests.

Earlier that week, when Shaw was briefed on the difficulties presented on the location of the terrorist and how important this target was, he immediately thought of Sylvio. Capturing or killing the man would put many lives in danger if Special Forces personnel were dispatched to attempt it. And they would be violating the sovereignty of a country that was barely on speaking terms with the United States. Shaw reviewed the options available for using conventional means that were presented to him, then proposed they ask Sylvio for his assistance.

To invade another country, they needed the consent of the president. His national security advisor would be at this meeting, along with the director of the CIA. They were coming to learn about the viability of

Shaw's proposal. I could feel myself grow paler by the minute as he spoke of who would be at the meeting.

I felt distinctly out of place. I am a very small fish in a very large pool, after all. Sylvio wanted me with him to read the feelings of those we were going to meet and report back to him what I found—also, because I could sense all magical beings and sometimes he could not, especially other witches. I was going in the guise of his personal assistant. I clung to my briefcase with white knuckles and willed myself to carry it casually at my side. Sylvio had loaded it with an office planner, stray papers, and a few sticky notes, all of them blank, in order to fool anyone scanning the case.

Werewolves can scent emotion. Before opening the door, Shaw turned to me. He'd obviously caught my unease that was rapidly growing to panic. "Some in this room are quite familiar with what werewolves can do," Shaw said. "We've been used in several operations over the years. A handful of those in this room know about vampires, but since appointments are transient, they've never met Sylvio. I don't advertise what Sylvio can do, and you are entirely an unknown. It will give you an advantage. And remember, no matter how high their status, in the end, they're just people."

Those last words helped calm me quite a bit. I rolled my neck on my shoulders, took a deep breath, and said, "Let's do this."

Shaw opened the door and gestured us inside.

In the center of the large room was a table made of cherrywood surrounded by black leather chairs. At the end of the table nearest the door was a tray with vegetables, fruit, and sweet rolls. A carafe of what I presumed was coffee and a pitcher with ice water were placed in the center. At one end was an open laptop, and past that at the far end was a screen. The table could seat more than a dozen easily, but there were only two small groups standing in the room, sipping coffee and talking amicably. They continued to chat with one another, but I sensed it as everyone in the room absorbed our presence and divided their attention.

When the chance presented itself for me to be at this meeting, Sylvio asked if I would read those in the room and relay messages to him. With trepidation, I opened myself to sense the emotions of those present. No matter how practiced I became at it, it still left me feeling vulnerable. I had to resist the temptation to be swayed by them.

What hit me first was the colonel in the group nearest us. When her eyes landed on Sylvio, terror swept through her. It was not a conscious thought, but a memory. That fear was mixed with desire. It was that odd combination of emotions that caught my attention. Without realizing it, her hand touched her throat. I understood then that she had been a vampire's victim, perhaps more than once. The memory still lingered in her inner brain, although she did not consciously understand her own unease.

Standing next to her was a bear of a man. The salad bowl of commendations on his chest was impressive. The stars on his shoulder indicated he was a four-star general. He was not hiding his displeasure at our presence. It was clear he did not believe either of us should be there at all. The glare he directed at us caught Sylvio's attention. When their eyes met, I felt amusement as well as a readiness to battle from Sylvio.

Since all those in the room were supposed to be on the same team, I thought it might be good to distract Sylvio. *"Do you recognize the colonel next to the general?"* I sent.

"No, why?"

"Well, it seems she's had a personal encounter with a vampire. Her fear is too visceral and real for anything else."

"That's good information. She will tell whoever enthralled her anything they want to know."

That hadn't occurred to me. Before I could ask one of the many questions I suddenly had, a man in a business suit stepped away from the other small knot of people and came over to greet us. From his manner, it was clear this man did not belong in a suit and tie. He moved with the precision of a soldier and was surely more at home in fatigues.

"Sylvio," he said as he came up to us and extended his hand. "So glad you agreed to help us out with this op."

I felt genuine comradery from the man. He knew Sylvio, not just that he was a vampire, but he considered him a friend. When I relayed that to Sylvio, he felt quite happy to hear it. This man was an older gentleman, and Sylvio relayed back to me that they had worked together on more than one mission in Vietnam.

"Barton, it's been a while. Glad to help," Sylvio replied smoothly. "This lady's name is Rachel."

Barton shook my hand and beamed in greeting. Unlike most people who met me and knew that I was a "pet," this man did not judge in any way. Instead, he was intrigued and genuinely interested in me. I liked him instantly. Flashes of his memories of Sylvio came through to me as Barton's hand clasped mine. They were images of jungle, and fire, and helicopter rotors making smoke swirl . . .

"Hello," I said, forcing myself to stay in the present.

"I'll introduce you, then we can get started," Barton said and led us to the nearest group. As expected, the greeting we got from four-star was barely civil. The colonel with the personal acquaintance with vampires was quite breathless in her greeting and could barely maintain her composure.

"Can you tell who has taken her before?" I asked Sylvio as he offered her his hand and she took it. I felt his brand of magic sweep around her.

"I can't scent them, so it hasn't been recent." He paused, then added, *"I can see his face in her mind. It was Jiang."*

I was quite relieved and sensed he was too.

"I'll find out from Shaw which operations she's been involved in," Sylvio said.

With that mystery solved, we were led to the other knot of people. One of the men in that cluster knew Sylvio already and greeted him with the familiarity and relief that Barton had. The others did not believe what they were told before the meeting was arranged. It was interesting to me because, for some reason, I thought such high-ranking people would be more open to the possibility that preternatural creatures existed.

The director of the CIA was interesting in that his emotions about Sylvio and me were undecided. This man was less skeptical to the possibility of magic than some in the room, but he had the same problem as the colonel at the gate. Believing something in theory was quite different from believing it in fact.

"Shall we get started?" Barton asked and gestured to the chairs.

People settled in their seats, and Barton began to speak, but Sylvio interrupted. In a voice that carried to all parts of the room, he said, "Rachel, before we begin discussing plans, will you ensure that we are not heard or seen by any others?"

I blinked at him and fought not to look astonished. He wanted me to use the spirits to find any electronic surveillance devices. I swallowed and said, "Certainly." I gathered the air spirits to me and asked them to find anything with electric energy that was covert. For good measure, I swept my arm in a half circle, which was totally unnecessary but made Sylvio's lip quirk up, and added, *"Quaero."*

Smoke curled from under the table, a sizzle was heard from something overhead, and a crackle and then a yelp from four-star. He stood up and slapped at the cuff of his fine-pleated pants, which now had a hole in them. A tiny blackened and charred thing fell to the floor. He bent down and flipped it over with his finger. Then he stomped on it and ground it under his boot. Clearly, he had not known it was there.

When he looked over at me, it was with a little more tolerance.

Barton was fighting the urge to laugh out loud. He said, "Thank you for that. It appears our sweep of the room was incomplete."

"Or others are aware of your methods," Sylvio added.

"We'll certainly look into that," the director said.

"Damn right, we will!" exclaimed four-star.

"Shall we get on with it?" Barton said and sat down. He was not disturbed by my little show, but most of the others in the room now felt apprehensive. They composed themselves and began by asking Sylvio if he had already been briefed on who their target was and what his role was in ISIS. The face of the man who was the target of this meeting was displayed on the screen at the end of the room nearest us. Sylvio assured them he had been briefed on the man already. They all felt relieved by that.

A display of a compound replaced the image of the man. The photo was obviously taken by satellite or high-flying reconnaissance drone. There was a walled courtyard which, from the size of the trees and walkways that could be seen, would be about the area of half a football field. A fountain was in the middle of the trees, and a large house was at one side. A second image was then overlaid on top of the image of the house, showing an architectural drawing of the arrangement of rooms. Each floor was displayed and described. The image stopped changing slides when their best guess about which room the man was most likely to occupy was shown.

The agent presenting the information was named Ramirez. Sylvio relayed to me that he was a senior analyst now at CIA and at one time was quite an effective spook in the field. They had worked together more than once. When Ramirez finished, all heads turned to Sylvio.

It wasn't only that they were waiting for Sylvio's response. He commanded their attention simply by being there. It's a vampire thing. Dominant werewolves are the same way, but in this room, it was Sylvio who captured their attention instead of Shaw.

Sylvio stood and walked to the screen. On the left side of the image, beyond the trees and the house, was what looked like a large gazebo enclosed by a rock wall. He reached up, not quite touching the screen; his hand hovered near the gazebo. "Falasa's palace," he said to no one in particular. He was simply thinking out loud.

At those words, four-star felt surprised. I'd already forgotten his name. He made a point of sitting across the table where he could keep an eye on both of us. He said, "You know your history."

Sylvio's eyes met his, but he wasn't focused on him; his mind was occupied with the past. My connection with Sylvio had evolved so that now I could read even small nuances in his mood. He knew that compound from the distant past. How distant I could not discern, but there were good memories—and bad ones. The memories unsettled him, but no one in the room would know that. He was a master at composing his face into what he wanted people to see. I tried to do the same but mostly failed at it.

Sylvio turned back to look at the image. That time, he studied the house, trees, and fountain. The images were excellent, and the details were quite clear. After a full minute ticked by, he turned to address Ramirez. "I can capture him for you."

Ramirez felt quite relieved. "Good to hear that. What can we do to assist you?"

Sylvio looked at the image again. "Does he have information you would find useful?" Which was another way to ask, as everyone in the room understood, if they wanted him dead or alive.

"What he knows could potentially be very helpful," was Ramirez' careful reply. Everyone understood his meaning too: alive, if possible.

"Do you have personnel in place in the region?" was Sylvio's next question.

"There are two who could be of assistance," Shaw replied.

"Have them meet me at the Mena House Hotel," Sylvio said.

The others were listening impatiently to this exchange. Finally, the man sitting next to four-star, introduced as deputy to the director, spoke up. "The hotel by the pyramids? That's miles from Dubai!" He was one of those who didn't believe, and he was quite angry at that moment.

Sylvio gave him a tolerant smile. "Yes."

The man was going to say more, but Ramirez cut in. "When should they meet you there?"

"In two days. I'll be there with the target when they arrive," Sylvio replied.

Ramirez was enjoying himself. He said, "Anything else we can help with?"

"That should be all." Sylvio walked back to his chair and sat down.

The feelings in the room were a mix of confusion, frustration, and incredulity from everyone who didn't know what Sylvio was capable of. Four-star growled, "This is highly irregular. There are things we need to know before we approve this course of action."

"Such as?" Sylvio inquired, his face unreadable.

"Who are your team members, besides this woman?" He gestured toward me. "They need to be cleared for such a sensitive operation. We need to know their plans and what kind of mess we're likely to land in if what you plan goes wrong. We need contingencies. We need a plan about what to tell the emirates. If you are such an expert and believe you can carry off this feat, why would you risk transporting the target to a luxury hotel clear on the other side of the Arabian Peninsula?" By the time he finished, he was nearly shouting.

Sylvio didn't reply for a few moments, letting some of the steam of the tirade dissipate. Eventually, he said, "There won't be a team, only me. There won't be a need for a contingency plan. Either I will be successful, or I won't. There won't be an indication about where I've come from or why. As far as transportation goes, I have the means to move him easily, which is the main reason I've been asked to assist in this. There are things I can do that others cannot."

The room was divided into two camps now, which was no surprise. Those who knew what Sylvio was capable of were amused. Those who did not know were confused. They were not satisfied by Sylvio's answer.

"But . . ." the deputy director began to object.

The director cut him off. "Mr. Costa, I gather that you do not advertise your abilities without need, but perhaps, given the highly sensitive nature of this meeting and the importance of a successful outcome, you would explain a bit more to those of us who are here? I assure you we will keep anything you may reveal in confidence." As he said those last words, he caught the eye of each person who had shown doubt about Sylvio, making sure they understood not to speak about what they might learn.

Sylvio considered that for several seconds while everyone waited for his reply. He said, "You've all been told magic exists. You saw a minor demonstration of it prior to our discussion. There are beings out there with power that is denied to most. We are each gifted with different abilities. My particular gift is teleportation."

They sat in silence and blinked at him. What I felt from them was surprise, and then doubt, like they wanted to say out loud, "No way, you're joking." I relayed this response to Sylvio. His eyes fell on Shaw, who gave a slight nod. Sylvio stood, stepped away from his chair, and said, "Perhaps a demonstration is in order." He offered me his hand. "Miss Rachel."

I took his hand and stepped beside him. He put his arm around my waist, locked eyes with four-star, and we disappeared.

He took us to his shop in Utah. A small room was set aside that was empty other than a couple of pictures. There were no windows. There was at least one room like that in all of his properties so he could hop to each place without anyone seeing. He grinned and kissed me on the forehead because he could.

Before I could respond, we were back in the conference room. Two of those in the room were startled enough that they flew to their feet. The smell of ozone that always accompanied one of Sylvio's jumps wafted away, and they stared at us in stunned silence.

The director cleared his throat and shuffled the papers in front of him to buy a little time to compose himself. "That does answer a lot of questions. Thank you for explaining in such a vivid way." He must have had more complete information than the others because he was now feeling wary instead of shocked, the way the others felt. I suspected someone had informed him that only a quite powerful magical being could teleport. Or maybe he knew that those who most often had that gift were vampires.

We took our seats again, and the two who had been standing when we reappeared slowly sank into theirs.

"Is there a limit to how far you can travel like that?" It was the deputy director speaking again.

"Yes," Sylvio said, but he didn't elaborate.

The man was annoyed at the incomplete response. He tried a different tack. "Can you teleport anywhere you want?"

"It has its limitations, but they won't interfere with this operation," Sylvio replied in a bland tone. The man understood then that he wasn't likely to get any details, and scowled. He fumed inside. He felt uncertain, too, unsure of his ground. I was certain that was something foreign to him.

The national security advisor spoke up. "Given the difficulties of capturing our target using conventional means, I recommend we go ahead with Admiral Shaw's proposal. Are there any objections?"

I realized then that I had felt no fear from her during this meeting. All the normal humans in the room deferred to her. It was interesting that she said "target" rather than "him." It meant she clearly viewed the man as an enemy and not a fellow human being. She was committed to the success of the operation. I wondered what atrocities the man had committed.

General Barton spoke up. "I can vouch for Sylvio's integrity." He looked directly at the deputy director and four-star. "In this case, it isn't really necessary for us to know *how* he plans to carry out this mission. We need to know that he can, and I have no doubts about that."

The room fell silent, but I could feel an accord forming. "Are there any more objections?" the national security advisor repeated. No one spoke. Four-star was now looking at us with speculation. He was no longer afraid and angry. He seemed to be considering the possibilities a being such as Sylvio could provide.

"Thank you, Mr. Costa, Miss Burns," the director said. She smiled at us both. "Admiral Shaw can work with you on finalizing the details and report back to us," she added, effectively dismissing us without having to say it.

Sylvio stood, and I joined him. He gave a small bow. "It's my pleasure to be of assistance. Good day." I nodded and smiled and followed Sylvio out of the room, with Shaw right behind us.

No one spoke until we rounded a corner and were in the large main hallway, then Shaw asked, "Why the Mena House?"

"Rachel has never seen the pyramids."

Shaw chuckled and smiled at me. "You're good for this old boy."

I grinned widely at the exasperated expression on Sylvio's face. "Good to hear it."

Sylvio turned on his heel and strode down the hallway. Shaw and I followed. We walked on a few more paces. When Sylvio spoke again, his voice was hard, and an icy chill permeated the hallway. "Where is Agent Donovan?" He didn't turn to look back at us.

I'd had a long discussion with Sylvio about the agent. I didn't feel capturing me warranted death for the man, especially when he believed that I was a black witch. Sylvio's perspective was different. He gave no quarter to those who injured people he cared about. He agreed to meet the man first, then make his decision. Sylvio's perspective about what warranted death was far different from those in this modern age.

Shaw said, "Take a left at the next hallway. It's the third door on the right." Shaw and I exchanged a look. Shaw and Sylvio had been friends for a long time—over a century. Shaw knew quite well what Sylvio was capable of and what his view of justice was.

"I saw that," Sylvio said without turning around to look at us.

We didn't speak the rest of the way to the room, even though we walked on for a couple of minutes. I was beginning to feel like the Pentagon was even larger on the inside than it was on the outside and wished I had worn flats instead of heels. When we stopped at the door, Shaw knocked once then immediately opened it.

It was a large conference room, and there were a dozen people there. I sensed that one was a werewolf; the rest were human. Sylvio stepped in and gave Shaw a look. Neither of us had been told there would be that many people at this second meeting. Shaw smiled benignly, but inside he felt uncertain. He knew Sylvio would do something to take care of the issue about what had been done to me, but wasn't sure what. I was certain Shaw had allowed so many to attend in an effort to keep Sylvio from taking drastic action.

The people in the room wore various businesslike expressions, but their true feelings were mostly apprehension, and for some, outright fear. It was obvious they all knew who and what we were. Unlike the meeting we had just left, these people believed we were preternatural. All four from the room I'd been captive in were there. I didn't recognize any of the others. The spirits gathered around me, always ready to come to my aid.

Agent Donovan was sitting at the far end of the room. Sylvio's gaze settled on him. He captured the man's mind in an instant. Sylvio strolled down the left side of the table and stopped across from where Donovan sat, not waiting for Shaw to make introductions. Sylvio reached out and placed his palm on the head of the man seated opposite Donovan. He had been one of those in the interrogation room I'd been captive in: Karl Beckman, the one bent on evil.

Magic pulsed in the room. The power vampires are particularly gifted with is controlling the bodies and minds of others. At Sylvio's touch, Beckman stiffened, feeling startled and angry. We had all assumed the target was Donovan. Beckman's body shook as he tried to move and realized he could not. Terror soon replaced his other emotions.

The room had been silent up to that point. Then a man I didn't know, who sat two chairs down from Beckman, reached under his jacket.

Shaw's deep voice rumbled through the room. He stood next to me near the door, appearing relaxed, and said to the man, "That would not be smart."

I was surprised. I'd thought guns were not allowed in a government building. I asked the spirits to bring any weapons to me. Sylvio might be impervious to bullets, but I certainly am not, and they wouldn't do Shaw much good either, especially if the bullets were silver, which these people might very well have used.

It happened too fast for them to do anything about it. Jackets fluttered and skirts lifted, then five guns and four knives slid across the floor to my feet. Shaw suppressed a chuckle. I glanced down at the weapons, then at Sylvio again. I felt humor from him as well. He pushed more magic into Beckman and the man gasped, causing the others to turn their attention that way.

"Show me," Sylvio commanded.

Beckman's eyes went wide and turned inward, seeing the images as Sylvio pulled them from his mind. Sylvio's expression darkened as a long minute ticked by. I knew then the man would die soon. The others didn't dare move. I was impressed with their composure; their faces did not reveal the fear that now permeated the room.

I could see the magical tie black witches had forged, like a braid of oily threads, between Beckman and Donovan. Sylvio was using it to relay what he saw to Donovan. Donovan's face darkened more than Sylvio's did during that interminably long minute. He felt betrayed. Any fear he had of Sylvio was burned away by his rage at the man he had considered a friend. Sylvio dropped his hold on the two men and at the same time severed the tie black witches had made.

Donovan lunged over the table, not bothering to go around, and took Beckman by the throat, hauling him out of his chair and against the wall with amazing alacrity. Sylvio moved out of their way.

"You bastard!" Donovan said in a low growl. It was more menacing than a shout would have been. Beckman couldn't reply even if he tried; Donovan's arm was across his throat. Beckman's eyes flicked from him to Sylvio, and he saw his death waiting there. The man seemed to deflate then. Donovan let go of him, and he slumped to the floor.

"Piece of shit," Donovan said as he looked down at his former friend, his hands clenched into fists. He was trying hard not to kick the man. Then he looked over at Sylvio, feeling startled to find himself so near a vampire.

"Nice to meet you, I'm Sylvio." He held a hand out, and Donovan took it.

"Sean Donovan . . . sir."

Shaw announced to the room at large, "You have a mole in your group. He's been working for our opponents." Then he asked Sylvio, "How long?"

"Months," Sylvio replied.

"Shit," said the man who'd reached for his gun. He was glaring at Beckman with nearly as much malice as Donovan.

Things went fairly smoothly after that. Sylvio asked me to put a bubble of air around Beckman so he could not see or hear what was said next. Sylvio then told them he would take Beckman into custody. Looks were exchanged, but no one protested that statement.

Shaw introduced us to each of them, and they asked some pointed questions about our capabilities. Sylvio and I relayed messages to each other, mind to mind. I needed his help to know how much to reveal out loud. Shaw had been *very* surprised to learn we could do that when we'd told him a few weeks before. Among werewolves, only mates could converse that way. An alpha could give a command and receive a response, but it wasn't a two-way conversation. Vampires could talk mind to mind if they were willing to expose themselves. But vampires didn't talk to their thralls that way. What Sylvio and I could do had not been heard of before.

Magic is as old as the earth itself; what could be done with it had been predictable until recently. It disturbed both Sylvio and Shaw that the rules were not set with me and my son Chris, or with Tim and his children. We were an unknown element, something new in the preternatural community. The people in this room didn't need to know any of that. All they needed to know was that I was a white witch—an asset for them should they need me, like Sylvio. It took a few minutes, but they began to believe we were sincere in our desire to stop the darker elements from wreaking havoc. There wasn't trust yet, but at least it was a beginning.

Their team had been created to help deal with the preternatural and learn more about it. Most investigated crimes that had unexplained or odd circumstances. They were sent in to determine if magic was involved. A few of them were also tasked with finding out how magic could be used to help American interests and humans in general.

Their questions became more pointed, and even Shaw was surprised at how candidly Sylvio answered them. I relayed to Sylvio that Beckman was the only dark soul in the room, and he took that news at face value. The others were trying their best to make the world a safer place.

What surprised me was that the truly dangerous one in the room was the werewolf who sat next to Donovan. Her name was Sasha. She was petite, with an attractive face that looked younger than the others, and I was very glad she was on our side. She let the others take charge and listened. They were all passion and fire, like Donovan. Sasha was ice. She noticed my interest and gave me a pleasant smile. I smiled in return, then pointedly stopped looking her way. The others who knew she was a werewolf didn't know the depth of her will. If she wanted to be viewed as a junior member of the team, I was not going to tip her hand. I wondered where she stood in the hierarchy of Shaw's pack.

They didn't ask me very many questions. They already knew quite a bit about white witches and the magic they could do. They had all heard what happened in the interrogation room, but it was only words—the electronics, including the video, had been destroyed. What heat and water hadn't ruined, the spirits had. Words don't have the influence that *seeing* does. They knew white witches didn't have the power of black witches, and Sylvio didn't ask me to correct their misinterpretation about me. Sasha was not fooled. Neither was Donovan.

They had all also heard what happened in the past couple of years since I'd begun staying with Sylvio. But he was present for each incident, and like many others, they assumed it was his magic that had destroyed those dark creatures. Now I understood why Sanders and Perkins weren't at the meeting. They worked closely with Shaw and knew what really happened. Like in poker, you keep your cards close and your knowledge secret as long as possible. If you reveal your skill too early, the payoff won't be nearly as great. Shaw obviously wanted these people to know only what Sylvio was willing to reveal.

℘ Chapter 3 ℘
Companion

I had been putting off starting the next section of Sylvio's history. Whoever pulls the strings on our lives had made quite a tangle of them recently. I had stopped at the point in Sylvio's story when Cyneric was made into a fledgling vampire. The reincarnated soul of Cyneric had come into our lives in the shape of Tim's son. I didn't want my feelings about Eric to be tainted with whatever I might learn about Cyneric. I now had a pretty good idea about the kind of person Eric was, so I was eager to start typing up the next section of the story as told by Sylvio . . .

℘ Sylvio ℘

I found Cyneric not long before dawn. He had run into the countryside. When I spotted him, he was climbing the cliffs near the sea, figuring out how to move in his new body as he did. He stopped on a rocky outcrop to stare at the ocean and wait for the sunrise. I knew he wanted to die a permanent death. But the demon, who now owned his soul, would not want that yet.

I stood some distance away and waited. When the sun topped the horizon and reached across the waves to touch the stone he stood on, he cried out in obvious pain—and ran. I followed him into the depths of the woods where the sun's strength didn't yet penetrate. He was moving slowly by then and finally fell to his knees. He began digging a grave in the soft, damp earth, but I wrapped my arms around his shoulders and teleported us to one of my caves.

When we landed on the cold stone floor, he rolled over so we were face to face. His expression of abject horror gave me physical pain. "Kill me, Sylvio," he whispered.

"I already have."

His eyes rolled over white as he fell into the sleep of the dead.

I teleported back to Niveus and found that no one had touched either Nyla's body or Malachi's. I finished severing Nyla's head. I could sense no life in her since she was so newly made, but I didn't want there to be any chance she would rise again. I burned Malachi's body as well and gathered both their ashes in separate piles. I turned to Gerald, who was Cyneric's apprentice, and asked him to find urns for the ashes and keep them safe. My people witnessed it all in silence. They had gathered around and watched as I burned the bodies. I knew they wanted answers, but I wasn't prepared to give them. I left Niveus to Gerald's care and returned to my cave.

When Cyneric transformed, Meri was standing mere feet from him, frozen by the horrible scene in front of her, and he'd ignored her. I sensed his hunger and knew he could smell her blood, and without any aid from me, he passed her by. When he ran away, he had not touched any of the others on the estate, nor had he bothered the animals in the pastures and forest, any of which he could have caught and killed easily. I didn't dare to believe yet but could not help wondering: Was there hope for him?

I watched for hours as he lay still and dead, waging an internal war. I could not bring myself to end him, although I knew that was truly what he wanted. Cyneric was a good, honest man; he deserved to move on to his next life. If his soul remained, he would grieve for his family and hate the thing he had become. He would have every right to hate me, too. And yet, I could not destroy him. I was too selfish for that. I wanted a companion, someone like me. I knew if my hope was wrong and he became the killer the demon wanted him to be, those deaths would be on me, not him.

Yet another selfish thought kept me restless and pacing the cave: Would I lose the gift of walking in the light of day if I let him live?

As the day passed and dusk came, I wrestled with the question of killing Cyneric before any deaths weighed his soul. For even if we are hidden from the sun, we can always feel its presence. He began to stir and opened his eyes. From habit, he reached up to rub his face and scored his cheeks with his new claws. He stared at his hands in horror, then looked at me. I watched many emotions pass across his face, finally settling on despair.

"Why her and not me?" he growled. His voice had the timbre of a vampire, and his eyes blazed red like coals in a fire. I could feel his hunger from where I sat, watching him.

He meant his wife, Nyla, who had nearly killed him when she transformed into a fledgling vampire. I gave him my blood to restore him. I had saved him one time too many—and he was now a fledgling.

"Let's find out if I should have," I said.

Before he could protest, I wrapped my arms around him and teleported us to an area I knew to be near a battlefield. When we appeared, the scents of blood and the dying were everywhere. Cyneric groaned. His need to feed should have overpowered any other thoughts, but he stood by my side and trembled from head to toe.

"Come with me," I said. "We'll find those Death is waiting for and free their souls."

I took his hand and led him onto the field. Dismembered and mutilated bodies littered the ground. Horses made large mounds on the trampled earth, casting deep shadows in the gathering darkness. Some of them still kicked and flailed, and a few even gave plaintive whinnies. Many more men than horses lay on the battlefield. They bled from all manner of injuries. Arrows stuck up out of their chests, legs, necks. Slashes from sword and lance had found gaps in their armor or pierced through so that you could see the gore of what lay inside their bodies.

Some of the men still cried out, but they were weak cries. Most of the bodies were already frozen in death. The armies had withdrawn, taking with them all they thought could survive. In the morning, they would dig ditches to place their fallen comrades in, and their foes. But the night was for us. The field was free for Death to roam—for that is what we are: Death walking.

Cyneric was hesitant at first, until the lust for blood overwhelmed him. We both feasted until we were bloated. Then, as my master did with me, we covered ourselves with cloaks and used scythes to remove the heads of those who still suffered, letting death take them in another way.

When that was done, I took us back to my cave and found clean clothes. Mine nearly fit him; he was only slightly smaller in stature than me.

He remained silent throughout, caught in turns by the wonder of his new eyesight, the power of his new body, and the desire for blood. He watched in fascination as the blood that covered his arms was absorbed by his new skin, now free of dirt or blemish without the need of water. His gaze strayed to the claws on his hands. He reached toward a small gold statue that stood on a chest and listened to his claws click on the metal as he tapped them slowly, one by one. Then he turned to me. His expression reflected wonder and curiosity instead of anger and dread. The blood had energized him. He truly was a vampire. Magic surrounded him.

"You can change back to your human form," I told him. "Imagine what you looked like in a mirror."

It took him several minutes, but he finally managed it. When he had done that, he stared at his hands, which bore old scars from working with the metal forge and with horses. His eyes settled on his wedding band, which was the only adornment I'd ever seen him wear. It was quite unusual at that time for a man to wear one, but he had wanted it, and I had helped him fashion both of their rings. He began to remove it, then pushed it back where it belonged. He stood for some time in silence then. I had the impression he wanted to cry, but tears didn't come. Eventually, I held my hand out to him, and he took it.

I teleported us away from the cave to the depths of a forest, where we wandered aimlessly under the thick canopy and stopped next to a small pond. I watched as he absorbed how different things were with his new senses. I waited while his body purged itself of all the fluids and refuse it no longer needed. When that was done, he removed his clothes and stepped into the pond to wash. When he was clean and dressed, we wandered the forest again. We encountered animals, and he did not attack them, though he could clearly smell their blood and hear the beating of their hearts.

I took him back to Niveus. My people had more than a passing acquaintance with vampires. They knew immediately what Cyneric had become, though he appeared in his human form. I saw a mix of fear, compassion, and sorrow on their faces.

With the death of his wife and son, the person Cyneric was closest to was Gerald. For a vampire, it is more difficult to curb our desires with someone we are emotionally connected to. It is far easier to stop drinking if they are a mere stranger. It is yet another way the demon within taunts us.

I called them all to me, all those at the estate, until they stood in a half circle in front of us, two and three deep. The scent of their blood had to be torment for Cyneric, even as sated as he currently was.

"Come, Gerald," I commanded.

He could not disobey, and I hated having to risk him, but I had to know. He moved in jerky steps, his mind attempting to resist. He stopped only a pace away from us, his eyes pleading with me. He did not want to die and was sure he was about to. I placed my hand on his cheek, sent a silent apology, then tilted his head, exposing the vessel in his neck, which was throbbing fast due to his fear. His will was strong, and yet he began to shake.

Beside me, I could feel Cyneric's anger and frustration, and his *need*. "Drink," I ordered.

Compelled by my command, Cyneric hissed and struck. His arms pinned Gerald to him, his new fangs sliced skin easily, and the sound of him swallowing was clear in the cold silence. I did not attempt to control him, did not make a move to save Gerald when he began to weaken and finally fainted. The fear my people felt as they stood in silence was a living thing, rolling toward us in waves. I kept them frozen in place and waited.

Gerald's heart began to flutter, as did his eyelids. He fell to panting and turned a ghostly white. For a few moments, I thought my hopes were dashed. Despair began to take me, as it had the silent crowd standing witness.

When Gerald's panting began to slow and his heart beat ever faster, Cyneric drew away. He licked the wound to stop the blood flowing and shuddered. He clenched his jaw and took a long, slow breath, visibly composing himself. Then he bit his wrist, as he'd seen me do dozens of times, and set it over Gerald's slack, open mouth. "Drink," Cyneric commanded.

I was instantly angry, the demon residing in me coming to the fore. How dare he take the mind of one of mine! I snarled and began to move. Cyneric turned to look at me, his eyes full of accusation . . . and understanding. It is not possible for a human to truly comprehend our motivations and desires. He knew what I was now, what he was, and had accepted it.

We locked eyes until he felt another new sensation: the pain of someone feeding from him. It is both excruciating and erotic at the same time. His eyes widened, and he looked back at Gerald, who was beginning to revive. Moments later, Gerald's eyes focused, and he gazed upon Cyneric with adoration.

Cyneric was surprised, then appalled. With dawning comprehension, he looked at me again. Controlling the minds of others is the most evil thing we do as vampires, more so by far than what we do to their bodies. The mind is the doorway to the soul. I could see he felt the same way.

What he had done finally struck me. I recalled the look on Adonas' face when he came down to my cell and found I had not fed from the two children he'd gifted me. Now I understood the look of pure wonder when he gazed at me. I'm sure my face mirrored his. I stepped over and embraced Cyneric and could not help it when my shoulders began to shake from sheer joy. I was not alone anymore.

✆ Chapter 4 ☞
Excess Baggage

I stared in disbelief out the hotel windows. The pyramids seemed so close I could touch them. Everything had a red-orange glow, and I thought it strange that it would seem familiar. The air felt like the desert did in southern Utah, and the sky was the same color of blue. But down on the ground over toward the pyramids, the people bustling about wore a mix of modern clothing and traditional robes. Camels and donkeys shared the roads with buses and cars, and most of the words on the advertisements were in the odd squiggles and dots of Arabic.

There was a thump at the door. I peeked through the spyhole to find Sylvio on the other side. His arms were full, and duffle bags were slung over his shoulders. He'd been gone all afternoon.

I opened the door for him and he swept past, dropped the things on the couch, and turned around. He was dressed in black and had changed his hair. It stuck up all over in a disheveled mop. He'd also gone out somewhere to bake in the sun. The skin that was visible on his face and hands was now a deep tan.

"Is this your spy look?" I asked.

"In this part of the world, it works well." He was feeling reckless and bold, ready for battle. I hoped he was disappointed and things went too easily for his liking.

"Who was Falasa?" I'd been burning to ask that question.

That brought him up short and changed his mood to wistful. He looked into the past. It was now a familiar expression.

"She was a princess. Her father ruled a large territory in what is now Dubai. Until oil became important, the Arabian tribes grew and waned like the dunes in the desert. Both her grandfather and her father were intelligent and powerful. They ruled a strong kingdom. Her father built the palace this terrorist is using as a base. They haven't changed the gazebo in the garden. I can easily teleport there."

"You liked her."

He smiled a wan smile and nodded. "Throughout all of time, women have been oppressed, lorded over by men. They still are, in many cultures. I admire those who fight against such bonds. Her brothers were idiots, too proud to see the lioness in their midst. She ruled the kingdom without their knowledge.

"The other sheiks in the area were not fooled," Sylvio said. "They knew who was the power and respected her. She lived to be seventy-three. Her only son died at twenty-one. When she passed, the kingdom fell."

The faraway look fell away from his face, and he focused on me. "You would have liked her, too." He brushed his thumb across my cheek.

I considered the things on the couch. They were all black, including the shotguns, of which I could see three. The rest of the pile seemed to be black clothes, and I was curious what the duffle bags might contain. They sounded quite heavy when he dropped them on the couch.

"Why did you have to come to the door?"

He looked embarrassed, which was something I'd rarely ever seen on his face. "I forgot which room we ended up in. I scared the maid in the first room I appeared in half to death."

It was Ramirez who had reserved the rooms. He'd left me in the lobby before I picked up the key card. I laughed. "I bet her face was priceless. What did you do with her?" I immediately wished I hadn't asked, but his answer turned out to be okay.

"I only made her forget." He gave me a thoughtful glance, then added, "She has witch blood in her and doesn't know it."

"Oh, what kind of witch?"

His eyebrows rose in surprise. "No idea. I doubt she's ever used her magic. She reminded me of you."

"Did it hurt?"

Witch blood has a backlash to it. Sylvio explained once that drinking a witch's blood was like touching an electric fence. Sometimes it was a pleasurable zing, and on rare occasions, it could zap hard enough to knock him out. I'd learned early on to regulate his pain and only allow him the pleasure. In addition to the danger that came from feeding from a witch, which seems to attract vampires rather than the reverse, it was also a more intense feeling than feeding from a normal human.

"Not much," he said. "She's not very powerful."

"I suspect she'll be visited more than once while we're here."

He turned away but could not hide his grin or the humor he felt.

"Perhaps, but let's get down to business."

He took his time putting on the black fatigues and loading the pockets. He ended by hanging a shotgun from his shoulder.

"Why a shotgun?" For some reason, I assumed he'd have a rifle in addition to his pistol.

"The SAW is good for close quarters, and it's easier to load than the Street Sweeper I used to use." He added another magazine to the side pocket of his fatigues, whose pockets now bulged. His belt was weighed down with hand grenades and what appeared to be flares.

"SAW?"

"The Mossberg Chainsaw shotgun," he replied as he patted the gun affectionately.

The gravity of the situation hit me as he finished putting on his gear. My husband had been in the military, and my oldest son still was, so the feeling of apprehension when they went into danger was familiar, but it had been some time since I'd experienced it. If Sylvio thought he needed that much firepower, this was a very dangerous mission. He sensed my growing unease and came to touch my cheek with his gloved fingers. Even his hands were dressed in black.

"Don't worry. Capturing the target won't be the difficult part. We haven't stirred the hornet's nest yet." He stepped away, and before I could even think up a reply, he vanished.

I stewed about him leaving me behind for only a couple of minutes before there was another knock on the door. I looked through the peephole to find Sanders and Perkins on the other side. I opened the door for them.

"Hi, Rachel," they both said. They weren't surprised to see me, so Shaw must have clued them in.

"Hi. You have good timing. Sylvio just left."

"Already?" Perkins said. "He doesn't waste time, does he." It wasn't a question.

Sylvio reappeared in the middle of the room, knocking Sanders sideways since he'd been standing where Sylvio popped in. Sylvio's hand was on the shoulder of a man who was thin, lithe, and rather small in stature. I had imagined a bearded man in a robe before the meeting at the Pentagon—maybe because when I thought of terrorists, I pictured Osama Bin Laden. This man was wearing only a pair of shiny red boxers. There was a lot of curly black fuzz on his chest, and his hair was cut short like a businessman. He didn't have a beard, either, just a good start on early-morning stubble.

There was only a moment to consider his appearance before his emotions distracted me. He was certainly more composed than I would have been. He took in his surroundings, obviously puzzled about where he was, and did not struggle against Sylvio's grasp. I thought it odd that he felt so confident. He suddenly spoke in rapid words I did not recognize.

"English," Sylvio interrupted.

The man became immediately angry. He glowered and shot Sylvio a defiant sneer, then jeered at the rest of us as he looked us up and down.

Sylvio shook the man's shoulder and said, "Speak English."

Another string of words that were unintelligible to me came from the man. The words didn't seem totally foreign to Sanders. His face darkened with anger. The man's meaning was clear, even without my ability to sense his feelings. He didn't intend to cooperate.

Sylvio stepped forward and held the man still with his gaze and allowed himself to transform. I felt the man's shock and then fear as he realized he truly was trapped. Sylvio did not mask the pain when he bit into the man's neck. A frightened cry escaped the man, which soon turned to terror as he began to realize it was not an ordinary human that had captured him, but something *other*.

Sylvio drank until his captive's eyes lost their terror and became blank. As he fed, vampire magic began to swell and fill the room. He stepped away and let go of the man's shoulder. The man stood still and could not even consider moving.

Compulsion is how vampires survive. They can make people believe what they want them to, make them dismiss the odd events they have seen and invent a plausible reason to replace the memory. Once their minds are captured, people will tell them anything they want to know.

Sylvio turned to Sanders and Perkins, whose expressions were devoid of emotion. They were caught in Sylvio's magic as well. He sighed and looked at me. "Can you shield them from my magic so they can think straight?"

Our captive must have had a strong mind, or Sylvio would have been able to isolate only him in the compulsion spell he'd woven. I sent a blanket of spirits to wrap around Sanders and Perkins. They twitched and shook themselves, licked their lips, and stared at Sylvio with an equal measure of anger and fear.

"Sorry, I didn't mean to catch you two as well," Sylvio said apologetically.

They blinked at him. "That was creepy as hell," Sanders said and rubbed his palms on his pant legs. Perkins shook himself again.

Sylvio turned back to our captive and commanded, "You will answer these men truthfully. If you do not, I will know. Understand?"

"Yes, sir," the man replied, his face and body entirely slack, without resistance. It was more disturbing than watching Sylvio feed from an unwilling victim. I sensed Sanders and Perkins thought so, too.

They produced a list of prepared questions, and the man answered them without hesitation as Sylvio's magic continued to pulse in the room. The terrorist's English was quite good, although he did have a thick Arabic accent. Sanders and Perkins were most interested in where the terrorist cell headquarters was, who the main players were, and what sort of plans they had been making.

I was appalled at what the man had done and what he and his team were planning to do. Innocent lives meant nothing to him. I could feel his true emotions under Sylvio's mask of compulsion. He had begun as a true believer, but now it was merely business. He felt nothing for any of those he harmed. The human lives he destroyed meant less to him than his fine silk briefs.

When they were finished, they transmitted the encrypted recording to Shaw and waited. It was an uncomfortable wait. Sylvio dropped the compulsion spell and fed from the man some more until he passed out, then lay him on the floor, away from where we were all sitting.

Sanders and Perkins were both very uncomfortable, given what happened to them earlier. I began asking Sylvio questions about the pyramids and the demons he found there. That distracted them enough that they asked questions too, and they relaxed quite a bit while Sylvio indulged our curiosity.

An hour passed before Shaw called us back.

Sylvio put the phone on speaker and asked, "Did you get what you need from him?"

Shaw hesitated, then said, "I think he's served his purpose."

We all knew what that meant. The man would not see another sunrise. That knowledge didn't bother me at all.

"Could you do one more thing for us, Sylvio?" Shaw asked.

"What is that?"

"Would you be willing to retrieve the records the man spoke of?"

"One minute."

Sylvio walked to the man lying on the floor and lifted his head. His eyes flew open in alarm, then he was caught once again by vampire compulsion and stared blankly into Sylvio's red eyes. Both closed their eyes at the same time, and a pulse of magic hit the man. This was an unfamiliar kind of power, but I could guess what Sylvio was doing. He was given the gift of reading memories from Liling, a vampire who kept him captive for a time and shared her ancient blood with him.

We waited in silence. When Sylvio let the man's mind go, his eyes remained closed and his face slack. I caught Sanders and Perkins shuddering but made sure they did not notice I had seen.

Sylvio addressed the phone, "He gave me a clear picture. I can retrieve their computers and records. They're not foolish enough to keep it all in that one place, but most of it is."

Shaw asked, "Is there anything you need from our end?"

"How about an Apache helicopter?" Sylvio grinned at the phone.

"And a battleship off the coast, ready to fire," added Sanders.

"Fresh out of those," Shaw added dryly. He paused a moment, then said, "We do have a strike force ready to go in if they are needed."

"I think it would be best not to risk too many," Sylvio replied. "The four of us should be able to clear things up."

"Four?" Shaw sounded worried.

"Antone will be here soon."

"Oh, of course." Shaw sounded relieved. I was sure he'd been concerned that Sylvio intended to take me along. "How much time do you need?"

"We can go immediately, before they have a chance to move anything. No one saw me take him, but I'm sure they've realized he's missing by now."

"Sylvio, we'll owe you big for this."

Sylvio didn't respond to that. "I'll call you when it's done," he said and hung up. Then he turned to Perkins and Sanders. "I assume you want to help? It will go faster if there are more hands, and I could use a lookout."

Perkins stood up. "Hell yes, I'd love something real to do."

Sylvio tilted his head and regarded them. "I'll have to teleport you there."

Sanders stood up next to Perkins. "I'm game." Perkins nodded.

Sylvio chuckled. "Gather your gear." He walked over to the terrorist one last time, kneeling with his back to us. We were quiet, though, and the sound of him feeding from the man was clear in the room.

I'd never witnessed him kill someone in that way before. He would not have done it then, either, not in front of us, except that teleporting tired him and he needed his strength for the new task. When he finished, he threw a blanket over the corpse.

None of us commented about the dead terrorist. Sanders and Perkins left to get the rest of their equipment.

"I'll go first and make sure the place is clear, then I'll come get them."

He didn't offer or even consider taking me.

I began to protest. My spirits could protect me from a lot of things. But when Sylvio looked me in the eye, I saw he was ready to argue so I didn't push the issue. He disappeared.

It's a good thing I didn't go with him. I could feel him through our connection, and he was suddenly in pain. It was remote but clear all the same. He didn't come back for several interminably long minutes, and his pain soon faded to a mere annoyance, but I paced the room anyway. He returned with an armload of files and two laptops. He dumped them on the nearby chair. The entire left side of his shirt was bloody, and the shirt itself was in tatters.

He felt strong and vital and was not in very much pain. I was sure that whatever blood he'd lost, he took back from those who shot him. Still, I put my hands on my hips and gave him a frosty glare.

"Are those *bullet* holes?!" It was not right that he was excited and animated and not concerned about being shot at all. Vampires are not quite right in the head.

He smirked at my expression and said, "I'll go change my shirt. No reason for Sanders and Perkins to see this."

When he walked past me to the bedroom, the holes in the back of his shirt were bigger than those in the front. I stalked behind him, certain he could sense my displeasure. When he pulled the shirt off, I could see three holes in his back about the size of a fifty-cent piece that were still oozing blood, although not nearly the amount a wound of that size would have on a normal person.

"Ever think of wearing a vest?" I asked sarcastically.

"Why ruin a good vest?" he quipped.

I sighed again. "Let me put a bandage on those so you don't destroy another shirt."

He indulged me and followed me into the bathroom. I'd brought a first aid kit with me—trained by my mom to always be prepared. She taught EMTs for years. I put some large square Telfa pads on the holes in his back. The holes in front were already sealed over and were only puckered dark-red circles in the area of his heart. Someone was a good shot.

Sylvio's skin absorbed the blood as it trickled down, leaving only a faint red stain. I got a washcloth damp and cleaned him up. I didn't say anything, but I sighed a lot, and I felt him trying not to laugh, which made me roll my eyes and sigh some more.

He was choosing a new shirt when Antone appeared in the outer room. Antone looked around, spotted the dead terrorist, and then gazed at Sylvio as he put on the fresh shirt. He raised a questioning brow but didn't ask why Sylvio had bullet holes in him.

"Thanks for coming, Antone. I've been shown where this cell was keeping their records and thought four of us might get things done faster."

Antone looked at me, puzzled for a moment. Then he sniffed the air. "Sanders and Perkins?" he asked.

"Yes, they should be back any minute."

I put my hands on my hips and huffed. Antone and Sylvio both chuckled.

"You're cute when you're mad," Antone commented. He looked down at his clothes. He was wearing tan slacks and leather shoes. His sweater was beige and looked to be some kind of soft, warm material. He shrugged at Sylvio.

Sylvio said, "I brought you something more appropriate. Your bag is over there."

Antone's teeth flashed white with his grin. He was feeling as reckless as Sylvio and crossed the room to begin changing. He glanced over at me and asked, "What are you in a snit about?"

Fuming at his patronizing earlier comment, I snarled, "Snit! I'm not in a snit!" I folded my arms and glared from one to the other, knowing he was right. "It's not decent that you two *like* this sort of thing." I slumped in a chair. I really did feel hurt. I thought I would be helping them, but it appeared I was brought along only so I could see the pyramids.

Antone chuckled. "I don't think 'decent' and 'vampire' go together anyway, do they?"

He started changing clothes, and I couldn't help appreciating his beauty as he did. The man was simply breathtaking. I let myself enjoy watching the ripple of his muscles and the golden highlights that stood out on his chocolate skin as he moved. With his back to me, I could ogle in safety. He didn't like his fine physique; it had cost him a lot of pain in the past.

I caught a hint of frustration from Sylvio and felt vindicated. He came over to me, removed one of his black gloves, and stroked my cheek. I tried to paste a look of anger on my face, but it didn't work. He kissed my forehead and said, "I won't risk you getting shot."

Once Antone was dressed all in black like Sylvio, he walked to the second duffle bag and checked the contents, loading the twin of Sylvio's SAW and his Colt .45. The big pistol looked small in his hands. It also looked like it belonged there. He added extra clips to the pockets on his trousers and snapped a KA-Bar knife to the strap on his left leg. I wondered absently why either of them even took guns with them.

Antone caught my expression and guessed correctly. "Sometimes, a plain old gun works better than magic, and bullets travel faster than we can."

Sanders and Perkins came in then, carrying duffle bags of their own. They nodded at us and headed for one of the extra bedrooms to change into their gear. For a moment, I was surprised they weren't geared up already. Then it occurred to me that people might question why they were wearing fatigues in a hotel.

They didn't take long and came out complete with camo paint. Both looked at home. Always before when I'd seen them, they seemed to be wearing costumes. They were men of action who were more accustomed to their current attire than the detective suits they used most of the time.

As it turned out, I was needed after all. Both Sylvio and Antone brought captives back with them: two women and three kids. They asked me to wrap them in air so they could be contained, and if more was needed to make them sit quietly until they were told otherwise. Then they both disappeared again. I put up a shield of air. Eventually, they all grew brave enough to touch their invisible barrier. When they did, their eyes grew wide with fear and uncertainty. The children were small and terrified. I added calm to the bubble of air the spirits erected, and the tension went down somewhat.

Time seems to move at a snail's pace when worry for others' safety is involved. Eons later, but only an hour by the clock in the room, Antone appeared again with an arm around Sanders, who was sickly pale and only half conscious.

Antone quickly strode to one of the bedrooms and laid him on the bed. I ran for the first aid kit that was still in the bathroom and hurried to Sanders' side. By the time I got there, Antone had ripped the bloody shirt off. Sanders moaned in obvious pain. Antone pulled the Kevlar vest apart rather than moving the injured arm out from under it.

I climbed on the bed next to Sanders, put a Telfa pad on the wound at his shoulder, and pushed. I looked around for more injuries and saw Sanders' scalp was bleeding freely, the injury hidden by his hair and black cap. I taped the first Telfa pad as tightly as I could while Antone tore strips of adhesive for me, then moved Sanders' head for a better look.

A bullet had grazed his scalp above his ear, and I could see bone, but his skull didn't appear to be broken. I took another Telfa pad and placed it on that wound, hoping I was helping and not making things worse. I wrapped tape around his head and put his black stocking cap back on to keep the bandage in place. I was dismayed at how fast both pads were turning red.

"He needs a doctor," I told Antone.

Antone didn't reply. Instead, he bit his own wrist and commanded, "Richard, drink."

Magic pulsed, forcing him to obey. His lips clamped over Antone's arm, and he began to swallow large gulps of that liquid fire. After a few moments, he began to shiver and shake, but at the same time, his color improved from sickly gray to a pale pink.

Antone let him drink quite a lot until Sanders' eyes fluttered open and then grew wide with comprehension. Antone sat back and licked his wrist lazily, reminding me of a cat licking cream off its paw. His feelings of apprehension and worry for Sanders changed to humor as Sanders attempted to sit up.

I put a hand on his good shoulder, and he flinched. I don't think he noticed me until that moment. Following Antone's lead, I used his first name. "Richard, you need to lie still. Let us check you over and make sure you don't need to go to the hospital."

"I'd prefer that to what *he* did," he snarled, but it was a weak snarl.

Antone gave him a sardonic smile and reached for the bandage on Sanders' head. Sanders began to move away, but Antone's magic pulsed again and he was forced to sit still. He scowled at Antone and began swearing as only a military man can. When we both ignored his tirade, he stopped saying anything and glared in mute fury.

Antone removed the gauze pad that was now soaked in blood. He bent and licked the wound until it stopped bleeding while Sanders shook with a frustration and anger that soon turned to fear at his own helplessness.

I went to the bathroom and brought back the water pitcher and a washcloth and began wiping off the blood. With expert and gentle hands, Antone examined the wound on Sanders' head and said, "It's only skin, nothing damaged, but I'm sure you'll have a killer headache for a day or two."

Antone removed the soaked pad from the wound on the shoulder and licked it to stop the bleeding as well. Then his large hands explored the bruises that were already turning an angry red where the vest had stopped more than one bullet. As Antone examined Sanders, it occurred to me that he would be quite familiar with bullet wounds. He'd fought in battles beginning with the Civil War and continuing to modern times.

Although now, his battles were more covert than they were in the past.

As his gentle hands probed, Antone declared, "Looks like three cracked ribs, but nothing major. The bullet that went through your shoulder was the serious one. An inch to the left, and it would have hit that big vein in your neck, and then not even I could have saved you."

While he probed, Sanders' anger diffused and he was now uncertain how he should feel. Antone kept him still while I finished cleaning the blood off his back, then he released his hold on Sanders' body. Immediately, he slumped and winced. The movement was painful.

"Shit, that hurts." He sat back up and winced again, swaying in place. Antone put a hand at his back to steady him.

I took out the vial of morphine Sylvio always kept in the first aid kit and gave Sanders a shot. He didn't protest.

"Let me help you take your clothes off, and you can lie down," I suggested.

What was left of his shirt and vest were hanging off his back. I began to reach for his belt, but Antone said, "Here," and lifted Sanders onto his feet with an arm around his good shoulder.

Sanders leaned on Antone, and I felt he wanted to protest but was out of steam. I carefully set his heavy utility belt down in a chair, then tugged his pants off and quickly wiped off the blood that had pooled around the top of his pants. I put fresh sheets on the bed and piled the pillows up so he wouldn't be lying flat, then Antone let him sink onto the bed. He groaned and winced but relaxed into the pillows once he'd positioned himself on his right side. His skin was looking gray again.

"I'll be right back," Antone said and disappeared.

I checked on our captives. The women sat huddled on the floor with their backs to the wall and the children in their laps. They stared at me with abject fear. No one had ever looked at *me* like that before.

I thought about telling them they'd be okay, but I didn't know if that was true, and they probably wouldn't understand me anyway. I went to the kitchenette and filled a pitcher with water then set it down near them with some glasses. From where they huddled, they could watch me do all of that, so they knew I hadn't put anything in the water, but they still eyed it with suspicion.

I went in one of the other rooms and brought blankets out to set near them. I was being careful not to get close enough for them to touch me, but even so, one of them made a sudden move to grab my arm and was stopped by the shield of air I'd placed around them. She gave a startled cry and sat back, rubbing her palm. The spirits had added a sting for good measure.

I returned to Sanders' room and realized that our captives could see part of what happened in the bedroom.

In a hoarse voice, Sanders said, "Those kids are terrorists in training."

I didn't have an answer to that. He was probably right, but they were still only kids. Instead of replying, I went in the bathroom and got out more Telfa pads to put on his wounds. I put antibiotic on the pads and taped them down as gently as I could. As I did, I marveled at what magic could do. The wounds appeared to be several hours old, and the skin was healthy around them. Then it occurred to me that I could do more. I called on the spirits and placed a hand over each bandage. I began the chant I'd learned from Micah and sent healing into his body.

Antone reappeared as I was chanting and did not interrupt. When I was tapped out, I sank into the chair next to the bed and smiled at the look of wonder on Sanders' face.

"Well," Antone said, "I intended to give Sanders here more assistance, but it appears it's you who needs it."

I thought it was a good sign that he was back to calling Sanders by his last name, honoring him for the soldier he was. Antone scooped me up, gave Sanders a sly grin, and carried me to one of the other bedrooms.

ೞ Chapter 5 ೞ
Who's in Charge?

As Antone set me on the bed next to him, I could feel his need rising, but I had to speak up. "What about Sylvio and Perkins? Shouldn't you be helping them? I'm okay, just tired."

Actually, healing Sanders had exhausted me so much I wasn't sure I could maintain the shield over our captives if they pushed at the barrier in an attempt to escape.

"That terrorist cell won't be a danger anymore," Antone said. "There are a few more women and kids to find a place for. The cowards use them as human shields. That's how Sanders got shot. He hesitated when the man pulled a kid in front of him."

"So Sylvio and Perkins are clearing things up before coming back?"

"Sylvio is scanning their memories, finding out all he can first. I don't have that ability. He sent me with Sanders so I could keep an eye on you and get help for him."

I wasn't sure "keeping an eye on me" meant what Antone was proposing we do. But it had been too long since we'd shared blood. Our bond was weakening. We had been told that Antone and I needed to keep our link, although Ramon had not elaborated on the vision he had seen. Not that I minded. Antone was a good man, no matter what fate turned him into. But linking with him was becoming increasingly erotic, and I knew that aspect bothered Sylvio.

Antone guessed my thoughts and said, "Don't worry, I'll behave myself."

It wasn't him I was worried about. My body *wanted* Antone with the same fierce need it wanted Sylvio. I was the one who needed to behave. I was the one in control when we linked, and my resolve grew weaker each time Antone and I shared blood.

Antone gently brushed my hair away from my neck. As he did, I felt his fingers change from soft skin to silken claw. Claws that now cradled my head as I leaned into his palm, gasping from desire as his fangs sank in.

We were instantly awash in dark euphoria. Always before, Antone put up barriers to block his need for blood and to protect the soul of the person he took from. He hated that need and the evil it brought with it. He hated what he was, too. Not now.

The earth spirit Patrick had taken the sorrow, anger, and guilt that weighed on Antone's soul and gave it to the fire spirit Salamander, who took that darkness away with her. He was free now as never before.

Tentatively at first, but then with wild abandon, I joined him in that pleasure. I maintained enough control that he didn't take too much, and he didn't try to hold back. He trusted that I would keep us both safe.

It wasn't long before I began to swoon. He drew back and slowly, sensuously, licked the wound on my neck. My whole body shuddered. He nibbled the nape of my neck, and I shuddered again. He gave a low, throaty chuckle and set me on his lap.

I was very glad he still had his clothes on. I was more than ready to rip my own off. He hugged me to him briefly then turned his head and pierced his neck with his claws. I began to drink. That familiar liquid fire coursed all through me, bringing life, strength, and lust with it. His soul was open, for the first time inviting me in rather than resisting. It was so full of light and joy that the tendrils of the demon could not even approach the sphere of his soul and instead circled the edge.

This time it was my own dark desires I held at bay. Although Antone's soul remained protected from the touch of the demon due to his newfound freedom, mine was quickly covered with black snakes that slid over the surface and fought for entry. I was barely able to push them aside and held on to the light of my own soul by my fingertips.

Need raged through me. I wanted to take all of him, body and soul. I knew he would let me if I led the way.

Instead, I kept my hands where they were: one fisted in his soft curls, the other grasping his shoulder as tightly as a lifeline, although it was like stone, only indenting a little no matter how desperately I clung to him.

I let his mind go and leaned my head on his chest, breathing hard. Both of us were shuddering at intervals. Our bodies had not been satisfied.

I sensed rather than felt Antone stiffen, and looked up. Sylvio was leaning on the doorjamb, pretending casual amusement. That was not what he felt. Perkins stood behind him, looking embarrassed. I felt a blush creep up my neck and heat my cheeks. Silently, Sylvio stepped next to us and held a hand out for me. I placed my hand in his and stood. Without a word, Antone left the room and closed the door quietly behind him.

Sylvio took me then, fulfilling the need my body felt and then some. He was more urgent and driven than ever before. He demonstrated that he was a master in many new ways. I was incapable of coherent thought when he finished with me and fell into a deep and dreamless sleep.

When I woke, it was dark; I had slept the day away. I sat up and began to rise, intending to find something to eat. I was starving. Sylvio came in the door then and closed it behind him. His eyes glowed in the dim light, lit with more than demon fire. Wordlessly, he began his seduction again, taking his time, enjoying every moan he coerced from me.

When he was finished, he led me to the shower and washed my body and hair with gentle hands. I marveled at his skill, not only as a lover but also because those same hands could easily leave bruises or snap my neck before I could even think of defending myself. Humans are truly helpless in the hands of a vampire, even me.

When he dressed me and brought me a plate of food, I was humbled. I was not the one with the power after all, nor did I really know or understand the preternatural beings that exist alongside humans. I was as a child, and I had a lot more to learn.

𝕊𝕠 ℂℝ

We spent another week in Egypt after sending Perkins and Sanders on their way, and Antone too. I didn't ask where the women and children were taken.

Sylvio booked the services of a personal guide for the two of us. We brushed by long lines of regular tours filled with people from all corners of the globe speaking all manner of languages. He took me around the city of Cairo and to the museum. I was fascinated with ancient Egypt even as a small child and never dared wish I would be so lucky as to see its ancient wonders in person.

At night, he took me on his own private tours. We hopped to spots either he or I picked out during the day, and we spent hours studying the hieroglyphs by the light of the small globe I created with the aid of the fire spirits, until the handbook I bought to translate the pictures was tattered and torn.

Sylvio could translate the pictures on the walls easily. He said that when he learned of the Rosetta Stone, he fashioned a copy and lived in Cairo and Luxor for two decades, posing as a scholar.

On one of those nighttime excursions, we were harassed by a poltergeist. It left Sylvio alone but tossed my hair, blew cold air in my face, and rattled the walkways that kept the tourists in line and away from the walls. With Sylvio at my side, I was not afraid of the ghost. It soon grew tired of us and went away. I couldn't help wondering how many apparitions Carlisle would see if he wandered those tombs.

Eventually, he took me home. I was glad to be back. Nero, the black kitten I recently brought home, didn't leave my side for a week and climbed in my lap anytime I sat down, unless Kita got there first.

Sylvio's house was now my home; I felt I belonged there, even if I was out of step with the others I lived with. They were captives, bound to stay by Sylvio's magic. Sylvio took broken souls from the streets or battlefields and brought them to his houses, where they accepted the price of captivity in exchange for a new chance at life. His home was a place where both their bodies and souls could heal.

The next time Antone dropped by, he gave me a wan smile and touched my cheek in a way that meant friendship, not love. I knew then that he had no intention of betraying Sylvio's trust. He may take my blood, but he would not take my body without Sylvio's permission. My cheeks colored with shame again that I had even considered it.

Something fundamental had changed between Sylvio and me, but I couldn't quite define it. It was still me who orchestrated the dance of our souls whenever we exchanged blood. I held the reins then, but he held them at all other times—or so I began to think.

ℤ℥

The next time it was Sylvio's week to be with us at our house, I lay with my head on his chest, sated from our session together, and listened as his breathing slowed. Then it stopped altogether, and he began to grow cold, like stone, as the dawn crept in the windows.

I propped myself on an elbow to ask him something and stared in disbelief at his face. He still looked human; he was not in his vampire form. But his eyes were half open and unmoving, with only the whites showing. He was a corpse.

I slowly crawled out from under his arm, which was stiff and heavy. I stood next to his bed and stared. He *never* slept the sleep of the dead where others might find him. If he was going to honor me in that way, trust me that much, I was going to keep him safe. I created a bubble of air spirits to protect him. I would know if anything came near.

The room began to brighten with a dawn that was promising sunshine after several days of rain mixed with sleet. I considered what to do. If I stayed up here to guard him, the others would come looking for me. I decided to go downstairs and act as if Sylvio had left, as he usually did once he was finished with us.

It was when I was cleaning up the kitchen after Lisa and I made breakfast that another thought occurred to me. While he and I were lying there, resting after our exertions, I had been thinking how nice it would be if he could relax, be at peace, even if it was only for a little while. Did *I* cause him to fall into the sleep of the dead? What would he think of that? I was certain he would not be pleased, even though it was accidental.

I would know by his mood when he did wake if it was me who did it.

I didn't need Sylvio waking up to get my answer. Shaw called right before noon, wondering where Sylvio was. Apparently, he and Sylvio were going to hash things over before attending a debriefing about the terrorist Sylvio captured and the encampment they destroyed. I told him I had a pretty good idea where he was and would remind him about the meeting. Shaw said it was odd for Sylvio to forget a meeting. I told him not to worry and hung up.

With trepidation, I went upstairs. I'd covered Sylvio with a blanket, so he looked fairly normal, except the bed covers weren't moving since he wasn't breathing, and I've decided there is an instinct in humans that senses when there is something dead nearby and when there is something dangerous.

I stood in the doorway, out of his immediate reach, removed the bubble of spirits that enveloped him, and said, "Sylvio, wake up."

Immediately, he sat straight up, not like a human would, but too fast, like he'd been jerked upright by a string. Spotting me, he said, "*Vaffanculo!*" I seemed to have a talent for making him swear.

He glanced at the clock by the bed and said, "*Mierde!*"

His swearing, which he didn't do very often, tended to be multilingual. He went into his closet and began to dress. As he did, his emotions went through several changes, from surprise and anger to frustration, finally settling on humor. From the depths of his closet, he said, "You should have seen your face when I woke up. Do I really still scare you that much?"

Did he? I thought for a moment then said, "I'm not afraid of *you*, but

I am a little afraid of what you can do."

"Hence standing at the door, several feet away, to wake me up." He emerged from his closet while he was tying a tie, which he could do with ease and without a mirror.

"Shaw called a couple of minutes ago and told me you are due at a meeting. How many bigwigs will be there?"

"The same crowd as last time. Want to come along?"

I was wearing my standard sweatshirt and jeans, wore no makeup, and my hair was in a ponytail. I smirked at him and said, "I think I'll pass."

He stepped over to me and kissed my forehead, then looked me in the eyes. "Did you do that to me to see if it would work?"

Surprised, I said, "No, total mistake. I didn't even know for sure it was me that did it until Shaw called."

He gave me a lopsided grin and vanished. I sank onto the bed, knees suddenly weak with relief. I didn't *want* to control Sylvio. I didn't want to control *anyone*. But I sure seemed to be doing that very thing more frequently as time went by. I sat on the bed and stewed over recent events for some time.

∽ Chapter 6 ∾
Sylvio: Ammit

Antone and I were playing chess. I didn't lose as spectacularly as I used to, but I was still no match for him. It was odd to feel happiness and peace from him instead of burning anger over the injustices he'd suffered. I wished there were some way to relieve Tim and Sylvio of their own burdens of painful memories and guilt.

Lucas came in the room and watched us for a bit, then decided to rub my shoulders. He was quite talented at massage . . . and other things. I closed my eyes and moaned with pleasure.

"I can make her do that in the bedroom, too, but not for the same reason," Lucas remarked.

It was near the end of our week with Sylvio. All of us living in the house were more than ready for adventures in bed. I turned to Lucas, knowing he could see the lust in my eyes. "Promise?" I said.

"You bet." He grinned wolfishly at me then nodded at Antone, who felt amused. "Can I catch a game next time you're hanging around?" Lucas asked.

"When you're not too preoccupied," Antone purred. His voice was always seductive, and he was largely unaware that it was.

"Deal." Lucas bent and kissed my cheek. "Later."

"See you soon," I said as he walked away.

"Counting on it," he said, then added, "Don't take too long beating her at the game."

It was times like that when I wished I was quick with a comeback. All I could think to say was, "Hey!" in an aggrieved tone.

Antone chuckled and moved his bishop to take out my rook. I sighed. It was always hard to concentrate when Sylvio's blood raged through me, and Lucas had not helped. I searched for something to distract Antone from the game.

"Did Sylvio own slaves?" I asked.

I knew Sylvio had bought Antone, but I'd never asked if that was something he did as a matter of course in those days.

Antone raised an eyebrow and regarded me for a few seconds. A small smile played on his lips. I suspected he knew why I'd asked. "You don't think the people he and I keep now are slaves?"

I sniffed at him. "You know what I mean." He was right. The people kept by vampires are slaves, even if some agreed to be captives, but it wasn't what I wanted an answer to.

"Yes," Antone said, "he did." He waited to go on and enjoyed the surprise and dismay he felt from me. Then he added, "After coming to America, he owned several slaves over the years who weren't kept for him to feed from. He'd buy them for one reason or another, usually due to sentiment. Then he'd take them north and let them go."

I slapped his arm for making me doubt Sylvio, which brought out another chuckle from him. It made me feel warm inside. His voice was mesmerizing, and the good mood he carried with him now was refreshing. But my ploy was not working; I was much more distracted than he was.

"The result was that he had very loyal employees for his own business enterprises," Antone added.

That gave me a new thing to think about. I wondered if Sylvio had plotted things that way, or if it was simply a nice consequence. "Why did he keep you enthralled, then?"

I had unexpectedly hit a subject that served to distract Antone completely. His eyes took on the same look I often saw in Sylvio's as memories came to the fore.

"I still marvel at what Patrick did . . . what you did . . . for me," he said. He put a hand over mine and gently squeezed. "Thoughts of the past used to make me so angry, but now I can look back objectively."

He leaned back in his chair and picked up a pawn, fiddling with it as he spoke. "My mind was unstable when Sylvio bought me. There isn't much I remember clearly about those first few weeks. We'd been at his estate for several days before I began to think coherently, only to discover I was captured by him far more completely than my former owner, even with her power as a witch. I've resented his hold on me all these years." He shook his head. "Now it seems like such a petty waste of time, especially since you emailed me his story—the parts you've typed up so far."

I was right in my guess that Antone had never asked Sylvio about his past. I sent him what I had transcribed after my recent visit to his building in New York City.

"Thank you for that," Antone said. "I understand now why slavery is appalling to him, and why he fights so hard to deny giving the demon what it desires."

"Glad I could help." I spotted something on the chess board I hadn't noticed until then. I moved my knight and said triumphantly, "Check."

Antone sat up and chuckled once more, then we continued our game. He won, of course, but not quite as easily as usual. Afterward, I went to find Lucas. When my body's lust was sated, I took out my laptop and started on the next part of Sylvio's story, eager to find out more about Cyneric.

ℬ Sylvio ℭ

Cyneric tried to carry on with his life. We spent the first few months living and working at the estate as though nothing had changed. He was confined to working only at night, and Gerald took care of things during the day. I spent my days impatient for him to wake up, and stewed for hours trying to figure out how to free him from lying still and dead during daylight. But Cyneric wasn't human anymore. The humans who were friends of his weren't enthralled by him, so they feared him, and he began to resent them.

There was a lot to feed that resentment. The humans at Niveus might have been my captives, enthralled by my spell, but they had far more freedom than he did. Immense strength, immunity to disease, immortality—to a mortal, those might seem wonderful gifts. But the cost is being a slave to desire. Our need for blood, sex, and bringing death is never-ending. The scent of a human is intoxicating. The beat of their hearts mesmerizes us. Even today, I often sit at the dinner table, appearing at my ease as my humans talk among themselves about their day, and become lost in that primal need.

At that time, I did not keep men fully enthralled as I began to later. It was only the women that I used to satiate my body's need. Since my blood drives them to a wanton desire for sex, they were free to satisfy themselves with any of the men at the estate who wished to join with them.

Cyneric had not indulged himself in that way. Nyla was fiercely possessive, and he loved his wife with all his soul. He never dallied with other women since marrying her. He believed in the teachings of Christ. He and his family attended church in Brycgstow with regularity, and

Cyneric truly embraced those ideals. I did not prevent my people from practicing their religion, whichever one they believed in, as long as they obeyed me and didn't plot my ruin. If I'd kept them as mine before they became believers, their faith did not weaken or harm me.

Now, according to the teaching of his church, Cyneric was damned to Hell. He was the spawn of a demon, driven to commit nearly every sin condemned by the commandments he once tried to abide by.

As a mortal man, his days had been occupied from sunup to sundown with the affairs of the estate. His evenings were spent in the company of his family and friends, his nights in his wife's embrace.

I thought I lost everything when I'd been taken as a slave for Adonas. But I was young. I'd never fallen in love or had a family of my own. There wasn't a religion that I embraced. What was stolen from me was only the promise of a full life. Cyneric had already experienced those things. At that time, I grieved for him, thinking he'd lost far more than I. Now, I'm not so sure. Which is the greater tragedy—to be torn from your mortal life before you've really ever lived, or to be torn from a rich life full of family, friends, and true love?

I don't have an answer for that.

It wasn't long before I realized Cyneric could not stay at Niveus. The anger and resentment he felt were beginning to consume him. He became almost violent when he would take the women to his bed, and his hunger could not be quenched. He would spend hours with the women, and the rest of the time he prowled the estate and woods, hunting animals. He always took more blood than his body needed, although he did still have the control to stop before he cost the humans their lives.

When he wasn't in pursuit of either blood or sex, he would sit and brood. When vampires are not trying to pretend to be human, we can stand in any position we desire, as still as stone statues, and that disturbs humans even more than the sight of our fangs. When any of the humans spotted him, they'd go out of their way to avoid him. His mood infected the whole estate. A gray cloud of doom lay over all of Niveus.

After six months, I was past feeling sorry for him. He was perched on the top of the entrance to the castle courtyard with his elbows on his knees and his chin in his hands. He looked like a gargoyle, hunched over as he was. I was riding Lucifer through the gate and reached up and knocked Cyneric off. He fell onto the flagstones with a crash, then jumped to his feet so fast Lucifer started and leaped sideways, nearly unseating me.

"What?" Cyneric snarled.

He was always too polite around me; a snarl was progress. "I've had enough of you pouting. It's time to get on with living. I've indulged you while you licked your wounds, but I'm done with it."

"I don't pout," he growled petulantly.

I looked at Gerald, who was standing nearby, waiting to speak with me. He was quite nervous, and I realized how drawn he looked, pale and uncertain. Not the man he was before Cyneric changed. It seemed it wasn't only Cyneric whose former life was lost. Gerald was Cyneric's apprentice and closest friend. They had spent their days together. Now Gerald avoided Cyneric whenever possible, although Cyneric did not feed from him after the one time I made him do it.

"Gerald, I'd like your opinion," I said. "Has Cyneric been pouting?"

Gerald stared at me, eyes wide and uncertain. He licked his lips and flicked a quick glance at Cyneric, then cast his eyes around nervously, not daring to look at either of us. Oh, yes, Cyneric was not the only one whose life was changed by that fateful night.

"Gerald," I prodded, "you know him as well as anyone. Would you put up with this sort of behavior from your friend?"

At the mention of "friend," Gerald's eyes snapped to mine, and he stood up straight. "Well, no sir, I wouldn't."

"What would you do to cure him of indulging in such a pathetic waste of time?"

Cyneric folded his arms across his chest and glared at me.

Gerald dared to grin. "Well, I'd kick his arse, sir."

I dismounted and handed Gerald the reins. "That sounds like a good idea. Cyneric, turn around and bend over. I want a good wide spot to aim at."

Cyneric said, "Sylvio, you're an ass."

Perhaps there was hope for him after all. He'd never called me a name before. I grinned. "I thought we'd decided that's what *you* are." I turned to Gerald. "Take care of things here, will you? Seamas and Mistress Harfor can assist you."

I didn't wait for his reply. I strode over to Cyneric and wrapped an arm around his shoulders. He stiffened and began to protest, but when we reappeared standing next to the Coliseum, he stood in the street and goggled with his mouth hanging open.

A carriage driving past nearly ran us down, causing us to dash to the side of the road. Cyneric tilted his head back, trying to find the top of the wall. He turned and walked down the road until he was far enough away to take it in. Then he stared, mouth agape.

I followed him, and we gazed at it for some time. Finally, I said, "The world is full of wonders. It's time you saw some of them."

He looked at me and smiled. For the first time since before he became a fledgling, there was a spark of life in his eyes.

ℰℴ ℭℛ

As time wore on, I would teleport back to Niveus to check on things. At first, I returned almost daily. Then, as the years went by, I visited less frequently, often returning after a span of weeks or even months. I didn't bring Cyneric with me.

Seamas fell in love with Ragna, who grew into a beautiful woman and a powerful witch. The clergy in the area kept their promise not to interfere with my estate, but they refused to perform a wedding ceremony for them. So Seamas and Ragna lived "in sin," and she bore him four children.

I was gone too often to keep my people enthralled anymore. I weaned them off the need for my blood until they were all free to go on with their lives. Most stayed. Life was good at Niveus under Gerald's stewardship, and time slid by.

Cyneric did not have the gift to teleport, so I would tell him about places I'd seen before, and he would pick one to visit. Some I could not take us to. They had changed too much, which made me curious, so we'd get as close as I was able to jump, then go see what had become of the place. Perhaps the biggest change was the city where Liling's palace once stood. When we arrived, the people had recently endured a siege, and rule of the area fell to Genghis Khan, whose name we had heard even as far away as our home in the British Isles. After conquering it, he changed the name of the city to Yanjing.

The city was prosperous when Pascal and I visited before. Since then, the area suffered constant rebellion or conquest. When armies clash, it isn't only those injured in battle who are brought to the brink of death. Starvation and overcrowding led to disease. There were countless humans to feast on—humans who welcomed death.

It is odd to me that later history books seemed to be written with the notion that countries were isolated. At later dates, some were—but during the time of which I speak, merchants traveled to China from all parts of the known world, and Europeans were as likely to be seen in China near the Silk Road as Indians or Arabians. Perhaps it was the general lack of education that later plagued Europe, or the lack of an easy means to communicate, that led to those ideas. In any case, we were not the only tall white men who wandered those cities.

While we were there, I saw the first paper money. I remember thinking it was a foolish notion. Why would a merchant honor a mere slip of paper? Cyneric became intrigued by the idea behind a central repository, a place where the common man, not only the nobility, could store wealth. I could see why that kind of security appealed to him. It was a simple matter for me to hide my wealth, literally. Such a thing was not possible for most.

I also saw the first hand cannon. That was something I could immediately understand. I'd been a soldier as a mortal man. The idea of being able to disable or kill an enemy at a distance with shrapnel instead of a tiny arrow was intriguing to me. One hand cannon could hurl many more projectiles than an arrow, though not with nearly the distance or accuracy of an archer. Still, the idea was fascinating. I found several of them to experiment with.

One night, we were wandering along the Qin Wall, which had nearly all been destroyed. Most of the Great Wall was yet to be built. The section we stood on was still quite impressive, and Cyneric commented that he couldn't envision man building something larger than the Coliseum. Adonas often felt I was but a child, no matter how long I had lived in years. I was finding that in having a fledgling of my own, I understood him more than before.

It was cold on that wall. Cold can't hurt us, but it is annoying. Besides, if we aren't wearing proper clothing, people tend to take too much notice of us. When Cyneric made the comment about the Coliseum, I turned and took his coat and hat off, and his gloves, and tossed them off the crumbling wall. He watched me take mine off too. There was a strong breeze that night. It caught my scarf and tossed it here and there. We watched it finally settle in the branches of a tree far down the valley. Finally, Cyneric said, "Sylvio, what are you about?"

Grinning like a loon, I put my arm over his shoulder and took him to the base of the pyramid of Khufu. I laughed out loud at his expression. After several minutes of staring in mute shock, and not even feeling annoyed at my laughter, Cyneric said, "Surely man didn't build this."

"Follow me." I led him away from the largest pyramid until we stepped to the side far enough to take in the other two. "As you can see now, it's not the only one. There used to be more than these, and there is an odd-shaped one farther down the valley. Things like this are not made in nature. Pascal said there are pyramids of nearly equal size in the lands across the sea."

Cyneric hadn't been interested in reading very much. That night changed him. I'd mentioned the pyramids to him many years earlier when he was mortal, but he'd been more intrigued with finances and managing the estate's records. He felt he didn't have time to read about lost civilizations. After that night, he consumed any book I brought him. I had amassed a large library by then. It contained scrolls and books in multiple languages. One gift all vampires are given is the gift of tongues; we can read or understand any language, although it does take practice to speak them. As with all things, some are more gifted than others, but we all share that ability to some extent.

Cyneric became fascinated with religions and read all those texts as well. He was surprised to discover how new Christianity was in comparison to older civilizations and cultures. It also shocked him how similar the metaphors and messages were through all the written records.

We traveled down the Nile and investigated the countless ancient sites as we went, finally stopping for a time at Thebae, which is now called Luxor. The people in the cities throughout Arabia were more enlightened and educated than those in the Christian countries once the Romans no longer ruled, not to mention much more clean. Bathing regularly was encouraged in territories controlled by the Muslims.

While at Thebae, we spent many nights digging around the ruins, looking for treasure like other thieves had done for millennia. We didn't find gold and jewels, but we did find tombs. They seemed to be everywhere in that valley. As always, the pictures on the walls fascinated me. It was amazing and humbling that a culture that lasted thousands of years could die so completely that no being, living or dead, had the knowledge to explain the meaning of those pictures.

Early one evening, we dug our way into a massive tomb with many rooms leading off the side of the main passageway. When we had wandered to the end, we came to a figure whose face was now familiar since it seemed to be on every third statue. At that moment, a presence made itself known.

An evil pall surrounded us. Always before, when I had encountered demons in the human world, I had only felt their presence. But this time, I could see it. It came from one of the side tombs and crept toward us on short legs. Its head was elongated, with jaws and skin like that of an alligator, but beyond its head, it had fur like a lion instead of scales.

Its eyes glowed crimson, lit with demon fire as ours are when we are in the throes of feeding. Its tail was thin like a whip. Its black tip was in the shape of a xiphos blade, and it lashed the air each time it took a step.

The thing stopped and regarded us. I had seen pictures of this being on the walls of the tombs, but they did not show it having a long tail as this one did. Its black tongue flicked out and was as a snake's, with a fork in the end.

A wind circled us and a voice whispered, but its mouth did not move. As the wind filled the chamber, we were compelled to transform, and soon both of us stood before the thing in our vampire form. This was a new kind of power.

Up to that point, I had made it my practice to avoid demons. Only their host can be killed; the demon itself is a thing not tied to this world. At most, they can only be temporarily banished to the realm they come from.

I reached out and grasped Cyneric's arm and attempted to teleport us away. Nothing happened. I tried again, and the magic reverberated, sending us both a step backward.

With an immobile face constructed of bone and scales, it should not have been able to—but the demon smiled.

Cyneric was no coward. He drew the sword he'd forged for himself when he was still mortal. It was in the Viking style and hung in a leather scabbard at his hip. He had christened it Ustus. As the blade slid free, he stepped to the side to give each of us room to maneuver.

I drew Muerte from the scabbard that lay between my shoulders and moved a pace to the other side, widening the gap between us. I feared that against this being, Muerte would be just a sword. Without a human body to reside in, a demon has no soul. Which is why they yearn to link with a mortal.

In a voice that was at once all around us and yet intimate, as though it had whispered only in my ear, it said, "Your hearts do not beat. They have been weighed already. Your souls are not mine to take." Its mouth did not move when it spoke.

The words sounded promising, but the demon was now between us and the hole we had dug. I was not certain what kind of foe it would be if it chose to fight us. We were in its territory, and it had already shown it had considerable power by stripping us of our human disguise.

Making no sound and moving on cat feet, but with claws that did not retract, it crept slowly out of the side chamber and into the circle of light from the torch Cyneric held in his other hand. The light of the flame guttered and flickered with the wind that circled us each time the demon spoke. Its eyes gleamed, catching the torchlight, as it gazed at Muerte.

I said, "Only curiosity brought us here. We want nothing from you."

The disembodied voice whispered to us again. "Flesh, whether living or dead, is mine to consume."

That did not sound promising. Without warning, it rushed at Cyneric, giving lie to its slow crawl before. In an instant, it was upon him.

Cyneric slashed at its jaw and jumped aside. Its teeth snapped shut, barely missing their mark. The sound made the space echo. I leaped over it, intending to lead the fight closer to the hole we'd dug. Its tail slashed the air and met me at the top of my arc. The blade on the end of its tail sliced through clothes, skin, and flesh with ease. It cut clear to my ribs and even scored the bones.

I crashed against the stone wall on the other side of the passage and clutched my side, more from shock than pain. Blood poured from the wound "Ah, your bodies are not entirely dead after all," the demon said. "You'll make a fine meal." It flipped its long tail and licked the blood off the blade. Again, it swept toward Cyneric.

Cyneric jumped to the side as it lunged for him and sliced down across its neck, where scales turned to fur, but his sword only sparked on the demon's hide. It launched itself into the air and twisted as it leapt, once again moving with a speed to match our own, and snagged Cyneric's leg with one clawed paw.

Cyneric crashed to the ground, making sand and gravel rain down on us. The demon's jaws opened wide and clamped down on his leg. He screamed in agony. Smoke rather than blood came from the mouth of the demon as its teeth sank through bone and flesh. He shook Cyneric from side to side, and I heard the bone crack.

I ran up the wall and launched myself at the demon's head from above and in front of it in order to avoid its lethal tail. I stabbed Muerte into its eye with enough force that the blade sank into the stone floor.

I haven't heard a roar such as the demon made before or since. It slung its head and tossed both of us up the long passageway.

We slid on our backs for several feet. Cyneric's torch was lost. The only light came from Muerte, whose blade glowed red, and from the tiny patch of pale starlight that lit the stone floor only a pace away. Down the passage, one red eye could be seen coming out of a darkness that was otherwise complete. I could hear its tail whip the air. The blade on the end sang.

The thought came to me of another stone chamber, and rock falling. I reached for Cyneric and hugged him to my side as I stood directly under that patch of light. I roared my own roar like I had those many years ago, and rock began to fall. As the stones of the ceiling rained down, I jumped with all my strength, and we burst through the hole we'd made earlier and up into the air. Then we fell . . . and kept falling as the sand gave way. The chamber beneath collapsed.

It's not often that I'm frantic—time has taken care of that—but at that moment, I was desperate to get away from that forsaken desert. I've no idea why, but the picture that came to mind then was of the altar in the Druid's glade. It was there that I took us. We landed on the soft grass with a canopy of trees surrounding us.

When I recognized where I'd taken us, I began to laugh. I was amazed that the glade was still there. Cyneric rolled away from me and looked concerned, as if he thought I'd gone mad.

Muerte still glowed red, so I took the blade and pressed it against the slice on my side. The pain was exquisite and turned my giddy laughter into a hiss. When the wound was cauterized and the blood stopped flowing, I stood and assessed Cyneric's mangled leg.

I handed him my cloak and said, "Tear some strips off that. I'll go get some sticks so we can bind it straight."

We must have been more distracted by our narrow escape than I realized, because when I turned around, five vampires were standing at the edge of the clearing on the other side of the altar.

℘ Chapter 7 ℘
Outsider

It was the full moon. Micah and I were on our way to a meeting of the Wasatch Coven, where I was to be accepted as a member, no longer a mere observer. We also intended to discuss what I learned from Sylvio during our meeting at the Pentagon about the black witches uniting.

Something was agitating the spirits, but I could not pinpoint what. Sometimes their intent was clear, as if they'd spoken words to me, but most often they were irritatingly vague. They rarely form words. Instead, they communicate with images and impressions.

The meeting was at Tawnya's cabin, which was partway up the mountain in Parley's Canyon. There was a stone altar and arbor in her back yard where the Wasatch Coven usually met for their full moon ceremonies. As we approached, there were more vehicles lined up outside than there had been the last time I attended a meeting at her place. We had to find a spot along the lane to park. Neither Micah nor I were really interested in socializing. She timed our arrival so we weren't late, but also not early enough that we'd be stuck having to chit-chat.

"Is it normal to have so many attend an initiation?" I asked as we approached the front door.

"No," Micah said. "Karen didn't say there would be extras." Karen was the leader of the Wasatch Coven.

I gathered the spirits around me, asking them for protection and to be still so I could concentrate. I knocked on the door. The spirits did as I requested but were vibrating with energy all the same. I was having a hard time keeping a mild expression. I've never had a poker face, but I was getting better at it. The spirits were very agitated and were too distracting. I could feel Micah's unease as well. She could sense at least part of what the spirits were doing.

Tawnya opened the door with a smile on her face that was forced, and she felt worried. When we stepped across the threshold, I scanned the room. Four in attendance were not from our coven. I recognized two of the four. One was Jean, who was a leader of The Coven. It made sense that she would be there, given our previous encounters, but her unease was a surprise. I thought we had sorted out the questions about whether I should be accepted or not. Her sister, Janice, sat beside her.

When I finished counting those present, I felt Micah stiffen and grow more alarmed, and the spirits came to attention. I did not get a sense of danger from them, but they made me feel uneasy.

On Jean's right was a woman with silver hair, dark skin, and strong Native American features. She scrutinized us both but was not looking at us directly. I realized she was concentrating on the aura of spirits around us. She was a native witch.

Next to her sat another white-haired elderly woman, but her skin was fair. I could feel her magic from where I stood. It dominated the room. There are two kinds of magic that witches are gifted with. Those with native magic can access the power of the elementals—earth, air, fire, water, and living things. The other kind can access magic through spells and enchantments—the kind European witches use. Both are gifts from the spirits, but native magic, although rare, is normally far stronger. By then, I could easily discern the difference between the two. This woman was an extremely powerful sorceress. Of those I had met so far, none of the European witches would surpass her power.

It took a moment for me to absorb that shock. Tawnya led the way across the room to introduce me to her first, indicating that she stood highest in the hierarchy of those attending. That puzzled me. I had thought, as a leader of The Coven, Jean would be highest ranking.

Tawnya said, a little breathlessly, "Gwen and Nascha, this is Rachel."

Gwen stood and pinned me with fierce intent when our eyes met. I received yet another shock. Hers were a deep dark green, like a pine forest, and flecked with gold. I had only ever met three people with that particular eye color: Tim and his two children. I studied her face and found other similarities. There was the same curve to the jaw, the same shape to the eyes, and the same laugh wrinkles, although she certainly wasn't laughing now. Tim's nose was more pronounced, while hers was petite and feminine. She was quite attractive, even at her age . . . if she hadn't been scowling.

The spirits stopped still when our hands clasped. The others in the room could sense the power that swelled in the room as her magic met mine. She had put up a block to stop me from affecting her and to mask her true feelings. The spirits prompted me to allow that block and not penetrate it yet. The expression on her face was one of suspicion and resolve.

"It seems this meeting is not about confirming me as one of the Wasatch Coven after all, is it," I stated.

Gwen's eyes narrowed, and her lips pursed. When she hesitated to reply, I let her hand go and scanned the other faces. They all knew I could read feelings. Some were even holding their breath. Micah stood behind me. She felt angry and was ready to come to my aid.

"We intend to find out how you were able to change Janice and Jean's minds in one brief meeting," Gwen said, accusation clear in her tone.

I understood then. They thought I had used compulsion, which was black magic and forbidden. I glanced at Nascha. While Gwen was fair-haired and lean, Nascha was dark and stout, with sleek black hair and a prominent nose. She stood up slowly and hit me with a spell the moment she moved. It washed over and around the shield the spirits had wrapped around Micah and me. Her eyes flicked to Gwen for a moment, then met mine again.

I held out a hand. She hesitated but then took it, and another spell hit my shield. I narrowed my eyes and said, "If you intend me to be honest, I expect it from you, as well. You've both attempted to ensnare me without warning. Why should I hesitate to use my own magic?"

Fear permeated the room then, but mostly from the others watching us—not from Micah, and certainly not from these two women. They were confident in their standing and their abilities. For a moment, I considered easing the emotions of the other witches in the room but then thought better of it. I might need all the power I possessed if this meeting went south, and they had all known there were inherent risks being around me.

I dropped Nascha's hand. The spirits gave me a mental push to speak what was tickling my mind. Everyone in the room was already so unsettled that I decided to follow the prompting of the spirits, but I could not guess where it might lead. I turned to address Gwen and said, "You lost a grandson when he was thirteen."

She inhaled sharply, and the shield she'd put over herself dropped. She composed herself an instant later and gave me a stern glare.

Tim told me once that memories of his family kept him sane when he was in the clutches of Dr. Sabin. He'd known the world he ended up in was not the real world. Reuniting him with his family might go a long way toward helping his mental state. As I was about to say more, Micah grasped my arm. She wanted me to wait, but the spirits prompted me to speak. I gave her an apologetic smile, then turned back to Gwen and said, "I know where he is."

The whole room inhaled. Gwen blinked at me, not sure if she should believe me or not.

I went on. "He's doing okay. Actually, amazingly. He's had a very hard time, but he copes with it all fairly well." I found, to my own surprise, that statement was true.

Gwen lost the glare and scanned my face as if trying to catch some sort of deception. Finally, she said in a whisper, "He's . . . alive?"

"Is his name really Tim?" I asked. She had forgotten about the shield she'd put up earlier. I wanted to keep her unbalanced. "He changes his last name but uses Tim for his first name, as far as I know."

"Timothy, yes," Gwen replied, but more to herself than to me.

"It *was* him," Nascha said. She put a hand on Gwen's arm and continued. "The man who helped the duke and his wife escape the kidnappers. You remember I dreamt that it was Timothy?"

Gwen was still trying to absorb this hit, which came from left field. Nascha asked me, "How do you know Tim, and how do you know he is Gwen's grandson? Unless I'm mistaken, you knew nothing about us until you walked into this room."

I wondered how the two women were related. Tim might have Gwen's eyes and bone structure, but his skin and hair were more like Nascha's. I looked more closely. Yes, there it was. This was where he got his nose, and their ears were the same shape.

"The spirits prompted me about what to say." I felt Micah's relief at those words. I added, "Gwen's eyes are the same color as Tim's. It is a unique shade."

Everyone else watched us in silence. Gwen glanced around the room, aware that she'd lost control of the situation. She looked me up and down and attempted a stern expression on the outside. Inside, her emotions were in turmoil.

I stepped to the chairs that were obviously waiting for Micah and me. They were set apart so we were facing the others rather than a part of them. I sat down and said, "Well, I'll be glad to discuss Tim once our main purpose is resolved." Micah followed my lead.

Gwen and Nascha glanced at each other. I could feel Gwen's annoyance that I had taken control. They resumed their seats, directly across from us, and Tawnya sat down as well.

I didn't wait for them to direct things. "I think you were implying that I used compulsion on Jean and Janice when we met in January.

The spirits prompted me to get them to tell me their true feelings, and why they held such anger and resentment in their hearts toward vampires." I looked around the room. "I have no interest in controlling others. The whole concept appalls me. I *live* with people whose minds are under the control of another. It is disturbing and wrong in the most basic way."

"And yet you are his ally. Some would even say his lover," Gwen countered.

"He didn't choose to be what he is," I couldn't help snapping back. "He has less control over how he lives his own life than those he keeps."

They all exchanged surprised looks. When I first became aware of the preternatural beings out there, I thought they would know about each other fundamentally. I had found since that there was much misinformation, especially regarding the witches' view of vampires. My perception of vampires was immediate and personal. It was witches I knew little about, even though I happened to be one.

Nascha asked, "How can we ever know we're safe around you or your son? Even native witches rarely have the gift to sense individual spirit beings. We cannot know if what we think about you are even our own thoughts."

"If I make you so uncomfortable, you do not need to include me in any coven," I replied. A part of me wanted to belong *somewhere*, to not be so unique and set apart. But I could live with things as they were. In my view, every breath I currently took was a gift. If I hadn't been led to Sylvio, my body would be moldering in a grave.

"We can't leave you without some sort of . . . guidance," Gwen put in. I was sure she started to say "control" and caught herself.

I spoke with a little more force than I intended. "I don't allow even Sylvio to control my mind and my will. Don't be under any illusions that I would allow a coven to do so."

Gwen's frustration was obvious, and she allowed it to show on her face. "We follow specific rules. It keeps us safe, and our families and friends as well. We require obedience to those rules because of atrocities in the past. There have been costly mistakes."

I said, "I learned, after the fact, that some things I have done are forbidden. But if I had not done them, Carlisle and I would be dead, Sylvio and Antone would be captives, and your safety would be compromised far more than it is by leaving me to my own devices."

They exchanged looks again. The tension from the others in the room had gone down quite a lot, but Gwen and Nascha remained frustrated and angry. Not at me specifically, but at circumstances.

"I will not make promises I cannot keep," I said. "If becoming a coven member requires that I make vows not to touch what you deem black magic, then I will have to decline."

Everyone exchanged startled glances at that statement. "You admit to using black magic willingly?" Nascha asked.

"I've used the magic that was available for the spirits to manipulate. I learned early on how to tell the difference between the two. It's saved my life and those I was with each time I've used it."

Micah spoke up then. "Magic is a tool. You all know I have argued that by refusing to use the spells and enchantments referred to as black magic, we are limiting our resources unnecessarily. It is certain there will be mistakes, large ones, if we begin to use what is now considered black sorcery. Such power is a temptation. But I say many more of us have died, and others have not realized our full potential, by limiting our options."

"Such talk is dangerous," Gwen cut in, "especially since you are already in violation of our rules. We haven't determined your punishment as yet."

I couldn't keep the frustration out of my tone. They weren't really listening. "If she had not helped me, I would be dead. She views Sylvio as he truly is, something the rest of you don't seem to be able to do."

It was Jean that spoke next. "Micah's decision to leave you in Sylvio's care was sanctioned by The Coven. Giving you her grimoire was in violation of a direct order."

"Ignorance is more dangerous than education," Micah retorted. She was not intimidated by Jean's glower. "Our practices are outdated. We need to rethink them and move forward. We are stuck in the past, afraid to change things. It will be our undoing."

"Without rules, there is anarchy," Jean said. "You know very well the danger in attempting new spells. A witch must *earn* the right to have a grimoire."

Micah's hands were fisted, and her usual calm composure was on the brink of collapsing. "Do you know that the most recent spell added to the grimoire is over two *hundred* years old? We've become too cautious, afraid to push the boundaries we have inflicted on ourselves."

"We stray from our objective," Gwen said. "If we accept Rachel into the Wasatch Coven, it will mean we sanction what she has already done, which is in violation of the very principles we stand for. If we do not accept her, then we release an untrained and powerful witch on the world, a witch who is under the direct influence of a demonic being."

I bridled at her words and began to attempt a reply. I didn't want

Micah to pay for helping me. But these women's minds were closed. They were hearing our words, but they weren't *listening*.

Karen interrupted. "The moon is at its zenith. I propose that we let magic decide. I suspect we would argue all night and get nowhere, otherwise. The moon goddess will choose the most appropriate spell as always and guide us on the correct path."

Her words served to cool the tension in the room. I took a deep breath and willed myself to relax. Everyone waited for Gwen's reply.

Finally, she said, "Yes, that might be the best course to take."

We followed Karen obediently out the door. Each of us donned the cloak she gave us and stood where indicated around the altar. Gwen stood where Karen usually did and gestured for me to stand at her right. I realized I had lost control of who was in charge somewhere in that exchange, but I could play nice if they did.

"Do not call your spirits to you in this," Gwen ordered. "Allow the magic to come as it always has."

"You misunderstand," I replied. "I am a conduit for the spirits, not their master. They do as they wish."

Gwen pursed her lips, but Nascha nodded and seemed reassured by my response.

When I stepped up to the altar, the spirits began to dance around the whole circle of women. But when the chanting began, they behaved themselves and did not influence the direction of the spell, only the strength of it. I looked at the ancient book and saw that the name of the spell the book had chosen was *Hundeb*. The page was covered in drawings of concentric circles, all touching each other. I recognized the rune for witch, and over it was another I thought I knew. I closed my eyes and pictured the page as it appeared in my mother's grimoire. It took me a moment but finally, I could see clearly the word she wrote under the title: Unity, with a tiny W after that, which meant the spell was in Welsh. I smiled and opened my eyes.

The spirits were continuing to dance in time with the chant. They had chosen to be seen this time and looked like thousands of tiny sparklers in a rainbow that swept around and through us. I glanced at Micah and could tell she could see them as well, and I was not surprised to find that Nascha could, too. Her dark eyes were wide and round, a look of wonder on her face, as Micah's had been the first time I participated in a moon ceremony and the spirits revealed their colors for her to see.

Karen's chants rose to a crescendo, then silence fell, and all of us absorbed the magic of the spell. It was warm and welcoming as it settled on my shoulders and wrapped me in a warm blanket. The tension fell from my shoulders, and contentment filled my core.

When it was done, Gwen looked like she'd tasted something bitter. I had learned that the magic people felt from these ceremonies varied, but I think her expression was more a disagreement with what the magic had shown rather than from having had a different experience. I could feel the accord in all of those present that we should be united.

Russell, one of the men from the Wasatch Coven, said, "I love it when you attend our meetings. There's always stronger magic, and for me, magic is joy, a wondrous gift."

His view of things was very refreshing. Yes, magic was a gift. I put a hand on his arm and thanked him without having to speak. They all seemed to be waiting for me to say something, however, so I said, "As much as I, too, enjoy the magic we share in these meetings, I think it's best if I don't join a coven." I felt surprise as well as relief from several of them. "I would like to join your moon ceremonies when the chance presents itself, though."

After a pause, Karen said, "We'd like that." Some nodded vigorously; others felt undecided but didn't voice an objection.

"I suggest you listen to Micah and not cloud your thinking with too many rules," I added.

There was another long pause, then Jean said, "We'll keep that in mind as we determine what to do about her transgression."

I could see arguing about *that* would get me nowhere.

It was clear Gwen did not agree with the accord that had formed, but she kept her silence after the ceremony. Nascha was not as reserved and became politely friendly as I helped them put the items used for the ceremonies away. After that was done, we all gathered in the house for more discussions about coven business. I kept quiet whenever possible and concentrated on the feelings rather than the words, unless someone was speaking directly to me, until the subject of the recent rise in the activities of black covens came up.

A lively discussion ensued. Sylvio, Antone, and I had been trying to find out who was behind it. Sylvio was sure someone was orchestrating events, although he had found no clue about who it might be. I gave them the information we'd accumulated, and they filled me in on their own discoveries. After that, even Gwen wasn't as uncertain about me as before. I'm sure the spirits were helping them accept me, even though I wasn't asking.

When the meeting was over, on the way out the door, Gwen asked me, "Is Timothy a witch?"

I kept my hand on the door and turned only slightly back. "Why do you ask?"

She hesitated, obviously unsure about saying more. I pushed the spirits to prompt her to speak her mind.

"My grandson's magic is . . . immense. He is too powerful. It bent his thinking." The spirits continued to pull more information out of her, although she fought it without knowing. "He was not . . . right. Dangerous, even. His access to most of that magic was blocked when he was a small boy. For his own sake, we made him think he was not gifted with very much."

Nascha's eyes went wide as she stared at Gwen, surprised she was telling me those things.

I couldn't help the sudden anger I felt from showing on my face when I turned to face Gwen. "You have *no idea* what that cost him," I hissed. "I'm not sure he could forgive such a thing, given what was done to him before he learned to free himself from that block."

She blinked at me, shocked by my reaction. "It was done for his protection." I could sense what she said was true. There was more to it, though, some bitter and sad memory she was trying to keep inside. "What happened to him?" she asked. "Since he's alive, why haven't we heard from him? He knows where his family is."

"Were his options limited truly for his protection, or for yours?" I asked. Everyone in the room stopped moving. "Some things are falling into place now. He credits the memories of his family with keeping him sane during all his many trials. He's also told me that he is not sure his family would be able to reconcile the things he has done in order to survive, and what he has become. Tell me, is your love of him unconditional, or are there limits?"

Gwen looked into my eyes and seemed to be attempting to find answers there without having to ask questions. Frustrated, she said, "What has he done?"

"So, the answer is your love is conditional?" I could see she didn't like to think that was the true conclusion. I hoped it wasn't. "It won't be difficult for you to determine who Tim is now that you know I'm connected with him, but I suggest you search your own soul before approaching him. He has powerful allies—not only his own magic, which, as you said, is considerable. Astounding and unprecedented, even. Among his patrons and protectors are Sylvio, Ramon, Chris, and me."

"Ramon! Why would Ramon be involved with my grandson?" She narrowed her eyes at me.

"Why would Sylvio and I?" I wondered why she was bothered by Ramon's involvement and not Sylvio's. "Fate has led him to us. Ramon says we are all connected, and that it is imperative we stay together."

I could see that Ramon's predictions held weight with everyone in the room. I could also sense that Gwen believed in his prophecies but did not trust him. I wondered why the spirits prompted this discussion. I did not see how these revelations would help Tim.

"I think it would be a good thing if Tim were reconnected with his family," I said, "*if* his family will accept him without conditions. If not, then forget I mentioned him."

"How can we do that?" Nascha asked.

"You believed he was dead. Carry on as if he were. I can tell you with certainty that Tim has a good soul, which constantly amazes me given the damage that has been done to it. The love of his own family would help him heal, but I won't risk you doing even more damage."

I turned to continue through the door, and Nascha put a hand on my arm. "Please, we need to know more," she said. Her expression held no command. Instead, she was speaking from the heart. "What has been done to him?"

I hesitated, but the spirits pushed me, impatient with my delay in answering. "I'm sure you've been advised of the experiments Dr. Sabin did. When Tim discovered his own magic, he escaped."

Gwen's eyes went wide, one hand over her mouth in shock. "What . . . what is he?" she asked in a whisper. At the same time, Nascha said, "He was in the hands of that monster!"

"A monster he couldn't escape because of that block," I said. They both blanched. Satisfied that they had absorbed at least a little of what limiting Tim's options had done to him, I added, "Sylvio says nothing like him has ever existed."

I saw the puzzle piece fall into place behind Nascha's eyes. She turned to Gwen. "He's the alpha," she said with a gasp. "The one Sylvio brought with him to his meeting with the other alphas." She turned back to me. "What is his connection with your son? They were there together."

"The spirits have forged a bond between the two of them, as they have with Tim and me."

I was having a hard time sorting out the emotions I was sensing from Gwen. Everyone was startled when I mentioned Sabin, so their mixed emotions and astonishment weren't helping me either. Gwen kept waffling between anger, remorse, frustration, sorrow, and fear. It was dizzying.

I closed my eyes and centered myself as Micah had shown me to do, then opened them and scanned the faces in the room and stopped at Gwen and Nascha. "I can see the news that he is a werewolf is troubling for you. I suggest you sort out your own feelings before you approach Tim in any way." I let the door shut behind me, leaving them all standing in the room, most of them with their mouths open.

When we got in the car, I asked Micah, "What's Gwen's issue with werewolves?"

She was reaching to start the car but stopped and sighed, feeling both sorrow and frustration. "When she was very small, a pack killed her older sister and turned her brother. He was not able to control his wolf, even after being sent to Ramon. Ramon had to kill him."

I stared out the window, stunned. No wonder Tim had made no attempts to contact his family.

Micah went on. "Gwen and many other witches believe most preternatural creatures should be destroyed and that witches should do it. She herself has killed more than one werewolf. She told me once, before I met James, that werewolves are an abomination and should be destroyed if there is any indication they give in to their desire to kill." She sounded bone-tired when she said that last, then added, "She feels the same way about vampires."

"In other words, she kills because they do? How ironic. Besides, vampires have no choice but to kill. Doesn't she realize that?"

"Rachel, neither do werewolves."

I stared at her, shocked.

"For a werewolf, it's the hunt, the chase, that drives them," Micah said. "It's not required for their target to be human. But human prey is much more satisfying to them than any other, as is true for vampires. There are valid reasons a great many werewolves are in law enforcement and the military. It's not only their strength and charisma that makes them excel at their jobs. It's because they get to hunt human prey."

"Gwen doesn't count witches in the same category as werewolves and vampires?" I asked. "We're all preternatural beings."

"Witches are human. Our bodies are not changed in any fundamental way by magic. Neither are our desires. When a witch goes bad, it is because of human weakness and human desire. We are not possessed or under the control of a demon."

I understood that distinction and was reluctant to admit Gwen was right, but when put that way, she was.

We sat in silence as we drove down the canyon. We were heading east toward Heber. The pack decided to gather at Micah's house that night to run during the full moon. I closed my eyes and concentrated on the part of me that could sense Tim. When I was able to isolate my connection with him, I could feel his joy. They were still hunting. I hoped revealing who and what he was to his family had been the right thing. With my eyes still closed, I asked, "Why would the spirits prompt me to tell Gwen about Tim?"

Micah didn't answer right away. Eventually, she said, "The leaders of The Coven have a hard time seeing between the lines, but most especially Gwen. Her world is black and white."

"While Tim, Sylvio, and I live in a world of gray," I finished for her.

I am a white witch who has mostly used black magic. Tim is a witch possessed by two kinds of demonic spirits who seem to have little or no control over him. Sylvio's soul is owned by a demon, but through his own actions, he was granted the freedom to walk in the day—by an angel. Yes, it was much easier to see things Gwen's way, but it was not the *right* way.

"I think we'll need their help soon." As soon as I said it, I felt the spirits' agreement.

"The Coven leaders?" Micah asked.

"Yes."

I kept my eyes closed and concentrated on Tim again. They had captured their prey and reveled in the kill, and the blood, and I marveled that I felt only happiness from him. There was no darkness.

ᔥ Chapter 8 ᔎ
Color-Blind

Tim chickened out when it came to teaching Eric to drive. Eric and Shena now had the bodies of sixteen-year-old kids, and they continued to mature in leaps and spurts. None of us knew when their rapid aging would stop, or even if it would—maybe they were destined to age and die quickly, like butterflies. We were encouraged by the fact that it did seem to be slowing down. Where before, a week was equal to years (so that at six weeks old they had the bodies of six-year-olds), now they were twenty weeks old but had the bodies of teenagers. It was fascinating and frightening at the same time.

I was showing Eric how to drive using the old Ford truck Sylvio kept at our place for puttering around the farm. We got it licensed so the twins could drive it around Willard. The twins were an enigma. Magic had never made creatures like them, at least not that Sylvio knew of—and if he didn't know, it probably had never happened before.

As a werewolf, Tim sired pups. His dog, Rain, was an ordinary dog; part wolf, German Shepherd, and Mastiff, but still only a dog. The spirits made shapeshifters out of the pups. They were the reincarnation of Atshena and Cyneric, two humans who had played no small part in Sylvio's life. The first time they saw Sylvio, Shena said that their memories as Cyneric and Atshena would fade—that Shena and Eric had their own lives to live. But so far, that hadn't happened. It was hard for me to fathom how they viewed their current life. And if it was hard for me, I didn't know how they even functioned.

Cyneric was born in the middle of the eleventh century in Ireland. Atshena was born to the Shawnee tribe in the mid-1700s. She was a powerful witch who was sent to destroy Sylvio and Marco when it was discovered they had come to America. She found instead that they were allies in the white witches' quest to rid the world of evil beings and dark forces.

Neither Shena nor Eric had a base of reference for living in the modern era. They had only been alive in their new bodies for a few weeks. The world viewed them as teenagers—a world they knew almost nothing about.

They were both highly intelligent. Not quite up to Tim's phenomenal brain, but close. Life experience is different from brain power. They were both wise in the ways of human experience, and at the same time totally innocent and unaware about the world they now lived in.

The twins were not able to completely control their shapeshifting until they were sixteen weeks old. They talked Tim and me into taking them shopping for groceries that week. We'd spent four hours there. Nearly everything in the store was foreign to them. Even many of the fruits and vegetables were not known or easily obtained when they were living their other lives.

Eric was fascinated by how things were made. Tim told him he should study to be an engineer. Shena was mesmerized by the people, and by the sheer freedom they had to wear anything they wanted and go where they wished. Both were fascinated by the mix of skin colors; people from all races and countries wandered the store. It gave me a fresh outlook on what once was ordinary and routine.

Being a teenage boy, no matter how atypical, Eric wanted to drive. Shena had no interest thus far, for which I was grateful. My nerves could only handle so much. I was trying to explain to Eric how to navigate roads and what all the symbols meant. We were in the church parking lot. The previous day, we'd driven around the farm. I was impressed. He had driven carriages and wagons in his previous life, so he understood how to gauge the size of the truck, turn radiuses, and things like that. But traffic laws were entirely foreign to him. Things we grow up with as kids and already know—like what the traffic lights and signs mean—he had to learn in addition to trying to drive.

I think I held my breath all the way to the church, which was only a half mile away down a rarely used road. Still, I was fighting to appear calm and in control as I explained what the white lines on the pavement meant and that he should try to line the truck up in a parking spot and stop.

Eric stopped the truck perfectly between the lines and didn't even bump the curb. He put the truck in park and said, "How about we sit here a minute so you can catch your breath." He turned to look at me with a shit-eating grin that was identical to the one Tim sometimes wore.

"Brat." I tried to scowl at him, but he wasn't fooled. As I looked at him, his eyes reflected someone far older. I thought now might be a good time to venture into the questions I'd been burning to ask. "Eric, what do you remember about your other life? You don't have to tell me if you don't want to, but both you and Shena seem to still recall how things were then."

He gazed out the window for a few seconds, then said, "It's so odd, not being connected to Sylvio."

I could think of a few hundred things that would seem odd to him in our world. I wondered why he'd picked Sylvio. "When did you first know him?"

The eyes that turned my way at that moment were not those of a man. They burned with the intensity of a vampire. It sent a chill down my back.

"Always." He blinked, and his eyes returned to their normal, warm, soft green. I breathed a little easier. He gave me a lopsided, wistful grin. "I was born at Castillo—Sylvio's property in Ireland. My father oversaw the estate, and I was his apprentice."

"So Sylvio didn't keep your family deeply enthralled?"

"Only the ladies at the castle were kept totally enthralled. For the rest of us, he maintained enough of a link that we wanted to stay and did not discuss what he was. But otherwise, we went about our lives undisturbed." He paused and stared out the window again. "I transformed because I'd accidentally taken in too much over my short life. As a kid, I seemed to pick up every disease that came through the area, and as an adult, I had a talent for getting injured. I was never totally enthralled, but he'd used his blood to save me several times. Even though my mind wasn't captured like the ladies at the castle or those that you live with now, he was always there, in my head. When I was seventeen, my father died while out hunting, and I took on his job."

Eric grinned at me wickedly and said, "We've been watching Dracula movies with Father the past couple of weeks. I guess you could call me Renfield. I did take care of his affairs when the sun was up."

I rolled my eyes. "Dracula movies, honestly. Do you like them?"

He shrugged. "Sure, they're fun. Shena thinks they're creepy because they don't get everything wrong. My favorite so far is the Abbot and Costello version. We watched that the other day."

"Have you seen the Mummy one?"

"No."

"Well, Abbot and Costello did all the monsters. You should check them out. There's a werewolf one too."

He chuckled and said, "I'll do that."

"No." I shook my head. "If you are anything like your former self, you aren't nutty enough to be Renfield."

He gave me a sideways grin.

"Did you know Celine?" I asked.

"No, she was after my time, but Father has told me about her."

"She talked Sylvio into telling her his story. She wrote it down, and he is letting me type it up. I've gotten to the part about Niveus and you."

He turned so he could watch my expression and asked, "How *does* what you've read about Cyneric strike you?"

I made sure he could see my heartfelt sincerity when I replied. "Dependable, down to earth, with your feet solidly on the ground. I'll bet the estate ran efficiently and did well when you were in charge."

He raised an eyebrow, which made him appear more like Sylvio than Tim. I could see he wasn't sure how to respond. He stared out the window again.

I hesitated, not sure if I should ask the next question. But, I've always been endlessly curious; it drives many of my friends and family to distraction. "Why were you able to control your desires as a vampire when none of his other fledglings up to that point could?"

Eric thought that over, then said, "I think it was because I knew him so well. I spent time with Sylvio every evening once I was handling the estate. I knew it was possible to control myself, because he could. It wasn't easy by any means, but I was able to because I knew he did it by choice. Later, when I met other vampires, some said he was odd and was given a rare gift, or that he didn't desire to kill as others did. That is not true. His desire for blood and bringing death is as strong, or even stronger, given his age and how close he is to the original source, than any other vampire. He lives as he does through sheer will. Most vampires simply won't bother fighting the demon's control."

The admiration in Eric's voice was unmistakable. I was surprised.

He added, "I wanted his approval and didn't want to cause him any more pain. No matter how angry I was at what fate did to me and my family, I knew it was not Sylvio's intent. I hated what he'd done to me, but I did not hate him."

He looked at me again, this time with concern. "Tragedy follows vampires. Death is their consort. Danger is ever present when you associate with any of them. Even one who attempts to deny what he is, as Sylvio does."

I put a hand on his arm. "Many have warned me about those very things. But Eric, my body would be rotting in a grave right now if I hadn't met him. I've already cheated death. Don't worry for me."

He searched my face, not sure if he should agree with me or not, so I said, "You know what really scares me?"

"What?"

"Teaching you to drive."

"Let's go try the highway," he suggested, Tim's grin on his face.

I went pale and gulped. He laughed and started the truck.

୫ ଓ

At dinner that evening, after having survived a road trip unscathed, Tim and the twins came over. Lucas, who couldn't help but tease, asked Shena if she'd noticed any cute boys in town yet. We could tell by her hesitation that she had. We were all instantly intrigued. Turns out, it was the middle son of the farmer east of us.

When Eric joined in on ribbing Shena, Lucas decided it was time to pick on him and asked, "What's the weirdest thing about being mortal again?"

Eric blinked, caught off guard, then replied, "Peeing. In fact, having to go to the bathroom is damned inconvenient."

We all busted up laughing.

"I do enjoy eating again, though, so I guess it's worth it," he added.

It took us a minute or two to stop chuckling. Lucas turned to Shena. "And you. What's the greatest difference now as opposed to then?"

She considered her answer for a few seconds, then replied, "I find it odd how people view me when we're out in public. As Tim's child, I'm not as dark as I was before, but it's still obvious I'm not white. In my other life, that's what people saw first, and often that's all they saw. They never looked beyond my skin color and my hair. In this time, people see me, and most of them dismiss the color and are curious about *me*. It's . . . nice."

We sat in silence then, thinking that over. Eventually, Eric added, "I must confess, I believed I was superior as a white man. That those with a different skin color were not as intelligent. It was simply the general belief people had. Until I became a vampire and could delve into their minds. It was a revelation to me how similar all humans are. Color is only their skin. It has nothing to do with what's on the inside, unless they let it."

Sylvio was watching our exchange from the end of the table. He sat twirling the wine in his glass and was feeling amused until that statement. Then melancholy took him. I searched for some sort of distraction from his memories.

I asked, "Why are you color-blind?"

Sylvio blinked and focused on me. "Color-blind?"

"About people. You don't care what color they are."

His lip quirked up. "Humans all bleed red."

He could tell we weren't going to be satisfied with that answer. He was silent for a bit, composing his thoughts. When he went on, it was in his "teacher voice" as Lucas called it.

"It's instinctive for humans to be cautious about things that are different. They would not have survived as a species if they were not. It's normal to be wary of people who look or act differently. My parents didn't care what color someone was. What they cared about was our own tribe. They were fiercely loyal, and since my people come from the north where white skin is prevalent, we knew those with other-color skin were not from our clan.

"People didn't intermarry or travel as widely in anywhere near the numbers they do now. It was easy to know where someone was from. Skin color was not the largest issue. It was the combination of skin tone, dress, and especially social standing that separated people from each other.

"One race enslaving another was never unique to America. Humans have always made slaves of each other, and they still do in some places. The Europeans like to say they abolished slavery before Americans did, but what they really did was trade that for indentured servants. They were slaves in everything except name. What *is* different about America now is the blend of people. Until this country was created, people identified themselves with the country their family came from."

He turned to look at Shena instead of me. "By the time white people came here, they had learned the value of uniting. The tribes, clans, and lesser monarchies in England bonded together to form a vast kingdom. The Indians were conquered in this country because the white people saw themselves as one—Americans. The tribes did not. Other tribes were their enemy. The few times they did unite, they won—decisively. But it was too late by then. What disease hadn't already destroyed, the flood of white people did. It was the same with the blacks in Africa. They quite happily sold their own slaves or captured enemies to the white traders. They did not see each other as the same race. They saw other tribes as competition."

Sylvio gave us a minute to think that over, then ended with, "I keep people of different races and cultures simply because I like variety."

That was one of the longest answers I'd ever gotten, which told me it meant a lot to him that we understood what he was saying. I wasn't sure I was getting it exactly, though.

"What's wrong about *my* perspective, then?" I asked. I didn't think I cared about what color someone was either, but maybe Sylvio saw something else.

He leaned forward and scanned all the faces at the table. Then he came back to mine. "Prejudice is worldwide, and it's always counterproductive. It is not instinct. It comes from culture and training. It feeds resentment and distrust. Americans like to place guilt upon themselves for things done in the past. It sets a bad precedent. A person is not *owed* anything as an individual, other than the right to be free to live their own life. It's up to them to make their own success. Blaming the past, or their color, on their lack of a good upbringing, is tempting, but not true.

"Like many white Americans, you worry too much about offending someone who is a different color. But many people who are another color don't worry about offending white people." He paused, then added, "If Claire had been white, would you have been as patient with her?"

Claire was a good person. She'd also been bossy and demanding, and I'd backed down to keep things running smoothly at the house. Would I have been as nice if she was another white woman? No, I admitted to myself, I wouldn't have. I *didn't* treat everyone the same. He did.

I said, "I'll see what I can do about that."

Sylvio smiled and sat back, satisfied that I'd gotten the message.

Dan, who was an alluring mix of Latino, Chinese, and Caucasian, asked, "Is it difficult sometimes keeping such a variety at your houses?"

Every house Sylvio kept had people of various colors and backgrounds in them.

"The new ones often have a rough time at first," Sylvio replied. "Most have been taught the wrong things about people who aren't their color or background. Vampire mojo helps a lot."

I laughed at his use of the word "mojo." The people in our house were all strong personalities. There would be more conflict between us, but Sylvio's magic made us get along and *want* to be together. Those he kept enthralled weren't interested in people outside our circle. It wasn't clear to me anymore how much of my need to get along was my own and how much was influenced by him, even though he couldn't enthrall me in the normal way.

It was a good thing we had that conversation, because Sylvio brought a new girl home only a week later, and she didn't like white people at all. It seemed she'd been taught all the wrong things. She had a foul mouth and no manners. She didn't know how to behave properly in any way, because no one had cared enough to show her. She was angry at the world and blamed everyone else for her issues. After the first week, I wondered if he picked her simply to teach me a lesson.

Lisa, Lydia, and I had speculated whether he would get another female to replace Claire or leave things as they were. The demon that gives vampires life exacts a cost. It desires blood, sex, and power. Sylvio keeps people to satisfy those desires. We soon lust after sex the week he's with us. So, to be fair to his people, he keeps both genders. The demon that drives vampires doesn't care which sex the human is—it wants to use their bodies. As a vampire, Sylvio *must* satisfy the demon's lust.

Lydia was an anomaly. Sylvio had set her free years before, but another vampire undid the block on her mind, so now she had to be one of Sylvio's people again until her mind had settled enough that he could let her go again. The other two weeks Sylvio wasn't with us, Lydia spent with her husband, returning to the life she lived once she was let go the first time.

After Claire died, it was Lisa and me living at the house with Ray, Lucas, and Dan. Lydia only visited, and during the week she was there, we were all preoccupied with Sylvio and our need for sex. It wasn't like how things were the other two weeks. It only took a couple of days without Sylvio's blood fresh in us for the lust to fade, and we lived like friends then. None of us were lovers. A vampire's magic prevents that complication.

The new woman Sylvio brought home was named Brianna. The first night he brought her home, it was hard to distinguish between what was blood, skin, and dirt. Her black hair was a mass of tangled dreadlocks, and her eyes were the color of dark chocolate. She glared with fierce anger at all of us except Sylvio. It was that will to fight through her pain that Sylvio perceived. It was the main reason he was sure she would survive. Brianna didn't know it yet, but Lisa and Lydia knew how she felt. Their beginnings had been similar to hers.

Sylvio preferred to find his females among those on the streets. It made sense for him to pick up people with no family—no one would come looking for them. But I had discovered he took them mostly because it made him angry that their lives had been thrown away.

Dan had gleaned a lot about medical care from Claire and Sylvio. He helped Sylvio stitch up Brianna's wounds and hook her up to an IV while Lisa and I went about cleaning her up. She was filthy, and it was mostly old dirt. She had the body of an addict—too thin, with needle marks up and down her arms from heroin instead of the rotten teeth that result from meth. She snarled insults at us whenever Sylvio stepped away from the room until he told her he could hear whatever she said no matter where he was in the house and that she was expected to treat us with respect.

The main emotion I felt from Brianna to that point was anger—not necessarily at us, but anger nonetheless, and we were the only handy outlet for it. When Sylvio gave her that command, she panicked, feeling true fear for the first time since he brought her there. She didn't know *how* to treat others with respect, and his command *must* be obeyed. Before I could reassure her, Sylvio added that we would all teach her manners and that he expected her to listen. He'd obviously dealt with that sort of problem before. She relaxed then, finally, and the morphine in her IV put her to sleep.

Brianna had been an addict long enough that pain killers didn't work predictably on her, and she had a difficult time sleeping. We regulated her morphine, and I stayed near so I could feel her true feelings rather than what she told us she felt. In only a few days, she was up and about. Her wounds were mostly healed, and she was learning to behave in a gracious way, if grudgingly.

A short time later, Sylvio taught me something else about human nature that I'd been vaguely aware of but hadn't contemplated in depth before. At first, Brianna resented Sylvio's edicts, but eventually, she embraced the concept of good manners. She would feel surprised when we treated her with respect and kindness. She hid it behind a blank face most of the time. She seemed unsure about how she should really feel.

Sylvio was with us for dinner; it was his week to be at our house again. We were starting on dessert when Sylvio announced, "Brianna, it'll be your responsibility to design the layout of the new pool house."

She stared at him with wide eyes, clearly doubting what she heard. She was seventeen and had dropped out of school in the fifth grade. She was truly at a loss for words.

"Dan and Ray are in charge of building it," Sylvio continued. "Lisa and Lydia are putting together colors, tile, interior decorations, and Rachel is designing the landscaping."

She still stared at him in disbelief. He put a hand over hers and said, "Don't worry. They'll help you find websites for ideas. But it's your project." He made sure to catch all our eyes then. We got the message: Help her, but don't take over. He patted her hand and caught her eyes last. "You'll do fine."

Over the next month, Brianna transformed. She threw all her efforts into the project and didn't mind having to do other chores, since she could concentrate on the pool house as soon as the regular chores were done. Sylvio was certainly wealthy enough to hire people to do things for him. He could have paid for housekeepers, landscapers, builders, farm hands, anything he needed done. But he understood that bored people are unhappy people.

I noticed before that he made sure we had enough work to do, but never too much. Each year, we had a large project to work on besides the farm. The previous project was re-chinking the logs and re-roofing the house. This year it was the pool house. The cow barn was being moved west, and a pool house would be built in its place. It had not occurred to me until Brianna came that there was more to it than keeping us busy.

Sylvio and I were studying the framework for the interior of the pool house that Brianna designed. It was certainly unique and innovative, but also practical. It would not be difficult to maintain. Brianna walked away to talk with Dan and Ray. We watched her approach them. She walked with confidence and was totally relaxed and friendly when she started speaking to them.

"It's only been a few weeks, and she's an entirely different person." I gestured at the plans she'd drawn up. "How did you know this project would help her so much?"

Sylvio was silent for a moment, thinking it over. "The cruelty abandoned children experience is not what is done to their bodies. It's that they begin to believe the labels people give them. Slut, whore, idiot, stupid—girls from her circumstances hear such things every day, most often with a fist to the face to enforce the words."

At that moment, Dan and Ray laughed at something Brianna said. It made us both smile.

Sylvio added, "Individual accomplishment is the best path to helping someone believe in themselves and feel they are of worth."

ဢ Chapter 9 ஐ
Sylvio: Feast

I think it was the scent of our blood that attracted them. Cyneric sat up. I stepped to his side and placed a hand on his shoulder, ready to jump us both somewhere else if need be.

They stood still as statues and did not even pretend to breathe. Only their eyes held any life. They were all far too thin and wore filthy rags. The veins on their arms stood out like ropes, as though worms slithered under their alabaster skin.

In Latin, I asked, "Where is your master?"

"*Ils parlent français,*" replied a voice from the depths of the forest. Back in the trees, I could discern a dark shape.

"My companion prefers English. Do you speak it?" I replied.

"I was told you never suffer those you've made to live. Or is this one with you stolen?"

I thought I recognized the voice. "Arkady?"

At the sound of the name, a ripple went through the brood standing witness, and as one they turned toward the voice. Arkady stepped out into the moonlight of the clearing.

I decided to pretend I was not worried about meeting him there, of all places. "Arkady! May I introduce you to Cyneric? He would stand, but as you can see, he's indisposed at the moment."

Cyneric nodded at Arkady and gave me a sardonic smile. He knew the confidence in my voice was false. He resumed tearing strips of cloth.

Arkady took in the sand that clung to our clothes, the blood on my side, and Cyneric's leg, which was nearly severed. Through the gore that had been his ankle, splinters of bone shone in the moonlight. Whenever I see an injury like that to myself or other vampires, I always wonder, what are we made of? Why would bones even still be there? Especially in a being as old as I am. Does the demon recreate us each time we feast on living blood? Does it use the blood to refresh our tissues and bones? I don't think even the demon has an answer to those questions.

Always polite, Arkady asked in English, "Where did you come from?"

As flippantly as I could manage, I replied, "Ran into a nasty demon in Egypt. Have you been there?" I began to dust my shirt off, then stopped and sighed. It was a lost cause with one side shredded. It hung in bloody tatters.

"Yes, I've seen its wonders." Arkady's eyes became fixed on Muerte, which I had not sheathed. Although the blade no longer glowed red and appeared now to be an ordinary sword, he knew what it could do. I had become used to the magic the sword was imbued with, and no longer noticed. I cleaned the blade on the sleeve of my shirt and put it back in its scabbard. That seemed to reassure Arkady. He asked, "How did you know of this place?"

The question surprised me. "Adonas was my maker."

"Ah, yes, I'd forgotten." He clapped his hands and rubbed them together, although the night was not cold. "Well, I let my brood loose to roust out some vagabonds that have been stealing from travelers. Their camp is nearby." He gave a flick of his hand, and his brood disappeared into the woods without a sound. "Would you like to join us when they catch them? Your . . . Cyneric, was it? He will need some blood, and perhaps you as well."

"Thank you for the offer. We'll wait here and see what kind of men your brood brings us."

Arkady gave a slight bow in our direction, then melted into the forest as silently as his brood.

After I aligned the bones in Cyneric's leg and bound sticks around the shredded muscles and skin with cloth, Cyneric asked, "Do you think mere thieves deserve the death that awaits them?" Pink sweat beaded his brow, although he had not protested as I worked on his leg.

I considered the question. "No, but perhaps they'll be more than thieves." I found myself wishing they were deserving of death, since that would be their fate anyway. I did not intend to battle Arkady over their lives. I also felt Cyneric needed to witness a brood feeding and to be part of it. When there is a group of us, it enhances the pleasure significantly.

They were gone for over an hour, so it wasn't as near as Arkady had implied. We heard them coming long before they arrived in the glade. Men were pleading and uttering threats at random, and I heard a woman's voice as well. In all, there were nine humans. Seven had the lean and tanned look of men who lived outdoors. The other two were a man with quite a paunch, and what turned out to be his obese wife.

The hunger and need Arkady's brood felt struck both Cyneric and me at the same time. He and I were quite hungry by then. We had both changed back to our human form when we appeared in the glade. I breathed in the scent of the humans—their sweat, and fear, and blood—and did not resist as I lost my human guise and fangs touched my tongue.

Four of the men were babbling in their fear, and one stank of urine. The others continued to claw at the hands of those who held them, but with mere human strength, they could not even begin to pry the skeletal fingers of their captors from the grip on their arms. Although these fledglings had no great power, they didn't even have claws.

Arkady took some rope out of the pocket of his cloak and bound the hands and feet of the paunchy man and his wife, saying, "We'll keep these two for last. They were directing the thieves' activities." The man began to plead as his wife wept. He offered all manner of compensation: money, land, slaves, if the two of them would be spared.

Arkady had remained in his human form until then. He stroked the man's quivering jowls and then his neck, and as he did, his fingernails became claws and his eyes shone with demon fire. The man's wife fainted dead away and slumped into her husband's lap.

In a quiet voice that was full of menace, Arkady said, "Ah, but all that was yours is now mine."

The man stopped pleading and gasped short breaths, as though ice had been thrown in his face, and knew that death awaited him.

Arkady stood from where he'd crouched to tie them up. With another wave of his hand, he signaled his brood. They released their prisoners. Some of them stumbled forward, catching their balance after their abrupt release. Their eyes darted around wildly, stopping momentarily at each of us, then taking in the altar, the small open glade, and the dark forest that promised at least a slim chance of escape.

Arkady's brood stepped back, giving them more space. As one, the men ran for the trees. The brood took their time catching them and brought them back, bleeding from bites either to their necks or their arms.

I put a hand on Cyneric's shoulder. He was shaking from the effort to remain where he sat.

Arkady took one of the men by the hair at the back of his neck—the one who stank of urine—and made him gaze into his eyes. The man stopped weeping and dropped the hands that had been clinging to Arkady's sleeve. Without resistance, he lay down on the altar.

Arkady commanded, *"Venez."*

Moving in perfect unison, his brood released their charges and swept upon the victim on the altar. They tore his clothes away as they sought a place to sink their fangs. When their fangs pierced his skin, the man began to scream, but it didn't last long. The other men stood frozen in place. Magic encompassed the entire glade so that Cyneric and I did not need to taste the blood to experience it. We all felt the soul leave the body and the euphoria that comes with that. It was too much for my fledgling. With a guttural snarl full of rage and desire in equal measure, Cyneric lunged at the nearest man standing at the edge of the forest.

His motion broke the spell on the captives. They scattered into the trees once more, but Cyneric caught his prey. I stepped to his side and gripped the back of Cyneric's neck, holding him still through our bond, and looked at Arkady. He nodded. I released Cyneric. Before Arkady's brood returned with the other captives, he had drunk the man dry.

After that, Cyneric joined in for each of the others as they were brought to the altar. Arkady and I watched, enjoying and absorbing the pleasure they all felt. Finally, when the last man's soul departed and the brood's lust had been sated, Arkady signaled them to stand back once again. This time, they were not motionless. They gathered in a group, licking the blood off each other. Cyneric was still with them. It was the first time I had seen him move as a vampire. It wasn't long before they finished. Then they proceeded to take the clothes from the bodies and replace their rags with new ones.

I felt Cyneric's shock when he looked down and saw the blood that soaked the collar and sleeves of his fine clothes. The sight seemed to break his link to the others, and he limped to my side.

It was only the fat man and his wife that remained.

The man had witnessed it all and stood staring with wide, blank eyes at the pile of bodies dumped at the edge of the glade. Sometime during the feast, he had lost his grip on reality.

His wife had roused during the feasting. Though her wrists were bound together, she put her arms over her husband's head and hugged him. She kept her face buried in his chest and whimpered prayers. I noticed a silver cross dangling between her ample breasts. But faith had come too late for her; it was not strong enough to keep us at bay, nor was it true. Her pleas to God were mere words.

Cyneric looked at the woman with uncertainty. His eyes met mine.

I stepped over to the woman and placed my hand on her head.

They say that women are the fairer sex. They are certainly more pleasing to look at than most men. But fair? I'm not so sure. This woman was the mind behind the thievery, debauchery, and killing that plagued the area. She was the one who found men willing to do her bidding, and her spouse went along with her plans, growing fat and wealthy as a result.

"They are the reason it took us a while to come back," Arkady said. "We went to their inn to capture them."

An inn. That would be a convenient base to discover the goods and wealth travelers might have with them.

"Care to join me?" Arkady asked.

I looked into the woman's eyes, which swam with tears. "With pleasure," I replied.

We took our time. Not long after we began, Cyneric joined us.

When it was done and no hearts beat in that glade anymore, Arkady signaled his silent brood to carry the bodies. I followed them with Cyneric leaning on my shoulder. As we walked through the forest, Arkady asked questions, curious about how we spent our time. I told him of Niveus, which he had already heard of. I knew other vampires spied on me but was a little surprised at how much he knew of my affairs. Finally, he asked why I let Cyneric live. When I said it was because he had the unusual ability to control his desires, I felt a ripple of surprise and then grief from the brood that walked in front of us. I was certain that none of them had chosen the life they now lived.

When we reached the inn, Arkady sent his brood into the building to dispatch the few travelers who happened to be there and to take any valuables they found.

I couldn't help thinking of the irony. Their actions weren't very different from that of the dead thieves that now lay piled in the main room of the inn. At what point did the potential for further violence outweigh the violence required to stop those men and the inn keepers?

Arkady's brood took the horses and other livestock from the stables and loaded a wagon with the goods from the inn. Then they set fire to the buildings.

Through all that time, Arkady's brood did not speak out loud. I didn't often open myself up to the voices of other vampires. I can often hear human thoughts if they don't guard them, and I can see the visions in their minds. I can do the same with other vampires, although it takes more of an effort. I don't want to hear them, so I don't listen. And I always block my own mind from them.

Spoken words have a value. There is more meaning behind it when we take the time to speak out loud.

"Can you hear them?" I asked Cyneric. I had never before spoken to his mind.

He looked over at me from his perch on the bed of the wagon. He was leaning against the side with his leg propped on a sack of flour and the other hanging down.

"If you wish, you can open yourself to their thoughts. Fledglings such as these will not be able to stop you."

Abruptly, the hum I heard from Arkady's brood ceased. They pulled the wagon to a stop and as one turned to look at Cyneric. I did not control Cyneric's actions as Arkady did his brood. Cyneric was more disturbed by them moving as though they were one band of marionettes, with Arkady as the puppet master, than he was by the prospect of speaking without words.

"Perhaps another time," Cyneric said out loud. In the silence of the forest, whose only other sound was the soft clink of the team's harness as the horses shifted, his voice rang out.

They drove south on the road, away from the nearby village and inn until the stars disappeared and the sky lightened from indigo to the gray of pre-dawn. They turned the wagon off the road and into a clearing. There, they tied the horses to some trees.

"I feel the sun coming," Cyneric commented.

Arkady nodded in agreement. "Yes, we must find shelter. My man Rene will find the wagon and take it to my villa."

I'd also sensed the coming dawn and knew of a place for Cyneric to be safe from it. I helped him out of the wagon. "There is a cave nearby. I sealed the entrance long ago, but I could take your brood there for the day."

Arkady regarded me, uncertain about my motives. I was fairly sure he would be able to remain conscious during the day, but his brood would be helpless. Older vampires, or those that simply woke sooner than others could, were those with the power to rule large territories, simply because they could avoid dying by the hands of their own kind. He was wondering how far he could trust me.

His brood stirred impatiently; the sun was on its way. "I am sincere in my offer," I said. "You will all be safe."

Arkady gave a small, polite bow and nodded.

"I'll take Cyneric there, then lead you to the place," I said. "It will only take a moment for me to return."

I jumped to the cave with Cyneric, and moments later returned to the clearing in the woods. "Follow me."

It would weaken me too much to teleport them all there, and though I was asking Arkady for his faith in me, I didn't quite trust him that far. I sped away, and they followed in my wake as trees flashed by. The cave lay on the western side of the hill, which was a stroke of luck for his brood; the sun was too near the horizon for them to dig a grave by the time we arrived.

I found a tree had grown at the base of the massive rock that sealed the entrance. Arkady helped me push both tree and rock until the gap was large enough for his brood to slip through. The sun crested the horizon and snaked around the edge of the hill. The last two of his brood fell and lay in the gap, caught in the sleep of the dead.

We took their arms and dragged them inside. Their skin felt hot under my hands, and steam rose from the dew that dampened their clothes as we ran through the trees and brush. I caught Arkady's eye and could see that he was not frozen as the others were. "I'll be back soon," I said and rolled the stone back in place from the outside.

Before returning to the cave, I walked to the top of the hill to watch the sunrise and bask in its light. As I did, I looked to the heavens, and though I dare not say a formal prayer, I did send my thanks. I never tire of watching the sun rise. I closed my eyes and let the sun bathe my face. I felt its heat warm me, the rock I sat on, the trees. I heard the chirping of the many birds in the forest as they greeted the sun with their own songs. I breathed in the fresh morning air. I did not feel worthy of the gift I'd been given. If any vampire should be granted the gift of seeing the light of the sun, it was Cyneric. I sat on the rock until the warmth of the sun soaked into my very bones, then I teleported back to the cave.

I landed on a body. One of Arkady's brood was lying where I'd chosen to appear. In fact, they were all lined along that wall, Cyneric included. Arkady had arranged them that way. He'd also lit the oil lamps that lined the walls near the entrance. When I caught my balance and looked around, he was sitting in one of the gilt chairs, studying the treasure that lay piled at the back of the cave.

"*C'est incroyable!*" he exclaimed as he gestured toward the treasure.

"It was Kumar's," I said. "Most of it, anyway." I took another chair from its place by the wall and set it nearer to his. "When did you begin speaking French instead of Latin?"

"Why do you speak English?" he asked. I smiled and shrugged, and we sat and stared at the treasure.

Presently, I stood and stripped out of my clothes, then found a brush and swept the dirt and debris from my body. From an old battered chest that lay to one side, I chose a silk shirt that was a deep shade of green, and from yet another chest, I took fine woolen pants dyed white. My boots survived our encounter with the demon unscathed. I dusted them off too. After that, I dressed Cyneric. He didn't like me to do such things to him while he slept, but I did it anyway that time.

As vampires, we can defend ourselves somewhat from intruders, even during daylight. There is some alarm in us if we sense we are in mortal peril. But we don't seem to feel or notice anyone near that is not a threat. So, I was able to manipulate Cyneric's body and dress him, and the only resistance was the leaden weight of his limbs—like a corpse that has been dead long enough for rigor mortis to have passed.

Arkady watched me in silence. He stared blatantly at the many scars on my body when I changed shirts, his curiosity obvious, but he did not ask, and I didn't venture to explain them. I considered myself lucky that my face had been spared such marks as a mortal man.

When I finished dressing Cyneric and replaced his bandage with a better one, he looked distinctly out of place in the middle of Arkady's brood. They lay still and cold in their filthy clothes. The vagabonds they stole them from had not been concerned with hygiene.

"I'll be glad to give them better clothes," I offered. "I'm sure I have sizes that will fit them, even for the women."

Two of his brood were female. I often kept the things from my victims, if they had any value. So, you see, I was no different from Arkady and his brood. Vampires are the ultimate thieves. We steal not only material things, but life itself.

Arkady was silent for a while as he considered my offer. He gazed sorrowfully at his brood. I understood his hesitation. Giving them fine clothes would remind them of a life and a freedom they most likely would never be able to have. Instead of replying to my offer, he shook his head and said, "How do you do it?"

I wasn't sure what "it" he meant. "Pardon?"

"How do you murder your own fledglings? If they become one of us, it is likely that you have known them for many years. How can you then destroy them?"

That hurt. Not the truth of what he said, but the memories I thought were long since buried. I could not keep the heat out of my voice when I said, "I would have preferred death to living as I did when I was newly made."

"And now?" He spoke slowly, taking care with each word. "Would you give up the life you have had once you learned control? Would you have wanted that chance denied to you?"

I turned away so he could not see my face. Adonas had not wanted to keep me in his dungeons. He was furious when he found he could not trust me. But he refused to kill me when I asked, and later I was grateful for that. I hadn't thought of it in the way Arkady presented it now. It had not occurred to me that Adonas' motivations were anything but selfish.

On the other hand, what right did I have to live? I enjoyed my life, for the most part. I treasured each night after seeing the light of the moon after so many years in darkness. And the sun. My heart burst with joy when I gazed at it as I had that very morning. And yet, we are monsters. We do not belong on this earth among humans and exist only on the fringes of humanity. Adonas laughed at me often, saying I should stop "clinging to morality" and simply enjoy being what I was. But if I did, what purpose would my life have?

I realized my arms were folded across my body as though I were hugging myself. Maybe I was. I dropped them to my side. More to myself than to him, I said, "If I were to let them live, the murders they commit would be on my hands. Think of the numbers, the dead, the souls taken from life too soon, which would all be because of *me*. I would rather kill the one before the bodies pile up, before they truly know what they have become." I turned to face him and could not help balling my hands into fists. "I will not keep others as I was once kept."

Arkady absorbed my words and shook his head once more. I wasn't sure if it was in disbelief or incredulity. He asked, "And Cyneric?"

"He had control from the start, even with someone he loved."

"Impossible!" he exclaimed, in an accent that was purely French with no hint of his native Latin.

I shrugged once more and took a seat next to him. "Yes, I would have thought so too."

We sat in silence for a time, watching the rainbow of colors play on the cave wall, reflected from the firelight striking the jewels and gold.

Eventually, my melancholy waned, as it always does, and curiosity won out. "Do you still have some in your brood who have learned control?" I was careful not to ask by name about Dabria, who accompanied him the last time we'd met. It was significant that she was not with him that night.

"They'll meet Rene on the road when night has fallen. There are two of them. The vagabonds seemed a good opportunity to give my young ones the chance to hunt."

He must have told them through their mental connection where to find the wagon. I left the question of Dabria unasked. I suspected she was older than either Arkady or me. I had not asked Arkady to verify that. I didn't want him to know I found her intriguing. When I last saw her, she clung to him as though to an anchor. She was afraid of the world she now lived in.

We discussed less weighty matters as the day wore on. I learned he recently moved to a property very near the place Adonas had owned. Recently from our perspective. He'd been there nearly a hundred years. As he spoke of his place and the mundane concerns that go with running a large estate, it occurred to me that I had not returned to Niveus in nearly twenty years.

We spent three nights in the company of Arkady and his brood at his villa. I was glad to find that Dabria still existed, but she had gone down into the earth before Cyneric was born and had not risen again. Arkady was certain he would sense it if she left this life.

The two favored of Arkady's brood were men. When we arrived, the other wraiths he kept were sent to their dungeon. I tried not to think about them while the rest of us enjoyed lively discussions and told stories of our adventures and our travels.

Cyneric did not attempt to speak with any of them mind to mind. The idea disturbed him. He shut his thoughts from them, as he always did from me. I did not attempt to break that block, although I was fairly certain I could have. Arkady was more stunned that he could do that last than he was that Cyneric had the will to deny the demon's desire to kill with wanton abandon.

We parted amicably, an unusual thing for vampires who aren't from the same brood.

Arkady awakened a curiosity in me about Niveus. As soon as Cyneric and I moved the treasure to other caves, I resolved to go there. I asked Cyneric if he wanted to join me. He said he preferred that I went first and found out how things stood. When the sun was at its zenith, and Cyneric lay safely in one of my caves, I returned to Niveus.

ॐ Chapter 10 ൠ
Catch a Tiger by the Tail

I was watching my granddaughter Naomi for the evening while Anthony and Tracy took the rare chance to go out together. Naomi and I were making faces at each other, and I was turning her mobile for her when I felt a shiver run through me. It was not the spirits. It was the mental connection I had with Sylvio, the people I lived with, and Tim. But I could not pinpoint who. Something was terribly wrong.

"Sylvio!"

I shouted his name in my mind and waited . . . nothing. No response.

Maybe the connection didn't work when he was so far away. Celine had invited him to visit her and Mateo, and it was not his week to be with us anyway.

I closed my eyes and concentrated on the feelings I was sensing from the others. The only strong sensation was from Tim. I focused on that and received feelings of pain, fear, and confusion.

The sudden sound of the theme from *The Man from Snowy River* coming from my pocket made me jump. It startled Naomi, too. She began to screw her face up, ready to cry. I placed a hand on her cheek and sent calm to her while wishing I could do the same for myself.

I took the phone out of my pocket and saw it was Ramon. He didn't bother with a hello; he started with, "Do you know where Tim is?"

I heard the concern in his voice. He would be able to sense Tim through their bond even better than I could.

A chill ran down my spine. "He and Ray went to the night rodeo up in Cody," I said. Many possibilities ran through my mind. Foremost was that Tim would have been hurt by a bull since he'd gone to ride. Something told me that wasn't quite the cause. Ramon didn't say anything right away, so I asked, "What are you feeling from him?"

"He's been hurt and isn't blocking the pain. He must be unconscious or unable to concentrate. The whole pack felt rage from him, more than the usual. Then a few minutes after was pain. And that's still there." He paused, then added, "I think he's trapped somewhere."

"Did you try his cell?"

"He didn't answer. But if he thinks I'm attempting to interfere, he might not answer me. Will you try him?"

Whatever happened was bad if the whole pack sensed it. Now it was me who felt trapped. I didn't dare take Naomi with me, not if what was wrong had to do with the preternatural, and I only knew a general direction to go. Anthony and Tracy weren't due back for another half hour.

"Sure," I said.

Ramon hung up, which I guess meant I was to get to it. I dialed Tim's phone and held my breath.

A strange voice answered on the third ring. A woman's voice said, "Hello." Her tone carried authority with it.

"Who is this?" I asked, willing whoever it was to tell me anything they could.

"Officer Michaels, Cody City police. Who is this?"

My phone buzzed, and I looked at the screen. Shena was calling me. I hung up on the officer and answered Shena.

"Father is in trouble," she said, sounding calm as always, which helped soothe my nerves. I could hear Eric mumbling in the background.

"Yes, Ramon and I felt it too. Stay at your house for now. I'll keep trying to get him or Sylvio on the phone. We need more information first."

"We're at Sylvio's."

"Even better. Stay with them, and I'll keep you all updated. Have you heard from Ray?"

"Dan says he's not answering his phone either." This time, I caught exasperation and worry in her tone.

"Okay, I'll call you back as soon as I know something. Sit tight." My phone buzzed again as Shena hung up and the screen said it was Tim.

I answered and said, "Is this Officer Michaels?"

"Yes, who is this?"

"Sorry, I had to pick up another call. I'm a close friend of Tim's. Where is he, and why do you have his phone?"

Her tone was puzzled when she answered. "This is the phone that called 911."

I felt the blood drain from my face. My knees buckled. Luckily, the couch was behind me. It was a moment before I could compose myself enough to reply. "What has happened?"

"We're trying to sort it out. What does Tim look like? Does he have distinguishing features?"

I assumed she did not mean fur and huge teeth. "Scars. Lots of them. And a large tattoo of a dragon on his chest."

She paused before answering. "I see. Have you been watching TV?"

Why *that* question? "No."

"You might want to turn it on. I need to check on something, and I'll call you back in a few minutes. Please answer when I do."

"You can be sure of that."

She hung up.

TV—damn, I thought. I sent another plea: *"Sylvio, we really need you!"*

I turned on the TV and changed it to a local channel. Sure enough, it said "Breaking News" at the bottom in big, bold letters. A somber-looking male reporter was in the middle of saying, ". . . officers to the hospital. The victim has also been admitted and is being treated at this time. We will update our viewers on her prognosis, and that of the officers, as soon as we hear from the hospital staff."

The anchorwoman broke in. "What about the suspect? Has he been taken to the hospital as well?"

"He's been taken to the local jail as a precaution. A team of paramedics has been dispatched to attend to him there."

The anchorwoman asked more questions. "Can you tell us more about this video? Why were there so many officers involved?"

The TV screen changed from the reporter to the start of a video. It began with a picture of a motel, and the sway as the vehicle the photographer was in lurched to a stop. When they opened the door to get out, a body was thrown through the motel window, which was already broken.

The motel room door was open, and a woman could be heard screaming hysterically over the shouts of the men in the room. The photographer focused through the window, and the scene was clear enough that they put blurry spots over the woman's face and private parts. She was obviously naked. Her feet were free, but her hands were tied to the headboard of the motel room bed.

I recognized Tim from the scars on his legs below the t-shirt and gym shorts he wore. He was standing on the other side of the bed from the door. Most of his upper body was not visible because a man was reaching for him. The room was full of men, but only the one going through the door wore a uniform.

I saw a flash of metal and realized Tim had handcuffs on one wrist, but whoever attempted to cuff him didn't have a chance to put them on the other. The loose handcuff caught the man reaching for him in the face as Tim's other hand struck him in the throat. The man dropped like a stone, and another one took his place.

It was horrific to watch—the kind of video TV reporters drool over. Another man sailed through the window to join the one who still lay crumpled on the sidewalk. There were only two men left standing now. The one in uniform grabbed Tim by his shirt collar, and they were face to face. Tim's eyes, which were bright gold, had been on the man he'd downed. When his eyes came up, they fell on the officer's badge.

Tim stopped moving and looked confused. Then the officer hit him on the head with a Maglite—one of those huge, heavy flashlights. Tim staggered, still looking at the badge, and the officer hit him again on the same spot.

I could see the flashlight sink in as the skull broke. Tim crumpled to the floor. As he fell, obviously unconscious, the only other man standing aimed a vicious kick into Tim's groin with his heavy boots. Then there was suddenly silence. The woman had passed out, and the men lying two deep on the motel floor weren't moving.

The video continued, but they muted the sound so the reporter could be heard. He was attempting to look somber while dollar signs floated through his eyes. That video and his report would surely go nationwide and probably hit the international news as well.

The reporter said that in the restaurant across the parking lot was a retirement party for an officer. That's why so many responded to the call. I didn't hear what else he said; my ears were buzzing. I'm not prone to panic, but it was starting to seize me. I watched as a few of the bodies on the floor began to move and emergency vehicles screeched to a halt. The photographer was made to move away and take a place back among the spectators. The strip of script at the bottom of the screen now said, "Local girl assaulted and taken to hospital. Several officers injured while subduing the suspect."

I turned the TV off, barely able to breathe. I sent a third plea and could hear voiceless tears in my tone: *"Sylvio, please come."*

I picked up little Naomi and hugged her to me, wanting to hug Tim. This was beyond disaster—Tim injured and locked up. Mentally, he would not be able to handle being in a cage, and the odds of him staying human under such conditions were not good. Plus, he obviously needed medical care—and how were they going to cope with an injured werewolf?

I found a bottle Tracy had prepared and warmed it up for Naomi. I knew I was stalling. I didn't dare call Ramon. He might decide things were safer for all the werewolves if Tim died. I started feeding Naomi and was pacing the living room when my phone began playing tunes again. It was Tim's number.

"Officer Michaels, what can you tell me?" I asked. "How is Tim?"

"I think it's *you* who needs to tell *me* some things," she replied.

"I can tell you for certain Tim would not have raped that girl."

I knew that people who have been abused often copy what has been done to them. They seem compelled to repeat the evil visited on them in a twisted sort of release from their anger. I was certain Tim had not taken that path. I would have known if he had. There was certainly another reason for his presence in that room.

I pushed the spirits to make Officer Michaels talk to me. I needed information. She said, "We're waiting for the doctors to give us permission to speak with her. She regained consciousness a few minutes ago."

"Where is Tim?"

"Currently, he's at the Park County Jail in Cody."

Sylvio appeared in the room. I jumped enough to pop the bottle out of Naomi's mouth. I was instantly angry, and scared, and relieved at the same time. I dropped the phone to catch the bottle. When I picked it up, I said, "I'll have to call you back."

I heard the officer shout a protest as I clicked off.

"What's happened to Ray?" Sylvio asked.

"Ray?" I was taken aback. "It's Tim I was calling to you about. He's hurt." I didn't know how to begin with the rest of it.

"So is Ray. My connection with him is wavering."

That meant Ray was near death. My heart sank even further. There had been no sign of Ray in that news report.

"They're in Cody," I said. "They were at the rodeo. Are you familiar with Cody? Could you take me to the jail?"

"Ray first." I saw the stubborn look on Sylvio's face and knew it was pointless to argue. He would defend and care for his own before he gave a thought to Tim.

"Ray was with Tim. He's probably in the same area. Would you be able to find him if you were near enough?"

He caught on to my thought in an instant. "I don't know what the jail looks like now. But I can take us to the park. It's right near the jail, and only a couple of blocks from the hospital."

I bit my lip. "I can't leave Naomi until Anthony and Tracy get back."

I knew he would not wait, but my concern was answered by a car pulling into the driveway. I was relieved but also worried. This was not going to be pleasant. Anthony would be angry that Sylvio was there.

I set Naomi back down in her cradle. She was wide awake, even after taking most of the bottle, and her eyes were following Sylvio, who could not stop pacing. I could feel his frustration. Anthony opened the door, spotted Sylvio, and glared at me. He started to speak, but I cut him off.

"Anthony, there isn't time to explain. Sylvio and I have to go. Tim and Ray have been hurt. Naomi is fine."

I put an arm around Sylvio's waist and hoped the look I sent Anthony and Tracy was sufficiently apologetic. I heard that familiar buzz; then we reappeared in a dark, empty space that smelled of pine trees and snow. I immediately regretted not grabbing my coat before we left.

"The jail is that way." Sylvio pointed to the right, where I could see the flash of emergency lights over the tops of the buildings. Then he pointed to the left. "Ray is that way. In the direction of the hospital."

Then he was gone. There was only a slight breeze to mark his passing. He hadn't teleported, he moved too fast to be seen.

I began jogging toward the jail and hit the button on the phone for Tim as I went. I hoped jogging and talking would distract me from the cold.

Officer Michaels answered on the first ring. "Don't hang up again!" she barked.

"I can't guarantee I won't. I'll be at the jail in a few minutes. Is that where you are?" I pushed the spirits again to get her to cooperate.

"What are you driving? I'll have them let you through."

"I'm on foot." I rounded the corner and could see the jail only a block away. "I'm coming from the park."

"What? On foot . . . what does that mean?"

"I'll find you when I get there."

Again, I heard her say, "Don't hang up!" as I clicked off the phone.

When I approached the building, I could feel a tableau of emotions from the crowd assembled near the entrance. The ambulance was parked at an angle to the curb with the back doors open. The paramedics were milling near the door. I sensed they felt frustrated and uncertain. A crowd of reporters were being kept at bay by several officers who were blocking access to the building. I stopped a half block away and scanned the people, asking the spirits to lead me to Officer Michaels.

She was standing outside the door, looking my way. Our eyes met at the same instant. After a moment, she held up the phone in her hand. I held up mine and began walking her way. She turned to speak with the two officers flanking her. One of them went back into the building; the other gave me his cop look—the kind of look that says, *We'll see if what you're saying is truth.*

Officer Michaels found her way through the throng, and several reporters watched her approach. I wasn't sure what to do about them. I held out a hand. "I'm Rachel, the one who keeps hanging up."

She was strong-willed and was fighting the compulsion to help me. I urged the spirits to gain her cooperation. Now was not the time to split hairs about right and wrong.

"Officer Michaels." She shook my hand and looked over her shoulder at the reporters. "Let's go in the back way, over here."

She led me around the building to a side entrance while the spirits kept the reporters from wanting to follow us. As soon as I stepped in the door, I felt magic—pack magic. I knew immediately where Tim was. I also felt fear and anger, not only from him but also from the officers still in the building.

As we passed the main entrance, I could hear the reporter on the TV stating, "The suspected rapist is still in the jail. The ambulance is waiting outside the entrance."

I fumed inside; trial by TV.

"Take me to Tim," I commanded.

Officer Michaels didn't hesitate, but turned and said, "This way."

We didn't walk far. I could have found the door without her guidance. Two officers decked out in riot gear and holding shotguns stood on either side of it. When we got there, I reached for the handle.

"What the hell! Take your hand off that door!" The officer who had been with Michaels at the entrance had followed us in. At his words, the two men in riot gear and Officer Michaels snapped out of the stupor my spell had caused, and all eyes turned to me.

The officer came close enough for me to be able to separate his emotions and aura from the others, and the game changed. This officer was a werewolf.

I looked up into his eyes. "The man in there is from Ramon's pack. He trusts me."

One of the riot gear officers said, "Lady, that thing is not a man."

I kept my eyes on the werewolf and replied, "Most of the time, he is."

The werewolf was not backing down. His eyes narrowed, and the green irises began to show a yellow tinge around the edge.

"Why would he trust a witch?" the werewolf asked.

Werewolves can smell a witch if that witch has recently done magic. I hoped he couldn't tell what kind of spell I'd been using.

The word "witch" brought the other three up short. Out of the corner of my eye, I saw them exchange glances.

"There is a bond between us," I said.

My eyes were beginning to water, and I was growing tired of this game as we stared each other down. I was gathering the spirits to push him out of the way when my phone began playing tunes again. He twitched and looked down at the phone. I caught a faint growl from Tim at the sound of the phone. I blinked furiously to clear my dry eyes and checked the screen. It was Ramon.

I answered without preamble, "I'm at the jail where Tim is. I was about to go in and see him."

"I'm sensing he is in a very bad place," Ramon said. He didn't mean the jail. "You might not want to approach him right now."

The werewolf officer was looking smug now. He could hear our conversation as well as if Ramon were standing next to us. I gave him a frosty look, and he dropped his eyes. Then his head snapped up again, startled, but the battle had been won.

Another officer shouted down the hall, "Officer Michaels, come here a moment." He was gesturing for her to come toward the front of the station. Michaels looked at the two of us, hesitant to respond, then went to see what they wanted.

I said into the phone, "I'll be careful, but he needs help now."

"Rachel, I can't see what the outcome is going to be."

The werewolf's entire demeanor changed suddenly, and I glanced at him. He was astonished and stared at me as if I had sprouted horns or something. "You're *that* Rachel?" he blurted.

"Who is that?" Ramon asked.

The werewolf swallowed, then composed himself. "Caleb . . . sir."

Officer Michaels came back down the hall waving a sheet of paper and said, "It wasn't him. The girl spoke to the doctors for a few minutes, then passed out again. It was kids from the high school. Officers have been sent to locate them."

I did some fast thinking. "Did you hear that, Ramon?" I thought I could see a way to get Tim to cooperate.

"Yes."

"Let me in with Tim," I ordered.

They all stared at me, then Caleb nodded slowly. He glanced at the door. "You heard that. We can help you if you'll let us." The answer was a muffled snarl and bang as Tim hit the door. It sounded oddly far away.

"I'm going in to talk to him. I'll call you back soon," I told Ramon and hung up. I knew I'd have to apologize to Ramon and Officer Michaels for hanging up on them, but right now Tim was my focus.

Caleb gestured to the men in riot gear and Officer Michaels. "We'll be in the observation room next door." He held the door for them to go in the room, but he didn't follow them in. Instead, he placed himself in the middle of the hall to block Tim from going that way. It was a brave gesture, and a futile one if things went bad.

"You're certain he trusts you?" Caleb asked.

"Absolutely," I answered and hoped he couldn't see my hands shaking as I grasped the door handle.

"The doors are unlocked from this side," Caleb explained and stood at the ready.

I turned the handle on the door and pulled. This was no ordinary door; it was twice as thick as a normal door, and heavy. On the other side was a small space and another door. Now I understood why Tim hitting it had sounded odd. I gathered the spirits around me, asked them to show me Tim's thoughts, and stepped into the room.

Terror—it was visceral, a living thing. I sank to my knees, unable to stand under the power of his magic. Images flashed through my mind: Tim tied and helpless as others used his body for their own sport; Tim strapped to an exam table as they gave him injections that made him convulse and writhe; Tim locked in a cage the size of a coffin made of stainless steel bars and sterile white walls; Tim shackled in the corner of a room with almost no light, watching the demon twist the mind of the woman who was its host until she was hideous and cruel; Tim as a helpless toy for that demon, who had no mercy, no soul, and fed off the pain it caused its victims; Tim attacked from behind by a werewolf, and the agony of changing without a pack to help him.

The room stank of bile, and I realized he had vomited into the corner near the platform that was bolted opposite the door. The blanket and the cot that had been on the platform lay in shreds on the floor under the observation window. The window had a green tint and felt heavy, even from where I knelt.

Tim's psychiatrist, Dr. Ross, told me that if Tim were ever caged again, it would most likely unhinge him completely. Through my tears, I looked at the werewolf that stood watching me from a mere ten feet away. Other than memories, all I could sense was wolf. There was no Tim. The wolf had gone silent when I stepped into the room, but now he began to growl. The growl was so low and deep that I could feel the vibration through the tile floor. He had *very* large teeth from my angle.

His appearance was far different from the wolf I usually saw. This was a man caught in the body of a wolf. He stood on two legs, his joints bent at weird angles, as part of him fought to be human and the other fought to be wolf. Fur did not cover him entirely. Scars and even the dragon tattoo were visible. His face was elongated into a wolf's muzzle, but the rest of his face was human. The eyes peering at me were golden and full of the pain he felt, body and soul.

I swallowed. He could tear me to bits in an instant. I gathered the spirits to me and with all my heart hoped they could help us both. I took a deep breath and said, "They'll get away with it," surprised that my tone was strong. With the aid of the spirits, my voice was clear and not broken, though tears had begun to leak down my cheeks. Moving slowly, I wiped them away with my cold palms and sat against the wall beside the door.

He stopped growling and blinked at me. His eyes were not tracking together, and his pupils were not the same size. I could see a large goose egg behind his ear, his left one that was missing the tip.

"Those boys that raped the girl you were helping," I continued. "They'll get away if you stay wolf and don't tell us what happened."

I wasn't sure that was true, but it was a possibility. The terror in the room went down a notch and was joined by confusion. I asked the spirits to continue to soothe his pain. He blinked again, his body melding and changing before my eyes into the wolf. He tried to sit down, but that hurt enough that he actually whined, so he stood back up again.

I brought my knees up, hugged them to me, and leaned against the wall. "You know, it's nice that you go out of your way to help strangers, but it has not been good for your health."

He tilted his head at me and winced. It appeared he couldn't block pain, as disoriented as he was, which made me wonder if he could even understand all I was saying. But he was looking more like a wolf all the time, and the terror that had filled the room began to dissipate.

"It'll hurt less if you turn back into a human. You look kinda funny in a t-shirt and shorts anyway."

He was still wearing both, although they had tears in them and would probably fall off once he was human. Ramon told me once that switching helps a werewolf heal—if I could talk him into changing back.

The wolf stared at me with inhuman golden eyes, but he wasn't growling anymore.

"I've learned how to use magic to heal things," I went on. "I can do a little bit. I'm not sure how much, but it's worth a try. I'll need to touch you, though."

He turned his head to watch me with the one good eye. There was intelligence behind the eye now, something more than animal. The other one was clearly out of focus and rapidly swelling shut. He started walking toward me on all fours. His hands had become paws, and fur covered all of him. It was obvious it hurt him to move, and he staggered a little, but he stopped with his right side to me and put his massive head in my hand. The human had lost the battle by the time he came to my side. Standing taller than I was sitting down, he was completely wolf. A very large one. Heat radiated off him.

"Oooh, you're nice and warm. I'm freezing." I swallowed the lump of fear that leapt into my throat and asked the spirits to keep my tone conversational. "I forgot my coat when we jumped here, and this room is cold."

I stretched my legs out so he could get closer. A separate part of me was thinking how easily those huge teeth could tear into my exposed throat or belly. Rip me to shreds.

I shoved that thought away and asked, "What first, your head or your privates?"

He took a step forward. Tim and I were close, but I'd been careful never to even give a hint of sexual intimacy, and he didn't like people to touch him—anywhere. He had allowed me to stroke his hair a few times. This was different, though.

"Um, okay, then." Still, I hesitated. Suddenly, I wasn't afraid but embarrassed. His wild emotions seemed to have affected my composure.

He huffed a couple of times, and his lip curled up. His teeth were very large, especially only inches from my face. But the pervasive feeling of terror had left the room.

"Are you *laughing* at me?"

His lip curled more, and he huffed a few more times. I felt much better. I took a deep breath and composed myself, calling on the spirits of living things to come to me. I felt them respond. Even in that cold room, there was space for them to come through the cracks around the doors and the vents in the ceiling. I borrowed them from the officers in the building, the crowd gathered outside, even the plants in the foyer. We're all made of energy, after all.

I let the spirits guide me to the spot that was causing him the most pain. When my palm met fur and skin, I could feel which parts were wrong. Energy flowed through my arm and into him. He hunched his back and squeezed his eyes shut but did not move away. His entire body shook.

I closed my eyes to better sense the spirits as they used me as their conduit to heal him. Then I felt something else; a different kind of healing from my own. Behind my eyes, a golden light came with that new magic: love. The pack cared for Tim with more than friendship, and their magic joined mine. I felt Tim's surprise. I was sure it had not occurred to him that the pack might care that much for him.

It did not take long. After a minute had ticked slowly by, he began to shiver and pant. The spirits stopped flowing into him, and he flopped down, trapping my legs. I was nice and toasty then.

I stroked his thick fur, then placed my hand gently on the bump on his head. The spirits flowed into him again. That took longer. The swelling only went down slightly; there is only so much that magic can heal. But he did stop panting and sighed, and I felt the bones in his skull realign under my palm. I scratched the ruff behind his ears and felt like I could sleep for a week. I was quite tapped out.

The phone in my pocket went off again. I twitched, startled, and Tim growled. "Oh, stop that," I scolded. I fished the phone out from under my butt.

It was Ramon. He's not into small talk. He started with, "He's much better now."

"We're in the holding cell together. I'll try to get him to change back."

"Thanks for helping—again. You do as she says, Tim." Tim's growl made my whole body vibrate. Ramon chuckled, relief obvious in his tone. "I'll be there soon. I commandeered Sylvio's plane." He hung up.

I waited, but Tim didn't move. He lay on my legs with his head on his paws while I scratched him. I wondered absently that Ramon knew not only how to get to one of Sylvio's planes, but also how to fly them. After a couple of minutes, I said to Tim, "You really should listen to your alpha."

He groaned as he stood up, shook himself, and stepped away from me. He deliberately put his back to the observation window, then began to transform. It was awful and fascinating at the same time. I could sense both fear and wonder from those behind the one-way mirror, and I could sense Tim's pain—until he was human enough to block it. When it was done, he sat crouched on the floor and shivered.

I crawled the short space between us and put an arm around him. There was a sheen of sweat on his back, half of his face and his groin were a hideous shade of blue-black, and his eyes still had the glaze of someone concussed. I looked over my shoulder at the mirror and ordered, "Bring him a blanket." His t-shirt hung off his left arm, ripped nearly in half. His torn shorts were pooled around his ankles.

Only moments later, Caleb opened the door, moving slowly and keeping his eyes down. Tim turned toward the sound, and Caleb fell to his knees and ducked his head. He held out the blanket as the door clicked shut. I felt it was safer to stay on Tim's level, so I crawled back to the door and retrieved the blanket, then went back and set it over his shoulders. He continued to gaze at Caleb, who remained on his knees with his eyes on the floor.

"Let him go, Tim, he has things to do."

The weight of pack magic in the room lifted a little.

Caleb licked his lips but didn't stand up. "Paramedics are waiting in the main lobby," he said, addressing the floor.

Tim gave me a panicked look. I touched the side of his face that wasn't damaged. "You really need a doctor to look you over. We weren't able to heal it all."

He shook his head a fraction, and I was at a loss about what to do.

When he spoke, Tim's voice was raspy and slurred, like a drunk. He said, "There were three besides the one in the bathroom."

"Okay." I was glad he was able to comprehend what I'd said earlier. "What did they look like?"

"Three are white kids, one is black. At least two will need to see a doctor. One had a broken arm. The other's shoulder is messed up."

Caleb chanced a glance to look up at Tim and said, "Got it. I'm sure we can track them down."

Tim stood up, swayed, then dove for the trash can. He didn't quite make it before he threw up.

"You really need to get checked out," I said.

Tim gave me a bleak look.

"Caleb, would the paramedics have any drugs that would knock him out?" I asked.

"It's not good for someone with a concussion to be tranquilized."

I'd forgotten that. Tim really needed to be examined by a doctor—werewolf superpowers of healing or not.

"You're gonna insist I go, aren't you?" Tim's tone carried a little bit of whine in it.

"Yes." I held my phone out to him. "Here, tell Shena and Eric you're okay and you're on the way to the hospital. Tell them the police here know you were not the bad guy."

I could see he'd forgotten about his kids, and I could feel his surprise that he had.

"Most doctors are good, Tim."

He sighed and spoke in his normal tone, "Try telling that to my subconscious."

I tried the door, but of course, it was locked from this side. I looked pointedly at the one-way mirror. Moments later, Officer Michaels opened the door. She was very much afraid and was only partially able to hide that. She glanced at Caleb and decided to copy his submissive attitude. Good for her.

We started out the door and down the hall to the entrance while Tim was distracted by talking to his kids. When he hung up, he felt better, but he stopped still when he caught sight of the paramedics standing next to a gurney that was positioned near the door.

"I'm not laying down on that thing," Tim announced.

"I'm sure they'll let you walk to the ambulance." I sent a wave of compulsion out to ensure they would do that.

We all headed out the door, with Tim in the lead. Camera lights were almost blinding as we stepped outside. It was like when one of those strobe things goes off at the fourth of July. The reporters all began shouting at once, and the tension in Tim and Caleb went up several degrees. I touched them both and sent them calm.

Tim said, "Thanks," and Caleb gave me a puzzled look.

We ignored the reporters. The paramedics and officers made a corridor for us to get to the back of the ambulance. The inside was crowded and too bright, but it was better than the noise and lights outside. Caleb stayed with us, and two of the paramedics climbed in, bringing the gurney in with them, which we sat on. One of them said, "Let's get you started on an IV." He reached for Tim's arm. Tim caught his wrist and held it. They were eye to eye.

"No," Tim growled.

The man went pale and dropped his eyes instinctively. He could sense that this was not a macho man trying to be difficult. This was something *other*. I started to speak, but Tim's mood swing distracted me. He had reached out with the arm that still had the cuff on it. His wrist was apparently near the same size as a wolf as it was when he was a man.

He let go of the paramedic's wrist, took hold of his own thumb, and jerked, dislocating it with a sick pop. He pulled his hand free of the cuff and let it fall to the floor with a clang. Then he twisted and pulled his thumb until it popped back into place with a loud crack.

I glanced at the other three faces in the ambulance. They were all wide-eyed, and the female paramedic even felt a little nauseous. I felt a little green around the gills too. She licked her lips and looked at me.

I gave her a reassuring smile. "He has lots of reasons not to like needles and doctors, and all the other medical paraphernalia. I suggest you move slowly and explain *everything* you are doing or want to do."

"Rachel, where are you?"

I jumped at least an inch off the gurney. I'd done far too much of that this night. They all stared at me.

"I'm with Tim. We're on the way to the hospital. Did you find Ray?"

"That's where I am, and I need your help. They won't let me in to see him."

One of my mom's favorite sayings popped into my head: *It never rains but it pours.*

ℰ Chapter 11 ℭ
Appearances are Deceiving

"**W**e'll be there any minute," I sent to Sylvio.

I was puzzled. It wouldn't matter to Sylvio whether he had permission or not. He could gain entrance anyway. So why hadn't he concealed himself and gone into the room? And what happened to Ray?

"*Where are you?*"

"*Outside ICU.*"

My heart plummeted . . . again.

Tim, distracted from his own issues, said, "What? You just went pale."

"Ray is hurt too. Do you know why?"

"Ray! No, he was in the motel room when I went jogging. I couldn't sleep."

Caleb suddenly felt alarmed too. "Is Ray . . . like Tim?" He'd started to slip up and almost said "werewolf," but he caught himself. He glanced at the paramedics, who hadn't moved, and who were feeling extremely frustrated. They were used to being in charge of their patients, not the other way around.

"No," I said. "He lives with me. He's a very good friend."

Caleb's eyes went even wider when I said, "Lives with me." I felt his unease increase. It was obvious that he knew who I lived with. I was wishing we had taken a cop car to the hospital instead of an ambulance. Then maybe we could have spoken freely. The two paramedics knew they were missing a big part of the conversation. They were looking from Caleb to Tim, and I could see things were adding up in their minds.

The female paramedic said, "Tim, will you let me at least take your vitals and administer some morphine?"

Tim's glare was enough to make both paramedics blanch. I was tempted to elbow him in the ribs but was afraid they might be sore too. "Let them do their jobs, Tim. They mean to help, not harm."

Showing uncommon bravery, the paramedic reached over and put a pressure cuff on Tim's arm and a clip on his finger. She explained every move she made and why they needed the data. Her partner sat quietly and handed things to her. When they took Tim's temperature, we were pulling to a stop at the emergency entrance.

"You have a fever."

Before Tim could answer, I said, "A high temperature is normal for him."

Those words seemed to confirm something for her, and she nodded to the other paramedic. A team of nurses opened the back door to the ambulance.

Caleb said, "We need Room D."

The small crowd in front of the ambulance door and the two paramedics with us stopped still. They glanced quickly at Tim and felt alarmed. "Right this way," the tallest nurse said. They did not reach for Tim but let us get out on our own. They backed away, keeping their eyes averted. Somehow, they *knew* what Tim was, and they knew not to challenge him.

Room D was the first room on the right. It had a massive, thick door like the one in the police station. Caleb immediately spun the dial on the lights to dim them, shut the door on the rest of our entourage, and clicked the two deadbolts. Even so, the smells and sounds of the hospital were becoming too much for Tim. I was using what little energy I had left to keep him human, and I was losing the battle. Stress, coupled with his concussion, were also making him disoriented.

As soon as the door shut, Tim lost the fight to remain human. He groaned, which quickly changed to a growl, and fell to his knees as his body parts began to rearrange themselves. Caleb sank to the floor too, caught in the more dominant wolf's power, his body twisting and contorting. I backed up and sat in the only chair there. I wasn't sure what I was going to do with two werewolves in the room, but I could not abandon Tim.

I looked around. The room seemed to be a normal hospital room at first glance, but there was no window, and everything except the mattress and the heavy leather chair I sat on was made of steel and was bolted to the floor or the walls. It dawned on me the room was made to contain a werewolf. But why would the hospital know to build a room specifically for werewolves?

The spirits still wrapped me in a soft blanket, but I could not enlist their aid. Healing Tim and keeping him sane enough to get here had sapped everything out of me.

Caleb had the presence of mind to strip his clothes off before he changed too much. Tim's blanket lay discarded on the floor.

Tim, as always, changed first. I didn't know if it was because of his odd brand of magic or because he could block most of the pain or some other reason, but he could transform faster than other werewolves. In only a minute, he was all werewolf. His yellow eyes gleamed in the dim light of the room. I had learned to tell when the human was in control and when the wolf was in control. My magic could control the wolf. I was not so foolish to try controlling the man other than to lend him comfort. The eyes that looked at me now were wolf eyes. He felt trapped and in pain. Not surprising.

He stood behind Caleb, who was still changing and could not control his movements. Caleb gasped and whined at intervals. I sat and watched, both fascinated and repulsed as joints popped and bent and body parts that belong inside showed on the outside momentarily. There was nothing else I could do.

I heard shouts out in the hall, and someone jiggled the door. Tim's snarl brought out a snarl in Caleb, who was getting to his feet. Tim's silver-gray coat glistened in the dim light. Caleb's coat was deep red, like some hounds. Not a color I associate with wolves. He shook himself and turned to peer at the door. It jiggled again. Caleb's ears went flat on his head, and his hackles came up. His growl held more menace than Tim's. Maybe it was because I didn't know him, but I was certain someone would die if they got the door open.

At that moment, I heard some words that were not in English. The handle turned as if it had no locks, and the door opened a crack. Caleb lunged for the door as Ramon slid through. The wolf checked his leap in mid-flight, turned, and fell against the chair I was sitting in. The recliner tipped over backward, and the wolf's weight pinned me to the floor, knocking the wind out of me. An instant later, Ramon picked Caleb up by his ruff and threw him onto the bed as if he weighed only ten pounds instead of 200. Magic followed him in.

"Tossing the dice as always, I see," Ramon commented, grinning down at me. He held a hand out to help me up, totally unconcerned about the two angry werewolves in the room with us.

"You get the award for good timing," I gasped, trying to gulp in some air.

James came in the door next and smiled reassuringly at me. He shut

R.E. Beebe

the door, clicked the locks back on, and put his back to it. Ramon picked the chair up and held my hand until I sat down. Then he walked over to where Caleb lay on the bed, unmoving, and petted his head. Caleb rolled onto his back with his tail curled between his legs, exposing his belly.

"You're having quite the night, Caleb." Ramon scratched the wolf's stomach. I could taste the pack magic as he settled calm into the other wolf's mind. "Thanks for your help. You should know that trouble follows Rachel wherever she goes."

Caleb turned over and put his head on his paws. Ramon began to scratch behind the wolf's ears. Caleb let out a contented sigh.

I crossed my arms and glared at Ramon. "I don't invite trouble. I led a perfectly normal life until two years ago," I protested.

"Trouble seems to find you more than it does Sylvio, and I always thought he was a marvel for getting into tight places." He continued to pet Caleb and spoke without looking at Tim. "Well, Tim, I can feel your pain. Rachel was not able to take all of it away. Come up here, and I'll see what I can do."

For a long count of twenty, Tim didn't move. Finally, he crept onto the bed and lay like a sphinx next to Caleb. James moved to stand next to Ramon and placed a hand on Tim's shoulder.

Magic vibrated and thrummed, pulled from the depths of the earth by Ramon. It met a wall for an instant while Tim decided whether to let him take over. Then he relented, and we all were compelled to close our eyes and open ourselves to that raw power.

Ramon was quite unassuming, easy to be around. He masked his strength quite well. But there was a reason he ruled all the alphas in the Americas. The spirits circled and wove around all four of us. I could feel them reach out and pull more magic into the room. As alpha of all the packs, Ramon had access to all the packs' magic. The room smelled of a pine forest, of the earth, and of life. It sank into all of them, and into me. I was no longer drained.

I opened my eyes and felt only peace from all four of them. I stood up and kissed Ramon on the forehead. "Thank you." My own spirits capered around the room.

"James and I will take care of these two," Ramon told me. "You go find Sylvio."

I didn't need to find him; he was standing outside the door when I went out.

"Tim okay?" Sylvio asked.

"He is now. Ramon fixed him."

"Ramon? How did he get here?"

"He took one of your planes."

Sylvio was feeling quite frustrated but chuckled in spite of himself. "Good to hear."

There were many eyes watching us. They were staying down the hall, away from the room, but all eyes were on us, and they *knew* we were not average humans. The knowledge behind their eyes was disturbing.

Sylvio caught my unease and said, "The area in and around Yellowstone is werewolf central in America. Most people that have lived here for more than a few years know about them. The problem is the hospitals around here routinely scan blood samples for traces of werewolf. Unfortunately, someone has shown this hospital staff how to recognize vampire as well. As soon as I walked in the door and asked to see Ray, they suspected what I am."

I could tell that bothered him quite a bit. He was used to moving through the human world as an unknown. Normally, his magic masked what he was.

"Where is Ray?" I asked.

"This way."

When we neared the area, I felt us pass through a bubble of magic—witch magic, with a new kind of twist to it. As we rounded a bend, I saw double doors that said ICU. In front of those doors were two guards. Not the sometimes soft and out of shape security staff that are often employed by hospitals. The two men were fit and would surely have been at home in fatigues and face paint. They held shotguns. I was willing to bet the shells in those guns were full of silver buckshot.

The two men in fatigues turned to face us. The one on the left said, "We're not to let you in until Dr. Swallow returns."

Sylvio felt angry, frustrated, and concerned for Ray. He looked at me with expectation. I understood then. Whatever spell had been woven on this place kept him from concealing himself and going in to see Ray. I thought about the meager knowledge I had learned about sorcery from the grimoire my mother left me, and from the one Micah loaned me. Nothing I'd read in those came to mind. My mother left notes and tips in the margins of most of the spells, putting things in plain English. I had found nothing so far about how to keep vampires out, other than not inviting them in in the first place. There had been nothing about undoing a spell of this type, either. I would have to try another way.

I pushed the spirits at the two men, compelling them to do my bidding. "May we please enter?" I asked.

They blinked, paused for only a few seconds, and then one of them reached out and punched a code into the panel by the door. It swung open. Sylvio's relief washed over me, and I smiled at the two men, feeling guilty as we walked through.

"He's that way," Sylvio said and turned right.

The nurses at the desk both got to their feet at the same time.

"Only family is allowed in here," the tallest one protested.

"We *are* his family," I said. "We live with him. He only has his sister, and even if she has been notified he's hurt, it will take her several hours to get here. He needs us now." Ray's sister lived in Boston. His parents and little brother had died in a car accident six months before he joined the Army. As far as I knew, he had not contacted any other relatives since.

I could see they were not to be swayed by what I said. I pushed the spirits at them to gain their cooperation. They both sat back down and blinked, first at me and then at each other. We continued down the hall. I reflected that it was getting to be too easy for me to resort to compulsion. Were my actions really justified? When we stepped into Ray's room, I decided they were. He was hooked up to various machines, including a breathing tube. That was problematic. How was Sylvio's blood going to help him if he was not able to swallow?

Sylvio stepped to the bedside and stroked Ray's face on the side that wasn't bandaged. Ray's other eye and most of his head were covered in sterile wraps. Sylvio put so much affection in the gesture that I was brought to tears. He usually avoided touching any of us with affection when the others could see. He was afraid for Ray, and worried, and angry.

"Take this off him," he ordered, gesturing to the breathing tube.

I looked at all the paraphernalia, dismayed. "I'm sorry. I don't know how to do it safely."

His anger spiked into frustrated rage. "I'll hurt him if I do it, and he needs my help *now*."

I asked the spirits to guide me once again. I didn't know if they ventured into modern medicine, but they moved my hands with purpose and soon it was done. Immediately, an alarm went off and was quickly silenced by the bubble of spirits around us.

Sylvio wasted no time. He gathered magic to himself, placed a hand on Ray's cheek again, and said, "Ray."

Ray's unbandaged eye flew open. I felt shock and confusion from him. Then Sylvio said "drink" and placed his bleeding wrist over Ray's mouth. Ray obeyed, and immediately became calm, totally absorbed in feeding. It was difficult for him. He was in a great deal of pain, but by the time he finished drinking, his breathing had evened out and his expression was peaceful.

The doors to the room were glass. I could see the nurses at their station. There were other nurses and guests walking to and from other rooms. The spirits kept them from looking our way.

I stepped up to Ray and touched him with both hands. I pulled at the spirits to heal him as they had done with Tim. I felt the spirits follow the path of Sylvio's blood and enhance the magic in it, stitching broken cells together, aligning bits of bone and sinew, washing away the bruises, and soothing his pain. When I was too tired to send anymore healing into him, I bent and kissed his forehead, and he fell immediately into a deep sleep.

The spirits dropped the bubble surrounding us. Immediately, the alarm went off again in the room and out in the nurse's station as well. The nurse passing in the hall rushed into the room.

"Can you replace it?" I said as soon as she entered. "He pulled it out."

More nurses responded to the alarm, as well as an intern. Sylvio and I stepped back and let them examine Ray. "Looks like he'll be okay without being intubated. He's much more stable now," the intern concluded. "Fasten his wrists as a precaution."

"What happened to him?" I asked the nurse while she checked the rest of the tubing attached to Ray, as well as the monitors, and the intern made notes on his chart.

"He was hit by a drunk driver. They ran a light. His vitals have been unsteady until now; he seems to be improving." She was confused for a moment and looked at me with a frown. "Who are you?"

"Family," I replied, and pushed the spirits to make her believe that. It wasn't entirely false.

"Well, he's not out of the woods yet, but he's doing much better." She smiled at us, all concern lost, and I was even more disturbed by that. Before they left, they fastened Ray's wrists to the bed frame with cuffs made of Velcro that had been hanging there.

Sylvio led me to one of the chairs, and I sank into it. All my energy had been spent. The relief that both Tim and Ray would probably be okay was sinking in. Sylvio settled into the chair next to mine, and we sat quietly, watching the monitors and listening to Ray take in deep, slow, healing breaths.

Twenty minutes later, my eyelids were drooping, and I had almost nodded off. Then I felt a stirring among the spirits and looked up to see the source of the spell on the area arrive down the hall. He was wearing blue scrubs and strode purposefully to the nurse's station, speaking rapidly while the nurse made notes on her computer. He turned and went to a room where two people waited, anxiously wringing their hands. He spoke briefly with them. They appeared to be relieved and hurried out the ICU doors. I didn't attempt to delve their feelings.

When he turned to go to the nurse's station again, he stopped and glanced at Ray's room, spotting us. His face, which was already dark, reddened even further. He turned and snarled at the nurses; his long white braid swung back and forth as he gesticulated. He was not a tall man and was clearly Native American.

He pushed magic toward the doors of the ICU until they opened, then snarled at the guards that were still standing outside the door where I had compelled them to stay. I dropped that spell so I could concentrate on this new threat. I could sense that my magic was weak after the night's events, which made me more worried than I might have been about this new threat. The man turned, and they all followed in his wake toward Ray's room.

We stood up, and Sylvio wrapped an arm around my waist. He backed us a couple steps away from Ray. He felt ready, calm. I was not. The witch approaching us had magic that was quite strong, about an equal with Micah, but his magic felt odd, different. He was more than human, but I couldn't tell quite what. I asked the spirits, who didn't seem concerned by the team converging on us, to help me see what he really was. Unfortunately, the spirits didn't have a clear picture or word they could give me in answer, other than "witch." I received images of water and earth in the form of clay. I had no idea what that meant.

"What is he?"

Sylvio had been intent on watching the group approaching us and felt a little startled by my question. *"I thought the spell on this place smelled like witch magic."*

"It is, but there's something more than that with this being. He's more than human."

They arrived at the doorway. The guards flanked the two nurses, with the doctor in the middle. He had been focused on Sylvio, but when he stepped through the door, he seemed to realize what I was. He blinked; his face went blank for an instant, devoid of any expression. I was once again sent an image of water, brown clay—hands molding a pot on a wheel was added. The spirits were so *frustrating* sometimes.

We were all waiting for him to speak. He seemed to realize that and cleared his throat. His black eyes took in Ray, the monitors, and the chart hanging on the bed. He took it off the hook and scanned the most recent notes. His eyes flicked to me, and then he turned to speak to the guards and nurses. "I was mistaken. These are not the people I thought were a danger to this patient. Please return to your posts and do *not* let anyone else in this room without my *express* permission."

The guards said "Yes, sir" at the same time the nurses said "Yes, Dr. Swallow." As they turned and left, he drew a small circle in the air, and I felt him add a shield around the room to block sound. The spell was witch magic, but with that same odd twist.

He watched them leave, then turned back to us, fixed Sylvio with a glare, and said, "More than one of my patients has been murdered by their owners. Vampires don't risk doctors knowing about them or their pets. Our lab results seem to disappear. We've learned to recognize the signs and analyze the blood before it goes anywhere. Your kind are parasites, living off the lives of others." He now had a strong European accent that did not match his appearance, and he did not sound like he had only moments before.

"Parasite, yes, a rather large one, too, and I must say I haven't heard it put quite that way before," Sylvio said, seeming unperturbed. "You're not far off the mark. Although I intend no harm toward Ray, no more than is required from one of mine." Sylvio's voice was silky, and his own accent stood out strong that time. "Tell me, what brought a nix to America, and where did you pick up how to perform a witch's spell?"

Nix? I wracked my brain for what I'd learned about them. Shapeshifters. Some said they were fae; some said they were not. All said they were associated with water. The images made sense now.

The nix's jaw became set in a stubborn line, and I thought it wasn't likely we'd learn the answer to Sylvio's question. Sylvio must have sensed the same thing, because he asked, "Who has been murdering their own pets? I'll pay them a visit." I found it fascinating how Sylvio could project menace with a few mere words.

The nix's face morphed again into surprise. "You must be the one they call Sylvio. I thought so, when I stepped in here and your pet wasn't dead. I've been shown a photo of you too, Rachel. I've been told you are trustworthy." He paused and looked at Ray. "We were plagued by vampires and werewolves in Mora. With the help of some white witches, it's not as pervasive now, but still quite frequent. If they had any connection to your kind, our patients would either disappear or die. The werewolves were less civilized but more honest." He turned and looked up at Sylvio again. "A colleague of mine knew I had experience with werewolves and asked me to help them here. She said things were different in America." He stopped and blinked, clearly wondering why he'd said so much.

"You don't even seem to use magic to do that," Sylvio commented.

"If you recall, I didn't know it had anything to do with magic. People tell me things. Where is Mora?"

"Sweden."

"What are Ray's chances for recovery, and what are his injuries?" Sylvio asked the doctor.

In answer, the nix handed Sylvio the chart then turned his attention to me. "I'm certain you know compulsion is not allowed. What you've done to the people here is punishable by death." He had no fear of Sylvio, which was quite unusual for someone who knew about him. He felt righteous and angry, but also undecided. He hadn't put conviction behind his words.

Before I could reply, Sylvio said, with his eyes still on the chart, "Actually, the edict states 'with evil intent.' Surely, helping Ray is not evil intent. Less harm was done to the staff here than would have been if I had been kept from coming to the aid of one of mine."

By the time he finished speaking, his eyes were boring into the nix. He set the clipboard on the bed next to Ray and kept his other arm around my waist. I felt him pull magic from the air. His sword, Muerte, coalesced in his palm and he looked past the blade to the nix. "Do not think I would allow harm to Rachel or to Ray. *Your* kind are even more indestructible than a vampire, but whatever body you reside in, your soul cannot escape this sword."

Unexpectedly, the nix smiled. "She spoke truth, then."

"Who?"

"Morgen. She said you protect those in the Americas and Brittania, most especially your own."

Sylvio relaxed a little bit. "Why haven't we met before?"

The nix hesitated, but then spoke truthfully. "I'm a half-breed, in more ways than one. I'm only seventy-three."

He looked like a man in his fifties, but I supposed he could look any age he chose.

"I didn't know nix could sire human children," Sylvio commented.

"It was quite a surprise for my father, too. Even more that I had any magic in me." His smile widened. "Call me Dr. Swallow." He offered his hand.

Muerte disappeared into the ether, and Sylvio took his hand.

The phone in my pocket rang, making me jump again. As I reached for it, I realized I was bone-tired. There had been far too much tension and fear, and I could see dawn approaching. It had been a *very* long night.

๖ Chapter 12 ൭
Sylvio: Niveus

When I strolled into the kitchen, the plump woman there dropped the pan of dough she was holding. At first, I didn't recognize her, although it was obvious she recognized me. It wasn't until she uttered a breathless "Master Sylvio" that I knew it was Meri.

When I'd last seen her, she was petite and pretty, with a voluptuous body and lips that were full and kissable. I actually like plump women. In fact, I like women in all their variety. When I was a young mortal man, what in the modern age is considered fat was the shape that appealed to most men. It was the other changes in Meri that were shocking to me, though, and not her weight.

Her face was wrinkled from age, and at that moment was a rosy pink shade from the heat of the hearth. The veins on the backs of her hands stood out. They were hands that were used to work, not petting her lord. She wore a full skirt and a long-sleeved blouse, which was cut modestly, hiding most of her fine bosom. As a young woman, she enjoyed the freedom I allowed my women to wear scant and alluring clothing when they were at the castle. Meri had put her hands up to her face when she spoke, and her cheeks were now dusted with flour.

I had to chuckle at her expression. I took her hands and held them out so I could get a better look at her. "My, you do look proper in that dress," I said. "Whatever brought that on?"

She blushed, turning her already rosy cheeks darker. It made the white flour stand out even more. "I, well, you've been gone so long, Master Sylvio. I . . . I'm married."

I caressed her left hand, whose fingers bore no rings, and raised an eyebrow.

She understood and stammered, "Oh, I take my rings off when

kneading the dough. They're over there on the sideboard."

I kissed the back of her hand then let her go. I strode to the nearest chair and sat down, leaning back with a boot on one knee. "I would imagine there have been many changes. Did you all presume I would never return?"

She bent and picked up the pan of dough, took it to the table in front of my chair, and dumped it out to begin kneading it. "We knew you weren't . . . gone." I could tell she had begun to say "dead" but caught herself, since of course I was already dead. There were many jokes that used to pass among my people at Niveus about me being dead but alive, some of them quite ribald. They were endlessly creative in their inventions as they twisted the meaning of words. Besides, they would have known if I died permanently—those who, like her, had been fully enthralled. When I grinned, she went on more boldly. "We had begun to believe you'd lost interest in Niveus."

Satisfied with that answer, I asked, "Do you have children?"

"Oh, yes, three girls." She beamed at the thought of them. "We were sure I was done bearing children, but three years ago God blessed us with a boy, too." Her hands stilled at what she said, and she cut a glance at me, and then out the window where the midday sun caused the trees to cast strong shadows on the flagstones. Reassured, she continued kneading the bread.

She'd said "God blessed" out of habit, but she believed the meaning of the words. If Meri was any indication, things had indeed changed at Niveus.

I said, "Why, that's splendid! Who is the father?"

She hesitated once more, then plunged on. "Jonathan Weaver." Another blush colored her cheeks.

I stared at her, astonished. Then, to be sure, I asked, "Robert Weaver's youngest son?"

Robert Weaver had been one of Father Clark's guards when he came calling. The man's faith drained my power from across the courtyard. I couldn't help it; I laughed until tears came and Meri smacked me across the back with her rolling pin, which made me laugh all the more. Curiosity about what would cause such laughter brought others to the door. Most of the faces I didn't recognize, but a few of them I did, and they knew me.

The news that I had returned spread like wildfire through the whole countryside. There were many changes. Gerald was now bent-backed with gnarled hands that bore bony lumps on them from long, hard use. His son Grant had assumed stewardship of the estate and was considered its lord by the other nobility. He earned his title fighting for the high king. I found that in my absence, Christianity had taken over Niveus as it had all of England. The pagan gods were almost forgotten, and the rituals were forbidden or were changed to suit the new religion.

Meri's oldest daughter was seventeen and was the mirror image of her mother at that age. In front of her husband, whose faith robbed me of much of my power, Meri said that if I made any covert moves toward her daughters, she would ensure I burned to a cinder. We all laughed, but she hadn't really been jesting.

On the third night, I convinced Cyneric to come back with me. They were holding a dance at the castle to celebrate my return and, though he still limped, his leg had nearly healed.

I chose for us to appear on the top of the northern guard tower next to the parapet. I'd discovered that the room below had been converted into a chapel. Two things made me think of it: I wanted to discover if Cyneric could enter the chapel as I could, and it was the best view of all of Niveus and the village beyond. We often stood there in the past and discussed what needed to be done to care for the property and its people.

Light was fading fast, and the torches had already been lit in the courtyard. Carriages could be seen coming up the long lane from the valley, their lanterns swaying, making the circles of light they cast dance. The clop of horses' hooves trotting and the murmur of cheerful voices and laughter came to our ears. With our keen eyesight, even in the dim light of late evening, we could make out the details of the surrounding fields, their edges lined with trees and stone walls. We could see a small herd of fine horses pacing along the walls and whinnying at the carriages passing by. I wondered absently if any of Lucifer's get wandered those fields.

After several minutes of silence, Cyneric said, "I had forgotten how beautiful it is. How simple and clean."

We spent a great deal of our time away prowling the cities, where it was an easy matter to find evil men or the dying to provide us a meal. Cities have their own appeal. They are complex and fascinating in their variety, and there is always someplace where things are happening, even when the dark night covers the earth.

It struck me then how sweet the air smelled. The scent of the trees, the fields freshly harvested, even the bare earth had its own scent. The air didn't carry soot in it or the stench of sewage, manure, and unwashed bodies that was so prevalent in the cities that you became immune to it. We stood and took it all in as the soft fall breeze brought a slight chill to our cheeks. Winter would blanket the land soon.

Eventually we were spotted, and voices shouted up at us, inviting us to join them. Cyneric could not enter the chapel, which saddened me, so we descended the stone stairs that curved along the side of the tower.

When we opened the doors to step into the castle interior, we were met by several of those we had known before. A cacophony of sound came from the ballroom below. Those who gathered to greet us stood back, unsure about approaching us.

Gerald was closest. Cyneric strode past me and embraced his old friend, and the small moment of uncertainty passed. Hands slapped our backs and shook our hands, and I had to take a moment to compose myself. I hadn't felt such joy in many years, and their scent, their blood, and the life it carried was almost too much. I stayed by Cyneric's side, aware that this was even more difficult for him than it was for me. I had ensured that we fed deeply before coming, so our need was present but not overpowering. Still, the combination of so many warm human bodies was a heady brew.

They led us down the sweeping stairway, asking endless questions as we descended to the base. They were particularly curious about Cyneric's limp. They knew of our strength and were intrigued that we could be hurt. Most of them believed we were impervious to any sort of lasting injury. When Cyneric answered their inquiries by stating quite truthfully that a demon tried to tear it off, they all stopped and stared, and silence descended on the little group.

In a lighthearted way that was not false, I said, "If you ever visit Egypt, stay away from the tombs. They're haunted by things even more frightening than us."

Gerald put a hand on the porter walking by who held a tray full of wine glasses. He handed us both a glass, and the others who didn't have one already took one. Grinning, he said, "A toast to your continued good health!"

They all shouted "Huzzah!"

Our little group spread out onto the main floor. We danced and partied until well past midnight. Even Cyneric took a turn now and then, sore leg or not. When he wasn't dancing, he was surrounded by old friends and some new curious onlookers, most of them women who were irresistibly drawn to both of us.

Gerald stayed at Cyneric's side nearly the whole time. His wife, as well as many of the children on the estate, had died from a measles outbreak five years before. Meri hadn't said it, but two of her children, those between the daughters she mentioned and the boy that clung to her skirt at the start of the evening, had died as well. Disease was an ever-present danger, and though we were always aware of it since many of our victims were those dying of such a fate, I had forgotten that for humans, a great many children did not live to become even young adults.

The villagers departed before midnight. It was considered unsafe and improper to stay up past then. There were chores to do in the morning. I could tell that this party was quite unusual for those at Niveus as well. When I resided there, the castle had been a hive of activity, day and night. They lived as normal humans now and slept the nights away.

As often seems to happen to me after a party, I was feeling melancholy. We said our goodbyes, and when Meri came and gave me a chaste kiss on the cheek, I felt despair creep in on me. I reached out and shook her husband's hand and wondered if my legs would hold me up. The aura of faith, of goodness, that enveloped him was so very powerful. I was glad for Meri and felt sorry for myself.

Cyneric stood behind my shoulder and bowed to Jonathan. He could not even touch the man. Although it appeared Jonathan was unaware of his power over us, I could see in Meri's eyes that she understood, and Gerald had seen it too. He clapped Cyneric on the shoulder and led him away, saying something about the improvements he'd made at the forge. I turned to trail after them, but Lini was suddenly at my side.

Age had crept up on her, as well. She always was tall and strong, beautiful in her own way, but not a woman who would catch the eye of most men. She had helped me train the horses and shared a life at the castle with Meri and the other women when I was there. I discovered that she had married Arthur, who had been a stable hand who earned the title of horse master. He also served the village as a constable and died while chasing bandits three years previously.

Lini placed a hand on my arm and asked me the question with her eyes, sure I would not want her. But to me, she was beautiful. The lines in her tanned face enhanced her strong character. Her long brown hair, which I knew she considered plain, was shot with gray and lay about her shoulders and almost to her slim hips. Her hands told a story of their own. They were broad and strong, with small scars here and there. They were hands that had been used to make a difference, to create, and to teach.

I discovered that, at Gerald's insistence, my rooms had been kept as they were when I left. Servants polished and swept, but they remained unused. I took Lini's hand and led her there, where we enjoyed the silk sheets, soft pillows, and each other until we drifted into blissful sleep. Even when living at Niveus, I rarely allowed myself to do that.

When I woke in the morning, sunlight streamed through the windows, and Lini was propped on one elbow, studying my face. I wondered what she saw there. I pulled her lips to mine and embraced her again, and we played with each other for quite some time. I even drank a little, and memories of the lust it brought flooded her mind. I hadn't known one time would capture her mind again. She was not a frail woman. She had a strong will and would be able to carry on without my assistance if I didn't feed from her too often.

There was a chill in the room, so I started a fire and sent for food to be brought up for her. When she had eaten and dressed, she took me out to the stables. I was not surprised to find they were well maintained, and Niveus retained its reputation for producing exceptional war horses. We met her sons there. Both were young men who favored their mother in looks more than their father. They eyed me with disfavor; they knew where their mother had spent the night. She told them without an ounce of shame that it was not their business to judge and to treat me with the respect I deserved as their lord.

The boys were separating the weanlings from their mothers, and the stable was a cacophony of plaintive whinnies. As I asked them questions, their dislike of me lessened somewhat, although it didn't go away entirely. I sensed that Lini was pleased rather than annoyed with their protectiveness of her.

In the late afternoon, a carriage arrived. It was flanked by riders in livery that indicated they came from St. Philips' cathedral, not the village as I assumed at first. Father Clark himself stepped out of the carriage. Like Gerald, his back was slightly bent, his movements stiff, and his face lined with age.

The sun was getting low in the sky, but it still shone brightly. Father Clark looked up at it and then at me and smiled. An angelic light surrounded him, and weakness swept over me. If anything, his faith and the power that came with it was even stronger than it was those many years before. The combination of his presence and that of his guards, who were men of faith as well, was overwhelming. I found that, even facing the demon Ammit, I had not felt such unease. Among humans, I counted on my physical power and my ability to control them if need be. If they wished, these men could destroy me with ease. I would not even have the strength to teleport to safety. It was an effort to keep that knowledge from showing.

I glanced up at the sun myself, then returned his smile. "Father

Clark, I'm glad to see the people in this area still have you to preside over their health and their souls."

His chuckle was raspy but genuine. "And I'm glad to witness that you still walk in the light."

"I strive not to do anything to compromise that gift. What brings you here?"

"I'm told one of my flock has returned with you." He leaned on his cane and pinned me with his clear blue eyes.

"Please, come sit under the trees." I gestured to the same spot where we had our brief meeting those many years before.

Gerald, Grant, and I had been discussing plans for the evening when Father Clark arrived. Gerald approached and said, "Greetings, Father. I'll have drinks brought out for us." At a look from him, Grant shouted an order and quickly strode away. Gerald accompanied me as I took my place at the end of the long table, where my back was to the wall and I could keep all of them in sight.

Father Clark's guards dismounted and gave their reins to the stable hands waiting to take them. They all walked to the small grove and sat down. The old wooden table had been replaced with stone and was much larger than the one that used to stand there, as were the trees. Under the shade of their boughs, the stone was cold. The breeze, which the courtyard wall could not block entirely, brought a chill.

We had settled on the benches when Grant returned with a servant carrying a steaming pot of berry juice as well as some wine, cheese, and fruit. The servant was dismissed, and Grant took a seat next to his father and me.

In answer to Father Clark's earlier question, I said, "Yes, Cyneric has come with me. I've been showing him some of the wonders made by man and by nature."

"Truly! That is good to hear. I would like to speak with him. It has been many years, after all. Bits of the stories the two of you told the villagers last night have already reached my ears. Is he well, then? Someone told me he was injured."

"Yes, he's quite well. His leg was broken but has nearly healed. Alas, however, he would not be able to speak with you while the sun shines. At least not yet, although I do hold some hope for him if it's possible for such a gift to be granted to more than one of my kind." I surmised that was why they came when they did: to see if Cyneric was about during the day.

Father Clark's guards stirred at my answer but settled when he gave them a quelling look. He boldly asked, "Are the people here or those in the village in danger from him or from you?"

I appreciated his frank honesty. "No more than they ever were."

He absorbed that answer while he sipped some juice, then asked, "Do you intend to take up your former place here?"

Did I? I thought of the pleasure of lying with Lini, the gracious greeting we received, the comfort and joy that enveloped Niveus once again. I realized as I considered those things that if we stayed, fear would creep in. I had seen it in the eyes of those who had known us before, an uncertainty they could not hide although they were truly glad to see us. I could sense that Gerald and Grant were sitting quite tensely at either side of me, waiting with bated breath for my answer.

I met Father Clark's eyes and said, "No, we're only visiting."

I should have directed my gaze elsewhere. He saw the pain that answer caused me and understood it all, and behind his eyes, I saw a realization he had not come to when we met those many years before. He felt pity for me, for my fate. It angered me, and he perceived that too. Neither Grant nor Gerald could completely disguise their relief as they let out a sigh.

Conversation was light and pointless after that. It wasn't long before they took their leave and I watched their carriage depart down the long lane, feeling a sadness and loss that made me as weary as any old human. My strength returned gradually as the carriage pulled away. I wondered, if they had known the depth of their power over me, would Father Clark have ordered his men to murder me? Would they have felt justified in that act to prevent me from killing anymore? Would the act taint their souls? Or would they be even more blessed than they already were once they destroyed a demonic monster?

Grant and Gerald were standing a little behind me, sensing that I needed a moment. When I turned toward them, I couldn't help doubting them, too. Even as frail humans, they could have easily overpowered me only moments before. I shook my head to chase such thoughts away.

Father Clark's carriage had only passed the gates down in the valley when I felt Cyneric awaken. I went to find him. He had hidden himself out in the woods, in one of the cellars we used to store goods at the north end of the property. He learned caution from me and did not divulge his resting places to anyone other than me. He'd taken a blanket with him to protect his clothes, so he still looked fairly presentable.

We walked in silence up the hill and across the fields. He could perceive my mood. Finally, he asked what was troubling me. I told him of Father Clark's visit and my decision, and he understood perhaps more than anyone else could.

We told them we'd stay for a fortnight. Only eight days later, a messenger came that changed our plans. We learned that Ragna and Seamas had moved away. The villagers never lost their suspicions about Ragna and did not welcome her, so Gerald gave them funds to go elsewhere. They moved to Amesbury, where it was rumored Ragna had gained renown as a healer.

The messenger's horse had been ridden hard, and the man was nearly as spent as his horse. He surprised me when he handed me the parcel he took from his saddle bags. It contained a short, simple note from Seamas.

In bold, black writing, the note said: *Sylvio, word has come to me that you have returned to Niveus. If you can, meet me at the southern end of the standing stones at Amesbury on All Hallow's Eve.*

The standing stones. Surely Ragna would have told him that the stones were a conduit for magical power. I had visited Amesbury out of curiosity many years before. It was a dangerous place for a creature of the night to wander. The old wizards had been strong so that even these many centuries hence, the protection they wove on those places did not welcome creatures such as I.

I smiled, folded the little note, and handed it to Cyneric, who also perceived that the lack of a formal greeting or any other cordial sentences conveyed a sense of urgency even more than the tired horse and its rider.

The celebrations beginning on All Hallow's Day and continuing with Allhallowtide were only two days hence.

"Come, Cyneric, we must prepare to leave."

ဆ Chapter 13 ෮
High Society

Tim was allowed to go home with Ramon the day after he was taken to the hospital. He wasn't ready to leave physically, but everyone felt it was best if he did. Caleb helped him escape the throng of reporters by taking him through the morgue and out a back entrance.

Ray was moved out of ICU the following day, but Dr. Swallow refused to release him for another week. He'd been hit on the driver's side, and his ribs were all broken or cracked on that side. One punctured his lung. His spleen was bruised badly enough that they removed a portion of it.

Nevertheless, Ray recovered quickly. By the end of the week, he was bored even with us hanging out in his room all day. Two of us stayed with him, taking turns 'round the clock. The local alpha put us up in their pack house so we could be near the hospital. Ray and the rest of us spent another week there until Sylvio felt it was safe to teleport him home. The rest of us drove down to Willard.

When we got home, we were all grateful to be back in Sylvio's house. It was our sanctuary. Staying in Cody made us keenly aware that we did not belong in the regular world—not while we were Sylvio's people.

Once Tim returned home, he began to sleep in wolf form to escape the nightmares that plagued him. Shena and Eric would shift into their wolf form to keep him company. I'd been able to soothe him in the beginning, but since the night the spirits changed Shena and Eric from pups to something much more, I hadn't been able to help him as much. Being captured and put in a cell had brought back old memories. Tim's nightmares weren't imagination; they were reality replayed in vivid detail. His memory was exceptional, which was not a blessing for a man with his past.

Ramon stayed for a few days to help him cope. He could feel the imbalance in Tim. Helping unstable werewolves was a specialty of Ramon's. But Tim's magic was greater even than his, and he wasn't able to soothe him as much as he could other werewolves. If the problem had to do with controlling his wolf, Ramon may have been able to do more. However, the problem wasn't his wolf. It was life as a human that Tim had trouble with.

I called Tim's psychiatrist, Dr. Ross, to see if he could help out. When I told him what was going on, he said he was planning to call me anyway. Curious, I asked, "What did you want to call me about, Ross?"

At Ross's suggestion, we left the title "doctor" off his name when speaking to him. Neither Tim nor Kelly were fond of doctors. It was best not to remind them that medical doctors and psychiatrists had the same title.

"I'd like to run an idea past you for your input," Ross said.

"My input?"

"Yes. I'm thinking a change of scenery and someone to help out might do Tim some good."

"Oh?" Of course it would. I was wishing I had called him earlier.

"I had an interesting visit from Dr. Oliver Hastings. He's a colleague of mine. Do you remember Darin, the one who survived Dr. Sabin's lab along with Kelly and Tim?"

"Yes. Is he still not talking?"

"No, but there have been some interesting developments since the director of the estate and the head nurse retired."

Dr. Sabin captured a vampire and a werewolf and injected their cells into the children he used for his experiments. What he created were creatures like Tim and Kelly—a mix of human, werewolf, and vampire. In addition, Tim was already born a witch. As with all hybrids, he was stronger from being a mix. Kelly was also a werewolf and had been given some traits of a vampire. Darin had not changed quite as much as they had, but I sensed from the other two that he was not a normal human, either. Tim helped them escape and tried rescuing more, but only the three of them made it out of the lab. Darin hadn't spoken since the rescue and didn't interact with people.

In his earlier visit, Ross told me that Darin would sit for hours, not moving, then suddenly he'd be busy at his computer. He took care of himself as well, but he wouldn't respond when other people were near. If they tried to engage him, he sat or stood and stared without any reaction at all.

The medical care for those who survived Dr. Sabin's lab and stable was paid for by the British government. Darin lived on an estate rather than in an institution. It was Dr. Sabin's family property. The doctor's assets were seized when it was discovered what he had been doing. There were other survivors from what Dr. Sabin called his "stable"— kids he rented out to wealthy pedophiles. His two daughters had managed the stable. They had orders to kill the kids if they were discovered by the authorities. When the fire broke out in the lab and it was clear the stable would be found, they shot all but four of the twelve kids there at the time, then shot each other.

I'd gotten to know Ross a bit when he came the last time to help Tim out. We spent a lot of time sitting in Tim's room waiting for him to come out of the stupor he'd fallen into. Ross was easy to talk to. It wasn't surprising that he was an excellent psychiatrist.

"What kind of developments?" I inquired.

"Turns out Darin arranged things to suit himself, rather than the other way around. If something happened he didn't like, he'd tear his room apart, especially when he needed a doctor's care."

"I'll bet he feels the same way about doctors as Tim does."

Tim's emotions were often in turmoil, but he rarely felt afraid— unless a doctor was near. I swear he can smell one a mile away. Tim and Kelly visited Darin once they found out where he was, but he did not respond to their presence either.

"It certainly appears that way," Ross agreed. "The interesting thing is, when he destroys his room, he doesn't touch his computer or his backup files. He's written several stories. The whole staff has read them and say they are excellent."

I couldn't help grinning. "So, he's only pretending to lose it?"

"Exactly. Oliver is a smart man, and unconventional. He took over the estate about two months ago and reviewed all the cases there. He discovered they would put tranquilizers in Darin's food when they needed to perform any sort of medical procedure." Ross waited to see what I thought of that.

"No wonder Darin was pissed." It made me angry to hear it.

"And justifiably so," Ross confirmed. "Not long after Oliver took over, they discovered Darin had a toothache, so Oliver went to his room. He said he chose to go talk to Darin when he was active and typing on his computer. The staff said he seemed more aware when he was moving and not simply sitting. He told Darin they needed to take care of his bad tooth, but that it would cost too much money to replace things when they get destroyed. He said the pills to put him to sleep would be brought with his breakfast. Then he hung a punching bag in the room and told him he was welcome to do whatever he wanted with the bag, but if he broke other things, his computer would be taken away."

"What happened?"

"He hit the bag."

"Cool. So he might not talk, but he is listening."

"Right. Oliver called me to find out if Tim and Kelly would be willing to see Darin again and maybe get him to respond."

"I know the answer to that will be yes. I'm sure you do, too. Why are you running this by me first?"

"I think it would be best if you went with to help Tim handle his emotions. I've also been asked to extend an invitation to Tim to attend a polo match with me, and you could run interference with the people there. People are always more curious than is healthy when it comes to anything to do with the royal family."

"What about the twins?"

"I think they should stay home for now, don't you think?"

It was decided. When I told Tim the plan, he was all for it. I told him Sylvio's people and Ramon would check on the twins while we were away. Tim wasn't too keen on leaving them, but they assured him they would be okay. Sylvio said he'd fly us over in his Learjet. He had been helping Tim get his pilot's license, and they both jumped at any excuse to fly.

A couple of days before we left, I called Suzette, feeling a little panicked. I had *no* idea what to wear to a polo match if members of the royal family would be attending. She lived in Antone's New York apartment and had taken me shopping in December, so I had some very nice clothes. She, of course, remembered what was in my wardrobe better than I did, and gave me recommendations. I thanked her profusely and packed up.

The afternoon we arrived in London, Kelly and Marta joined us. When Sylvio offered to get us a room, Ross said he was sure he could find us enough space at his place. His place turned out to be a sprawling estate. The massive brick mansion commanded the end of a long tree-lined drive. He had inherited the property and explained when we arrived that the north wing was now used as a bed and breakfast.

Kelly was a rather intense man, polite and personable but quiet. He was tall and ruggedly handsome. He always wore black and gave the air of someone dangerous but trustworthy. His business, in addition to hunting criminals and their victims, was security. I was sure his mere presence gave his clients confidence in his ability to protect them. The steady, focused feeling I'd get from Tim when he was hunting seemed to be Kelly's mood nearly always.

He and Marta were a calming influence on Tim. By the time we decided to turn in for the night, Tim was more relaxed than he'd been in months. Kelly proposed they change into their wolf form and sleep in front of the fireplace. Tim agreed, so Marta and I slept on the plush couches while the two wolves curled up next to each other.

Kelly's wolf form was larger than Tim's, black with silver highlights. He wrapped himself around Tim and lay his head on Tim's shoulder. Tim didn't even dream that night, spared from the nightmares that usually plagued him.

$$\wp \; \wp$$

The Beaufort polo club was beautiful. I had expected the sweeping lawns, aged trees, and equally aged buildings, but the crisp, white canvas pavilions were somewhat of a surprise. There was enough space that we were not crowded, and we made our way to our assigned table. We arrived not long before the first chukker. Ross didn't take us around to mingle until the second one was over.

He led us on a tour of the grounds and explained the history of the place so that it seemed only by chance when we came upon the Windsors. As we approached, they caught sight of Tim and smiles lit both their faces.

"John, how are you?" Lady Windsor kissed Tim on both cheeks with genuine warmth, then Lord Windsor shook his hand with both of his, saying, "So good to see you, old boy."

I shouldn't have been surprised that they would be using Tim's middle name. The name Tim was not a difficult intellectual leap to "Sir Timothy."

Ross introduced the rest of us, and we chatted amicably about polo horses in general until the next chukker began. They invited us to stay with them to watch the remainder of the match.

The Windsors and their entourage were surprisingly easy to get along with. We discussed the polo horses and which breeds were best suited for that. Then I found that Lady Windsor had learned to ride after Tim rescued them and would be competing soon in her first horse trials. I'm not good at small talk, but that subject was an easy one to delve into.

After the fifth chukker, Lady Windsor asked if we'd like to join her and her husband while they went to mingle at the appetizer tent. It was an entire tent filled with tables for different categories of food and drink. We followed in the Windsors' wake while they went to the table that held seafood. There was an exquisite ice carving of a mermaid as the centerpiece.

Tim was walking beside me, and he whispered, "Do you think Undine would be pleased with that representation?"

We had both seen Undine, the embodiment of the water spirits, not long before. She appeared more like a sea serpent that time, not human in any way. Although, it was generally agreed that the stories of mermaids were either Undine herself or other water spirits with enough power to take on the shape of a human body.

I studied the ice mermaid a little closer. "Well, she certainly is pretty. I think Undine would be pleased to be represented that way."

Tim chuckled, and we each picked up a plate then hesitated, looking at all the food. There were too many choices. The Windsors had caught our exchange, and Lord Windsor studied the sculpture with interest for a moment. Tim asked Lady Windsor what she thought of our conclusion. She laughed and gave him an eyeroll. I moved forward with Lord Windsor.

In front of me, a burly man was filling his small plate with shrimp. He distracted me because he was one of those people who carry a black cloud around with them. His wife stood beside him. She caught my eye and gave me a fake smile. I returned an equal smile.

The man raised his head and looked past me as if I didn't exist. He said to Lord Windsor, "Who is this young man chatting up your wife?" He had an accent that made me think of Sean Connery, and I wondered if he was Scottish.

Lord Windsor turned to gesture to Tim and said amicably, "John, I'd like to introduce you to Sir Gordon."

Tim stepped to the side around Lady Windsor and began to reach out to take the man's hand. Sir Gordon's feelings were odd. I sensed humor with a smug undertone, topped with maliciousness. I didn't have any time to puzzle that out. The spirits coalesced around me.

When the two men's eyes met, Tim's feelings flashed into an explosion of surprise, boiling rage, then deadly calm. Without hesitation, Tim hit Sir Gordon's face so hard and fast that the heavy man flew backward several feet. His cheek and nose were instantly a bloody pulp.

His wife let out a scream and ran to her husband. She sank to her knees beside him as he lay flat out and unconscious on the ground. Then she turned to glare at Tim. All eyes followed hers. "How dare you strike my husband!" she snarled.

In a growl that was deep and menacing, Tim replied, "That man is vindictive and cruel. He *enjoys* torturing children."

The crowd around the pavilion went still. The buzz of polite conversation stopped.

Tim began to scan the people, his eyes burning bright gold—wolf eyes. He shook from the effort he was expending to not transform then and there. "How many of you *know* what he is and have done *nothing*?"

Some of them could not hide the truth in their eyes. They all stared at the scene with the same shocked faces, eyes wide and mouths open but not saying a word, stunned into silence.

"You can't accuse him of such a thing!" the man's wife hissed, indignant.

I had a moment to consider—how did she know what "thing" Tim meant if she didn't already know the man was guilty?

"Don't pretend you don't know what he is!" Tim snarled. "What you care about is status and the image you present to the world. He gets away with it because such things are not talked about in polite society, and certainly not in present company. I don't *care* what titles he was born with. What matters is who he is as a person, and that man is *evil*. He cares only for his own pleasure, no matter what the cost is for those he persecutes."

Tim scanned the crowd again. Many were looking quite chagrined and cast their eyes down. That was best; meeting his eyes at that moment might be courting death. Even Sir Gordon's wife could not look him in the face anymore. She began to scan the crowd herself and found that they knew truth when they heard it. She paled and looked down at her husband. I saw the realization that the fantasy they had woven as people worthy of high social standing had all crumbled.

Kelly materialized at Tim's side with Marta beside him. Kelly looked down at the man and his hands clenched into white-knuckled fists. His feelings were not a wild mix of emotion like Tim's. He set off alarm bells in me. While Tim was fire, with passion behind his rage, Kelly was ice. I got the sense he was even more deadly in his pursuit of justice than Tim. I pushed the spirits to calm them both.

Tim turned to Lady Windsor and said, "I'll be going now." His voice was amazingly steady given the depth of rage I sensed in him.

She touched his arm and looked at him with concern etched on her face, not afraid to meet his eyes. "I understand," she said. "It's okay." She reached up and placed her palm on his cheek. I was impressed by her bravery and compassion. She knew what his golden eyes meant.

Kelly looked from Sir Gordon to his wife, who still crouched beside him, and her face drained of color. Terrified, she fainted dead away.

Marta grasped Kelly's arm. He twitched and turned slightly so I could see his face. His irises glowed with an eerie golden light. Tim's aura was always an odd mix of magic. It was rarely focused on any one thing unless he was in his wolf form. I had assumed Kelly and Tim would be the same. I was wrong. Kelly did not fear the wolf inside him or the power he held as a werewolf, nor the part of him that was vampire. He was truly in harmony with his whole being. Menace radiated from him, but it was entirely under control. His eyes burned with the presence of his wolf because he allowed them to, not because he had no choice. He didn't need my help to calm him. When he scanned the crowd, every one of them dropped their eyes. Some even took an involuntary step back and bowed their heads.

At that moment, several men in tailored business suits that were nevertheless cut a little too large came forward. They were the Windsor's bodyguards. When their eyes met those of Kelly and Tim, they stopped in their tracks. Low murmurs had begun among the crowd until the bodyguards appeared. Now silence fell, and several seconds ticked by.

Lord Windsor cleared his throat and said, "These gentlemen are our guests. They are free to go."

Lady Windsor turned to me. Her own eyes held resolve, as did her husband's. "You take care of John," she commanded, "and Kelly."

"I certainly will, my lady," I promised.

For a brief moment, her eyes held appreciation and relief. Then she was in command again. I felt sorrow and distress from the Windsors, but not embarrassment. They went up even more in my estimation. They believed Tim and would side with him no matter what the consequences.

"Nigel will take you wherever you need to go," she added.

Nigel was apparently one of their security detail. He was standing quite near us, a hand in his jacket, ready to protect his charges if need be. He felt startled when she said that, but his face did not change. "Yes, ma'am," he said, holding out his free hand to show us the direction to go, and followed us across the lawn and under the trees that lined the parking area. Ross stayed behind to smooth things over.

The next day, charges were brought against Tim for assault. Tim went to the police station to give a statement. He was advised not to leave the country until the matter was settled. The day after that, Sir Gordon and his wife committed suicide. That very afternoon, the couple's children dropped the charges. Having more honor than their parents, they did not dispute the charges Tim made against their father. That act, more than any other, cemented the belief in those who had been there, and the press who now mobbed Sir Gordon's estate, that Tim's accusations were true. I wondered what kind of hell Sir Gordon's children had lived through.

The news about the suicide reached us as we were leaving Ross's house to visit Darin. I felt both relief and regret from Tim and Kelly. The regret was not that the two had died, but that they hadn't been the ones to mete out justice. All in all, they were in a surprisingly pleasant and calm mood as we drove to Dr. Sabin's former estate.

The estate was rambling and peaceful, with sweeping green lawns bordered by trees and aged brick buildings. The staff called the homes the tenants lived in "cottages" although they were nice-sized houses. We were informed that three patients lived in Darin's cottage with him, and a nurse was always in attendance in each residence.

As we stepped into the area that served as Darin's living room, he was sitting in a chair facing a TV. His appearance was a bit of a surprise to me. He was not tall and handsome like Tim and Kelly. He wasn't homely, either, just ordinary. He had sandy-brown hair, gray eyes, and skin that was too pale. It was obvious he didn't spend time outdoors. He wasn't overweight, but his body was soft. He was sitting in a chair staring blankly at the TV and did not turn to acknowledge that anyone else was there.

I followed the rest of them through the doorway and scanned the feelings in the room, which had become a habit by then. I stopped in place, stunned. Darin was not a werewolf; not a vampire, either. An odd kind of magic pervaded the entire room. It felt a bit like Dr. Swallow— fae magic. I shut the door and caught Tim and Kelly cutting a glance at me. I folded my arms and shot them a glare. "Was he born this way, or was he made?" I asked. I didn't like that they had kept me in the dark.

Both Ross and Oliver turned and looked at me, puzzled. Tim and Kelly appeared contrite. Silence stretched as both doctors caught that they were mere observers in this scene. It was Tim who was brave enough to answer. "He's yet another abomination of Dr. Sabin's."

"Well, where is the real Darin?"

They blinked at me, showing genuine surprise. I scanned all their faces and discovered Ross and Oliver were clueless as well. Tim and Kelly didn't seem to know the whole truth either, so they hadn't held back as much as I thought they had when I first delved Darin's feelings.

Ross cleared his throat and ventured to ask, "What do you mean?"

"That body is an empty shell. There's no person in it." More blinks, from all of them. I asked Tim and Kelly, "Did you know he could do that?"

They exchanged glances, and slowly I could see things fall into place. It was clear then that they had not known exactly what Darin could do, but they had known part of it. Slow smiles crept onto their faces.

"*Putain! Nous sommes fous,*" Kelly exclaimed, a wide grin on his face now. Marta put a hand over her mouth and clicked her tongue at him in disapproval.

Tim began to chuckle. Ross and Oliver were looking at each of our faces, trying to figure out what was going on. It appeared Oliver knew French because he asked Kelly, "What do you mean we're fools?"

Kelly said, "I'm sorry, but he hasn't been stuck here all these years after all."

I decided to rescue Oliver. "Welcome to our world . . . Oliver." I caught myself before I called him Dr. Hastings. "Magic, that's what Kelly means. Darin is able to leave his body behind and go elsewhere."

He eyed us all suspiciously, then asked me, "How can you know that? I was told you've never even seen him before."

"I'm a witch. My particular gift is reading feelings. Souls, really. The essence of a person. What's sitting over there is only a body. There is no spirit being in it."

"Spirit being? What do you mean by that?" Ross asked.

I hesitated, trying to think of how to put it into words. "Our mortal body is only a shell. We use it to live in this world. Our essence, the part of us that is eternal, is our spirit being. It is more than a soul. It is a combination of our soul and the energy we are made of. The stuff of stars." That explanation was the preface to the section about spirit beings in both my and Micah's grimoire.

There was a lively discussion about that for a few minutes. Oliver was having a difficult time absorbing the news at all. Ross was simply bemused and went to stand in front of Darin, studying the body as though he were in a museum looking at a manikin. Tim and Kelly drilled me about how to sense when a spirit being was missing from a body. They could scent it when a spirit had moved on and all that was left was the corpse. They could not sense that Darin wasn't there. His body was clearly alive and breathing. They could hear his heartbeat.

I suggested they see if they could smell the difference when Darin came back. We all picked a spot to settle and wait for Darin to return. While we sat, we filled Oliver in about magic. I confessed I had heard of astral projection but didn't know it could be done with magic. I assured all of them that I would know when Darin's spirit being returned.

It took three hours. Tim and Kelly began to wander the room restlessly until Oliver suggested they read some of Darin's stories. They were soon absorbed in that, staring at the computer screen while the two doctors discussed other things. Marta and I watched TV, and I asked her questions about her life with Kelly.

I felt Darin's presence come through the window and hover near the ceiling. The spirits welcomed him, and I caught his surprise. Out loud, I said, "We've been waiting for you, Darin. I'm Rachel, but I'm the only one who can sense your presence while you're like you are now. How about joining your body and saying hello to long lost friends? Kelly and Tim have come to see you."

Everyone had frozen in place when I began to speak. Their eyes followed mine to the spot above the window. I felt Darin's indecision and pushed the spirits to get him to have faith in the truth of my words. Thirty very long seconds ticked by while we waited.

He moved slowly from the window and along the wall, keeping himself well away from me. He hesitated when he was at the far side of the room very near to where Ross stood by his body. I sent calm and peace out into the room and willed the spirits to help him feel safe.

I felt his spirit travel next to his body and hover there for a moment. Then his spirit being slowly sank down through the top of his head and into his limbs until I could no longer distinguish it from the mortal body he'd rejoined. He took two very long deep breaths, blinking rapidly. Slowly, he turned his head and stared at me.

"Hi, Darin, that's a pretty fancy bit of magic you can do." I was careful to remain where I was. I could feel his confusion and fear about being found out. "Tim and Kelly are eager to talk to you. They've missed their friend."

Moving slowly, Tim picked up the chair he had been sitting in and set it down so he was directly in front of Darin. He was careful not to crowd too close. "It's time to get on with living, Darin. Why let Dr. Sabin take even more of your life than he already has?"

"*J'eccepte*," Kelly said, also moving closer.

Darin blinked some more and licked his lips. His eyes kept traveling from Tim to Kelly and back again. He rubbed his palms on his knees and swallowed. In a voice that had obviously been unused in a very long time, Darin said, "Are you . . . real?"

It wasn't long before the tears were flowing from all of us, even Kelly.

ಹಿ Chapter 14 ಲ
The Cat's Out of the Bag

It was a troll that did it. No one in the preternatural community had predicted that. Everyone assumed it would be a witch caught performing a spell that couldn't be explained away. There had also been speculation that a werewolf would reveal themselves, having lost control. There was a werewolf involved, and a witch, but the troll was the star of the show.

Instant streaming from dozens of cameras was too much for magic to conceal. Hundreds shared their posts before the videos became corrupted. Later, when all the film footage was ruined, making it impossible to view what had happened, it cemented the idea that what the hundreds who witnessed it in person, and the millions who watched it unfold online, was real. After all, only Hollywood could have pulled off such a stunt, and they would certainly view the film as a golden ticket and keep it safe.

It started on a fine sunny Saturday morning. A tour boat was cruising under the Brooklyn Bridge. The platform on top of the boat was filled to capacity with over a hundred passengers. The ship had cleared the bridge on its way to Lady Liberty when a passenger cruiser going the other way suddenly veered out of control and slammed into the bow of the larger ship. Moments later, there was a massive explosion that tore the front quarter of the tourist ship off.

The troll had been strolling along the walkway in the center of the bridge. The explosion captured everyone's attention, so the only video of the troll was from a distance. It showed him climbing the cables and steel to the top of the bridge, growing larger by the second until, when he leapt across from the center to the side and then into thin air, he was the size of King Kong. The resemblance ended there. He seemed to be made of rock. His skin was mainly white with streaks of other colors throughout, like marble, and it was all in motion, all the time. His parts kept rearranging.

Several cameras caught the immense splash he made as he dove into the river. Only a few seconds had gone by, but the boat was rapidly sinking. The deck had been covered in simple folding chairs. Now a pile of chairs and people slid toward the front of the sinking ship. The ship's cabin was keeping the people from falling into the river, but if the deck tilted much more, they would topple over.

Then the boat began to rise, seemingly of its own accord, until the head and shoulders of the troll broke the water where the bow had been. His head was nearly as wide as the boat by then. He headed for Brooklyn Park. The boat lifted and dropped a few feet with each step he took. As he neared the shore, he turned the boat around and pushed its broken bow up onto the bank. When the boat was wedged into the earth and rock so it wouldn't tip sideways and toss people overboard, he let go of it and walked out of the water, shrinking as he went. By the time he stepped onto dry land, he looked like a handsome young man with a bodybuilder physique. Not a thread of clothing had survived his transformation.

Cameras caught another phenomenon. A second body followed the troll into the river from the bridge. The miniscule splash he made in comparison to the troll's was masked by the waves. With astonishing speed, the creature could be seen swimming toward the shredded bow of the ship. It looked like a man. As the bow was lifted from the water, he climbed up the twisted remains like a squirrel and disappeared into the gaping hole.

The cameras that were aimed at that part of the ship caught the flames that the water had been unable to quench. Soon, the man reemerged carrying two bodies. They were on fire, and the man's clothes were burning too. As soon as the bow crunched into the shore and came to a stop, he leapt over the mountain of rock, cement, dirt, and ship remains and dashed with his burdens up onto the grass berm.

A witch was among those on the shore. She could be seen in the background, wand in hand and performing some strange gyrations with her arms. Then she pointed her wand at them and shouted a command. A blast of air and something more shot at the man and the people he held under each arm. The fire was quenched immediately, and all three were covered in what appeared to be snow.

By then, it was obvious the man was more than a man. He set the unconscious people down onto the grass and shook himself, sending pieces of his melted jacket here and there. The witch ran past him, stopped where the ship met the shore, and flung the same spell into the depths of the fire. Moments later, steam and smoke rolled out of the gap in the ship and the witch collapsed.

Charging back into the steaming ship, the werewolf returned in less than a minute with two more people. He repeated that feat three more times, looking less like a man after each trip, and cameras caught every second. The troll joined him for the fourth and fifth trip, bringing injured out with him too.

A news helicopter arrived, and the scene unfolded on international TV. A Coast Guard cutter and harbor police boat appeared at the same time, followed quickly by firetrucks, police cruisers, and ambulances.

When the swarm of human rescuers arrived, the troll and werewolf stopped to catch their breath. The werewolf now looked less human and more like a wolf. His face sported a wolf's muzzle, and his hands ended in paws with long black claws. Fur peeked through where his clothes had burned away. He still had his pants on, but his legs and feet were bent at an odd angle, making him crouch.

The last scene was a shot of the two of them taken from the news helicopter now hovering over the river. The troll could be seen looking around. He appeared to be surprised by the crowd of people, although no one had approached either of them. Even the paramedics near the ambulances were giving him and the werewolf a wide berth as they secured the injured to gurneys. The troll stopped scanning the crowd and looked at the werewolf. He shrugged his shoulders, and the werewolf responded with a toothy grin. The troll turned and walked casually down the bank and disappeared under the waves of the East River.

The werewolf took one last look at the ship. Firemen had leaned tall ladders on the side and passengers were coming down. He shook once more, dropped to all fours, loped into the river, and swam away.

I wasn't the only one who recognized them. Reporters were soon swarming both of their apartments and the hospital Amanda had been taken to. I'd met Andrei the same night I'd met Trevor the troll (yes that was his real name—at least in this century). I'd danced with both of them. I had delved their souls as we danced, since that was why Sylvio and I were there. Our main target had been black witches, but in any case, Andrei's soul glowed like the dawn. It was no surprise to me that he would risk everything to save a boatload of strangers. Trevor, the troll, liked humans. He enjoyed their company and found them to be endlessly entertaining, and he liked to dine on them, too, on occasion. I couldn't guess what had motivated him to jump in that river.

Amanda was my son Chris's mentor. She was the first to explain to him that what he could do was sorcery. She was also a detective for the New York Police Department, but on that day she was simply another tourist. Relatives had come to visit, and they went down to the park to walk the bridge and take a ferry to see Lady Liberty.

Between tourists and crew, there had been 149 people aboard the ship. Only nine died, and three of those were on the smaller boat. Experts debated for weeks on how many would have perished without the aid of all three of them, especially Trevor. The river is quite cold in late March, so even if some of the tourists had been in decent shape physically, they still would have had quite a swim to get to shore, or to a ship attempting a rescue. Their muscles would have probably cramped up before they made it very far. Besides, I knew from experience it's very hard to swim when fully dressed and wearing a coat.

Trevor got tired of the reporters after only a week and disappeared. I'm sure he's still out there. He just doesn't look the same. Unfortunately, Andrei didn't have the option of changing his appearance. Ramon and Andrei's alpha, Brett, convinced the alpha of the Estes Pack in Colorado to take Andrei in and reveal other pack members too—at least those who were willing. About a fourth of them chose to move to other packs.

The pack's combined properties all bordered the Rocky Mountain National Forest. Their pack house was far enough from the main road to be a nice buffer between them and the reporters and gawkers. Two pack members had become local heroes a couple of years earlier after rescuing several people during a freak storm that had washed away one of the main roads and flooded half the town. The pack alpha, named Luke, was photogenic and possessed a cool head. He handled the press well. It made sense why Ramon picked their pack to be the public face for werewolves.

Amanda chose to continue working as a cop in New York after she recovered. Using such a strong spell had nearly killed her. After she got out of the hospital, she did well handling the reporters in the beginning but soon proved she was a little too hot-headed as a spokeswoman. The Coven chose a handful of men and women to represent witches in the role as consultants, and Amanda was glad to have someone to refer people to.

The fae kept quiet. It was a simple matter for them to conceal themselves. But they didn't object to the werewolves and witches talking about them as long as what was revealed made them appear benign.

Scientists, government officials, even several in the media came forward to say they already knew of the existence of such creatures and had been studying the phenomena for years but hadn't spoken up because of the fear of ridicule. Now, the flood of information and disinformation was staggering. It was all anyone talked about.

People seemed to have no problem grasping the concept of werewolves. The idea that a human could be inflicted with it like a disease was not a hard pill to swallow. The magic the European witches performed wasn't too hard for people to accept either. When witches began revealing simple incantations using wands or other objects of power and the ingredients for making modest potions, it made sense that some might be able to use things like that if they were gifted with a particular talent.

Scientists, however, were at a loss to explain how a two-hundred-pound man became an eighty-foot wall of moving rock, or how snow could be conjured out of thin air. *The Tonight Show* host suggested that coaches should line up at Andrei's door and convince him to play for the NFL.

It surprised me how little was said about actual magic, given all the news reports and "experts" the media trotted out for their talk shows. They skirted around the darker aspects of the stories and "fairytales" too. The world seemed to be in a Pollyanna state of mind. I worried what would happen when people began to ask sticky questions. Like if there are werewolves, are there vampires too?

On the heels of the revelation that magical creatures were real, a reporter for the *London Times* added two and two and came up with six. Reporters and photographers had not been invited to the polo match we attended, but these days cameras are in everyone's pocket. Some who were there dared to risk not being invited to a private party with the royal family in the future. Videos of the scene between Tim and his tormentor hit the internet. Those photos ended up blurry and eventually were unusable, but not at first.

The *London Times* reporter recognized Tim from having seen him on the cover of *Sports Illustrated* when he'd been tossed into the air by a bull. He'd also been on the scene for the whole saga when the duke and duchess were kidnapped. At that time, he overheard snippets from hospital staff that made him wonder about exactly what had rescued them. The video of Tim tossing policemen around in Cody did not become corrupted. Tim hadn't been using magic to fight them. But he moved a little too fast, and he was a bit too strong for anyone who is only a man. In addition, in the video from Cody, his eyes blazed golden, but after he was released from the hospital, his eyes were green.

One afternoon, shortly after the episode at the polo match, Shena was teaching me how to use potion ingredients. Eric and Tim were tooling a leather scabbard for the puukko knife Eric had helped Tim make. We were all in the kitchen with our projects spread out on the long marble countertop when the reporter from the *London Times* showed up on Tim's doorstep.

We'd decided a couple of weeks earlier it would be best if the twins called their father Uncle Tim. He wasn't quite old enough to have teenage kids, and since they were making an appearance around town now, we'd come up with the story that he had taken them in. When people asked about them, we were vague on details about why they came to live with him.

When the doorbell rang, we all stared at each other. Tim didn't have callers who were unannounced, and the spirits had not warned me anyone was coming. Tim and the twins were too absorbed with their projects to notice someone approaching. I thought that was a good sign. Tim was not as tense or hyper aware as he had been when I first met him.

After a moment, Tim stood and headed for the front door. The three of us lingered in the archway between the kitchen and living room, curious about who had come calling.

The reporter was direct and to the point. As soon as Tim opened the door, he said in a nifty British accent, "Sir Timothy Martin, I presume?"

He was a couple of inches shorter than Tim and me, with brown curls that he tried to tame with a short cut, and skin that was fairly light. His facial features hinted at an African ancestry, and he was attempting to hide his triumph with a mild smile. Our collective stunned silence had given him the confirmation he needed. "Mick Collins, *London Times*."

Tim slowly reached for the man's outstretched hand and said, "Please come in."

They shook hands, and Tim stepped to the side. I was surprised to discover that Tim mostly felt amused rather than angry.

"Is this your family?" Collins asked as he stepped into the room.

"Rachel is a friend." Tim paused, then said, "The other two are my niece and nephew, Shena and Eric." The feeling of humor in the room now encompassed all three of them, which made me smile.

Collins nodded at us and gazed with curiosity at everything in sight as he sat in the chair Tim indicated. I headed for the couch. No way was I going to miss this unless Tim ordered me from the room. Shena and Eric followed me. Tim quirked a smile at us when we had settled, then asked, "What can I do for you, Mr. Collins?"

"Please, call me Mick, everyone does." He leaned forward but didn't look Tim directly in the eyes. "I'd sell my firstborn for an interview."

Tim grinned and asked, "Do you have a firstborn?"

Mick chuckled and said, "Afraid not. Married to the job, you see. But the sentiment is true."

Tim leaned back in his chair, appearing at ease, which wasn't that far from reality. "All right," he said with an amused drawl, "I can give you a few minutes, as long as I get to read the story before it's sent."

"Brilliant!" Mick clapped his hands together and looked like Christmas had come early, which for him it surely had. "I had quite a list of questions I planned to pick from, but yesterday things changed. My business is about cultivating friends, contacts in various fields. Years ago, I asked one of them to monitor some funds for me. One of those accounts has had only one transaction, albeit a rather large one. It was to buy this house." He'd been addressing Tim's collar rather than looking in his eyes, but he flicked a quick glance at them when he said that, checking for a reaction.

It dawned on me that Mick suspected Tim was a werewolf. He knew not to stare directly into a werewolf's eyes.

Tim's face went blank for an instant before he masked it with a smile, but it was enough to confirm things for Mick. Tim felt alarmed and uncertain; the humor in his expression was pretense now.

Mick's next question caught us all by surprise, although I wasn't sure what I thought he might ask. "Why did you do it?" he asked. He wrinkled his brow, genuinely puzzled.

Tim's face went blank again, this time with bewilderment.

Mick decided to explain himself. "I mean, you can't have a very high opinion of British people. No one would blame you for that, mate, but you went out of your way to rescue the Windsors. Put yourself in the line of fire to save people you'd never met. Wealthy people." He dared another glance at Tim's eyes. "Why?"

Tim sat quite still as he considered his reply. His emotions were a jumble, finally settling on resolve. I was thinking it was no accident that Mick had added all the pieces together. Mick was highly intelligent and intuitive. He perceived the deeper aspects, not what was on the surface. Later, when Sylvio and I investigated his background, we found he was not a member of the paparazzi. He did not write for the social columns. He was an investigative reporter who wrote mainly about political and social news, with an occasional human-interest story thrown in.

"They had grit," Tim answered.

Mick's eyebrows rose. He sat back and nodded. He didn't need more words to discern what had motivated Tim. He let the admiration he felt show on his face. "Well, Sir Timothy, you are a quick judge of character, and an accurate one. The duke and duchess are genuine, without guile." He let that statement sink in for a few seconds. We could all tell by Tim's body language that he agreed.

"So, the next question I have is, are you a werewolf?" He was addressing Tim's collar again. He added, "I have connections at the hospital, too."

Tim glanced at me. I shrugged in a "why not" manner. The atmosphere in the room changed. Werewolf magic is subtle, even if their appearance isn't. Still, the room filled with a sense of danger, like how you feel when you're alone and you think there's something hiding behind the couch. Tim wanted Mick to know that werewolves were not to be taken lightly. Tim closed his eyes, and when he opened them, he compelled Mick to meet them. His eyes blazed golden now. "Yes, Mr. Collins—Mick. Yes, I am."

Mick was unable to look away. For the first time since coming into the house, the man felt afraid. He licked his lips and cleared his throat. "Did Dr. Sabin do that to you?"

Tim dropped the magic and let Mick glance away. "He began the process, but it was an actual werewolf that finished it."

"The one he kept in the lab?"

Tim's surprise didn't show on his face. "No, I had escaped by then."

Connections indeed. Not many knew there was a werewolf held captive in that lab. If he knew that, did he know there had been a vampire, too?

Tim said, "Those in the British press who know have not revealed what kind of experiments were done in the lab. I trust you will honor that silence?"

"Until recently, I didn't lend those rumors credence. My friend at the hospital told me you were a werewolf. I figured they kept your identity hidden and destroyed the photos and videos because there aren't many people who suffer from hypertrichosis, and it would not be hard to track such a person down."

Tim grinned and rubbed his chin, which was clean shaven. "And I'm damn glad I don't have to deal with *that* affliction." Being part Native American, he didn't grow a great deal of body hair.

Mick relaxed a fraction. "Was Dr. Sabin some kind of sorcerer?"

Well, I thought, *this guy gets to the meat of things in a hurry.*

Tim glanced out his big picture window that overlooked Willard Bay and the road up the hill to his house. I sensed a sudden alarm in him and turned to see what he'd seen. Sylvio's silver Bugatti was coming up the long drive.

Mick caught our expressions and glanced out the window too, but turned back when Tim said, "Yes, he was a black witch."

That was another carrot reporters had been reaching for—the question about whether there were witches who used magic for evil purposes.

"A wizard?"

"Yes, that's another name that could be used. Magus, warlock, wizard, witch, sorcerer, take your pick."

"I thought witches were women," Mick said, distracted from his planned line of questioning.

Tim smiled. "Well, it's easier to say witch. It's like we do with cows. Everyone says cows when they see a bunch of them, but really, the herds are a mix of cows and steers or even bulls."

I had been expecting Sylvio's voice, so I wasn't surprised when he sent me the message, *"Whose car is that in the driveway?"*

"We have company," I answered. *"A reporter has figured out who Tim is, and he's quite well informed."*

"Damn."

I had to grin in spite of myself. It wasn't me that had caused Sylvio to swear that time.

"I'll leave, then."

"He's already seen your car."

"If he inquires, say I was dropping something off."

Great idea. Relieved, I said, *"Okay, that's a good plan. I'll let you know when he leaves."*

"Yes, we'll have a lot to discuss then. I'll get ahold of Ramon."

"Okay."

Shena was looking at me curiously. I smiled and sighed with relief, then patted her knee.

Mick was grinning at Tim's answer and thought that was why I was grinning too. He took in our smiles and said, "How about you three? It's obvious you knew all the things I asked, but did you learn them recently, or have you known for some time?"

Shena appeared at ease, as did her brother. She said, "Oh, Eric and I have always known about magic—real magic." Eric nodded emphatically.

Everyone turned to me. I said, "I only found out a couple of years ago."

Mick nodded slowly. I could see wheels turning in his head and hoped he would be satisfied with simple answers. He asked Tim, "Is it true that children from a werewolf are born human?"

"Yes, kids born when a werewolf has a human mate don't have any magical traits." Which Tim could say with absolute truth, since Shena and Eric were not exactly either werewolf or human. They did not have to answer the call of the moon goddess.

Mick seemed satisfied with that answer, and I felt Shena and Eric's pensive feelings calm a bit, as did mine.

Sylvio's car going back down the drive made us all look that way. Mick said, "Is there another house up here? I thought there was only yours?"

"Oh, he's Tim's neighbor," I said. "He was dropping something off for him."

Tim raised an eyebrow at me.

"Nice car," Mick commented.

"No kidding," Eric added. Sylvio had let him drive it earlier that week.

Mick seemed to dismiss the mystery of Tim's neighbor. "Well, I have to say I was sure I'd get the door slammed in my face when I got here. Why give me your time?"

That got a chuckle out of Tim. "Well, it's a given if you've figured this out there will be more like you. Why not reward the first one off the mark?"

"I appreciate that."

I'll bet he does, I thought. He'd broken the story nearly every reporter would give their eyeteeth for. Sir Timothy had disappeared from the palace as soon as he was able to walk. Since then, speculation had been rampant about who he was and where he'd come from. The fact that he was a werewolf would give the royal family an out—they could say they kept his identity hidden because of that. They'd taken quite a lot of flak about keeping silent on the subject of their rescuer.

Next, Mick asked, "Do you intend to press charges against those officers in Cody?"

Tim was taken aback for a moment. Such a thought hadn't occurred to him, and that was obvious on his face. Reporters speculated for several days about it—both officers had obviously been carried away by hitting Tim when he stopped fighting. The officer who kicked him in the groin was put on a leave of absence for a week.

After the police learned why Tim was there, all charges against him for the scene in Cody had been dropped, even resisting arrest. The girl's father insisted on being allowed to thank Tim personally and bullied the hospital staff and security guards into allowing him to see Tim. Ramon had been there, so things went smoothly. He told me that Tim really didn't know how to receive the man's thanks, but when he asked Tim why he would fight four strangers over a girl he didn't even know, Tim had replied, "I've been where she was." Then the girl's father asked how he knew she was in trouble, and Tim said he heard her cry out when he was jogging behind the motel, so he called 911 and climbed in through the bathroom window.

Tim's response surprised me. "Hell no! You don't walk in on a scene like that and ask, 'Please sir, could you explain yourself?' You go get the bastard! I'd maimed three boys and scared another nearly to death (one kid had hidden in the closet) for the same thing those officers thought I was guilty of. They couldn't have known what was really going on, and there's no way in hell the policemen could have guessed what would happen when they tried to put handcuffs on me."

That response left Mick speechless for several seconds, which was something I thought didn't happen to him very often. He wanted to laugh but wasn't sure if he should. When Eric and Shena busted up, he figured it was okay to join in. After a bit, Mick asked, "Did you hear what the *Tonight Show* host suggested police officers should do the next time they spot you?"

Tim looked blank, but Eric snickered and said, "Yep, he said, 'In all fairness, Tim should wear a sign that says Approach with Caution.'"

We all laughed a little at that too.

"Should we?" Mick asked.

Tim raised an eyebrow in answer.

"Approach with caution," Mick added. "You seem fairly friendly to me."

"Well, would you reach out and grab a wolf if you saw one walking by?" Tim countered.

"Not likely." Mick tilted his head inquiringly. "You consider yourself a wolf, then?"

"No, I'm afraid it's not that simple," Tim said. "We have many of the same tendencies as our canine brethren, but a werewolf is more than a wolf. Our minds are human."

"Being human," Mick prompted, "why, then, the stories about the dangers werewolves pose?"

"We are as varied as any other creature. Who we are as a werewolf depends on who we are as a person. The magic takes our basic nature and enhances it, makes it more ... large." Tim's face reflected his frustration. The blend of wolf and man that becomes a werewolf does not lend itself to a description with words.

"So, you're saying if the person is bent on destruction, the werewolf will be more so?"

"Yes, and of course the reverse is true."

"Making a decent man a hero." It was clear Mick meant Tim.

For the first time, Tim was uncomfortable. He didn't want to mislead Mick, but he didn't want to tell him the whole truth, either. Werewolves are violent. They *must* hunt, and they *must* kill.

Tim gave a noncommittal shrug.

Mick looked down at his notepad for the first time and seemed to consider whether to ask the question his eyes caught. Making his decision, he looked up.

"Do werewolves actually howl at the moon?" His tone was lighthearted, but his face transformed into astonishment and his mouth hung open by the time Tim had finished with his answer.

"Werewolves are linked to the moon goddess. Her call is strongest when she is full. We answer her call with a song of our own."

Mick shut his mouth with effort and licked his lips. The man knew truth when he heard it, and what Tim said did not reconcile with his perception of reality. He cleared his throat. "The moon really makes you become a werewolf, then?"

Tim shook his head. "No, it is a matter of inner strength. I would not ever have to transform if I did not wish it."

Mick had been leaning forward, fascinated by every word. He sat back and looked at all of us in turn, then watched Tim carefully for his reaction to the next question. "But others who are werewolves, what if they don't have the wherewithal you do?"

"That's why the moon goddess created alphas."

℘ Chapter 15 ℘
Sylvio: All Hallow's Eve

I learned about the gods at my mother's knee. I was taught all their names and the powers they held. I pretended to be various demigods as my playmates and I acted out the fables or made up our own. So, although I was not raised to be a devout follower of her religion, I did know the basic precepts. Both she and my father instilled in me a curiosity about history and how religion plays a part in it, and I've never lost that interest.

I was considered odd by Adonas' other fledglings because I collected books and read all the ancient texts I could find, including those about religion. They would scoff at me and ask what did the past matter, why should I care what humans had done?

The early Christians were careful to ensure that their celebrations coincided with the pagan festivals so they could worship their own version of an event, or a saint, in safety. The actual date on which some celebrations occur has been moved many times to fit the needs of the worshipers. After all, what does a date matter? The calendar itself has been rewritten more than once. Still, the meaning of most of those events has carried through time.

The people of the stones, whose very name and religion have been lost, built circles of stone and circles of wooden posts, or more stones, inside berms dug in the earth—a circle within a circle within another circle—to symbolize those objects man has known throughout time hold power over their very existence: the sun, the moon, and the stars in the heavens.

A circle, or a similar shape with a continuous line, is a powerful magical form. It is endless; there is no corner, no weak point for the power to leak out. Unless something of equal or greater power breaks that circle, or unless the maker of the circle breaks it, the magic will remain.

Even today, thousands of years after those who built the stone circles have gone away, the magic they imbued into those places remains, even when the logs rotted, the earthworks were filled in, and many of the stones were carried away.

The people of the stones celebrated life and re-birth in the spring. They honored the dead and the long sleep of winter in the fall. There was no one left alive who knew the old stories or the names of those they worshiped by the time I was born.

When I first traveled Ireland, the Celts celebrated Samhain in the spring. It was meant to give honor to the dead, to those who have seen Heaven, and those dead who, in life, helped others earn the right to see Heaven.

The Germans had a similar celebration that they conducted in the fall, and the two were combined as the Germanic tribes had blended with the Celtic ones. Samhain became All Saints Day. But the meaning didn't change: to honor those who did God's work (or the work of the gods) on Earth and have now moved on to Heaven.

Today, the beginning of the celebration is named Halloween, a short version of All Hallows' Eve. The next day is devoted to honoring the saints. The day after that, the faithful pray for those in Purgatory, to plea for their acceptance into Heaven rather than Hell. In any case, the meaning of the holiday throughout time has been to honor those worthy of Heaven.

The magic in the stone circles has always made me uneasy. I can feel when I cross one of those boundaries, even if it can't be seen anymore. It doesn't make me weaker like those with strong faith in Christ do, but I don't belong there. My soul is not destined for Heaven.

I explained the purpose of the stone circles, as I had surmised them to be, to Cyneric as we prepared to meet Seamas. He was surprised. People fear things they don't understand, and by his century, the stone circles were considered unclean, as anything linked to pagan practices was considered evil. People avoided them. To be seen investigating those sites would bring that person under suspicion. Curiosity about anything other than the ruling religion was thought to be heretical.

At that time, very few people in Europe were educated. They only knew their own small world and were taught to be suspicious of any free thinkers and of anyone who questioned their religion. Superstition abounded. I found it depressing that the people didn't know the meaning of the place. Amesbury is ancient. Humans worshiped there even before the pyramids were built. The people living in Cyneric's century were ignorant of their own history.

Ragna had fought the boundaries set by the Church and by society, and so was shunned by most. I doubted things had been much different for her and Seamas in their new home.

The witch families throughout all time have vied with each other constantly over position and prestige. Even today, when the white witches have long since learned the value of uniting, they cannot seem to keep politics and intrigue out of their associations with each other. In Seamas' time, such conflicts were not as civilized as they are now. Also, the Church had begun to hunt witches along with other dark creatures. Witches tend to be highly intelligent; they would not have survived over time if they were not. They educate themselves and therefore begin to question those in authority. The Church feared the power of the witch families and believed the Bible, which states quite clearly, "Thou shalt not suffer a witch to live." Later, during and then after the Great Plague, such fears led to the deaths of thousands, most of them innocent of causing harm. The witches even in Seamas' time had learned to hide their power or die at the hands of a mob, or at the hands of the clergy.

The Christians and the Hebrews before them were not actually wrong in their beliefs—not usually. Witches can tap into dimensions beyond the one humans reside in. The beings most willing to lend their aid to a person attempting to gain power are demons. Far too many witches release demons upon man, either by accident or by design. That, or they become possessed by one, believing they can control or overcome such a tainted being. Demons are masters of deception; they encourage the witch's belief that they are superior. The demon pretends to be an ally, even a friendly spirit, and disguises its true nature until it has the witch ensnared. Once it does, the witch will be more powerful than any mere human, and far deadlier. They become twisted and evil and wreak havoc on all who encounter them and, sadly, on those they once cared the most about.

The place Seamas asked me to meet him was at the largest stone at the north end of Amesbury—inside the inner circle. But he didn't know that. I don't know that anyone during his time did, although a few, such as Ragna, would have been able to feel the magic in the place.

The stone circles were more complete in that century than they are today. Many of the smaller, outer stones were still there, although the Romans had taken several away centuries earlier. The earthen berms were certainly more apparent as well.

I'm not sure I would have recognized the man waiting by the

standing stone. I had chosen for us to ride there rather than attempting to teleport since my only clear memory of the place was in the middle of the circle of stones. He was mounted on a horse as fine as ours, which was unusual for someone not tied to an estate. His cloak and the sword at his hip were of high quality as well. It was his face that was different. He had a full beard now, shot with gray. His short, curly hair had been jet black, but now it had more gray in it than his beard. There were deep wrinkles around his eyes and mouth from smiling, and his face was tan—so perhaps the lines were from squinting at the sun instead. I prefer to think they were from smiling since his nature was to see the good in things from the beginning.

I could sense he had been worried I would not come. I saw the relief on his face when he saw us riding up the road. It was a while before his human eyes could make out who we were for sure, but when we were near enough, he rode over to greet us.

"Master, I'm so very thankful you've come."

"It's nice to see that you are in good health, Seamas, but please call me Sylvio. I am no longer your master."

He was surprised at that, then his smile grew wider. "Huh. I suppose that is true, isn't it?" He scanned Cyneric up and down, taking in the fine clothes he wore, then studied his face, pleased with what he saw. "Cyneric, you look well."

Cyneric replied, "That I am." Seamas' face lit up. "And how is Ragna?" Cyneric added.

Seamas lost his smile and bowed his head, staring at his hands resting on the pommel of his saddle. He hesitated, looking for the right words.

I asked, "Has she turned to using black sorcery?"

His head snapped up, and his eyes lit with fierce anger. "No, no of course not, how could you suggest such a thing!"

I was not insulted by his anger. I was reassured instead. I asked with genuine concern, "What has happened with Ragna?"

His anger cooled, and his shoulders sagged. "It's not her. It's our daughter, Kerri, she's our oldest. She's a good girl but stubborn. She is so strong, like her mother. She doesn't see the purpose of hiding her abilities. The other witch families have taken notice."

His eyes wandered as he considered what to say next. "Then, a week ago, representatives from three families came to our house when I wasn't there. It was only Kerri and Ragna, and my youngest boy. The sheriff was with them, and two deputies as well. Ragna told Kerri to go with them and we would sort it out when I got home. But when the sheriff's men took her arm, their clothes started on fire. They let go, and Kerri ran for the woods. The witches did not want to reveal what they could do in front of the sheriff and his men, so they didn't try to stop her. The witches said that was proof Kerri is possessed, and at that point, the sheriff and his men agreed. They have sent for Father Clark. They mean for Kerri to be purged."

"Purged" meant burned. To chase the demon out of the person. It works. Not because of fire—demons are often creatures made of fire—but because the host dies.

Cyneric asked, "Have you heard from Kerri?"

"Ragna gave me a bundle of food and clothes to take out to the woods and tie up in a tree. There is a clearing there where she and Kerri practice. I went to check yesterday, and the bundle was gone. She left a note that said she will find her own way." His gaze finally settled on me.

I understood. As gently as I could manage, I asked, "Are the other witches correct, Seamas?"

He blew out a sigh. "I honestly don't know. She has been acting odd lately, but Ragna has not felt evil on her. She doesn't think Kerri could hide it from her. Do you think she could?"

"There are some demons who could mask their presence from a witch's senses, but they are rare."

From his manner, I could see he had been hoping I would say no. Deflating a little, he picked up his reins and turned toward the town.

I added, "If you can lead me to her, I'm sure I would be able to sense a demon if there is one, no matter which one it is."

It was clear Seamas loved his daughter as only a father can, but I could also sense that he feared she had fallen into that trap. He knew what I thought of black witches. He had to be desperate to ask me for aid. If she was possessed, there was only a slim chance to save her. It is rare that a demon can be banished without costing the human their life.

The town of Amesbury was ancient even at that time but was still a small village. We skirted the edge of the village in the growing dusk. Between the gaps in the city wall, we could see a bonfire burning in the town square. People were making their way toward the square. They wore masks or had painted their faces like death masks with white paint and charcoal. They were singing hymns and carrying candles on their way to join the crowd around the square.

Seamas led us along the road that skirted the outside of the low city wall, clearly not wanting to encounter residents from the town. We followed that road and then turned onto a track that led into the woods. We continued on for about a half mile until we came to a rather large dwelling with a tightly thatched roof. Chickens and ducks were queuing up to get in their coop and settle for the night. Some pigs lined up at the low stone wall of their pen as we reined in.

A boy who was the mirror image of his father at that same age came out of the house, followed by another smaller boy with his father's face but with his mother's red hair—the color of aged cherrywood.

The oldest boy, like his father, had no magic in him, but his little brother did. When we dismounted, the boys came to take our horses' reins. Seamas introduced them as Hugh and Sean. Hugh was clearly intrigued by us but didn't hesitate to take the reins of two of the horses and start toward the barn. Sean, who appeared to be only eight or nine, stood and stared at us.

Seamas put a hand on the boy's shoulder, and he twitched. "Sean, take Lord Denman's horse to the stable." His tone was kind, but it was also clearly a command.

The boy stared at us a few more seconds with his bright-green eyes, then blinked and followed his brother. When the boy was far enough away that he couldn't hear us, Seamas said, "It's difficult for him. He feels things and notices things that most of the rest of us can't. I can't imagine what it was like for his mother growing up. Her family was afraid of her. Sean is easier for us to deal with since we already had practice with his sister."

"What do you think he saw in us?" Cyneric asked.

"He's always been able to feel magic, whether it's in people or simply in the air. I'm not sure what he sensed about you, but he would be able to tell you are not like me, and that you are not like him."

I asked, "What else can he do?"

"Magic comes out of him at random moments. We moved out here when Kerri was small, so there was less chance of those in town noticing when she did something odd. Ragna fears Sean may be more powerful than even she or his sister, but it's unformed and untrained in him as yet. She has sent out a request for someone to teach her how to block his access to his magic until he is older."

"That would be wise," I said. "A child with such power is a danger to everyone, even themselves. Ragna's family was not wrong to be afraid, but they were wrong to shun her."

Seamas paused and turned to look at me. We had been walking toward the house. "Do you know how to create a block like that?"

"I'm sorry, I do not." But I considered his question. Perhaps it would be prudent of me to learn about the spells and enchantments witches used.

I'd noticed a line of stones in front of the house as we rode up that appeared to circle the house. Cyneric strode along ahead of me, and I was curious if he would feel the magic I was sure was there. He stepped over the stones and paused, looking down at the line of rocks, which he hadn't noticed until then. He glanced over his shoulder at me.

"A protection spell," I explained. Curious, I asked, "Does it feel oily, or like a fresh breeze?"

Cyneric tilted his head. "Like a breeze."

Relieved, I stepped over the stones. "White magic. Black magic would feel . . . wrong."

He narrowed his eyes at me. "You let me walk into this first to see what might happen to me."

He was gaining wisdom with age. "Which of the two of us would be better equipped to get us out of a trap?"

Seamas was attempting unsuccessfully to hide a grin. "Come this way, gentlemen. Ragna is waiting for you."

The house was big enough to have four rooms, which was unusual for common folk in those days. There was a large open area and three smaller rooms beyond that. Ragna was standing at the hearth, stirring a pot full of what smelled like stew. Without turning, she said, "Master Sylvio, Cyneric, it is good of you to come." I noticed her left hand was wrapped in a bandage of white linen.

"As I told your spouse, I am no longer your master. Simply Sylvio will do."

I sensed uncertainty in both Ragna and Seamas, but I did catch a smile on the side of her face I could see. She seemed to steel herself and took a deep breath, then turned to face us. Ragna had been not only beautiful but stunning, adding to the suspicion and dislike the women in the village near Niveus felt for her. Men could not help but be attracted by her dark tresses and fair skin. She appeared delicate, with small hands and fine features, and was anything but. One half of her face was marred with an angry red burn. The burn was quite recent, only a day or two old. I strode over to her and placed my palm on the left side of her face, where it wasn't scorched.

Magic, as I had suspected. This had been done with sorcery.

Seeing the pain in her eyes, I said, "Would you like me to help you heal?"

The thought had not occurred to her. Her eyes widened, and that caused her pain. Seamas came to her side and said, "Love, come sit down, the children can take care of things."

I dropped my hand, and he led her away. She sank gratefully into a wooden rocker next to the hearth.

"Once will not tie you to me," I assured her. "You never were deeply enthralled." I hated to see her hurting, and she needed her physical strength to battle any black magic that might be threatening her family.

Eyes full of agony met mine. She nodded. I glanced at Seamas; his jaw was clenched. He didn't like the idea, but he liked her hurting even less. He gave a stiff nod.

I stepped to her side and slipped one hand behind her neck, tilting her head up so she would meet my eyes. She hesitated, looking at my chin instead of into my eyes; then she slowly looked up. She gasped when I captured her, and instinctively fought it. I knew this was going to hurt, but at the same time, I was excited by her intoxicating scent and the pulse of the vein in her neck. It never gets old, feeding.

Her magic slammed into me, bringing with it an equal measure of pleasure and pain. She had been more injured than she let on. Burns are so terribly painful, but she was not only hurt physically— emotionally she was spent. I drank until she swooned, then commanded her to drink. The pain shot through me and my vision went black. She was far stronger than she had been as a child. It was not entirely white magic, either. There was a darkness there, but it was outweighed by the good. When she had taken all I dared give her, my command to stop came out in a whisper. I was spent.

Cyneric was puzzled. He could feel when I was weakened. He was wise enough not to say anything as I moved away from Ragna and Seamas took my place.

"Give her a few minutes," I said. "Cyneric and I will go hunt in the forest."

Seamas' head snapped up.

"Not for Kerri," I added. "When we return, you can explain how this happened." I could sense Seamas had not told us the whole story. There was more to it than Kerri.

We didn't go far. Usually, I prefer to hunt rather than call animals to me, but as soon as we were in the shelter of the trees, I sent out a quest for them to come to me. After only a few minutes, a trio of deer walked into the clearing.

Cyneric had not known we had that ability. He petted the doe with wonder, and I saw the pain in his eyes, the sadness over what he was about to do, and the hunger.

"They're beautiful," he commented as the doe allowed him to stroke her soft hide. She stood placidly, without the slightest fear. "And yet," he continued, "even though I know I could walk away, I won't."

Speaking mostly to himself, he added, "I want the life she holds."

When we had stolen their lives, we slung the deer over our shoulders to take back to Seamas. There was no reason to waste meat. For humans at that time, fresh meat was a rare treat.

We walked slowly back to the house, at human speed. While we did, Cyneric asked, "Why were you in so much pain when feeding from Ragna, and especially when she took from you?"

"Witch blood. You'll know it if you ever happen upon one unaware. But the pleasure matches the pain. Surely you could feel that too."

He paused, then said, "I mostly sensed the weakness it caused me."

That had disturbed him. I realized I hadn't told him very much about vampires, about how we are connected, or anything, really. "Your strength is tied to mine. I'm not sure how long it will take for you to be independent of me, if you ever can be."

Again, we walked on a few steps before he asked, "How long did it take for you?"

"My maker did not want me to be independent. It wasn't until I could teleport that he allowed me even a small amount of freedom, and even then it was with reluctance. I was tied to him and to the vampire who took me away from him for half a millennium. So, I don't have an answer for you. It may be that I could have been free of that tie decades or even centuries earlier. I don't know."

He had stopped in his tracks when I said half a millennium. I turned and smiled at the astonishment on his face. "Come," I said, "let's find out how Ragna was burned."

The atmosphere in the house was subdued, mostly because of the small boy, Sean. His brother was not in the house. Sean was busy carding some wool as we came in, but when he glanced up at us, he was distracted momentarily, blinking and staring, not directly at our eyes but with a wandering gaze. I realized he must be seeing an aura of some sort.

Seamas cleared his throat, and the boy bent to carding the wool again, but not before glancing at his mother with a guilty look.

I made a guess and said, "Was it Sean who burned you and those men?"

They all stared at me; Ragna, Seamas, Sean, and Cyneric. Then Ragna shook her head and smiled, "Master . . . I mean, Sylvio. You always did see to the heart of things." She smiled kindly at her son, who returned her look with one of guilt and sorrow. "He meant to protect me, but my hand was on one of those men, and I was close enough that when their clothes caught fire, it got me as well."

Unable to contain his curiosity any longer, the boy asked, "Are you wizards?"

"I think it's best if he learns to recognize what we are and be warned, don't you?" I asked his parents.

Reluctantly, they nodded in agreement.

"Sean, we are vampires. Make note of that. We are not benevolent beings, any of us, although Cyneric here might be considered such."

The boy's eyes were wide. He looked at his parents with confusion and uncertainty.

Seamas said, "Sylvio and Cyneric are okay. They do not mean harm. Your mother and I asked them here because they might be able to help Kerri. We do hope that is true."

Sean narrowed his eyes at us. "Help her how?" The boy had steel in his backbone, like his mother. That was a good thing. He would have a hard life with his abilities. It was not likely he would survive his childhood. Disease was not the only danger he faced.

"I can sense evil beings because I am their kin," I said. "I will know if a demon has captured Kerri when I see her or catch her scent."

Sean absorbed my words, appearing then to be much older than he was. "You think you can find her?" he said doubtfully.

"I'm certain of it."

Ragna looked sharply at her son. "Do you know where she is?"

Sean blanched and bent to card more wool. He shook his head.

In a soft voice, yet with authority, Seamas said, "Son, look at me and tell me where she is."

The boy didn't address his father but looked at me instead. "She's found a . . . door . . . to somewhere else."

Seamas' eyes met mine, and we both had the same thought: Underhill.

ℬ Chapter 16 ℭ
Reunion

"**W**hy haven't you contacted your Dad yet?" Tim asked me. We were sitting in his living room. Darin, Kelly, and Marta were with us. Tim had invited Darin to live with him. Nothing had been decided about how long he would stay, but Oliver and Ross felt it would be good for them both. Kelly and Marta had also come to stay for a few days to help Darin settle in.

I'd asked Darin if he wanted us to help find his family. He was startled by the question. I guessed Tim wanted Darin to have a little time to consider his answer, so he decided to pick on me.

Why hadn't I contacted my father? I'd been coming up with excuses not to; it was sure to be an uncomfortable meeting. If I were being honest with myself, I was afraid his true feelings would betray him. I would *know* if he was glad he had a daughter or not, no matter what he said.

"Okay," I said. "I'll make an appointment to see him." I couldn't help sounding a little breathless. Tim raised a suspicious eyebrow. "Soon," I added.

He grinned. The others felt puzzled and curious but were too polite to ask, so I explained: "My father doesn't know I was born. He was a teenager when my mom came to live with him and his parents. James and Ramon found out about my father and my mother last summer. She died giving birth to me, and I was adopted a few weeks later and raised by another family."

Before they could ask me more, I decided to turn the tables on Tim. "Tim, did you know Micah and I went to that coven meeting?"

"Yeah," he replied. "James said it didn't go well. They're still undecided about you and Chris, and what sort of discipline to mete out on Micah." His tone made it clear what he thought of that.

"Yes, well, I plan to have a talk with them about that soon, but I've been wanting to tell you, I met your grandmother Gwen and your aunt Nascha at that meeting. They would like to see you."

There's a well-used phrase: You could have heard a pin drop. Well, you could have. We all waited in silence for Tim to decide what to say. Even the spirits stopped moving. His emotions ran the gamut, not settling on only one.

Into the silence, I added, "What werewolf killed Gwen's sister?"

Leaping at the distraction, Tim said, "He was new. He didn't even know what he was, what he had become. Grandma has never been told which one it was." He met my eyes.

"But you know."

"Andrei."

We all absorbed that. Werewolves policed their own, and their rules were brutal: obey or die. Those who survived a werewolf attack were rare. It required someone with an unusually strong will, someone who fiercely hangs on to life long enough for the magic to take hold. If a new werewolf changed without knowing they'd become a creature from legend, and they killed accidentally, they were forgiven those deaths. If allowances were not made, there would be even fewer werewolves than there already were.

The preternatural community has never been large. Although some have magic that should make them immortal, preternatural beings tend to live shorter lives than humans because their lives are dangerous. Also, it's difficult for beings with magic in them to reproduce. By far, the greatest numbers are the witches, because they are simply humans gifted with the ability to tap into magic.

Fae are born magical and can only make a pure fae child if they reside in a place seeped in magic. The magic in such places was diluted with the coming of the industrial age and its cold iron. And, in the modern era, electronic signals invade the very air. In addition, it's not often that female fae bear children, and the few male fae who take a human wife don't often father a child with any magic in them. It is only recently that fae numbers have dwindled enough that those remaining began to cooperate with each other. As much as many of them dislike humans and would prefer eating children, recently they have been promoting marriages with human partners in an effort to increase their numbers.

There are now more vampires than fae, but there have never been very many. It takes years to make one, and then that fledgling is most often a danger for some time and must be kept under tight control.

Vampires are by nature possessive and combative and tend to associate only with those in their own broods. They are far more inclined to fight with or even hunt other vampire broods than become allies with them.

So, there aren't many preternatural creatures out there, and maybe that's as it should be.

Darin chuckled at the news that Andrei the hero was the killer. It was good to hear. Even when he stayed in his body, he didn't talk very much. I guess he wasn't used to it. He tried, though. He would be in his own world, and then he'd noticeably make an effort to engage with those around him. Both Tim and Kelly said Darin had been an animated kid, full of fun. Bits of that personality were beginning to show occasionally. But he had a long way to go.

Darin was half human and half fae. When under Dr. Sabin's control, he hadn't been able to figure out how to change his own body unless he was under severe stress. Eventually, he had learned how to make a separate body into what he wanted it to be, like a Nix or a Jinni could, or even remain invisible. It had taken him several years to prefect it so the body looked normal. Before then, he had invaded live human bodies and lived with them for a while. He said most had not known of his presence, other than the weird and disturbing dreams they were suddenly plagued by. So, he had quite a lot of experience in observing life, but he hadn't truly lived his own since the kidnapping.

I told Darin if he tried invading my body, I'd turn him to ash. Being a smart man, he believed me.

"Sabin targeted kids with magic in them, didn't he?" I asked the room at large.

Kelly said, "Yes, at least those from families whose history meant the kids might be magical, although some of us had shown no signs of it."

In my view, all small children were magical in their own way, but I didn't say that.

"I can see why Tim would be reluctant to contact his family, and Darin has only now joined the real world. Why haven't you told yours?"

Kelly let out a bitter laugh. "My family is even more anti-werewolf than Tim's."

I considered that, but I'd done a lot of thinking about Gwen and Nascha. "I think you'd be surprised. Anyway, a reporter has discovered Tim. It won't be long before they've caught on to you two, as well. Your families are going to find out. It would be best if they found out from you."

As it turned out, it was already too late. Mick had written a poignant and even heart-rending article. It was not sensational; in fact, it rang of truth. He painted Tim in the light the world saw him after he rescued the royals: the quiet hero. He also revealed that Tim was a werewolf. No other thing could have promoted good relations more between werewolves and normal humans. More of the alphas considered letting their pack members reveal what they were, although very few did.

Mick hadn't drawn a map to Tim's place, but it wasn't difficult for other reporters to figure it out. The Willard police were constantly making the reporters move off the highway. Paparazzi also drove up on the canal road until a policeman was dispatched to chase them off. New "No Trespassing" signs cropped up in the farmers' fields surrounding Tim's place, too. Those few in town who knew Tim before the news broke liked him. Many others pretended they knew him for the attention. But even so, their stories tended to show him in a good light, since that was the way the prevailing wind of sentiment blew.

We hadn't really appreciated the long lane that led up to Tim's house, but now it turned out to be a blessing. No reporters or gawkers could approach the house easily. The closest access was the canal road above his place. For a while, there was a sudden increase in four wheelers, dirt bikes, and horses riding the road. Then Tim had exercised his right to protect his property, which was on both sides of the canal road, and had stationed security personnel (who happened to be Ramon's pack members) at each end of his property and at the new gate at the bottom of his lane.

Only seven days after the story broke, a van pulled up to the gate on the lane. I happened to be in Tim's dining room, although I no longer came up there on my own; Sylvio or Antone would teleport me to the study across from his bedroom. It was inconvenient, but it was better than leading reporters to Sylvio's house. Kelly and Marta hadn't yet returned to France. We'd been playing a game of *Redneck Life*, which Eric especially thought was hilarious.

Justin, the werewolf guarding the gate, radioed up that some people were there to see Tim and his friends. They claimed to be family, not reporters. He asked what we'd like to do.

Everyone in the room felt shocked. I hadn't tried sending the spirits out quite that far before, but I asked them to delve the souls of the people in the van. They did as I asked. What I got back was a tableau of uncertainty, fear, anger, grief, and a touch of hope—certainly not paparazzi trying a new angle.

"The spirits are telling me they aren't reporters," I said.

Everyone stared into space, trying to absorb the news.

Kelly said, "Ask them what happened to Darryl's little brother."

With a puzzled tone, Justin said, "Okay." A minute later, he radioed back, "They said Casey drowned in the irrigation ditch when he was two."

The three men blinked at each other. Tim croaked out, "Send them up."

The radio clicked off. We all sat motionless for a few seconds, then Shena jumped up and said, "I'll get some drinks ready."

"I'll help," Eric said.

"I'll go to the door and meet them," I said. "Find out how they feel."

The three men stood in the doorway between the kitchen and living room as I went out the door. They felt so lost at that moment.

I stepped out onto the porch and watched the van come to a stop. It was a green passenger van with rental plates like the kind that shuttle people at an airport. I wondered randomly how many people might be visiting, and then the doors began to open and magic washed out of the van. Some of those in the van were quite powerful.

Rain had followed me out and lumbered down the stairs to sniff at their legs and wag her skinny tail. They were a little taken aback at the size of her but could sense right away she meant no harm.

Like me, the spirits simply waited, ready for whatever might come as the people stepped out and began to assemble at the front of the van. It was not a surprise to see Gwen. I didn't recognize any of the others. A spell that felt like it was searching for something washed past me and circled the house. It came from a man who was climbing out of the van. He was some sort of fae. Fae magic is often unique to the being that wields it, and his was certainly different. His spell returned to him, and he felt satisfied with whatever it told him as he rounded the end of the van. They all looked up at me, but it was him that I concentrated on. When his eyes met mine, I sent the spirits to delve him.

Time stopped, because for him it had a different meaning. Images and memories began to scroll through my mind. He was an ancient being, nearly as ancient as the spirits themselves. His existence had begun in a time before the standing stones were being erected, before the first blocks were laid for the pyramids. He had lived countless lives, had existed in the bodies of all manner of creatures, men and women being only some of them. He had followed them into death and found the realm I'd recently glimpsed, where demons and dark spirits reside, and was trapped there for a millennium. Then he found love, another fae with whom he spent hundreds of years, and when she died, he could not bear the pain of it. He ceased to exist in any real form for yet another millennium and wanted only for it to end. He eventually began to live again, existing only in the bodies of simple creatures who did not think about past or future, but only of the now. While living as one of them, he had become trapped in Underhill. And time passed.

Upon his escape from there, he began to live as a human again. He'd been a street walker, an actor, politician, sheriff, judge, acrobat—an endless list of occupations. He preferred not to be human, though; his basic nature was not predatory. His affinity was for the gentle beasts, the browsers and grazers. Although he had countless memories and experiences he could draw on, he didn't often recall those other lives. It would be too much, after all, for one mind to contain.

He was not powerful in the beginning. His only magic had been to transform. Time—surviving—had given him strength. Then, when he despaired again and wanted to cease being anything at all, he'd fallen in love. With a human, of all things.

I hadn't wanted to know all that, but soon it was not me scrolling through his memories, but him giving them to me. He took my own memories as well and absorbed those. It left me feeling naked, exposed, raw. In that moment, I understood to the depths of my soul what I had only grasped intellectually before. Stealing into the minds of others is a dark art, an invasion.

When he came to my current life and discovered who I lived with, I felt his surprise. He had met Sylvio in the distant past and had been careful to avoid him ever since. For a few moments, I was afraid of what he might do to me, but he meant no harm and understood that I intended none as well.

He let me go. Suddenly, everything was back in focus, and I saw that mere seconds had passed in our world. It took me a moment to compose myself; I had been so deeply lost in his memories. They were standing at the front of the van, waiting for me to speak. The fae had soft brown eyes, and he allowed me to see that the pupil was oblong, like a sheep's. Then he changed them to normal human eyes with a gray tint and smiled at me. He was shorter than most of the others. He was only then coming up to them, having been the last to exit the van, and he turned to nod at Gwen.

Their purpose here was to see their children. They wanted nothing more than that. I introduced myself and Rain, then led them into the house.

Eric was bringing chairs out from the kitchen to give us all a place to sit. No one was ready for that yet. They stared at each other, unsure of what to do next. Then the fae crossed the living room and embraced Darin. Darin's mother was right beside him, and the hugging and crying began. Kelly's parents were there too, and they hugged and patted and cried, and included Marta in it.

As soon as Darin's parents embraced him, Gwen and the man with her, who turned out to be Tim's father, John, crossed the room and hugged Tim. I saw actual tears in Tim's eyes and was overjoyed. The rest of us—Eric, Shena, and the other three people who had come—stood silently weeping, feeling a bit awkward.

Eventually, they stepped back and everyone took a seat, although they kept a hand on each other, either on a knee or a wrist, or clasping hands, afraid if they lost contact their child would disappear again. The twins came with me into the kitchen to bring out drinks, and we handed them around.

Three of those who had come didn't have someone to hug. The boys knew why they were there. They were not strangers. It was Kelly who composed himself first. He introduced me as a good friend, and Eric and Shena as Tim's niece and nephew. Gwen shot me a sharp look at that news. I was sure she could feel the aura of magic on the two of them. She did not interrupt, though. Tim's father looked puzzled but didn't say anything.

Two of the others were Leonard's parents. They dared to hope that their son was alive too but had known when witnessing the others hugging their lost children that their own was truly gone. Kelly told them that Leonard had died on the plane before ever reaching London and added that he was the lucky one. Leonard's parents didn't agree, but Kelly was speaking the truth as he saw it.

The remaining man turned out to be Darryl's brother. Kelly explained that it had been Darryl who started the fight with Sabin in the lab. He had opened Tim's cage only seconds before his injuries from the fight took his life. All three of the boys said they owed Darryl their lives. But it turned out that was not all they felt they owed him.

It had been Darryl who'd kept them sane. When they would despair, Darryl would remind them of their homes and their families, make them tell each other stories of fond memories, and describe the faces of their loved ones. He refused to let them forget and maintained that they might someday escape the hell they'd been taken to and see their families again. It was Darryl who insisted that each day was a chance for a new beginning.

The depth of sorrow they felt because Darryl never saw that day caused me physical pain. I had to excuse myself and escaped to the fresh air and sunshine on Tim's back porch.

Sylvio found me there. I don't know if my emotions brought him to me or if he came on his own. He suddenly appeared on the patio beside me. He didn't say anything as he held me while I sobbed into his shoulder. He quietly rubbed my shoulders, and eventually, the emotions washing out of the house became bearable again.

It was Devin who came to find me. That was his name—the fae who had fathered Darin. I dried my wet face with my palms and shirt sleeves and took the handkerchief Sylvio handed me to wipe my nose. Sylvio was watching the fae warily; he could sense that he was quite powerful, but he didn't recognize him until Devin held a hand out.

"Thank you," Devin said. "I didn't think I would ever escape from Underhill."

Sylvio was so startled that he reverted to Latin. *"Es Devin?"*

Devin smiled, and Sylvio shook his hand. *"Duis te,"* Sylvio added. Then he composed himself and asked me, "What's going on?"

I swallowed and hoped I could speak in a fairly regular tone. "Devin is Darin's father. Their parents came a few minutes ago to see their kids." I had *almost* managed to sound normal.

I was surprised that Sylvio chose to follow me back to Tim's living room. He arranged for Dan to take Leonard's parents home. The rest of them stayed well into the evening, including Darryl's brother. They told stories, and Tim gave a more detailed account about the rescue of the royals than I'd heard previously. Darin told of some of his adventures, and all of us laughed at his descriptions of how weird it was to be in the body of a woman. Kelly left out names but added his own stories about people he provided security for. Some of those had us all laughing too.

The families of the kidnapped boys all kept in touch through the years and remained friends. It was unusual. Most often, a tragedy like they had experienced drove people apart. People often want someone to blame. Their community was full of those with magic in them. Those who knew about magic—real magic—tended to band together if they were bent on white sorcery and not black.

At around eight in the evening, Sylvio called Ray to come take Darryl's brother home. When they departed, the other unspoken questions that had been hanging in the air could be asked.

John spoke up first. He kept his eyes down and his tone neutral as he said, "Tim, I understand why you would say Shena and Eric are your niece and nephew, but where did they come from really?" He raised his eyes and looked from Shena to Eric. "Who are your parents?"

Eric smiled and bent down to pet Rain, who was lying in front of his feet. "We don't know what we are. We can shapeshift into wolves, but we are not werewolves, and we are not fae, nor are we witches. Sylvio himself has not heard of beings like us before."

Shena asked Devin, "Have you?" He shook his head, and she said, "Tim lets us stay here. He takes care of us."

John seemed satisfied with that answer, and although Gwen was not, she did not press for more. She felt frustrated but had kept herself in check all evening, and I appreciated that.

Kelly's parents had absorbed the night's revelations with a sense of equanimity. I could see where Kelly came by his calm nature. The raw emotions I suddenly felt from both of them was a surprise.

In a voice that was little more than a whisper, Kelly's mother said, "We know about Dr. Sabin's stable and what you kids there were used for. Oh, God, I'm so sorry you suffered so." She had to compose herself for a few seconds before she could go on. "What . . . happened in the lab? What did that monster change you into?"

Kelly's answer was straightforward: "Monsters." He had been staring at the floor when he spoke, but then he raised his eyes to meet his mother's, and they held a little bit of a challenge in them. "We're werewolves, Mother," Kelly said. "Tim and me. We also crave blood, like a vampire does, but it would seem it's not possible for us to be both."

I felt a spike of alarm from John. He fidgeted nervously at the word vampire. Then he forced himself to sit still.

Kelly's father, Don, asked, "But as a werewolf, do you have to answer the moon's call?"

Kelly sat up straight and looked his father in the eyes. He allowed his eyes to morph from their normal dark chocolate to golden as he did. "We are completely werewolf."

Don dropped his eyes to stare at his hands, which I realized belatedly showed signs of hard use, as did his face. He would have been a handsome man at one time, but he had scars that appeared to be from claws running down from his eyebrow to his chin and across his left eye. At first, I didn't recognize he was a witch. Devin and Gwen's power combined was so great that they eclipsed Don's. I could guess now where those scars had come from.

He had not lowered his eyes in submission, but rather in guilt. I sensed a tide of regret that threatened to swamp him if he gave in to it. This man and his wife had been the most composed of any of the visitors. People like that are often misinterpreted. They may not show it outwardly; they may appear distant, unfeeling. But it isn't true. Kelly and his parents cared deeply about a great many things.

Quietly, Don said, "Son . . . what I did in my youth . . . I regret that." He steeled himself to look Kelly in the eyes. "I know now that even when the monster is in control, the human rarely means to cause harm."

Kelly's mother squeezed Don's hand and smiled into her son's golden eyes. "We love you. We will not risk losing you again."

Kelly closed his eyes, and the tension in him fell from his entire body. It wasn't until he relaxed completely that I realized I had never seen him that way. Marta leaned on his shoulder, and silent tears fell down her cheeks.

Into the peaceful silence that followed, Devin asked, "And you, Darin, what did they make of you in that lab?"

As family, it was not wrong of him to ask, but it was too much for Darin. He left. I felt his spirit, the essence of his being, lift out of his body and drift away up the hillside until I couldn't feel it anymore. Everyone was looking at Darin, and those who had come calling were all puzzled by his blank expression and the stillness of his body. It still breathed, and the eyes blinked occasionally, but that was all it did.

"Sabin could trap Darin's body in a cage," Tim explained, "like he could the rest of us. He was fascinated with Darin because if he tortured him enough, he could make him change into other creatures. He did much worse things to Darin than he did to the rest of us. Darin was tougher than we were, too. He could take more pain. After a while, he stopped talking, even when it was only us in the dark lab after Sabin and his aides left. He would scream when Sabin tortured him, but that and the little sounds that would escape him afterward when moving hurt were all we heard from him. Then, a couple of weeks before the fire, he stopped responding, even when Sabin tortured him."

They had all been looking from Tim to Darin as Tim spoke. Darin's body remained motionless except for an occasional blink. Devin reached over to touch Darin's arm, and his eyes flicked up to meet mine. Comprehension lit his face.

I nodded and said, "He's not there. He has left his body behind."

Darin's mother was alarmed, and she took one of the body's hands in her own, staring into its eyes, searching for some sort of response. "What did you say?"

"Sabin tried to change Darin like he did with Tim and Kelly," I answered, "but it didn't work. Maybe it has to do with his fae blood. Anyway, Darin found a way to escape. He can leave his body and change into someone else, or float around like a spirit does."

I felt Gwen had been entirely too quiet all evening but was relieved she hadn't been confrontational. Now she gasped, "That's . . . simply amazing." She turned to Devin and then Sylvio. "Have you ever heard of such a thing?"

Sylvio shrugged. "No. It seems Dr. Sabin created new kinds of magical creatures."

As the evening wore on, John had begun to glance at Sylvio when he thought we would not catch it. He felt suspicious and unsure, and a little afraid when he did. He said to Gwen, "Several times today, you have asked Sylvio about magic. What's more, you value his opinion about it, as does Devin. The study of sorcery has been your life's work. Why do you defer to him? Frankly, I'm surprised."

I often forgot that, to those who didn't know him, Sylvio appeared to be a young man. He'd only been in his late twenties when he died.

I learned that evening that Tim's mother had died while experimenting with a spell when he was only nine. I was surprised to find that Gwen, who was John's mother-in-law, had not cast the spell to block Tim from his magic. She said his mother had done it when he was eight, after he set the house on fire when having a fit of temper like any normal little kid—but normal kids don't send jets of fire from their hands. John had Native American blood. Nascha was his sister.

Gwen smiled and patted John's hand, then said simply, "John, this will be difficult, but you should know, Sylvio has studied sorcery for centuries. He's a vampire."

John, who was sitting next to Sylvio, leapt out of his chair and spun around to face him, backing up as he did. "Jesus Christ! Vampire!"

He stared at Sylvio with terror in his eyes and then quickly glanced away. One hand was clasping the cross on the choker at his neck reflexively. John knew what a vampire truly was and believed what Gwen said without question. Gwen was shocked at his reaction and then felt chagrined.

Tim stood and held his hands up. "Dad, it's okay. Sylvio is a good guy. He and Rachel have helped me a lot."

John looked at me. "Are you his?"

"Yes," I said, and John's eyes widened. "And no. He can't capture my mind like a vampire usually does. I'm a witch. The kind Nascha and Micah are."

John scowled at Gwen. "What the hell! Since when do the covens let a vampire keep a witch captive?" His back was to the door now. He wanted to escape, and he knew, really knew, that attempting to run away was hopeless.

"Who kept you?" Sylvio asked John. He was guessing, but it had been an accurate one as we could all see from John's face. He did not reply. "And how is it that you are free now?" Sylvio added.

John still couldn't quite bring himself to speak, so Tim said, "Mom rescued him." He looked at Sylvio directly. "From Irene."

Sylvio blinked, surprised. Then the humor he'd felt moments before vanished, replaced with a sorrow that was bone deep. He bowed his head. I was sure it was so that none of us could see the expression on his face. Addressing the floor, he said, "She was in the coven that destroyed Irene?"

I felt a sudden anger from Gwen directed at Sylvio. She glared at him, then explained to me, "Antone and Carlisle helped them. Sylvio couldn't bring himself to do it."

Sylvio ignored Gwen. "Your mother was very brave, Tim. All of them were that day. Irene was very strong. She had lived a long time. But it had to be done. Her mind was . . . lost." Sylvio's voice faltered at that last word.

Gwen's expression turned from righteous wrath to surprise. It was clear she hadn't understood the depth of feeling Sylvio had for Irene, or that he had agreed she must be stopped.

Tim put a hand on his father's arm. "Dad, please, there is no danger. Come sit down." He led John to one of the chairs on the opposite side of the room from Sylvio. Reluctantly, feeling like a trapped deer, John sat down. I sent a sense of calm and safety to their part of the room, which helped quite a bit, and Tim smiled at me.

Sylvio caught John's eyes but did not attempt to hold him with his gaze, and John looked away. Sylvio said, "I'm sorry about what was done to you. I didn't realize . . . didn't want to see . . . what she had become."

Another silence ensued.

"Well, hell," Don said to Sylvio. I noticed he was no longer worried about looking directly at Sylvio. "This is a sticky business. If you're good friends with Tim, how are you going to keep the press out of it? I'm sure there aren't any plans to bring vampires out to the public. That'd be too much of a pill to swallow, don't you think?"

Sylvio smiled at Don, although he couldn't keep his smile from being a little bleak. "Luckily, I can teleport, so we can still visit without leaving a trail to follow."

"Sylvio," John whispered to himself, but we all heard. "I remember now. She told me about you, and Antone. He was the tall one, right? The black guy who looks like a model?" He didn't wait for Sylvio to answer; he wasn't addressing anyone in particular. "She said you are free to walk around during the day because . . . because you're on the side of light and white magic." He glanced up at Sylvio, and then quickly away. "Like today. The sun had not set when you came in the back door." His face reflected wonder now instead of horror.

Sylvio nodded, then turned to Gwen. "How did you keep Irene's brood from losing their minds? Did you give them to another and not tell me?"

Gwen's face showed compassion and love, and an apology, too, as she gazed at John and Tim. "Marie found a spell that she believed she could tweak so that it would work to free their tie to Irene without damaging their minds. It worked for four of the nine."

I realized that memories had been blocked from John, and we'd undone that block tonight. He was remembering it all now. Tim's was not the only damaged soul in the family.

"I would like to know how that spell is done," I said.

Gwen sighed, and with pure, open honesty, said, "It was an invention of Marie's. How to do it died with her."

Into the quiet that followed, Darin drifted back into the room and sank into his body. He took a deep breath, rubbed his face, and eyed everyone with a sheepish look. Puzzled by the charged atmosphere, he asked, "What did I miss?"

Kelly and Tim started chuckling, and soon we were all laughing, even John. We needed that release from tension.

℘ ෬

Two days later, emboldened by what had happened with Tim and his friends and family, I walked into my father's office.

"What can I do for you, Miss Burns?" he asked politely. He held out his hand and his brow furrowed when we touched. "Do I know you? You seem familiar."

I saw that we shared many similarities. I got my height and bone structure from him, and my large hands and straight hair. His hair was darker than mine, but his eyes were bright blue, while mine are usually hazel. I appear to be Caucasian, although my skin is a little dark. I'd learned this was because in the distant past, my ancestors had been Shawnee. But his was darker still, and even at nearly sixty, he was not soft. He clearly pursued more physical things than work in an office.

I smiled as I shook his hand and found I could not speak at that moment. So I sat in the chair on the other side of his desk and clutched my small handbag in both hands so they wouldn't wander or fidget. The name plate on his desk read Ryan Lakose.

Taking a deep breath, I said, "I've been trying for weeks to think up a way to ease into this, but there isn't one that I can see." I gazed directly into his eyes and said, "My mother's name was Ashley. Your family took her in as a foster child when both of you were teenagers. You're . . . my father."

The spirits were there with me, but I didn't ask for their aid. Somehow, that felt like cheating. I thought how horrible it would be if he didn't even remember her. He was blinking at me, trying to compose his thoughts enough to say something, so I rushed on.

"A nurse at Cook County Hospital told everyone I died. Then she kept me safe until I could be put in an orphanage. I was only a few weeks old when I was adopted. I didn't know about her or you until last summer."

"Safe?" he croaked.

"We don't know who exactly was after my mom, but . . . I'm sorry, she died right after naming me the night I was born."

In a whisper, he said, "She told me . . . people were after her."

Relief began to wash over me. He did remember after all. I could breathe again.

He was still grasping at straws. His hand wandered to a picture frame that stood on the corner of his desk. He picked it up and looked at it, then at me. Then he turned it around.

The only picture I'd ever found of my mother was one of those tiny ones in a school yearbook I'd been able to locate. The girl in that photo looked very much like I had as a teenager. In the photo my father now held out, my mother was holding hands with a boy who wasn't quite a man yet. It was a snapshot someone had taken of them at what appeared to be an amusement park. But—it was on his desk. He was near retirement age; he'd kept the photo close to him for over forty years.

ᔕ Chapter 17 ᘓ
White Magic?

I was glad to be at home doing something normal finally—or, as normal as things ever got anymore. I was practicing with Otis in the indoor arena. I had decided to show him in an eventing competition, so we were working on dressage and jumping. I'd become used to spirits wandering the same space with me by then. I was never without them anymore. They weren't invasive; they were simply always there. Most were good spirits, so they weren't disturbing. I wondered why they hung around. There must not be much to do when you're only energy filling up space. What an odd existence they must have, at least from a human perspective.

Otis had just completed a very nice lead change. I stopped him so he could take a breather and think about it. Shadow and Missy were lying nearby, watching me. They suddenly jumped up, barking, and startled Otis as they charged for the east end of the arena. The big door was open, and a woman was standing there. I had not sensed her presence until that moment.

The spirits gathered around me in a thick blanket; they were alarmed enough that I became nervous, and Otis caught my change in mood. He began to fidget. I sent some spirits her way to delve what she was as she petted the dogs then walked casually toward me.

Fae; that was the answer I got. Someone with very strong magic. It was midday and sunny behind her, so I all I could see at first was her outline. As she drew nearer, I noticed she had long, raven hair with a hint of red in it. Her eyes were the pale-green of sea foam, and her face was short of stunning. Enough to turn heads, but not enough to be a total distraction to the men she met. She stopped six feet from me.

I wracked my brain for some reason *she* would be here.

"Rachel, perhaps you remember? We've met briefly once before."

Her voice was seductive, her manner alluring. She exuded feminine grace, and she wasn't even trying.

"Morgen, yes, I remember." I was truly stumped and didn't have any idea how I should react to her presence. Sylvio didn't trust her, but they weren't enemies. As I dismounted, I asked, "What can I help you with?"

Morgen smiled and stepped past me to pet Otis. He calmed under her touch, although she did not use magic to achieve that. I noticed she was quite relaxed, but the spirits still wrapped me in a protective shield.

"You're not often alone," she said. "I've been looking for an opportunity to speak with you without others interfering."

It was not Sylvio's week with us. Kelly and Marta were at Tim's place with Darin. The others I lived with had gone to town to pick up supplies. I hadn't thought about it until then, but she was right. It was quite rare for me to be alone. Then I wondered how she had known. How had she been watching the house without the spirits telling me someone was spying?

Morgen continued petting Otis. She scratched under his mane, then wandered along his side and stopped to scratch his hip. She seemed to know that was one of his favorite things.

What did I dare ask? I didn't want to tip my hand and let her know I was unaware I had been under surveillance. She didn't seem to notice my hesitation.

"I can enlist their aid too, the spirits," she said. "If my motive is benign, they would have no reason to warn you."

Chills ran down my spine. Did she know what I was thinking, or was that merely a good guess? I found my voice. "I'm glad to hear your purpose here is benign, but what is it you wanted to tell me where keen hearing would not catch it?"

"They have some colorful phrases to describe feelings these days. Scared shitless comes to mind." She turned to look at me. "You scare the hell out of all of them. Everyone is keeping you in the dark."

"I've guessed as much already. The Coven doesn't know what to do with me or Chris, and they don't want to teach either of us anything." I knew my tone sounded a little petulant.

Morgen shook her head. "Of course they haven't." She fiddled with Otis's mane and seemed hesitant to speak. I waited. Finally, she looked over his neck directly at me. "Rachel, I said *everyone*."

I scowled and didn't worry about it showing on my face. A hint of what she meant was teasing me, but I couldn't quite puzzle it out.

She knew that by looking me in the eyes I would know her true feelings, no matter how powerful she was, and yet she still held my gaze.

"Sylvio has been careful not to reveal what he knows to you," she said. "He has hunted witches for centuries and none of them, even when they've united, have defeated him. He knows more about sorcery than any living witch and could teach you more than even Gwen and Nascha, or that grimoire your mother left you."

I was annoyed. She was not the first one to try driving a wedge between Sylvio and me. I narrowed my eyes at her and was ready to voice a protest, but she had more to say.

"Love has blinded you, Rachel. You live with your greatest teacher, if he were willing. Sylvio fears your power. He hasn't survived so long by trusting others, and certainly not a witch. *Any* witch."

I absorbed that and felt the truth of it from the spirits as well. They were more energized than concerned now, anticipating something important happening. "Why tell me this?"

"You're on the right track, although you don't know it yet. You have the ability to find and destroy our quarry if you are shown how to use your gifts."

Our quarry? Recently, a black witch coven had opened a portal to Hell. Or so I assumed that was where demons and the like came from. We had closed that portal, and it had cost us all a lot to do it. Since then, Sylvio had been systemically finding and killing the black witches involved, but none of them could provide him with a clear picture of who was driving this rise in evil—at least that he had told me about.

"Are you offering to teach me?" I asked.

"Some things, yes. Others, I have no gift for. But with the aid of Sylvio, and that slip of a girl and her twin you and the werewolf brought into this world, you and your son will be a force to reckon with."

It was a certainty she would not grant such a gift without cost, and I was still puzzled why she would offer. "What do you want from me in return?"

"Let's say your quarry is also an enemy of mine."

The light went on. Morgen feared what we were after. She would not risk her own life to pursue the black witch, or witches, we were hunting—if it even was a witch. I made a mental note to ask Sylvio if our quarry might be a fae. After my brief time in Underhill, I had read all I could find about the fae, and although much of it was impossible to distinguish between fact and fiction, there were some themes that carried throughout. One was don't strike a bargain with a fae; if you end up owing them, it will probably end badly.

I sent the question out to the spirits surrounding me: Should I agree to this? What I got back was not a resounding yes. They were pensive about Morgen, but not about what was about to happen.

"Okay," I said, "what is it that you want to show me?"

Morgen felt surprised then, and relieved. I hadn't been able to distinguish her feelings up to that point, and it occurred to me that until that moment she was unsure herself how to feel. She had truly wanted me to agree to her proposal but thought I would not.

She smiled mischievously and said, "This." The air split beside her, and an opening appeared, like a doorway. Beyond that opening were marble floors I had glimpsed once before. I hadn't known fae could do that. She'd done something similar in Underhill, but I thought it was because of where we were, not because of any particular talent of hers.

She stepped through and reappeared at the north entrance to the arena where I had first seen her. Otis began to dance around me and jumped sideways and snorted when, moments later, the doorway opened next to us and Morgen returned. Otis backed up several feet before I was able to calm him down. While I was petting him, Morgen said, "You would not be able to call Sylvio to your side if you did not have that same gift yourself."

And how had she learned I could do *that*?

Hoping to buy myself time to absorb what she was implying, I said, "Before you do that again, let me put him away." Being busy unsaddling Otis would give me a few minutes to think.

She followed me to the aisle by the tack room. I could feel her amusement as we walked.

"You think you can teach me to teleport?" I asked as I took Otis's saddle off.

"Oh, I'm sure I can. You only need enough motivation."

"Motivation?" I was suspicious. "What do you mean by that?"

"The Coven sent a cadre of witches to capture Chris. I imagine they've accomplished it by now."

I glared at her, having no one else to focus my anger on, and said with considerable venom, "Where is he?"

The spirits swirled around me, ready to do my bidding. It takes a lot to make me angry, but she had accomplished it. The very air began to vibrate; a faint clink and rattle came from the tack room as the things hanging there began to shake.

Morgen's eyes widened, and she spoke very fast. "You will not be able to travel someplace you haven't been, in the beginning. I'll have to take you there, but first I need to show you how to come back once you get there."

Things moving of their own accord spooked Otis again. I had to soothe him, which helped me calm down too. I put him in the corral, and as soon as I let him go, he took off to join the other horses huddled in the far corner. Animals are quite perceptive. Shadow and Missy were now cowering under the bench by the tack room door. I felt guilty and sent a wave of peace out. They didn't need to pay for my anger.

"Show me," I commanded.

Morgen's smile was triumphant. She told me the main thing that blocked a witch from the gift was the disbelief that it could be done. I didn't have that problem. I knew it was possible. She had spoken truth when she said it. In fact, nothing she'd said so far was in any way false.

The next step was to wrap myself in a cocoon woven from all four elemental spirits. Which, she said, was not how fae did it, or vampires, so she couldn't describe that to me, but she was certain the spirits would help me. It took more than an hour to figure it out. Once again, it was *not* trying too hard that caused it to work. I had to let it happen.

Morgen said that next, I needed to visualize the cocoon in that other place. She pointed out that the cocoon needed to encase everything I wanted to move, or it would be left behind. I couldn't help picturing the sight of my own severed foot sitting lost and forlorn next to the tack room door.

It took many failed tries; I was sure I looked like an idiot. Then, finally, I ended up on the other side of the arena where we'd put a bucket as a target, with all my parts intact.

Morgen clapped her hands and actually squealed with delight. Somehow, that seemed out of character for her. I asked the spirits if I was on the right path. Should I be listening to her? Their response was still positive. Yes, I should do this.

"What's next?" I demanded.

She sobered up immediately. "Okay, now we need to find out how far you can go. That seems to vary with the few who can perform this kind of sorcery. Come stand beside me."

When I did, she wrapped an arm around me like Sylvio always did. This time, it was different; everything was, when she did it. I didn't feel a blast of cold when we teleported. Rather, it felt warm and humid.

We took a step through her doorway, and it felt like I was being squeezed from all sides. The air around us stank like fish, not ozone. We stepped through onto a balcony, and I couldn't help gasping, glad to be able to breathe. The air was fresh and smelled of pine. Behind us was a house big enough to be called a mansion. In front of us was a mountain lake surrounded by trees.

She only gave me a few moments to get my bearings, then said,

"Now, take us back."

I stared at her. "But I don't even know where we are," I protested.

"Where you *are* doesn't matter. You need a clear picture of where you're *going*."

I blinked at her, trying to wrap my mind around it.

She pursed her lips, frustrated. "Come on, don't waffle on me now. Get on with it. Chris is waiting."

That did it. I wrapped the cocoon around both of us. She tightened her grip on my waist. I visualized the aisle by the tack room, all the details, even down to the pieces of hoof that had been left there after trimming Otis before I rode.

It took longer than it had when she did it. It wasn't cold; it was *frigid*. We were in a vast, black, airless sphere, like space but without stars. It felt like we'd be stuck there forever. There was something else there with us. It was surprised, and it was not pleased. Then we were back in the aisle by the tack room, standing by the hitch rail.

As soon as we appeared in the aisle, I said, "Take me to Chris."

"What are you doing?"

I had to turn away to hide my expression. I didn't think it would be a good thing for Morgen to find out Sylvio and I could communicate that way. *"Trying something new."*

I felt his surprise, and then Morgen put her arm around my waist, and I was being squished into too small a space again. We appeared in an alleyway. A cat was standing on the edge of a dumpster right next to us. It hissed, jumped up, fell into the dumpster with a crash, and immediately bounced back out and sprinted down the alley.

Morgen and I both jumped too. I said, "I think we scared a couple of lives out of that cat."

She was still watching the cat run, with a smile on her face, and that was a good thing because next, I heard: *"Merde! Where are you?"*

I was making him swear again. *"Actually, I'm not sure."*

"Are you okay?"

"I'll get back to you on that."

"Rachel, damn it!"

I felt his push to come to me and pushed back. *"I'll be sure to call you here if I need you."* Silence—and that was a lot scarier to me than his anger.

"Rachel?" Morgen was looking at me with concern.

"Sorry." I stepped to the side, away from her, and looked up and down the alley. "Where are we?"

Instead of answering, she said, "Can't you sense where they are?"

I put thoughts of Sylvio aside and focused on the spirits. It took me a moment. I had assumed that, since Morgen told me they took Chris, it would be black witches or some other being who used dark magic. That's what I delved for first. But it was not black sorcery. They were in the building on our right. Always before, my enemies had clearly been evil. But I was at a loss about how to proceed.

"The beings in there aren't black witches," I said.

Morgen didn't question that. She simply said, "True, but they are getting in the way."

"I intend no harm to innocent people, even if they are misguided."

She put her hands on her hips. "What makes you think they're innocent? A great many wrongs have been committed by those with good intentions."

And once again, she spoke truth. I saw something else in her eyes then. She had not lied to me at any time. But that didn't mean this wasn't a trap. If I harmed those in the building, my potential allies would become enemies. The question was how to get to Chris without causing harm?

Before I could say anything, I felt a pulse of power strong enough to send me reeling backwards. Sylvio appeared where I had been standing. He let out a roar that hurt my ears and hit the dumpster, collapsing one side of it. Then he looked at me with eyes that blazed crimson in the dim alley.

How had he found me? I had put a block up so he could not jump to where I was. As calmly as I could, I said, "Sylvio, thank you for coming. I wasn't sure what to do next." I prayed fervently that he would play along and make Morgen believe his anger was at her and not me.

Morgen was standing behind and to the side of me. I could sense fear in her now, and annoyance. She had not wanted Sylvio to interfere. She disguised her feelings with a tone of mild amusement and said, "Well, I think I'll leave it to you two to sort out how to help Chris."

I turned so I could see her. She gave Sylvio a coy smile, opened the gateway to her palace, and disappeared.

Some of Sylvio's fury washed away, and I stopped holding my breath. He looked at the huge dent in the dumpster and back at me. "I thought you knew enough not to mingle with a fae. Why did she bring you here, and what did she mean about Chris?"

"She appeared at the arena and told me I'm being kept in the dark on purpose. And she said Chris has been captured by The Coven."

He growled, "Did it occur to you that doing that would be a handy way to capture you, too?"

Now I was the one who was angry. I put my hands on my hips and glared at him. "Sylvio, I know I seem like a child to you since you have lived so very long, but I'm not an idiot."

He ran his hands through his hair in frustration. "How am I supposed to protect you if you do things like this?"

"Why haven't you shown me how to teleport?"

He stared at me. I reached for his feelings and was met with a wild contrast of emotions. I understood his anger. He kept himself under such strict control at all times that, when he could not do that, it frightened him. It was so tempting to use compulsion to calm him, but I didn't dare do it. He had fought for centuries to be free of the control of any other being, even the demon that gave him life.

He stared at the space where Morgen had disappeared. "Is that what she was up to?"

"Yes, she said you could teach me a lot about sorcery, more than anyone else."

His anger drifted away on the soft breeze that blew down the alleyway. The overriding emotions he had at that moment were frustration and fear. *Why fear me?*

"If I teach you," he said, "I'll have to explain the rules too."

I understood then. He was afraid for my safety. I already knew that. He'd said once, "It's not breaking a rule if you don't know there is one." My anger subsided, but I could tell that was not the whole reason for his unease about teaching me.

"So, if you teach me the rules, I'd have to abide by them?" I asked.

He sighed. "The Coven and I have been skirting the law. They don't have to confront you if it's clear you have not been trained."

Again, I got the sense he was speaking the truth, but not the whole truth. However, now was not the time to discuss that any further.

A side door on the building Chris was supposed to be in opened, and nothing came out that could be seen, but I could *feel* him.

"Antone?"

Sylvio put a hand on my shoulder and said, "Did you think I would leave Chris without protection?"

So *that* was how Sylvio had teleported to where I was. He'd jumped to where he knew Antone to be.

Antone dropped his concealment charm and said, "Good evening, Rachel."

I kissed Sylvio's cheek. "I'm sorry," I said. Then I turned to Antone. "I'm so glad to see you. Is Chris in there?"

"Yes," Antone said. "Chris is in a cell much like the one in Sylvio's basement. He's been drugged and is out cold at the moment. Rick is being held in another room. Looks like he put up a fight. He has some cuts and bruises on his face. He's out too right now." He paused, then added, "There's a spell I'm not familiar with around the cage."

As he spoke, he was looking up and down the alleyway and sniffing the air. He would be able to smell fae.

"Morgen brought me here."

Antone was surprised by that news. Then he glanced at Sylvio, who was still angry and frustrated, and felt amused. He felt it was a good thing that keeping me was a challenge for Sylvio.

"Did you sense anything besides witches in there?" I asked him. His humor was not helping Sylvio's mood.

Antone glanced back at the door. "No, and these are not black witches."

"And there's my quandary. I sense no black magic either," I said. I realized I was wringing my hands. I had no idea how to proceed.

Sylvio wrinkled his brow and put both hands on my shoulders. "Rachel, it's the same idea. You need to get something done, and the spirits are available for you to do it. All you need is to be clear in what you want from them."

I couldn't help it; I had to hug him, even though hugging a vampire is like hugging a rock. Vampires are full of contrasts, inside and out. Their skin is soft as silk, and their bodies hard as stone.

How obvious it suddenly was. He'd given me that same message time and again. Magic is a tool.

I gathered the spirits around us and sent them the message that I needed to find and free Chris and Rick, and that I didn't want to harm anyone. They felt delighted to do something new. I followed the rainbow of color as the spirits went through the door. Sylvio kept a hand on my shoulder, and Antone was a pace behind us. It was a stairwell. We were led up the stairs for three floors, then turned left down a long corridor. It turned out to be an office building. Most rooms we passed had clear glass windows showing cubicles inside, but the door they led us to was at the end of the hall, and it had solid walls on either side.

I wondered how to go in there and not be seen. In response, the air spirits gathered around me. An odd sensation started at my feet and wound around my body. I looked down at my shoes, and they weren't there.

Sylvio chuckled; all of his anger had gone. I felt both he and Antone as they wrapped a concealment charm around themselves. It was not like the one the spirits had woven for me, not even close. How strange.

Things were about to get even more weird. The spirits didn't open the door; they pushed us *through* it. I could actually feel my body blend with the wood fibers in the door and the metal of the handle. Sylvio and Antone were both startled. I could tell they hadn't ever done *that* before.

There were thirteen witches on the other side of that door, and they were having a lively discussion. I had learned that the number thirteen increased magical power. I could see the weave of magic that encircled the cell Chris was in. Tendrils of magic led to a room I presumed Rick was in. In addition to the witches sitting in a circle, there were others in the big room, people without magic. A few were unmistakably bodyguards.

I didn't know if the invisibility spell that concealed us would hide sound, so I sent to Sylvio: *"Can they hear us if we talk?"*

Sylvio kissed the back of my neck. *"You figure that out."*

Duh, I thought. Of course, the spirits would follow my lead. Still, I couldn't help whispering when I said, "Antone, will you go to the room Rick is in and wait? I'll signal you when it's time to take him away. I'd like to listen in on their discussion first."

It was not a surprise that no sound escaped our little circle. Antone stepped away, and a little cloud of spirits went with him. His grin was wide when he got to the closed door and slid sideways through it.

The witches had put up a charm meant to reveal magic. The spirits were able to bypass that easily, but how had Antone come and gone without their notice?

"How come they didn't know Antone was here earlier?" I asked.

"Witch sorcery, and how to counter it, is a pursuit of his," was Sylvio's reply.

Of course; if it would have done any good, I would have slapped myself on the forehead. I focused on the witches' discussion. I recognized some of them. One was Delilah. She had been at the first meeting I'd had with The Coven when Sylvio made it clear he intended to keep me. Three of the others had been at Brett's pub: Sherry, Joshua, and Staci.

Joshua was saying, "I agreed to this in the beginning, but now it feels wrong. We can't keep him drugged all the time, and we have no way to predict what he will do once he is conscious. He's bound to be angry, and I wouldn't blame him for that. Besides, I like Chris, and his mother seemed okay too."

"We have his boyfriend, he'll cooperate," a strange warlock said.

Staci said, "You didn't need to be quite so rough on him."

The strange warlock snorted. "Don't be fooled. He might look like an easy target, but damned if he didn't know a thing or two about fighting."

Staci said, "Well, if we intend to gain Chris's cooperation or his mother's, then doing harm to an innocent is not a good start."

"I'm still not clear how capturing Chris will gain us leverage with either of them," said another witch I didn't know.

Delilah said, "This was Nicole's plan, and I agreed with it. Regardless of what you know of Chris, they both need a lesson in humility, especially his mother. They are much too arrogant, and they believe we fear them. They need to be shown that we do not."

Which was a lie. They *did* fear us, or they would not have attempted such drastic action.

The name Nicole was familiar to me. Delilah had been standing in for her when I was first summoned before The Coven, so I knew Nicole ranked high. But I had never met her.

I moved toward the metal cage. There was a circle drawn in white chalk around it. Points led out from it, forming a pentagram. A white candle sat at each apex. Next to each candle lay a different item for each point. I recognized a white feather in the closest one but couldn't make out what the other ones were. A second circle was drawn around the outside of the pentagram. The witches sat in a third circle outside the other two, facing the cage.

When my foot broke the first circle, I felt a shimmer in the spirits. I hesitated, but the invisibility spell held. I took another couple steps, and as my foot crossed the inner circle, the enchantment surrounding it vibrated and my progress was stopped.

All the witches in the room had felt the thrum as the spell reverberated. They sat up in their seats and began to look around. Each of them whispered different words and held either a knife or a wand in their hands. I felt various spells waft around and through us.

Sylvio chuckled. *"This is fun. Who'd have thought the spirits could bend magic that way? Even delving doesn't show the witches where we are."*

His humor calmed me down. I had thought we were stuck. I reached up and touched the barrier softly so it would not vibrate. It was so weird to reach out with my hand and not be able to see it.

The barrier felt like the shield Sylvio kept around the homes his people lived in. Slowly, my hand slid into it. It was cold and thick, like passing my hand through Jell-O. Thinking to make myself smaller, I turned sideways and kept moving. It was not a bubble; I didn't emerge on the other side. It encased all of the space within that circle. I pushed my way through the bars of the cage with the help of the spirits until we stood next to Chris. I put a hand on his arm and asked the spirits if we could teleport away.

The answer was no.

"Any ideas what to do now that we're here?" I asked.

"Can you wake him? I'll bet the two of you combined could break this spell."

The witches in the room could sense something was happening, but not what. They kept trying to use their eyes to spot the problem. They should have been concentrating with other senses. It was Delilah who figured it out first. She focused her power on the cage and sent a strong spell our way, which once again passed through us, but then it bounced back. The spirits were not prepared for that.

The circle of witches was linked, so they all felt the spell wrap around us on its way back. It did not let go; it became an extra layer to the invisibility spell.

"Shit, now what?"

"Wake him up!"

I was annoyed that Sylvio seemed to be enjoying this. I was about ready to hyperventilate.

I touched Chris's forehead and willed him to push the fog of drugs away and look at me. At the same time, I heard Delilah say, "Now!"

A lot of things happened at once. All the witches spoke out loud, but they were not the same words, so I couldn't tell what they said. The door to the room Rick was in slammed open to reveal Antone standing inside with Rick cradled in his arms. The bars on the cell we were in caved in toward us, then expanded out, like the cell was breathing. The bars made a hideous creak and whine. Chris sat up and threw a blast of air spirits out that sent the witches tumbling backwards, and the spell that Delilah had wrapped around us evaporated. So did my own concealment charm. Chris sent another wave of power out, attempting to blast through the thick Jell-O surrounding us, but that didn't work.

All the others were picking themselves up off the floor and staring at us, but Delilah was not a member of The Coven for nothing. She sent out a spell I had not encountered before. Thick ropes appeared out of thin air and snaked around us all, Rick and Antone included.

Chris pulled fire spirits from the candles encircling the cage, and the ropes burned to ash in seconds but left us unscathed, even our clothes. The smoke from the burned ropes set off the building's fire suppressor system. Water sprayed down on us all.

Chris was delighted by that. He had a particular gift for water. He got off the bed, started to sway, and then Sylvio took his arm to steady him. Chris combined water and air, and everything surrounding the cage began to spin—chairs, candles, bodyguards, and witches.

I saw Antone move. He'd set Rick on his feet. The spell that had been tied to the room was gone. Rick was blinking at the scene in front of him, dumbfounded. Antone nodded at us, and he and Rick disappeared.

Chris saw them go too, and when they did much of his anger went with them. I put a hand on his shoulder and said, "I think that's quite enough for now."

Chris dropped his spell, and everything landed on the floor with a crash.

The three of us wiped water from our eyes and surveyed the mess of candles, chairs, and people in front of us. They were slow to move, more from caution than hurt, as they picked themselves up off the floor. None of them was injured to any great extent. They watched us warily.

I realized they were all in front of us now. I didn't know if that had been Chris's intent, but we could see everyone without turning our heads.

Sylvio could not contain himself anymore. He started to chuckle. "Well, Delilah, this was a *brilliant* idea."

I had to give her credit; she looked dignified, even soaking wet. None of the others could pull that off.

She glared at him. "They're a danger even to themselves, and you know it."

Sylvio laughed. "I'd say they're a danger to their enemies. Do you want to be counted as one?" To me, he added, *"Think up a way for you two to break this annoying glue."*

I said, "Chris, open yourself to the spirits, but don't think too much. Think only of being free of this stuff we're encased in. Empty your mind of everything else, even trying."

I wished I could talk to Chris mind to mind too, because Delilah's eyes lit up. She was sure the Jell-O spell could not be undone.

Chris looked at me, puzzled. I didn't want to explain more; not in present company. But I could see he did not catch what I meant. "Let it happen, don't try to *make* it happen."

"Think on it, Delilah," Sylvio said with a slight drawl. "I am quite familiar with the human mind. These two will not use magic for evil purposes. The spells you invoked tonight are deemed to be white magic, and yet consider what you've done with that magic." Sylvio was not only chiding them; he was attempting to buy us some time.

I felt the power from both Chris and I meld, become one. It was yet another new sensation. Then a cloud of sylph gathered around the three of us, and the air began to sparkle and fizz into tiny fireworks. The sylph tumbled and twisted like miniature ballerinas, and every movement they made created more sparks.

I looked at the witches and bodyguards. Every one of them was now staring open-mouthed. I was not the only one who could see the spirits this time. The cloud of sparks spun a golden web around us then expanded, and the glue spell disintegrated until they had consumed all of it. I could hear a tinkling of laughter right before the sylph wafted away.

"Take us to Antone's," Sylvio sent to me.

"Me!?"

"Yes, my love, you."

My heart soared. I felt I could do anything after what he'd said. I wrapped the three of us in a cocoon, making sure all of our parts were encased in it, and after a moment we reappeared in the bedroom I had occupied twice now while recovering from other adventures.

Not ten seconds after we appeared in the room, Antone opened the door, and Rick charged in. He and Chris hugged tight and started showering kisses on each other, which quickly morphed into a full-mouthed kiss that went on for several seconds.

Sylvio cleared his throat, and they broke apart. With mischief in his eyes, Sylvio patted himself. Then he looked Chris up and down. When he got to me, he turned me around completely, grinning like the Cheshire Cat the whole time.

"What are you doing?" I asked, befuddled.

"Checking to see if all your parts are still there."

I backhanded him in the belly, and he pretended it hurt. I shook my stinging hand and said, "Jerk."

Chris had caught on. *"You* teleported us back here?" He felt more alarmed than surprised and patted himself front and back like Sylvio had done.

I folded my arms and glared at the both of them, which made Antone and Rick crack up.

"You're not helping," I said.

Sylvio sobered up a bit and said, "What I want to know is why Morgen would show you how to do that, and what is her sudden interest in you?"

None of us had an answer for that.

ᔕᎧ Chapter 18 ᥄Ꮻ
Sylvio: Amesbury

"**T**ake us there," I commanded.

The boy knew he was caught. He stood and brushed wool and dirt off his trousers and followed his father meekly out the door, but the aura of magic around him had increased. I kept him in sight rather than let him trail behind us, as was expected of youth in those days. Magical children are dangerous simply because they are untrained.

We went to the stables and found Hugh was still there. Instead of being annoyed at having to help saddle the horses he'd barely untacked, he thought it was amusing. His personality was like his father's—ready to see the humor in life.

While they saddled up, I teleported to one of my caves and gathered some supplies, then loaded them into a saddle bag that I brought back with me. Everyone eyed the bulging bag but didn't ask about it or about the long iron bars I lay across the bag and strapped to the top.

Ragna was waiting outside the door, her traveling cloak over her shoulders. She wore a look of defiance on her face.

"Ragna, love, you can't come with us," Seamas said.

"Meri returned while you were in the stable, so Hugh won't be alone," she replied in a clipped voice.

Now I understood the other human scent I'd noticed. Amused at the exchange and certain that Seamas would lose this battle, I interjected. "Meri?"

Ragna glanced my way, and her voice softened when she said, "Meri was always kind to me, so we named our second daughter after her." She folded her arms and shot a piercing look at Seamas. She was not going to be deterred.

He sighed and said, "Hugh, saddle the mare for your mother."

Grinning even more, Hugh headed for the barn.

Cyneric said, "I'll help him." He handed me his reins and caught up to the boy. While they were doing that, Meri stepped onto the threshold. She bobbed a curtsy at me and said with a grin, "Lord Denman, Mum and Papa have told us stories about you."

I had to smile at the mischief in her eyes. I could sense no magic on the girl, but Seamas and Ragna certainly had their hands full with their four children.

ℰℭ

As I had suspected he would, Sean took us around the outskirts of the town toward the standing stones. I caught Kerri's scent crossing our path more than once. She had not taken the route we did, but she had been that way that very night.

When we rode along the outer edge of the town wall, we could hear the revelers singing and chanting. The light from the bonfire in the center square carried all the way over the wall, casting us in a deeper shadow than we would have been otherwise. It had become tradition to light fires to chase away haunts.

As we approached the wide plain where the circle of stones had been erected, I felt us pass the magical barrier. At that time, the woods had reclaimed the area, so the ancient ditch and earthen berm were not very far from the forest. Cyneric reined in his horse and looked over his shoulder at me. He raised his eyebrows.

"It won't harm us, the magic is old—a leftover," I explained. "What else do you sense? Can you sort out the scents we are searching for, and more?" Men had followed us from town. I wondered if Cyneric had noticed.

Sean, who was riding behind his father's saddle on a blanket folded across the horse's loin, had turned to look behind him more than once. I was certain he noticed we weren't alone.

"The girl has been here tonight," Cyneric answered. "Who are the others?" he added. "They don't feel like normal humans."

Seamas and Ragna looked puzzled; then she peered back the way we had come and pursed her lips.

Pleased with Cyneric, I said, "Father Clark and some of his men have trailed us from town. They are men of true faith. That's the difference you feel. We could use their help. It is not only Kerri who has come this way."

Seamas and Ragna passed a hopeful look between them when Cyneric said Kerri had been there, but at the mention of Father Clark, Ragna's face darkened. "They aren't here to help," she snarled.

"I think you might be surprised," I countered. "There is a great difference between those who merely parrot the words of God and those who truly believe in them."

We rode on, leaving the shelter of the trees and riding out onto the plain. The moon was quite bright that night; it was almost full.

Father Clark and his men stopped in the deep shadow of the trees. It had rained the previous day, so the trail was damp, muffling sound. What is more, the men were clearly experienced woodsmen, and I doubted Seamas and Ragna heard them as they came closer. But to a vampire's keen hearing, their horses' hooves and even the creak of their saddles was clear.

I reined in and spun my mare around when we were fifty yards from the woods where we could easily be seen—and shot with an arrow. Cyneric heard their bows being drawn and scowled at me, wondering why I would allow us to be clear targets. His palm rested on his sword hilt.

I spoke to the men in the woods, "Come on out, gentlemen. We are in pursuit of the same quarry and could use your assistance if you would be willing."

Those with me had all been peering at the standing stones, but Ragna's head snapped around at my words, and she glowered at me.

Loud enough for all to hear, I asked, "Cyneric, other than the humans, have you sensed anything else?" The scent was faint but there nonetheless.

Cyneric hesitated a moment, trying to puzzle out what I was up to. He replied, "The place reeks of brimstone."

Seamas' horse was standing an arm's length from mine. I heard Sean gasp. He mouthed a spell silently, and I felt the air around us spark with magic. A boy gifted with such power was rare. If he survived, he would be a formidable wizard.

I whispered to Sean, "Hold that power for later, to help your sister."

His green eyes met mine, and he clenched his jaw in defiance.

"You listen to Sylvio, boy," Seamas growled, "and we might actually be able to save Kerri."

Sean twitched at the heat in his father's voice and looked down, thinking. He didn't let the magic go that he'd gathered, but he wasn't as ready to fire it off, either.

I addressed the men hidden in the woods once again. "Father Clark,

Ragna's daughter has been captured by a demon. Will you help us free her from it?"

After perhaps a half minute, Father Clark led his men slowly out from the shelter of the trees. Two of his men stayed behind. Six men flanked him still, their crossbows drawn but not aimed. They had come prepared to do battle. They wore armor but had muffled the sound of it with cloth in the joints, and their horses' tack was plain leather, not the normal jointed armor. They had intended to mask their presence. Father Clark and his men believed not only in their God but also in the power of witches and vampires.

They reined up when they were ten yards away, but their faith preceded them, weakening me even from that distance. Cyneric fidgeted with his reins and eyed me with uncertainty.

"Captured, you say?" Father Clark's doubt was clear. He was certain Kerri was in league with the thing.

I had yet to discover if that was true. I hoped Seamas and Ragna were correct in their belief in their daughter.

"Witches are not inherently evil," I explained, "but they are often tempted or tricked by demons. Demons covet the depth of emotion and the freedom humans have. They prefer witches as their victims, which the witch will eventually become, even if they invited the demon in originally."

Father Clark considered my words, as did his men. The man on his right was both broad and tall, with a hooked nose. He scowled at Father Clark, then voiced his thoughts. "We intend to burn the evil from the witch, and from this place!" he declared.

The other men murmured their agreement, and Father Clark did not admonish the man for speaking.

Seamas' hand grasped the pommel of his sword, and Ragna gathered magic about her. Sean spread his fingers, and the smell of sorcery became strong enough to override the scent of demon in the air. Cyneric moved his horse sideways so he could see both the boy and the priest's entourage.

I hoped the boy could maintain his control. Addressing Hooknose, I said, "Burning the human only makes the demon seek another victim. Would you like to be such a one? Killing an innocent will certainly make you vulnerable to invasion."

Father Clark had been bent in the saddle, weary after the long ride. He sat up straight at those words, scanned all our faces and that of his men, and asked, "You believe the girl is innocent?"

"I haven't met Kerri yet. I have faith in Seamas and Ragna, and they have faith in their daughter."

"A witch is a danger to everyone," Hooknose snapped, his eyes on Ragna.

She lifted her chin and returned his glare.

Sean's magic was so strong now that the hair at the back of my neck was standing on end. "Magic is a tool that a rare few have access to," I said. "Those who wield it must always be careful to use it wisely."

Sean looked from his mother to me. He knew I was speaking to him. He pulled his magic back into himself.

"What do you propose?" Father Clark asked.

"Let's ride on to the edge of the hanging stones, and I'll explain."

They hesitated to follow us further out onto the plain, but then Father Clark kicked his horse into motion and his men did the same.

When we were near the largest of the hanging stones, I got down from my horse and pulled two casks out of the saddle bags. "Sean," I commanded, "take this cask and sprinkle the salt around the inside of the ring of stones. Not the hanging ones; the ring outside it. Ragna, you do the same on the other side until it makes a complete circle."

Seeing the look of understanding on his mother's face, Sean did not hesitate to begin the task.

"I doubt we have much time for you to decide, gentlemen," I said. "Neither a demon nor a witch can remain in Underhill uninvited for long."

Hooknose spoke up again. "Underhill? What is that?"

"A place you would prefer not to know about."

He was affronted and began to snarl a reply, but Father Clark put up his hand and the man bit back his retort. Father Clark dismounted. "What would you have us do?"

"Have a couple of your men take the horses, ours included, to those men in the woods. They'll stampede from fright, and we'll lose them all if they are near the demon when it shows itself. Then we need your other men to stand outside the circle Ragna and Sean are making." I turned to Hooknose. "You stand next to Father Clark and protect him."

It was a rather redundant statement. The man had already dismounted and was clearly ready to defend the priest.

The men hesitated, unsure if they should listen to me. Impatiently, I took the saddle bags off my horse and reached in to take the Bible and cross I'd brought from my cave out of the bags. I handed them to Seamas. "Take these to him," I said and nodded at Father Clark. I doubted I could get close enough to hand them to him myself. "I trust you read Latin, Father?"

He nodded mutely as he reached for the Bible and cross.

"Choose verses from there and speak them out loud when Kerri appears," I said. "Concentrate on that and on your belief in your God, no matter what happens inside this circle."

Father Clark and his men stared in astonishment at the Bible and cross. Their doubts assuaged somewhat, they began to dismount.

Looking down at the worn leather binding of the old Bible, Father Clark cleared his throat and asked, "Which passage do you recommend?"

"It doesn't matter. It is the strength of the faith you and your men have that will drive the demon away."

I tossed one iron brand to Cyneric and took the other, then stepped inside the circle. I was unnerved by the magic of the place and the weakness caused by Father Clark and his men, and I hoped my pretense of authority and power was fooling them all. It helped when two of his men rode back to the woods with the horses.

While we were waiting for the men to return, Father Clark said, "I have missed you and your family, Cyneric. I was sorry to hear what happened to them, and to you." His voice was sincere.

I felt a flash of pain from Cyneric, then annoyance at Father Clark, but he answered with an expressionless face. "It was a tragic night for all of us, but I have moved on." Turning to me, he asked, "What can I do?"

"Draw your sword. You're likely to need it." I reached over my shoulder and slid Muerte from its sheath. The magic in the blade sang.

Ragna and Sean had completed their task, and when Sean approached, his eyes grew wide as he stared at the sword.

Turning to Ragna, I said, "Create the strongest protection spell you can think of and close it off inside the circle of salt."

Instinctively, she paced to the space in front of the largest stone where the magic was centered and spread her arms wide. Her voice rang through the clearing. "*Ein diogelu!*"

Sean copied her.

I felt the magic swell and expand, attaching itself to the circle she and her son had made. The power of it surprised me. The ancient magic already there lent itself to it, and the dome of protection snapped in place.

"Seamas," I said, "you guard Ragna and Sean. Stay outside the circle. Cyneric, mirror me." Then, addressing Father Clark's men, I said, "Whatever comes out, keep it inside the circle, and try not to harm Kerri. Stay outside the circle of salt or the demon may very well abandon the girl and capture you."

They looked at each other, and one ventured to ask, "Out from where?"

"There's a portal here. You'll see soon enough."

We waited. The priest's soldiers shuffled their feet and, unable to see or feel the magic, cast nervous glances at the salt and the massive stones.

"Did you say Underhill?" one of the men scoffed. "Surely you don't mean the stories the folk from the north tell are true."

"Underhill is the realm of the fae. The world between worlds," I explained. "The fae have been given many names and come in many forms. Few realize those stories carry more than a little truth. They are shapeshifters. They are ancient, and they are not human."

They stared at me, mouths hanging open. All exchanged incredulous looks and glanced at Father Clark, who regarded me for a moment and slowly nodded his head. He opened the old book, located the chapter he wanted, and marked it with a gnarled finger. He held the cross in his other hand at the ready.

Taking their cue from him, the men changed their stances. They had been ready to defend the priest from us, clearly fearing a trap. Now they were ready to defend against what might come.

Cyneric had also been staring at me. It occurred to me that perhaps I should tell him more about my life. I tend to look forward rather than backward. The past can't be undone.

Another thought occurred to me, so I spoke it out loud. "It's also possible Kerri has found a path to and from Purgatory, not Underhill."

Father Clark's gray eyebrows knitted together. He lifted the Bible in his hand. "You've read this?"

"Certainly."

More looks passed between the men. This was clearly not what they had in mind when they followed us through the woods.

"*Are* demons from Purgatory?" Cyneric asked.

"That, I don't have an answer to. There are both demons and angels there, as well as souls awaiting their destination, but I know no more than any of you where those beings who never were human actually come from."

"Father, surely you don't believe the things he says," Hooknose protested. "He's attempting to sway us from our course."

Father Clark's eyes met mine. I wondered what he saw there. Then he looked at Cyneric, who was scowling at Hooknose. "I believe in being open to possibilities," the father said.

Another of the men began to speak, but then the ground under the largest hanging stone split into a jagged crack as wide as a horse, and Kerri scrambled out. She took one wild look around, spotted her mother, and ran toward her. Ragna stepped inside the circle, intending to hold the terrified girl in her arms. Sean took her place, his hands out to the side and above his head, fingers splayed to spread out the magic. I hoped he could keep the dome in place all alone.

"Ragna, step away, it's not safe," I commanded.

Ragna did not listen. She wrapped her arms around the girl and hugged her close. Seamas took a stance between Ragna and Sean, his sword held ready.

Dirt flew from the hole Kerri had crawled out of, and a massive arm with clawed fingers slammed onto the ground, followed by another arm. A head the size of a large boulder came next. As the rest of it emerged, it had the appearance of a naked tiger with too many muscles. Its gray skin was streaked with black bands. It snarled an oath in Gaelic and lunged for Kerri. Ragna twisted and stepped back so that she and Kerri were outside the circle.

The troll was intent on Kerri and didn't notice the salt until its foot touched it. The thing howled, an unearthly noise, then stumbled backward and went down on all fours. It bared its teeth at Kerri with its ears laid flat and its tail lashing the air.

I threw the iron bar like a javelin, and it slid into the creature's shoulder and out the other side like a knife through butter. It shrieked and twisted and spun to face me, forgetting about the girl. Its face kept changing shape, contorted with rage and pain. It began to grow larger, but then Cyneric's own javelin struck its thigh and pierced the leg through. Smoke curled from the wounds, and the thing's pale skin turned bright red, as though all of it had been set in a fire.

It roared in defiance, turned, and dove back into the hole. The black, loamy dirt flew up in a fount, then settled back down. A wave of fae magic swirled in the air, and the earth where it had come from appeared undisturbed. Even the grass over the hole had returned.

The priest's men converged on the area where the troll crawled out, but they stayed out of the circle as I had commanded. They were momentarily confused. It all happened so fast.

A shout of pain from Cyneric made me turn around. Father Clark, having followed my instructions, and having mistaken the troll for the demon, had begun his prayers. Where he stood outside the magical dome, the night still reigned. But inside, it glowed as bright as day. Cyneric, intent on helping fight the troll, had not noticed the light and was now caught in the priest's power.

Fearing the demon would escape outside the circle, I abandoned Cyneric and ran to Ragna. I pulled Kerri roughly out of her arms. The girl stumbled forward with me but didn't protest until the thing inside her realized where I was heading. With inhuman strength, she tore her arm free. Demon fire shone in her eyes, and her hair whipped around her although the night air was quiet and chill.

The priest and his men had too much power over me, and Cyneric could no longer stand. But I had succeeded in pulling Kerri into the dome. Moving too fast for a mere human, she circled the stones where the light had not yet penetrated but was unable to find a path through the protection Ragna had built.

Ragna started to go to her daughter again, but Seamas took her arm and shouted, "Help Sean! It's too much for him."

Looking from her son to her daughter, Ragna made her decision and left her daughter for me and Cyneric to save.

The light had expanded to encompass half the dome. I stayed out of the light, but the priest's prayers were making me weak even without the light touching me. Muerte felt uncommonly heavy in my hand.

Two of Father Clark's men stayed beside him. The other four paced outside the stones as instructed, attempting to keep even with the girl/demon.

Kerri stopped running, and the demon glared at me. Perhaps sensing my weakness, it stalked toward me. In a voice that could never have come from such a small being, it said, "What is this girl to you?"

"I've never met her. It's you we're after."

"Misguided, puny creature such as you? These mortals mean nothing. Their lives come and go like the day and the night."

The demon moved closer to me. I could see that the girl herself was exhausted, perhaps beyond what her body could endure. Her clothes were in tatters, her mane of red hair a wild tangle. Hoping to lure the demon nearer, I sank to one knee. It wasn't entirely an act. "What do you know of me?"

"You are forsaken by all, shunned by your own kind. You are not truly a demon, nor are you human. Your purpose is to feast on the living, as mine is to make puppets of them. Why would you deny what you were made to be?"

Was it the stories Kerri's parents had told her that the demon was drawing on? Or did demons converse with each other? No matter; they were not worth debating with.

The thing was near enough now. I lunged forward with Muerte held so that the flat blade would touch as much skin as it could without harm to Kerri. The demon bellowed as I pushed it backward.

Kerri's heels struck Cyneric's prone form. He was on his hands and knees, having become too weak to stand, and was trying to crawl toward me. Kerri fell into the light cast by the priest's prayers.

With a shriek that matched a vampire for volume, the demon began to rise out of the girl's body. It was made of smoke, its body in the shape of a dog with wings. Only its eyes were clearly defined. When the last of it left her, I jumped over Cyneric, up into the air, and plunged Muerte into the space between the demon's eyes and down into its center.

At the same time, Cyneric rolled over and swung his sword in an arc, slicing through its body. Our swords clashed in the middle, forming a cross. It may have been chance, but perhaps a greater force was guiding us.

The demon exploded, knocking me back so far and fast that my body struck one of the capstones. Lights flashed in my eyes. I hadn't hurt like that in a very long time. I didn't even try to brace myself as I fell to the grass in the shadow of the stone. It hurt far less to land there than it did to remain in the sphere of angelic light cast by Father Clark's prayers.

Cyneric was bowled end over end and was stopped when his body crashed into a pillar. But he was now out of the light.

I lay there assessing our situation and watched as Sean released the magical bubble and ran to his sister, but his parents made it there first. Kerri was very pale, but not unconscious. She clung to her father as he lifted her into his arms. Tears of relief streaked her dirty face.

A bit of strength returned to Cyneric and me. We got to our feet. I could feel broken ribs, and one of my shoulders was mangled, but they would knit soon enough.

Father Clark stopped chanting his prayer, and the light faded, leaving us all in the glow of unobstructed moonlight. His men were staring about, at Ragna and her family, at the stones, their stares finally settling on me and Cyneric.

"Thank you for your assistance," Cyneric said to them. He appeared much more composed than he felt; I was impressed. "It would have been far more difficult to save the girl without men of faith to aid us."

Hooknose said, "Doesn't seem like we did very much."

I could see that one of Cyneric's shoulders was broken like mine. He rolled his neck and said, "Your belief in your God and His teachings are a greater weapon against demons than any sword, even the one Sylvio carries."

Not being gifted with magic, the men could not sense the power in the sword. Father Clark eyed the weapon, which would look plain and small to their eyes, and asked, "What is special about your short sword?"

I held Muerte up, my shoulder protesting with stabs of pain as I did. I soaked in the pain. It was a reminder that though I may be demon-possessed myself, I was alive. I watched the moonlight play on the blade and felt the heat the metal still carried from the demon's fire.

"It was re-forged by Death as a gift." I swung the sword over my shoulder and into its scabbard. The men's eyes followed it.

Father Clark looked from me to Cyneric, absorbing my reply. Then he seemed to realize he still held the Bible in his hand. "Where did you get this? The text is not the same as those I have studied."

He didn't need to know I'd stolen it from a victim, so I said, "It's quite old. You may keep it, and the cross. I have others."

He shook his head, not in protest but clearly trying to come to terms with all that had transpired—events that ran against local belief and custom. After several seconds of silence, he said, "Thank you," and pocketed the book.

"Are Ragna and her family in danger from you and your men?" I asked.

"Not from us, not now." He glanced back toward the town. "However, even if we explain the circumstances to the townsfolk, I'm not sure they will be safe." He looked toward the woods and then at Hooknose. "Benjamin, go help Paul and Michael bring the horses here."

It was significant that the man didn't protest and left the priest with us, striding quickly toward the woods.

Father Clark turned to Seamas. "My men will escort you home and help you pack your belongings. We will shelter you at the cathedral until you decide where to settle."

"Sylvio and I can ensure you are paid for your property," Cyneric offered. "And move you somewhere safe."

To Father Clark, Ragna said, "You would shelter us?"

He smiled benignly at her. "I'll do better than that. It seems you have a wedding that is long overdue."

She blinked at him then turned away, placing a hand on her daughter's hair and keeping her face averted so he wouldn't see her tears.

"Seamas, do you agree to this arrangement?" I asked.

He twitched. His attention had been on the girl in his arms, and on Ragna. He looked up and scanned the faces of Father Clark and his men, then nodded at me. His grin was a familiar sight. "I'd like that,

Father. I truly would."

଍଍ ଼ୡ

Cyneric and I returned the horses to Niveus. We said goodbye to the people there, and they knew it was a final one. That done, he and I stood once again on the parapet at the top of the tower and surveyed the frost-covered fields below.

I fingered the fine wool of his coat. "We don't need this, you know," I said.

He arched an eyebrow. "What do you mean?"

"We don't need the trappings of civilization, these fine clothes, or even a home. We can sleep in the earth, or I can take us to one of my caves."

He regarded me for several seconds. "What are you proposing?"

"Would you like to wander the wilds with me? I haven't even taken you into the sea yet. What kind of creatures do you think are out there in the ocean, and on land? What kind of wild men might we encounter?"

Smiling, he said, "Let's find out."

๕๐ Chapter 19 ๙෪

An Eye for An Eye

The unusual events of the last several weeks kept distracting us from our main goal: finding whoever was behind the activities of the black covens. Or so it seemed, at the time.

However, I had learned from Sylvio to believe in the power of intention. Even though we kept getting sidetracked in our pursuit, the thought was out there in the ether, helping things fall into place.

And now there was yet another issue that had me sidetracked. I meant to let The Coven know that what they did to Chris was over the line. I fumed every time I thought of it. Teach *me* not to be arrogant and proud, like hell! I knew my own shortcomings. I could certainly use a stronger dose of humility, but they were the arrogant ones. They had played their hand. I intended to trump theirs.

To say I was pissed would be an understatement.

The following morning, I waited impatiently for it to get late enough in Utah so that calling Micah would not seem too out of character. I did have a different question I'd been meaning to ask, so I started with that. I had been attempting to copy my grimoire to make one for Chris, but it wasn't working. The spells on the page were only words and symbols; they had no magic in them. I asked about that first and found, to my dismay, that the book must be written where there is no interference to the magic. And, Micah added, in a place with magic already native to it. Frustrated, I asked the question that I really wanted an answer to.

I began by circling around my goal. I chatted with her about how the covens worked, and who was in charge of them, and how that was decided, and then finally to when they met. I was genuinely curious about all those things, so she didn't pick up on my true reason for wanting to know.

Finally, I felt it was safe to zero in on what I wanted. Were there meetings between the covens, including The Coven, besides the moon ceremonies? Micah said that all those in The Coven only met at the summer and winter solstice, and during the Harvest Moon. I found out that impromptu meetings were held, but it was only the trio in charge that met regularly once a month to conduct business. She told me the next meeting of the Albens Venificus Consilium was in five days. I'd asked her what that meant. She said it was the Latin name for the three who ruled The Coven: The White Witch Council.

Five days.

I got to work immediately. They knew what I could do with the aid of the elemental spirits—native magic. They feared that. They knew I had been taught next to nothing about European sorcery. They believed they could control us with the use of spells since they had ensured neither Chris nor I had been shown how to use them.

That afternoon, Chris came to my room and looked around. He noticed the bed was not slept in and that my breakfast had been cold for hours, although I did drink the orange juice. He came over to see what I was writing. Little post-it notes marked the spells I'd found that might help, and I'd written a list of their names and what their purpose was.

Wordlessly, he watched me for a minute, then patted my shoulder and left the room, taking the tray of food with him. I watched the door close, then rubbed my bleary eyes and turned another page.

Five minutes later, he came back. The tray now contained cold cuts, cheese, apple slices, and fresh juice, as well as a glass of rum and Coke. He set the tray on the small table in front of the opposite chair. Then he came around to my side and took the pen out of my hand. With his other hand, he tugged at my chair so I would get up.

"Eat," he commanded. "Then go to bed. I'll take up where you left off."

Around midnight, I heard him click the lamp off, but it's never totally dark in New York City. I saw him close the heavy book and set the pen down. He rubbed his own tired eyes, then stood and said, "See you in the morning, Mother."

"Goodnight, Chris, kiss Rick for me."

I felt his smile, and the door clicked shut.

The next morning, Chris and Rick returned to Antone's while I was having breakfast with Antone's people and explaining why I was there. Antone had told them it was up to me to reveal what I wanted to them. I felt there was nothing wrong with them knowing the truth, although I didn't go into details. I told them The Coven had arranged for Chris and

Rick to be detained, and I had objected. I said Sylvio and Antone helped us free them. They were satisfied with the short version, and Chris and Rick didn't elaborate. The ladies fussed over Rick and his bruises, which he enjoyed immensely. He would be fine.

It was convenient that both Antone and Sylvio were in Europe at a meeting to discuss selling a shipyard they owned. Plus, it was not their week to be in either Utah or New York in the evenings.

After breakfast, Chris and I shut ourselves in the bedroom again and reviewed the ingredients and tools we would need to go with the spells we had chosen. We made a list and divided it between us. Then we asked the spirits to guide us as we stepped out into the city.

Chris and Rick went together, and Tommaso insisted on coming with me. He said he didn't want a lecture from Antone about letting me go out alone. I was relieved; I *really* hadn't wanted to try driving around the city myself. When we climbed in the car and he asked where we were going, I said, "South."

He glanced over at me. "Can you be a little more specific?"

I shook my head, smiled, and pointed. "Not yet. I just know we need to go that way."

"Is this some sort of witch thing?"

"Yes, exactly."

"Alright, then, south it is."

New York City is not the place to wander, and it takes forever to get anywhere or find a parking spot, but the spirits led me to each place. Usually, we had to circle around because we'd pass the spot before I'd feel we had gone too far. On the other hand, probably only in New York would we have been able to find what we needed. There are a great many Wiccan practitioners in the area, and they had nearly all the items, but not in the same places.

We visited several. There were also a lot of stores with "natural food" where we could find fresh herbs and oils. Some things were so simple we found them at Walmart: chalk and gauze pads, paint brushes of various sizes, lengths of rope . . . Tommaso became more intrigued as the day wore on and didn't complain about my odd directions after the first hour.

Chris and I met that evening and enjoyed an early supper with Antone's people, then we closed ourselves in the room again and sorted things out. We'd been able to find more than I had counted on, and we accumulated enough to create five complete spells.

The next part was a little more problematic. Where to practice? I knew we had to get out of the city to somewhere remote, and I could think of only one place. Could I teleport us and all the stuff that far?

I asked Chris if he was game, and he said he was. I put us in a cocoon, careful to encase us and our supplies completely. I thought of the old abandoned ranch with all the details I could picture in my mind: the huge cottonwood, the cedar logs on the roof, the doghouse made of rock.

We arrived standing in front of the old house next to the stone slab that had served as our bench when Sylvio took some of us there to round up stray cows. It was miles from any paved roads, and even dirt ones didn't lead there.

We checked ourselves over to see if all our parts were intact and set the items on the sandstone slab. I sighed with relief, then jumped about a foot off the ground when I heard Sylvio in my head: "*What are you up to?*"

Chris noticed, puzzled and a little worried that I may have left a toe behind or something. He began looking me over closely. I put a hand on his arm and smiled reassuringly, then replied, *"Practicing."*

Sylvio didn't answer. There was a ... shudder ... in the magic around us. I hadn't felt anything like it before. Sylvio stepped out from behind the old house and said, "You feel like the wolves."

It was Chris who jumped about a foot that time. "Shit!" He spun to face Sylvio. "How the hell did you find us?"

"Rachel and I have a connection," Sylvio said, looking at me. He had somehow figured out a way to keep me from blocking him from teleporting to where I was. I shouldn't have been surprised that he would. "What are you hunting? All your thoughts are intent on something."

I assumed he meant the werewolves; he'd kept a small pack of them enthralled at one time.

Chris and I looked at each other. He delved my feelings, and I let him. He shrugged. He could sense that I would not lie to Sylvio, even if I could pull it off, which I highly doubted.

"I intend to show The Coven the error in their thinking," I said.

Sylvio studied my face, the anger at The Coven that reflected in my eyes, the set of my jaw, then said, "They're not the enemy. They're just ... human."

"They think their knowledge of spells and enchantments has us at a disadvantage, which is true. I mean to show them they're wrong."

He glanced at the bags sitting on the bench and looked in one of them. His furrowed brow cleared. After a moment's thought, he said, "It won't work very well if you build them here."

Chris had caught up. "Why not?" he asked.

In answer, Sylvio said, "I'll take you someplace that will work better. It's not far."

I picked up the bags I'd set down, and Chris followed my lead. Sylvio stepped between us. That familiar bitter cold and waft of ozone hit me; then we were standing on a flat gravel space. A dirt road with a wooden sign was on the right, but directly in front of us was a rock face that I recognized.

"Newspaper Rock," I said. It sits in an odd place, near nothing special, in a stretch of unassuming desert. I had wondered, when I first saw it, why there of all places?

Sylvio was surprised. "You've been here?"

"Yes. Lance was stationed at Hill Air Base when the boys were small. I think you were six or seven when we came to see it, Chris. Do you remember?"

Chris didn't reply. He stared at the figures drawn on the sandstone. Then he walked to the side of the rock and touched the wall a little past where the pictures were. He paced in an arc to the other side with his hands out and his palms up. A flash of memory came to me. While Lance, Anthony, and I had been standing in front of it making guesses at what the rock pictures meant, Chris had walked back and forth like he was now.

"I could feel it then, but I didn't know what it was," he said. He stopped and stared at both of us, his eyes open wide with wonder.

I closed my eyes and willed myself to stop thinking, to wash away all those busy thoughts that constantly tumbled over each other in my mind, to quell the seething anger I felt. And there it was: magic. It seemed immense suddenly. It flowed around the rock in an oval that expanded outward so that it encompassed the entire area. I could feel the energy coming from the life all around us, the scrub brush, the little rodents, the salt grass, the birds, even the bits of lichen clinging to the stones. Its power centered where Chris had touched the wall and surged down into the rock all the way to the center of the earth, where Salamander resides, anchoring it to the spot.

I kissed Sylvio on his cheek. Then Chris and I set about assembling the items. After watching us lay the things out, Sylvio said, "It doesn't have to actually be what is listed in the book. You can use similar items you have on hand. Although those things will hold the power best." Then he added, "You can link the spell to another item if the first one gets used up, if you do it fast enough."

I thought, to myself, *I wished I had known that earlier today. We might have picked different spells to master.* Out loud, I said, "Thanks for letting us know that."

Sylvio gathered wood to make a fire while we set the things in the right order. When the small blaze was crackling, eating the dry sticks of sagebrush, Sylvio asked, "Which spells are you attempting?"

I opened the grimoire and showed him.

He shook his head. "These are advanced spells, all five of them. Do you even know how to speak the words?"

Feeling defeated, I said, "No."

Sylvio looked at Chris, who shrugged and sighed. Sylvio felt undecided, conflicted. He simply stood there for several seconds. Then he softly brushed my cheek with the back of his cold hand and gazed into my eyes.

I sent him a silent plea. He returned it with a sad smile, and I thought for an instant we were at an impasse. I could not understand why he continued to withhold his knowledge about witchcraft from me.

Then he said, "You can't practice saying the words in order. It will invoke an incomplete spell, and that is highly dangerous. Speak the words only at the proper moment as you prepare the incantation. Then only speak the complete command for the spell when you're ready to use it."

He spent the next two hours helping us practice the words in random order. We had quite a challenge in front of us. Three spells were spoken in Welsh; two were in Latin. We had to get the tone, accent, and inflection right.

When he was satisfied, Sylvio said, "Call me to you if you need help," and he vanished.

It was full dark by then. I knew the people in his Colorado house needed him.

We practiced the spells for two nights until I finally dared to suggest we try them out. Chris wisely suggested we try them on inanimate objects and insects first. It was a good plan. It took us well into the next morning before we dared try them on each other.

We spent the next day looking up everything we could find about The Coven headquarters and how the building was laid out. I hadn't been paying enough attention when I'd been there before. I remembered being surprised that it was a large home on the outskirts of the city. The only thing I remembered in detail was the parquet floor in the meeting house and the large bench the women had sat behind. Not the place I wanted to pop into.

It took us a while, but eventually we found a picture of it that was clear enough I felt I could try teleporting there. The problem was, it was of the front of the house, exposed.

I teleported us to the Utah house first. We had decided I would go see what things were like before bringing Chris with me to The Coven's headquarters. We took the little mundane things we had imbued with magic out of the bags and put them in our pockets: a handful of sticks, short pieces of rope made of hemp that smelled of the coconut oil we'd soaked them in, white chalk, an old mirror set in silver, and the ancient black obsidian knife with the deer antler handle Micah had given me.

We had fashioned charm bracelets made of strips of leather with a silver chain in the middle. The leather was made of deer hide that we soaked in various herbs then dried and oiled. We tied them to our upper arms. We didn't want them to be obvious. The charms attached to them for the spells we were using were three dried lizard tongues that gave off the scent of jasmine, a silver pentagram, and a rabbit's ear. We each wore an additional pentagram. Chris's was on a new silver chain around his neck; mine I'd added to the necklace Sylvio had given me with the key that held white magic.

We were as ready as we were going to get. I could feel the magic of the things I now wore and wondered if that alone would reveal me when I jumped to the edge of the large house in the deep shadow cast by the sycamore tree that stood sentinel over the front yard. It was late evening, a half hour after Micah said they would begin their meeting.

I looked around. The only thing watching me was a calico cat sitting on the sill of the big window next to the entry. Its tail swung lazily back and forth; its blue eyes seemed curious rather than surprised. As I watched, it jumped down from the windowsill and disappeared behind the rose bushes that lined the wall. I could see glimpses of it as it walked lazily around the corner of the house.

The building they met in lay behind and to the side of the residence. I could feel them there. I didn't delve them any more than to be reassured there were only three souls in the room. I teleported back to Utah to pick up Chris.

Right before leaving, we held the pentagram hanging at our necks and said, "*Ein diogelu.*" A soft breeze touched our faces, and I felt an inner peace, an assurance that all would be well.

I chose a spot closer to the building to return to, under the darkness of the veranda, beside the large windows with stained glass panes. When we appeared, I was surprised at how tired I suddenly was. Teleporting that much in such a short time had sapped a good deal of my strength. I hadn't counted on that.

It hadn't taken us more than a minute or two to get there, but as soon as we landed, I felt a spell wash over us and return to the sender.

A voice that was not muffled by the brick wall or fancy windows said, "Is that you, Rachel? And now there is someone else with you. Chris, perhaps? Please join us. This is rather convenient. You were the main topic of our meeting tonight."

Another spell came out of the building and wrapped itself around us. I felt compelled to go into the building.

I reached in my pocket and held one of the short sticks in my hand. I snapped the stick while whispering the command, "*Ad conterum incantores.*" The spell they sent our way broke. I felt surprise from the one who sent it, and Chris nodded at me.

There was no point then in attempting to be covert anymore. We ascended the steps, and I took another stick out of my pocket as we opened the doors and stepped inside.

The same pretty parquet floor that I remembered greeted my eyes. The interior looked like an old courthouse chamber. There were rows of chairs on each side of the aisle. They were heavy, with embroidered seats and dark polished wood that glowed with the patina of age. There was a rail in front of the chairs and a raised bench. The three sat behind it: Gwen, Jean, and a woman I did not know. The calico cat lay in front of her, its tail still swinging lazily, and I would swear its expression looked smug.

Jean and Gwen were trying to hide their feelings of surprise. Their faces certainly didn't reveal how they felt; on the outside, they appeared composed.

Jean said politely, as if she'd been expecting us, "Rachel, Chris, I don't believe you've ever met Nicole."

I didn't see it at first. It was covered in layer after layer of dense protective spells: a complete mask—an amazing construction of concealment. I focused all my attention on the creature in the center that was still languidly petting the cat. I reached up under my sleeve and pulled the bracelet down to my wrist. I jerked one of the lizard's tongues off the bracelet and held it tight in my fist, then said, "*Sairad qwir.*"

I opened my hand and blew on my palm to send the spell at the thing. The spell hit the cat instead. She leapt to her feet, arched her back, and hissed at me. I grabbed another lizard tongue and repeated the spell. That one hit the creature pretending to be Nicole.

Puzzled, not seeing the thing for what it was but following my lead, Chris took the rabbit ear off his own charm and said, "*Auris adhebio.*"

He blew on the rabbit's ear, and the spell settled on all three of them.

Angry and alarmed, Gwen snarled, glaring at the two of us, "What are you doing? What is the meaning of this?" She began to rise out of her chair.

But Jean was looking at what she had believed was Nicole, whose layers of protection were beginning to slide away and fall onto the bench. They made a slithering, slapping sound as they hit the floor.

"What is your true name?" I shouted. I repeated the same command in Latin—"*Quod verum est in nomine tuo?*"—hoping against hope that the little bit of Latin I had studied was right since that phrase was not one we practiced.

The cat leaped from the bench toward us and hit the protection spell Chris and I had already placed over ourselves. Like a cartoon character, she was stopped in midair when she hit our shield. I felt rather than heard the spell that had been on the cat pop. She landed on the floor in front of us with a thump, ran in place for a couple of seconds on the polished wood floor, and streaked out the open door. It would have been funny if the demon wasn't starting to move too.

It didn't want to answer my question. If you know a demon's name, it gives it less power, and you more. Lesser demons can be made to do your bidding, at least for a while, if you have their name. I doubted this was a lesser demon.

I took the small mirror from my pocket, turned it toward the thing, and shouted, "*Ostende te!*"

It hissed like the cat had, only a lot louder, as the name "Rahovart" was forced from its mouth. It acted before I could begin to think up a use for our new advantage.

It sucked power from somewhere in the direction of the house and pulled it toward us. A gust of wind surged through the doors, causing them to slam shut, buckling as they did. The building shuddered from the force of it, and the lights sparked and went out, plunging us into a darkness that was blacker than the night should have been.

Chris said, "*Cynuea*" and an orb of light lit the space near the bench.

I couldn't help the brief smile that crossed my face; I'd shown him that spell over Christmas.

The demon swung its head back and forth. I sensed it was testing its power. It sneered at us and began to grow. The fingers on the bench stretched and spread wide. The skin on them cracked and flaked away. The lacquered red nails lengthened and became black talons.

The mask that had been Nicole's face split and peeled off. Nostrils like a pig's showed first, then yellow eyes with slits in the irises. Its muzzle was like a pig's too, with tusks showing at the sides. Then a forked tongue, incongruously pink in that blackened face, slithered out and in like a snake testing the air.

Leather wings expanded outward as the last bits of the concealment shields fell to the floor. The wings took up the entire space behind it, all the way to the high ceiling. It began to climb over the bench, heading for me.

I found the obsidian knife in my pocket and pointed it at the thing. I started to say, "*Yn eu dal,*" but only got the first syllable out when it countered the spell with its own.

The demon's voice was a rumble that brought despair with it and sank like ice into my very core when it growled, "*Tene linguam.*"

I wondered randomly why a demon from Hell's voice would feel like ice. Then my tongue cleaved to my palate, my mouth shut tight so fast it hurt my teeth, pain lanced through my bitten tongue, and I couldn't breathe. I looked at Chris, panicked.

By then, both Jean and Gwen had scrambled down from around the bench to stand beside us. Gwen and Chris pointed their wands at me and said in tandem, "*Ad conterum incantores.*" They blinked at each other.

I sucked in air. It tasted like sulfur and made me cough, but I could breathe again. We all turned toward our foe at the same time. The wood on the bench began to smoke where the demon's clawed feet touched it. Traces of red light showed where its joints were, and when its ribs rose and fell. The veins in its wings were like snakes full of red flame. It looked like lava flowing under cracked black obsidian.

Chris took the short lengths of rope out of his pockets and held them tight in his fist. "*Yen eu dal!*" he shouted.

Gwen repeated the spell, pointed her wand at the ropes, and added a few more words.

The ropes flew from Chris's hands and slithered around the legs of the beast, around its neck, and hind legs. Its body slammed down onto the bench as its feet were jerked out from under it.

I had a moment to shout *"Yes!"* inside my head, then the ropes burst into flame.

It wasn't enough. We couldn't steal all its power, and I was out of ideas. Certain I was too late, I sent, "*Sylvio, help!*"

The demon sprang back up. The bench began to crack. The claws of one hind leg gripped the edge of the bench. It was poised to launch itself at us. Jean hit it with a different spell, but I couldn't hear the exact words over the sound of the wood splitting. Gashes appeared on its skin, from shoulder to hip, and it howled.

I couldn't help clapping my hands over my ears automatically. I did it hard enough that the bone handle of the knife in my palm hurt my ear.

Chris wasn't out of ideas. I felt him reach for the spirits. Dirt flew in a fount outside the windows. A shriek of wind imploded the windows, all of them at once, and glass rained down on us.

Distracted, we all looked out the gaping holes where the windows had been, even the demon. What at first looked like white snakes coming up out of the ground became PVC water pipes that Chris was pulling from the earth. They began to snap, sounding like a cacophony of gun shots. Water shot out of them and hit the demon like a brigade of firemen was standing outside the windows.

On the heels of the jets of water, three figures hurled through the gaps at either side of the building and collided with the demon, ripping and shredding it with claws and teeth. Werewolves—I couldn't begin to imagine how they had come to be there.

The demon stood on its hind legs, and the bench collapsed entirely beneath it. The biggest werewolf clamped its jaws on the thing's throat and hung there, twisting and pulling with its jaws and clawing with all four legs. Streaks of red began to show, and smoke curled from around the wolf's jaws. Burnt flesh was added to the sulfur and ash stench of the demon. The water was beginning to quench the lava inside its skin. Steam curled up from the injuries we had inflicted on it.

It attempted a roar, but it came out as a guttural cry instead. The other two wolves had its arms in their jaws. It was attempting to shake them off, and they flopped in the air. Finally, it spun a circle, and the two smaller wolves lost their grip on it and crashed among the chairs behind us. The wolf in the middle still hung on. I saw its left ear was missing the tip, and realized who the three wolves were. The demon raised a hind leg, clawed Tim from neck to groin, and kicked him. He flew past me and hit the rail in a crumpled heap.

The battle of water against fire made the air scalding hot. I shook my soaking hair out of my eyes and wiped my face, not sure if it was sweat or water that I wiped away. I pulled on the spirits of the water and asked them for guidance. A creature manifested out of the stream closest to me. I couldn't quite make out what it was. It was built somewhat like a lizard but more sinewy and sleek. Its form was rather creepy, but its scales shimmered and gave off a luminescent light of their own—a light that was greater than that of the demon's fire.

I understood. I pointed the obsidian knife at the demon as it opened its mouth to roar in defiance at us and shouted, *"Mors ad te Rahovart!"*

Undine dove down its throat, and the knife shattered into tiny shards from the strength of my sending.

In an instant, the jets of water stopped, the darkness lifted, and starlight came through the empty windows, making the bits of glass and puddles of water shimmer. The demon's fire had gone out. No streaks of lava showed now, even where Tim and the twins had flayed its skin from its ribs and shredded its neck. Only its yellow eyes seemed to have life in them still.

Undine's battle with the demon wasn't quite finished. The demon's body began to expand. It swelled until its eyes bulged and its body looked like a bloated toad. The yellow eyes that glared at us were malevolent pools of hate. Then it exploded.

Flesh that stank like tar, blackened skin, and ectoplasmic goo covered all the surfaces, and us.

The force of the blast knocked me off my feet. My heels thumped into the body of the wolf behind me. Tiny bits of glass were embedded into my skin. I fell backwards. My lower back hit the rail. I flipped over it, upside down. My head hit the floor the same time my shins smacked into the wooden chair arms.

I had an instant to think *That's going to hurt* before I blacked out.

ೲ Chapter 20 ೞ
A New Beginning

I was awakened by someone pulling shards of glass out of my face. I tried to push their hand away, but they pinned my hands with their other arm and continued until my face and arms were clear of glass. I could feel thin trickles of blood sliding down my cheeks and arms, and a thousand tiny needles pierced me from the many stinging cuts. I stopped wriggling since I'd figured out who had hold of me. Arms as strong as iron bands were the giveaway. Then he licked the blood off.

"Ewww," I croaked and wriggled in Sylvio's arms. My voice was hoarse from inhaling soot and shouting incantations.

Sylvio chuckled and ignored me. He took his time, lazily healing me, enjoying the zing of pleasure the blood always gave him. When he finished, he bit his wrist and commanded, "Drink."

I was bone-tired, I ached all over, and my back was sending spasms of pain down to meet the agony in my shins. My head was telling me I was going to have a killer headache. I felt nauseous, which meant I probably had a concussion. I kept my eyes shut due to my pounding head, but I could sense we were not alone.

I didn't want to be more of a spectacle than I already was, but I simply didn't have the energy to defy him, and I knew that liquid fire would bring vitality and magical healing with it. I drank.

When that was done, I heard Sylvio purr, "Would you like me to assist you two as well?"

I ventured to open my eyes a crack. I was lying on a patio lounge chair in Sylvio's arms. The only light came from the moon and stars and a small lamp set on a log bench nearby. Shena, back in her human form, was tending to the cuts and burns on Gwen and Jean. Their skin had been scorched where the demon's flesh had hit them. I realized that, in addition to the cuts I'd had, my skin was burned here and there. Their hair was frizzed and had been burned in a few spots as well.

Jean and Gwen attempted to fix Sylvio with a disapproving glare, but they were too tired to look very intimidating. Gwen spat out, "Of course not."

Sylvio chuckled. I reached up to touch my hair and felt some of it break off in my hand. It appeared I'd have to put up with short hair again, at least for a while.

Tim lay in his human form on a matching lounge chair, looking dazed. He'd put some pants on but not a shirt, and angry red streaks showed on his chest and belly. They were already mostly healed. He was watching the activity happening across the back yard.

Eric and Chris were digging around what appeared to be a window well that had been filled with dirt. Chris was using the earth spirits along with a shovel, but he was tired. It was slow going. Eric was making more progress than Chris was, digging at the dirt with his claws. The calico cat paced back and forth behind them.

"Why don't they go in through the basement?" I asked, still sounding like a frog.

"It's been bricked up," Jean explained, "and whatever spell is on the door was not of the demon's making, so it still holds. We're afraid to break it. It might hurt Nicole."

"Nicole is down there?"

Sylvio nodded and smiled down at me. He kissed my forehead while Gwen looked on. She pursed her lips in disapproval. It made me smirk.

Tim began to stand up, intending to go help the other two. Shena snapped, "Stay." He sank back down with a groan.

That struck Sylvio as funny. He began to snicker, and when Tim gave him an exasperated scowl, Sylvio laughed out loud. After a few seconds, Tim couldn't help smiling too. Shena shook her head at them and continued putting salve on Gwen and Jean.

"You all stink to high heaven, you know," Sylvio said. "Except Shena." I realized he was right. We all smelled like brimstone with more than a hint of sewage mixed in.

Sylvio asked Shena, "How did you end up smelling normal? In fact, your skin smells like you recently came from the shower, and your clothes are fresh and clean. Plus, once you transformed, there isn't any sign of scorched skin or cuts."

When he said that, I noticed there were a few spots missing fur on Eric, and he still had sores on his sides, but they appeared to be days old. Chris also had patches of his clothes missing, with angry, red burns peeking from under the holes.

Shena glanced quickly at Sylvio and the two coven leaders, thought it over, then decided to answer. "When I pictured what I wanted to look like, it was like this."

"*Ut 'admirari*," Sylvio said, shaking his head in wonder. I didn't know that phrase; I'd have to look it up. Then he asked me, "How are you feeling?"

I did a quick assessment. "I'm fine, thank you. Just a little rough around the edges."

He stood and gently set me on the lounge cushion. Then he went to the window well, moving fast. Before he got there, his fingers morphed into claws. Faster than the rest of us could really take it in, he knelt in front of the window and slammed both hands through the remaining dirt and wood behind it. He ripped the plywood out of the wall, threw it aside, and disappeared through the hole. Eric jumped in behind him. The calico cat was right behind Eric.

Chris leaned down to look through the hole. There was the shriek of metal and a crash from inside. We waited. A minute later, Eric came through the patio door in his human form, looking clean and wearing a t-shirt and jeans. Sylvio followed him, carrying a woman, and stopped outside the patio door. The cat stropped Sylvio's legs and meowed.

Nicole's hair hung in twisted, filthy dreadlocks. Her skin was a sickly brownish-gray, her eyes listless and seemingly without color. She was much too thin, and her clothes were stained and stiff. She smelled even worse than I did. Her thin hands clung to Sylvio's arm as he cradled her.

Sylvio looked over at Tim, who willingly gave up his spot on the lounge chair, albeit moving slowly. Sylvio sat down with Nicole in his lap and brushed her tangled hair off her face. The cat jumped up beside them and kept meowing plaintively, fixing Sylvio with an intense stare.

Their feelings hit me then. Sylvio was undecided, torn between opposing convictions. Nicole felt panicked. She knew what sort of creature held her, but she also knew her life was slipping away, and she was bone-tired. The demon had used her life force to create its disguise. It had trapped her soul, stolen her power, and kept her alive those many months with its will. Now she was only herself again, and her body had suffered too much.

Sylvio tilted her head so she looked in his eyes. "Nicole, do you want to live? I can ease your pain and release your soul. You won't suffer anymore. Or, I can save you and you can carry on with the good work you pursued before the demon captured you."

I could feel her life slipping away. There wasn't much time for her to decide.

She stared into his eyes, but he hadn't attempted to capture her mind. He was not going to sway her decision one way or the other.

The panic she felt changed to resolve. I felt a glimmer of her strength of character find its way out of the despair she had fallen into under the spell of the demon. She gave a tiny nod.

Sylvio turned so that her long, tangled hair hid his face. She gave a weak cry when he bit her neck. I felt it as their souls combined, and her horror at the feeling of intense pleasure that comes with a vampire feeding thrummed through her body. But she was very weak physically. Sylvio couldn't take too much. It wasn't certain if he would be able to form enough of a link.

I snuck a peek at Gwen and Jean. Their emotions were understandably conflicted. Their expressions kept changing from disgust and fear to hope.

After only a minute, Sylvio drew back and licked Nicole's neck. He bit his wrist, then adjusted her so that the blood dripped into her slack mouth. Her eyes were fluttering, and she breathed in short, quick gasps. Nothing happened for several seconds. Then her jaws moved of their own accord, and her lips curled over his wrist and clamped on.

I felt pain lace through Sylvio for an instant, then they were lost in the pleasure of it, the life it brought with it. Her body began to shake and shudder, and her hands clung so tightly the thin skin on them turned pale. Her broken fingernails pressed into his arm.

He let her drink until he was quite weak, but only Chris and I were aware of that. As always, Sylvio's face reflected what he wanted others to see. Only a slight tightening around his eyes belied the pain he was feeling.

Finally, he whispered, "Stop."

Nicole shuddered again, then went still when he took his arm away and licked his wrist. Her eyes opened and gazed at him with adoration, then they went wide from comprehension and she sat up. Sylvio slid out from under her hip and sat beside her. The cat jumped in Nicole's lap and began rubbing against her chest, purring loudly as its tail stroked Nicole's jaw and chin.

Nicole picked up the cat and hugged her. The purrs got louder.

Sylvio left her side and came to sit next to me again.

Nicole's wide eyes followed him. Then she looked around. She took in the white pipes strewn everywhere and the pools of water bubbling, adding to the stream that trickled down the driveway. She stared at the meeting house, at its empty windows with water dripping from the blackened sills, and at the doors that lay broken and sagging in the entry. Then she made herself look at Sylvio again.

"Thank you," she said with genuine, heartfelt honesty. She turned to take in all of us. "Thanks to all of you."

Gwen said to Nicole, "I'm sorry, we didn't realize . . ." Her voice trailed off.

Jean said, "I fear what may have happened if Rachel and Chris hadn't come."

Chris quipped, "Well, if we hadn't, Nicole's place would not be in such sad shape."

Nicole was still quite weak; it was taking time for her tired brain to catch up. She stared at Chris with no expression for several seconds. Then a hint of a smile touched her lips. A moment later, the name got through the fog in her brain. "Rachel—the witch who destroyed that black coven and Arturo?" Her eyes settled on me.

"What's the last thing you remember?" Jean asked her.

Nicole bit her lip, thinking. It made her look younger. "We had set a date for Sylvio to bring her to answer for what he let her do. And for keeping a witch as a . . . captive." She took in the fact that I was sitting next to Sylvio, and that we were holding hands. A hint of disapproval crossed her face.

"Then," Nicole continued, "I got a message from Grace in Alberta. She said they had a problem with . . . with . . ." She couldn't go on. Her face crumpled, and she began to sob into the cat's soft fur.

Gwen stepped to her side, sat down, and patted her shoulder. Jean came over to sit beside her too.

Gwen said, "It's alright, Nicole. Let's get you cleaned up. In fact, all of us could use a nice, long shower and something to eat. Do you think one of you guys can figure out how to turn off the water to the yard? It doesn't appear that the house pipes were damaged."

"Sure, I'll go see what I can figure out," Chris offered. Tim and Eric moved to follow him.

"No, we're not done here," Sylvio said.

All of us stopped moving. The command in his tone had been unmistakable.

Sylvio's voice was imposing. "It's time to decide things. Chris and Rachel will not be bound to the rules of any coven. They will not be restricted in their activities or in the kind of sorcery they pursue. It will be up to them to determine where to draw the line between black magic and white."

"It is not your right to decide such things!" Jean said hotly.

"You may be an ally, but you cannot dictate to us," Gwen added.

Sylvio gave a slow shake of his head. "I'm not the one who has made those decisions. What I stated is not a proposal. It has already been decided. The two of them have shown us all how things are to be."

The night became entirely still as we absorbed his words. Even the cat stopped purring. Eventually, Sylvio spoke again.

"Change is inevitable. The endless march of time is relentless. It is the bane of my kind." His head was now bowed, his hands clasped in his lap as if he were praying rather than teaching. "For the first time in a very long time, I do not know what is going to happen next. I must confess, that frightens me. Chris and Rachel, Tim and his children, are a new kind of magical being. They belong to the new millennia."

He paused. I could feel astonishment from both Gwen and Jean that anything frightened Sylvio.

"They are compelled to move ahead and drag the rest of us with them, those who are willing to change, anyway. If we are all to survive, if we want to carry on, we must follow their lead and give them what knowledge we can so they don't die from mere ignorance as they forge ahead.

"They don't need a coven. They don't need the ceremonies to aid them or to increase their power. There was no one there to tell them the rules when they were young and accepting. There are no blocks on their minds. Their future is full of endless possibilities."

He stood and helped me up. Chris, Tim, and the twins came to stand next to us so that we faced Jean, Gwen, and Nicole.

"The question," Sylvio continued, "is not whether they should ask for your acceptance, but rather if they should accept all of you. Will you follow them into the future? Will this be a spring from which you can grow into something more, something better? Or will the covens wither and die as the leaves do in the fall?"

A cloud that had been masking the light of the stars moved away. Moonlight flooded the stones on the patio and reflected in the eyes of the three women seated before us. They were afraid, uncertain, but I did sense a small glimmer of hope in them, too. None of them spoke.

"Miss Rachel, will you take us home?" Sylvio said.

I hesitated for an instant, thinking of how many of us there were. Then I remembered the words he'd spoken to me not long after I learned about the preternatural world: *"You do things with apparent ease because no one has told you it can't be done."*

I wrapped a cocoon around all of us, nodded at the three women staring at us wide-eyed, and took us to the house in Willard. My home.

℘ Epilogue ℘

We were celebrating the opening of the new pool house. Brianna had outdone herself designing it. Sylvio and Antone had flown their people there from the other houses, so although the pool house was obscenely large, it was filled to capacity. The party had gone on through the night, and dawn was approaching. But then we were all used to being up at odd hours. We also had a bit more stamina than usual, because Sylvio and Antone had snacked on each of us and given us a little in return.

I watched as Antone jumped off the rafters and swamped the whole patio with his cannonball. Sylvio came over to stand beside me and brushed my soaking hair out of my eyes. I'd been too close to where Antone landed, and the wave flopped my hair over onto my face. It was almost long enough to put in a ponytail again. He took the opportunity to kiss me. Then, by some unspoken agreement, we were all leaving the pool and heading for the showers and into the house to crash.

When I woke, Sylvio was sitting by my bedside reading a book. I couldn't decipher what language it was written in from the cover. Greek, perhaps?

"Good morning, Sunshine," he said.

"Is it still morning?"

"No, actually, it's about two o'clock." He gestured to the tray full of pancakes, bacon, and fruit that lay on the small table beside my bed. I realized that was what had awakened me. I quickly dressed and, as I ate, I noticed he was feeling impatient.

Curious, I asked, "What's up, why are you in a hurry?"

"I want to show you something." He was literally bouncing on his feet with excitement by then.

I scarfed down one last piece of bacon, chugged the orange juice, and said, "Let's go, then."

He wrapped an arm around me, grinning ear to ear. We reappeared in a large, dry cave. The top of the chamber we were standing in was so high that I couldn't see it, but there was a little light seeping in. It wasn't a hole directly to the surface; the light spilled down from rock to rock.

Sylvio sent magic out, and several lamps came to life. They were old-fashioned oil lamps that gave the entire space a golden glow.

Sandstone. I recognized the feel of the cave, the smell of the air, the red rock. This was southern Utah. The first time I visited there with Lance and the boys, it felt like I was coming home. Some part of me belonged in that country. I wondered, even then, if I had lived there in some past life.

I began to turn a slow circle. In the center of the chamber was a large fire pit. Hanging on a cast-iron stand with an arm that would swing was a massive cauldron. Smaller cauldrons alongside a collection of mortar and pestle bowls sat on a stone table to one side. On the opposite side of the fire pit was an altar. It gave an impression of great age. The top was flat; no runes or symbols had been carved on it. It was made of white rock brought from somewhere else, not the sandstone or even limestone found in that part of Utah.

Against the far wall of the cave were shelves lined with jars made of both old bottle glass and pottery. The glass glittered in the light cast by the lamps so I couldn't see what they contained. Sprigs of plant stems stuck out of some of the pottery jars.

The wall beyond that was where I presumed the entrance to the cave had been. Massive stones were set there. They fit perfectly, like a giant sideways jigsaw puzzle, so they needed no mortar. As I gazed at the stonework, Sylvio said, "We're in Glen Canyon. Lake Powell lies beyond that wall."

Meaning the cave was now underwater. The thought was slightly creepy. I continued to turn and saw other objects lined up next to the wall Sylvio had made. Staffs fashioned from a variety of woods and metal leaned on the rock, bracelets not intended as jewelry but as conduits for magic hung on pegs driven into the stone.

To the left of the staffs were more shelves. They contained books, most bound in leather, and stacks of scrolls. In front of the bookshelf was a large table with an oil lamp on top. An ink bottle and quill stood poised on one side next to a pile of blank parchment paper. The carvings on the table legs were of runes rather than animals. The top was black marble chased with golden streaks.

I could tell most of the items in the cave had not been there long. Dust had not begun to accumulate on the edges and crevices, which it will do eventually no matter how diligent the housekeeper.

I turned to see what was behind us and stopped, dumbfounded. Treasure lay piled in the farthest corner of the cave. Mounds of it. It was somewhat organized. There were stacks of gold, silver, and bronze coins. Necklaces, bracelets, broaches, and even snuff boxes lay in heaps to one side. The farther back the treasure stretched, the larger the items became. The myriad colors of the jewels they contained reflected on the cave wall, dancing in the lamplight to form a rainbow. It was breathtaking.

Sylvio gave me time to absorb it all, then he said, "When they proposed building the dam, I saw what an opportunity it was for me. At that time, one of the caves in Turkey that I kept treasure in was found. They had blasted the hillside to make a road. I moved most of my treasure that I didn't keep in banks to caves in this canyon and walled them up."

I blinked, stuck on the word "caves"—as in more than one. I said, rather breathlessly, "The perfect hiding place."

"*Castifico.*"

I smiled; I was getting better at understanding Latin.

As I completed my scan of the cave, I found the final wall had been left untouched. The cave itself was not round or oval. The treasure chamber lay down a smaller alcove. The wall to the left of there was at an angle so that it would catch the light best from where the cave entrance had been. That last wall was covered in ancient rock art. Sheep and bison and human figures vied for space with spirals and lines.

Sylvio explained, "In this country, the places with magic in them are where the pictures can be found. The Indians could sense that magic and tapped into it."

I felt tears on my cheeks. For some reason, I was crying.

"It's for you, Rachel. These are the things you will need to learn to use more than what the spirits can do for you. Since you can now teleport on your own, you can come here to practice and study. It's remote. There is little activity in this area. The magic done here will not interfere with any electronics, except for maybe a few passing boats. Spell casting and the modern age don't blend well."

He petted my hair and stroked my back as I continued to weep. It was so overwhelming.

"Some of the ancient witch families in Europe were incredibly powerful," he said. "They could perform magic that has been lost to time. When I saw what was happening to the old knowledge, I began to collect their things, even though most of it is of no use to me. I have studied the books. I understand the spells and how they should be performed, even though most of them don't work for a vampire."

I turned around and hugged him. It wasn't necessary for me to say thank you. He could feel it.

After a moment, power flashed from his hands, and the fire came to life under the massive cauldron.

Sylvio brushed a thumb across my cheek, wiping my tears away, and said, "Shall we begin?"

ജ About the Author ര

R.E. Beebe lives on a small farm in Northern Utah. She has two beautiful daughters and lots of pets—the normal kind. *Sylvio: Revelations* is her fifth novel. To be notified of further releases, or to contact Ruth, visit www.beebebiz.com.

Other books by R.E. Beebe:
Sylvio: The Preternatural
Sylvio: Past and Present
Sylvio: Spirit
Sylvio: Sunrise

৪০ About the Publisher ৫৩

Glass Spider Publishing is a hybrid micropublisher located in Ogden, Utah. The company was founded in 2016 by writer Vince Font to help bring to light the works of underrepresented authors. To learn more, visit www.glassspiderpublishing.com.

The following is an excerpt from R.E. Beebe's forthcoming novel *Sylvio: Vengeance*.

Visit www.glassspiderpublishing.com for updates on its availability.

It was getting close to Halloween, so we went to Halloween City on Riverdale Road. I found the perfect ghoul to hang in the trees in front of the house, and an actual witch costume—the kind that looks like an old crone. Green makeup came with it, along with a hump, warts to stick on, and a long nose.

When I showed them to Sylvio, he commented, "A hag is not a witch. It's fae." He patted my cheek while I blinked at him, and continued. "Witches are ordinary people, with extraordinary abilities. Hags are green, like mold, and smell like that, too, when they aren't covering up their actual looks with glamour."

I found my voice and asked, "Do they have warts?"

"Yes, everywhere," he replied, sounding positive.

"Everywhere?"

"Yes."

"How do you know?" I asked, because he was feeling uncomfortable and even a little embarrassed.

He sighed. "That's not fair, you know, reading me like that."

Grinning, I asked, "What did she do?"

"Do you want me to buy the things in the cart for you?"

"I have my own card." I took it out of my phone case and waved it at him. "There's no escape now. I want the dirt. What did she do?"

Sylvio looked around the store. There were several people close by. He wheeled the cart to the checkout and used his own card to pay for the stuff.

On our way out the door, I asked him again. He gave me a put-upon sigh and said, "We were . . . enjoying ourselves, and she got a little too . . . distracted. Her glamour fell off her."

I was trying to hide my snicker, and losing. "Couldn't you smell that she was fae?"

"Not always, not like Antone can. It's not one of my gifts. Some fae are very good at masking their magic."

Intrigued, I asked, "What does a hag actually look like?"

He opened the back door of the car and I put the bags on the seat.

"A lot like E.T."

Nonplussed, I said, "What?"

"You know, that creature in the movie. They look like that thing, only hunched over and green."

"And warts," I added.

"Yes," he said, smiling finally.

Sylvio walked around the front of the car and opened the passenger door for me. We were parked at the back of the lot to minimize the chance of other car doors hitting his. There were several people in the parking lot walking toward the store. I began to slide onto the seat when I realized something was wrong. None of them were looking at the car. Whenever we went somewhere in one of Sylvio's exotic cars, people always stared. Then the other thing that was missing made itself clear: No spirits surrounded us. My eyes met Sylvio's, and he saw the fear in them.

I delved for the spirits, all four kinds, and felt them then. They could not reach us. A bubble of magic surrounded the car, even into the ground underneath it.

At that moment, the world tilted, the circle constricted, and I felt as though my whole body was being squeezed through a tube. My shoulders hugged my ears, my arms were pinned to my side, and my legs were straight as sticks. I couldn't breathe. Whatever I was encased in was too tight.

Suddenly, everything let go and I stumbled to my knees, gasping for air. Sylvio was still only a couple of paces away. He didn't fall when we were let go. I immediately sent out a quest for the spirits and felt their shock at being held back. The bubble of magic had come with us, but the car had not.

Sylvio stepped to my side and helped me up. He put an arm around my waist and held his other hand out. I felt the magic as he sent it out, then Muerte materialized in his palm. Slowly, he wrapped his fingers around the hilt of the enchanted blade.

We were standing in the middle of a large stone courtyard in the shape of a circle. Five vampires stood at the edge of the courtyard, their backs to the low stone wall. The vampires didn't move. They could have been alabaster statues if not for their eyes, which were very much alive and riveted on Muerte.

The bubble of magic felt a lot like one of my own cocoons. I calmed my scattered emotions as Micah and Sylvio had shown me how to do, and I began to build my own shelter inside the bubble using normal witchcraft, since I couldn't access the spirits. I focused all my thoughts on the anger I felt at our captors. I let that rage build, to add power to my spell, until I literally saw red. My breath was coming in short gasps by then.

The vampires surrounding us looked at me. They mistook my expression and breathing for fear. They began to move toward us as one, not walking like humans do, but in the slow, robotic steps vampires use when they don't care to hide what they are. These vampires were dressed in ordinary clothes, and they weren't skeletal like fledglings usually are. The lone female in the center seemed to be in charge. The others moved in sync with her.

I waited until they were about two paces away. I could feel the spirits coalesce around the barrier, ready to come to my aid.

"*Blutio!*" I snarled into the little rock crystal on my bracelet. The cocoon I had built inside the barrier blasted outwards in a ball of air and fire.

It was deafening. The force of the spell sent the vampires flying backwards into the courtyard wall. Their clothes began to smolder and their skin was scalded from the heat of the blast. The wall itself collapsed and fell in a heap. Dust and smoke shot up into the night air and curled along the ground, covering us all in dirt.

The barrier spell bounced back for a moment before it unraveled. The backlash knocked Sylvio and me off our feet. The dust settled and I waited, ready for the vampires to get up and come for us.

They didn't move. They weren't unconscious. The spirits were back with me again and I could feel they were aware of us. I realized belatedly that the vampires were in pain. Their pain had not been caused by my spell. Someone or something had harmed them before we appeared.

Sylvio waved the hand holding his sword in front of his face to clear the air. His other arm was still around my waist. He'd kept me from falling backwards farther when we were knocked off our feet. He began to chuckle, his weird sense of humor coming to the fore. I stood up, trying not to show that my butt was as sore as it was.

Sylvio stood with ease in one graceful motion. He held Muerte in front of his face and watched the light play on the sword, then looked over the blade at the vampires lying in front of the ruined wall. He began to speak. Then he stopped and tilted his head, listening. After a few seconds, I heard it too.

Out of the haze of smoke and dust still filling the air walked a tall figure wearing a long cloak and carrying a staff. Boots and staff alternated a steady clomp, clomp, tap, clomp, clomp, tap on the flagstones as he came forward out of the swirling cloud. On his head was a worn cowboy hat whose brim had seen better days and dipped where it shouldn't have. Under its brim was salt-and-pepper unkempt hair, which peeked out from under the brim and draped in a tangle of waves down past his upturned collar. His short beard was the same mix of black and gray, and could do with a trim. His jeans were faded and worn. They matched the leather duster I had mistaken for a cloak. The hand on his staff had rings connected with fine chains to a bracelet that vibrated with power, as did the wizard himself.